The Heirs of Lydin

THE AP'LYDIN CHRONICLES

The Heirs of Lydin
The Slaves of the Horned God
The Tears of the Divine (2019)

THE TALES OF AELZANDAR

The Grey Mage
The Errant Princess (2018)

THE HEIRS of LYDIN

Book 1 of the Ap'Lydin Chronicles

AIDAN HENNESSY

Published by Atallas Publishing 2017

Cover Design by James, GoOnWrite.com

Cartography by Sebastian Breit

ISBN: 0648186458

ISBN-13: 978-0648186458

For Nona, who helped make it happen, and for Jan, who made sure that it did.

THE LANDS OF
EMPARIA AND GORIINCHIA
0 25 50 75 SCALE IN MILES
· YEAR 234 OF THE THIRD EPOCH ·

PROLOGUE

Winter, Year 24 of the Third Epoch

A wolf's howl cut through the night.

In the valley below, banners fluttered in the cool breeze, surrounding a circle of hide tents. The smell of campfire smoke hung in the air.

The exiles had stopped to rest, temporarily halting their weary journey north. Haggard and carrying little more than the clothes they wore on their back, they were a defeated people.

The Wars of Pacification had ended with the followers of the Horned God victorious in Goriinchia and their enemies scattered to the winds. Chief among these enemies were the followers of Mael, warlord and apostate.

Mael had been born to the most ardent of the Horned God's followers, but turned against his faith and became the chief rival of Ygarak, self-styled Prophet-King of Goriinchia and chosen of the Horned God. The war between them had lasted years, but eventually Ygarak triumphed, winning a series of bloody battles, and brutally slaughtering the bulk of Mael's loyal followers.

Mael, the one-time warlord, terror of the north, and so-called scourge of the faithful, sat in his tent brooding. Thoughts of failure and loss hung over him. Even the mulled wine his servant poured for him, once the warlord's favourite drink, did nothing to ease Mael's pain.

"Defeat," Mael mused. "Total defeat. This was not what I was promised. Bring him to me."

"My lord?" the servant said.

"The warlock," Mael growled. "Bring me my warlock."

"Yes, my lord."

The servant disappeared through the tent flap, returning some moments later with a hunched and cloaked figure.

"Leave us," Mael said, and the servant departed, bowing as he left.

Mael stood, passing around his throne, turning the goblet over in his hand. He looked at the figure in front of him and then, with a snarl, threw the goblet to the ground.

"Ailill, you still answer my summons, do you? Still following my voice like a loyal hound?" Mael said to the figure. "Or is this your idea of mockery?"

"Not at all, my lord," the cloaked figure said, inclining his head towards the warlord. "I am, as ever, your humble servant."

"Enough of your lies, warlock," Mael growled. "Have you not destroyed enough already?"

"My lord?"

"Don't play coy," Mael said, pointing angrily in the warlock's direction. "You made promises. You spoke of prophecy. You said that Ygarak would be defeated. You said that the followers of the Horned God would fall to our armies. You lied to me!"

The warlock's voice came, as cold as ice. "Indeed. I did speak of prophecy. I did make promises. I did say Ygarak and the Horned God would fall. Perhaps then, I was mistaken."

"So you admit it then, that it was all lies?"

"No. The specifics of the prophecy are clear. The *what* and the *when* — there is no question of that. All that needs answering is *who*. I thought that *you* were the Heir of Lydin. Perhaps it is there that I made my mistake."

"Is that so? Then why, pray tell, did you recruit me for this? Why did you draw me from the Horned God's path, only to see me fail? Was it not you who forged Kaltban for me with your bare hands? Did you not encircle my brow with the Tears of the Divine? Did you not burn the mark into my very skin? And now you claim to have had clouded vision?"

Ailill's face hardened. "Do you feel that I have cheated you, Mael? Do you feel that I have been unfair? Did I not make you into a great hero? Did I not give you the chance to rule a free Karlicia? Did I not give you the power to save your clan?"

"Save my clan?" Mael said, exploding into fury. "My clan is dead! Hardly a dozen survive. Old feeble men, womenfolk and children — barely a single soul fit to bear arms. Most of them won't even survive the trek over the mountains. You have killed Clan Lydin, warlock, and you stand here with the gall to judge me."

With that Mael swung about, and drew Kaltban from its scabbard. The sword shone with its queer blue light, and, with a yell, Mael advanced and thrust the sword deep into the warlock's chest. The warlock made no sound as the blood seeped through his robes, merely regarding Mael with a look of equal part amusement and disappointment.

"I am sorry, Mael, but this changes nothing. I die, but you will soon follow me, and with this knowledge in your mind — that you are not the Heir."

The warlock slumped to the ground, his blood pooling around him, and

Mael, his voice hoarse, called again for his manservant.

"Remove this corpse from my sight."

"Yes, my lord."

Mael pulled his sword from the warlock's body, wiping it clean. "And call the clans together. We will leave as soon as they are ready."

"Where are we going, my lord? Back home?"

"No. We can never go home," Mael sighed, walking to the tent's entrance. He gazed out to the horizon. "To the south lies only shame and defeat. To the north, the unknown. Let us see what it can offer us."

CHAPTER 1

Autumn, Year 234 of the Third Epoch

All things in Aderilund were beautiful.

To its people Aderilund was called the Aspen Kingdom, and the name was well chosen. Sunlight streamed from above through the tall, ancient trees of the forest, swathing elegant Aderial with a patchwork of dappled light and shadow. Foremost of Aderilund's cities, nestled in a fertile valley, Aderial stood serene and unchanging throughout the centuries.

Aderial the proud, Aderial the beautiful.

In its forests were wild flowers of all colours and varieties, and beasts both fair and foul, but striking in their own way – shining coats, brilliant plumage, sparkling scales, or a call that sang like a thousand musicians in harmony.

All who came to Aderilund agreed: of all things in the world, the elves were the most beautiful of all.

The elves of Aderilund knew their place in the order of the universe. They were the firstborn, the "Children of Hydria", the *Eldara*. They knew that the other races of the world paled in comparison. The Eldara knew that they were the pinnacle of divine creation, angels in a world of beasts.

Their cousins far to the north, the Eldara of Liderial, wore shimmering gowns and robes of silk and fur, and let their long hair, golden as the sun, flow over their pale, snow-white shoulders.

In Aderial the Eldara were not the same as their northern brethren, but they were no less stunning. They favoured garments that were more subdued, but still breathtaking in their magnificence. Their locks were not fair, but dark, rich mahogany or deep velvet black. Their eyes were even more exquisite – almond-shaped orbs of glittering green or blue.

One thing in Aderilund, however, was not beautiful, and the elves had scorned it from the first day it came to their idyllic kingdom.

"Mal-halyth," they uttered, expressing their distaste aloud.

Mal-halyth – a weak one. An ugly, unfortunate being. A thing to be pitied.

A human.

***

It was raining.

Bellaydin sat in the drizzle, letting the light drops fall on his eyelashes as he stared towards the ocean. His black hair was damp, plastered across his skull, and his clothes were soaked, but Bellaydin didn't care. He was alone, and he was at peace, for the moment.

The bluff was some days north of Aderial, but the path to it was well marked, and quick to travel upon. Bellaydin had lived in Aderilund for twelve of his seventeen years. He had been coming to this particular beach for ten of those.

A gull swooped overhead, its squawking bringing a smile to Bellaydin's lips as the bird wheeled around in the sky above, perhaps looking for food. Feeling hungry himself, Bellaydin reached for his pack, rummaging through its contents. As he felt the few rations that remained, he grimaced. The supplies he had dutifully packed two days before were now getting low. It was probably time for him to return home.

Home.

It still seemed strange to call Aderial that, even though he had lived there for more than half his life and barely remembered the land of his birth. Of that place, nearly nothing remained for Bellaydin – a few blurred memories, some half-remembered names. He wasn't even sure if he really remembered any of that, or if he had reconstructed the memories from what others had told him.

He knew he was born in the distant land of Emparia, in a place called Genio, but he wasn't sure if it was a village, town, city or even a settlement at all.

His parents were named Alusine and Eleanor Ap'Lydin, but that was about the extent of his knowledge about his ancestry. He knew they were both dead, but how they had perished he had never been told, and any time he brought the matter up, others would deftly change the subject. Bellaydin suspected some tragedy in his long distant past but those close to him conspired to keep the truth hidden.

He had been barely five when he came to Aderilund from Emparia. Old enough to have acquired some memories of his youth, but not old enough to be able to retain any of them. Perhaps it was this dull, peaceful land he had been brought to. Perhaps it had some stupefying effect on his brain.

At the very least, he wasn't alone in this place. Bellaydin lived with his sister Polnygar, who was his elder by five years.

In truth, she was his half-sister. They had only a father in common – the late Alusine. It had been Polnygar's mother, Saegralanna, who had brought Bellaydin to Aderilund upon the death of his parents. For the last twelve years, she had been the only parent he had ever known and had raised him with the same love she would give her own child.

7

And yet, even though he barely remembered them, he still missed his true parents. He had been told by his foster mother that his father was an attractive man – dark and brooding, and with a winning personality.

"He was charming, your father. Very captivating," Saegralanna had said wistfully. "Witty too, with a self-confident gaze that hinted of invincibility. He took everything life threw his way with the sort of dry humour that endeared him to even the most aloof stranger."

"And of course he was irresistible to women, a very handsome man – "she had noted. " – for a human," Saegralanna would add as a defensive-sounding aside, as if trying to justify the relationship she and Bellaydin's father had shared.

Eldara society did not approve of relationships with humans, a fact that Saegralanna was reminded of constantly, to her own shame. But although she never voiced them, her own feelings were never far from the surface, and Bellaydin noticed that when she mentioned Alusine's name, Saegralanna would stare off into the distance, a dreamy look in her eyes. Perhaps he was even more handsome than Saegralanna cared to admit.

Bellaydin had to concede his sister must have received the lion's share of that inheritance, with her thick raven hair, sultry eyes and full lips. Bellaydin, on the other hand, had a somewhat sinister, unappealing look – almost black deep-set eyes, a prominent aquiline nose and unruly hair that, even at its best, tended to stick out like the straw on a scarecrow. At the moment it was tangled, knotted and soaked from the rain, and, though it was almost as long as his sister's, that was hardly noticeable from its current appearance. A cut across his top lip as a child had left Bellaydin with an ugly scar, something that did nothing to accentuate his features.

Of his own mother Bellaydin had few memories, and of her appearance he had even less of an idea, but Saegralanna had said that Eleanor Ap'Lydin's most striking features were a full head of fiery red hair and intense blue eyes. Bellaydin had a faint and uncertain memory of such a woman, but he was never sure if it was indeed a true recollection from his childhood or if again, as he suspected, it was merely a reconstructed reminiscence, pieced together from the explanations of others. Other details about his birth mother were not forthcoming, and Bellaydin assumed it was a sore point with Saegralanna, due to his father's relationship with Eleanor coming swiftly after the end of his relationship with Saegralanna.

The rain had eased.

Above Bellaydin's head the sun had emerged from behind the clouds, though it sat low on the horizon. Soon, one by one, the four moons would appear in the sky and the night would be upon him. The afternoon was slipping away from Bellaydin, and he knew that if he was to reach home by tomorrow, he would need to leave soon. He stood, breathing in the fresh air and savouring the sea breeze one last time. Then, shouldering his pack, he turned and made his way back up the path.

He wondered what tomorrow would bring.

***

Dawn.

The sun rose over the Halls of the Ancients, the centre of life in Aderial for generations. It had been here, nearly three and a half thousand years ago, that the Eldara Prince Aderias had arrived with his followers and proclaimed the birth of the city of Aderial.

It was here, under the gaze of kings and lords long gone, that the heads of the Houses – the High Council of Aderial – had met for centuries thereafter.

It was here that the Council had gathered again, summoned by the word of one of its most powerful members – the spellweaver Lord Ivellios.

Lord Ivellios was a tall and dignified Eldara lord, his silver hair long over his shoulders, his eyes a cold slate grey, like the long robes he wore. He held himself with a proud and haughty air, but that was hardly something that set him apart from his peers. The spellweavers were the masters of the Art among the Eldara. This skill, called "magic" by the unlettered, gave them power beyond equal. With the Art, there was no end to the wonders the spellweavers could create, limited only by the power of their own minds. Humans would call spellweavers "wizards", but the Eldara considered the term undignified. spellweavers were considered the guardians of the celestial tapestry and occupied the highest strata of Eldara culture, acting as the keepers of the tradition, history and protocol of their civilisation; they were advisors to the king himself. The influence they wielded was great, and amongst the spellweavers, Lord Ivellios was greater still.

Ivellios stood in the centre of the grand hall, as many generations of spellweavers had done before him, and as many would do so after him. His powerful presence and rank added a solemn weight to the words he directed at those present, reinforcing his message.

"If I may remind the Council of the reason we are gathered here today." He paused, waiting as eyes settled upon him with expectation. "It is, of course, the matter of the make-up of Lady Saegralanna's household." There was fervent discussion, in hushed whispers, as Ivellios directed his gaze towards a single member.

"Indeed, Lord Ivellios," said Speaker Quarion, "And it is a tale we have heard from you on many occasions already. Yet you wish to discuss it again. What has changed since last we met?"

"Nothing, my Lord Speaker," said Ivellios, "That is precisely the problem. Another year has passed and still the stain remains, still Lady Saegralanna has done nothing to address that which she shelters under her own roof. I begin to fear that she will never respect the sanctity of our fair land."

Among the Eldara, Lady Saegralanna was an oddity. She was the only child of the deeply respected Lord Saegras, and thus, heir to the House Aelsar. Saegralanna had two uncles, centuries older than her, and so it was tribute to the power and influence of her father that Saegralanna had come to a position of leadership in House Aelsar at all. It had certainly not been to the taste of her uncles, who departed from court and into seclusion at their estates the moment their niece's ascension became confirmed.

Saegralanna's father was a respected diplomat and a powerful spellweaver, an advisor to the Aspen Throne for over two hundred years. He had travelled the world forging peace between the Eldara kingdoms and the other races of the world. Saegralanna was his only child, and she had been spoiled and doted on. But despite this favour, or perhaps because of it, she had rebelled as a youth, left her father's household and disappeared into the outside world. When she returned it was with a child.

Her child.

Worst of all, the child's father was human. Although they did not cast her out, many of the older elves began to view Lady Saegralanna with suspicion from then on – as a dangerous subversive. Some even suggested Lord Saegras' untimely death was caused by the stress his only child put him under; though few were brave enough to mention this in Saegralanna's presence.

"The contents of my household are the business of House Aelsar, Lord Ivellios, not this Council," Saegralanna said firmly.

"Actually, Lady Saegralanna," Lord Ivellios interrupted, "It is most definitely the business of this Council, charged as they are with the protection of Aderilund and its ways. We have tolerated your eccentricities for a long time, my lady, mostly due to the respect with which we hold your late father and his advocacy of House Aelsar. This tryst of yours, the results of which is a half-human abom –" He paused, noticing a few frowns.

"You refer to Lady Saegralanna's daughter, I presume," Speaker Quarion prompted.

"Ah yes, of course. Her *daughter*," Lord Ivellios said, the words forming harshly on his tongue. "As I was saying, we tolerated that child because she at least shared some modicum of Eldara blood, tainted as it was. But this other child – why do you sully your household keeping a human amongst you?"

"That *other child* is my daughter's half-brother, Lord Ivellios." Lady Saegralanna said, anger flashing in her green eyes, "And he is also an orphan. Surely you, of all people, respect the sanctity of the family. Are you suggesting I rob Polnygaranna of her only sibling?"

"Of course not," said Lord Ivellios. "I have only the greatest respect for the concept of the family. The *Eldara* concept, mind you."

He turned to the rest of his audience and declared, "Brethren, let us not muddy the waters here with these emotive arguments. The issue is clear. We have a human child, living here among us in Aderial. What is next? Mountainfolk in our gardens? Hsien or Nemoi in our libraries? Orschans?"

Ivellios' last comment brought about some consternation in his audience. The Orschans were a barbaric and violent people who dwelled in the lands to the south, renowned for their savagery.

"Surely, Lord Ivellios, you are not comparing human children to Orschans," Speaker Quarion said, raising an eyebrow.

Ivellios smiled, "Of course not. I was just illustrating my point." He then added quietly, "Orschans have far better manners."

Some delegates heard his remarks, and the hall erupted into a mixture of jeers and cheers.

"Order," yelled Quarion. "Order! Watch yourself. What was that comment, Lord Ivellios?"

"A slip of the tongue, my Lord Speaker," Ivellios said quickly.

Quarion continued, "Very well, Ivellios. A slip is sometimes unavoidable, but you should remember that High King Talan himself has been very clear on the importance of our alliance with the civilised human nations. He would hate to see it jeopardised by *ill-advised* comments. Enough, Ivellios."

"Oh you misunderstand me, Speaker. I have nothing against humans –"
Pausing, he then added, a little more quietly, "– in their own lands."

He smiled wryly as he returned to his seat.

Speaker Quarion sighed, looked over at the assembly and said, "Very well. I think we have entertained this discussion enough for one day. The Council will be adjourned."

Ivellios smiled again – a twisted, crooked grin – and bowed. "I have every confidence that your Eminence will give this matter the attention it deserves."

Quarion waved away Lord Ivellios' sarcasm and rose from his seat, bowed to the assembled nobles, and left the hall with his entourage.

"Give my regards to your family, Lady Saegralanna," Ivellios said pointedly.

"Arrogant oaf," Saegralanna said under her breath.

Quarion looked in her direction, and frowned as if he had heard her comment. "Please, all of you, before you leave," Speaker Quarion said. "You will be required to attend tomorrow. The Emparian ambassador will be making his address. The Emparians wish for us to honour the promises we made to them. And it would not serve High King Talan's wishes if the ambassador were to leave offended."

CHAPTER 2

As the assembled councillors departed the halls, the Emparian ambassador in question was occupying himself as best he could. Like many first-time visitors to the Aspen Kingdom, he was sampling what Aderilund had to offer in goods and crafts.

The markets of Aderial were busy. Harvest had finished and farmers from all over Aderilund had brought their produce for sale, accompanied by craftsmen, artisans and merchants of all stripes.

Augustin Bauer, First Baron Bauer, looked with interest upon the wares of a weaponsmith. One item, a particularly finely forged sword, had caught his attention.

Augustin was a brawny and middle-aged human, his auburn hair greying at the sideburns. An old war wound had cost him one of his eyes many years ago, and he covered it with a patch. This had caused some level of unease as he arrived in Aderial, as most Eldara found physical disfigurements discomforting. By now though, Augustin was used to the stares, and concentrated his attention on the weapon in front of him. The sword was unlike any that he had used during the many years of military service

"Magnificent," Augustin said to himself, as he ran his fingers along the blade of the weapon.

He took a few practice swings with it and then, suitably impressed, placed it back on the merchant's stall. The merchant eyed Augustin expectantly.

"You there," Augustin said to the merchant. "How much for that sword there?"

The merchant muttered something in the elven tongue. "Quei?"

Augustin went to repeat himself. "I said – "

A voice behind Augustin interrupted him. "He doesn't speak your common tongue, human."

"What?"

"Emparian. This merchant can't understand it," the voice said.

Augustin turned, and looked at the newcomer. It was a young woman, an elf, judging by the pointed, lobe-less ears. Standing some seven inches over five feet, her hair, like most of the inhabitants of Aderilund, was black, and contrasted with her green almond-shaped eyes. She was rather oddly dressed for an inhabitant of Aderilund. While the clothes she wore were of an expensive cut, the entire outfit was mismatched, and the girl wore them untidily.

"This merchant only speaks Eldaric," the girl said.

"I see." Augustin narrowed his eyes. "What is your name, young woman?"

"Polnygaranna. But most call me Polnygar," she said.

"Polnygar? Isn't that the name your people give to a purple flower?"

"Blue," the girl corrected. "And who are you?"

"Straight to the point, I see. My name is Augustin Bauer, that is to say, *Baron* Augustin Bauer. I'm ambassador for Her Majesty Queen Amaryllis of

Emparia. I'm here to negotiate with your High Council. Diplomatic treaties, trade rights, that sort of thing."

At the mention of 'Emparia', Polnygar's eyes lit up. "You come from Emparia? Tell me, have you been in many battles? Against the Goriinchians, I mean?"

Augustin was intrigued. An elf with knowledge of human affairs was rare. Even rarer was one with an interest in it. But this was an elven *girl*, of all things. It was most astonishing. He would humour her, for the moment.

"A few," Augustin replied. "But there hasn't been a full-scale war against the Goriinchians for years. Not since they were crushed at the battle at the city of Genio fifty years ago." He smiled. "I heard it was a glorious victory. If only I could have been there."

"Sir William Ap'Lydin fought in that battle, didn't he?" Polnygar said.

Augustin raised an eyebrow. "That's right, girl. Ap'Lydin was the commander in that conflict. Even his death could not take victory from us. The Goriinchians fell in their thousands." He paused, turning to her. "I'm impressed. How did you know that name?"

"He was my grandfather," Polnygar said.

Augustin laughed. "I'm afraid, girl, that you are mistaken. Sir William was a human, just as I am. You are an elf."

The girl smiled. "An *elf*?"

"Oh, I forgot myself. I forgot my manners," Augustin said.

To almost any inhabitant of Aderial, the word "elf" would have stung as badly as any shot from an arrow. Elf was a human term that the Eldara found demeaning. Most humans, however, were unaware of any inference, and used the term cavalierly.

Polnygar however, took no offence. In fact, she smiled, ever so slightly, as if amused by Augustin's discomfort.

17

"Are you not offended?" Augustin ventured.

Polnygar shook her head. "I've been called worse in my life. And sometimes, being surrounded by Eldara and their diplomatic, well-trained tongues, well; it sometimes makes me long for human brevity."

"So, I am not mistaken. You are Eldara, yes?"

"Yes and no. My mother is Eldara. My father was human," she said, shaking her head with amusement.

Now that he took a second look at her, Augustin had to concede that he could see traces of human ancestry in the young woman. Her height and build was indicative of it, and her face was less chiselled and delicate than that of a full-blooded elf.

"I see," said Augustin. "So who are your parents, then?"

"My mother is Lady Saegralanna, Head of House Aelsar."

A tap on his shoulder distracted Augustin from Polnygar's words. The elven merchant babbled something incomprehensible into his ear. "I'm sorry?" Augustin said testily.

"He wants to know if you are going to buy anything," Polnygar offered.

Augustin frowned, and waved away the merchant's objections with a negligent gesture. He turned back to Polnygar, and took stock of her once again. "So, the Lady Saegralanna is your mother," he said. "She is on the – what is it called? – the High Council of Ancients, is she not?"

Polnygar nodded her assent.

"Interesting," Augustin said. "I'm due to meet with them tomorrow. And your father?"

"My father is dead," Polnygar said.

"Oh," said Augustin. "I'm sorry to hear that. What was his name?"

"Alusine Ap'Lydin."

Unlike many from his homeland, Augustin Bauer was well-travelled, and had seen many things in the world. In his youth, a half-elf claiming an Emparian knight as her father would have caused him equal parts shock and astonishment. Now, he barely flinched at the information, and took it as calmly as he might the news that his favourite horse needed reshoeing.

"Ah," said Augustin. "Lord Alusine. The late uncle of the Earl of Genio. Yes, I know of him, and now that I take another look at you, girl, I can see a resemblance. I was not aware he had a daughter." He paused momentarily, gathering his thoughts. "Nor, young woman, was I aware that he had indulged in a dalliance with an elf maid. But I can imagine why he would have kept it a secret. I can't imagine that your parents were ever properly married at any stage. Not according to any damn churchman."

"Does that really matter?" Polnygar said tersely.

"More than you would think. The Church of Ralom is quite powerful in Emparian politics, and they don't look favourably on what they term *illegitimate* pairings. A bastard may rise in Emparia, but only on his own merits." He shrugged. "Not such a bad thing though, in the end."

Polnygar frowned, but said nothing.

"Now, girl," said Augustin. "If you'll excuse me, I must retire to my lodgings and prepare myself for tomorrow. It has been interesting talking to you, to say the least."

***

The most prominent families of Aderial mainly dwelt in the inner, most ancient districts of the city, their elegant estates clustered around the central Palace of Karn-Raka.

Among these estates, the one belonging to House Aelsar was particularly noteworthy, though not for its size or even its lavishness. After all, elves did not go for ostentatious displays of wealth. Humility was a virtue – flaunting wealth was a trait belonging to "crass" humans, not to Hydria's chosen. If any Eldara exhibited such a ridiculous affectation, they would risk being shunned by their social betters.

Aelsar Estate, ancestral home of House Aelsar, was noteworthy because of its peculiar architecture, a design that set it apart from the other buildings in Aderial. It was a strange, eclectic blend of styles from around the world – stately halls like those found in the depths of Relon Möker, minarets from Qarld, a barbican matching those found in Lerid and a traditional Tarkenese courtyard, to name a few of its features. This unusual design was the brainchild of the late Lord Saegras who had travelled widely in his centuries of service to the King. His taste had been considered eccentric by other Eldara, to say the least.

Bellaydin frowned as he approached the gates of the estate grounds. To him, the building highlighted how alien this place felt – a feeling that had persisted his entire life, even though Aelsar Estate was the only home he'd ever known.

He reached the gate, unlocking it and stepping down the path that led to the manor. He was not even halfway to the front door when he became aware of someone else walking quickly behind him. Suddenly, he was punched in the arm.

He cursed loudly.

"Come on Bela, what's the matter? What's with the frown?" Polnygar said.

"Oh, you know how it is…"

Polnygar laughed. "You were at the bluffs again, weren't you?" she teased.

Bellaydin said nothing, but offered an enigmatic smile.

"Don't worry," Polnygar said. "I won't tell Mother. You're just lucky she's been away these past three days."

"What's been going on, Pol?"

"The High Council is preparing to receive the ambassador from Emparia. Mother had to-"

"Did you say Emparia?" Bellaydin said.

"Yes, yes," said Polnygar. "But I'm not sure why you find that-"

Bellaydin shrugged. "I guess I still think of it as home."

Polnygar looked at him. "You know, I lived there for longer than you did, brother."

Bellaydin nodded quietly. That much was true, at least. Polnygar had lived with their father in Emparia for just over five years. When Bellaydin was born, Polnygar had been sent to live with Saegralanna, likely at the instigation of Alusine's new wife.

"I know, I know," Bellaydin said. "Gods, sometimes I find it as ridiculous as you must, Polnygar. I mean, I've not even seen the damn place since I was five. But I can't help thinking about it, especially when I'm alone."

"Well there's your problem, Bela," Polnygar said, "You spend too much time alone."

They reached the front door together and Bellaydin opened the great doors. Waving his hand, Bellaydin let his sister enter the manor first. The doors opened up into a large sitting room, with a grand marble staircase leading up to the upper levels. As usual, Bellaydin's eyes were drawn elsewhere, to a wall dominated by a huge and ornate map of the known world.

The map had been commissioned by Lord Saegras in his days as ambassador, and it depicted all the lands he had set foot in. An elaborate border framed the map, with the corners holding stylized representations of each of the four moons that illuminated the night sky. As Polnygar sat down and stretched, Bellaydin went over to the wall, tracing his fingers over the map. Aderilund and the city of Aderial were situated in the very centre, but as far as Bellaydin felt, it was far away from anywhere important. To the south of Aderilund stretched out the great continent of Orspederia, through the Mokerian Plateau all the way to the Shattered Empire of Orscha. To the north, across the sea, was the continent of Carurlonia, and then, just to the northeast of that, Emparia. He placed his finger on the kingdom, his lips moving as he silently said the names of its prominent towns and cities, including Genio, the city of his birth here nothing more than a black dot on an unfamiliar coastline.

Polnygar came to stand next to him. "Looking at grandfather's map again?"

Bellaydin smiled, "For now, it's about as close as I'm going to get to Emparia."

"Look, Bela, I don't blame you for hating this place," said Polnygar. "Living here, around these – what can I call them – pious asses all the time gets on even my nerves, and I share blood with them. Though not much else." She paused, and then shrugged. "It's why I'm planning on getting far away from here, as soon as the opportunity arrives, Bela."

"I've heard this before," Bellaydin said. "Where are you going to go? Emparia?"

"No, probably not. I want to broaden my horizons a little more." She placed her fingers on the map, to the lands north of Aderilund. "Maybe Carurlonia. I've always wanted to see the cathedrals of Ralom, or the frozen wastes of Skurj. Haven't decided yet."

"Have you told Mother then?" asked Bellaydin.

Polnygar laughed. "Of course not. You know how over-protective she is. She nearly burst a vein when I asked her last year. She's not going to let either of us go, you know that. It would break her heart."

"So what are you saying? We're both stuck here for the rest of our lives?"

"No, what I'm saying is that if either of us wants to leave, we're not going to get Mother's approval, we'll just have to do it, no matter the consequences. If you're not prepared to do that Bela, well, you'd better start planning for a long, dull life here." She paused, and then gave him a mischievous look. "Still, it could be worse. There's famine in the lands to the south these days. At least in this place there's never been so much as a failed harvest, thanks to the spellweavers." She smiled slightly, and nudged her brother. "Those pompous gits are good for something, eh?

"So," said Bellaydin, after a few minutes. "What's it like?"

"What's what like?" Polnygar said, her eyes focused on some distant corner of the map.

"Emparia."

"You're asking this *again*?" said Polnygar. "And to think mother is always talking about your perfect memory."

"Humour me," said Bellaydin.

"All right, fine," said Polnygar. "It's dirty and crowded, the rivers are brown and the air stinks. And the people who live there are such miserable bores. Happy? Oh, don't give me that look. You wanted to know."

Bellaydin sighed. "I guess Mother will be home soon anyway."

"Indeed she will be, let's make sure we both greet her with a smile, yes?" Polnygar said.

"I *am* smiling."

"That's not a smile, little brother," Polnygar said, somewhat cheekily. "I think that's what they call a grimace."

Bellaydin smiled wider.

"There, that's better. Everyone's happy now. Remember that for when she's home."

"Of course my darling sister." Bellaydin said with a sarcastic tone.

"Well, you've certainly convinced me," Polnygar said. "Anyway, I think I'm going to take a bath. I'll leave you to your map. Oh, and little brother –"

"Yes?"

"Smile."

Despite his mood, Bellaydin could not help but crack a grin. Polnygar had always had a knack for cheering him up, even when nothing else did. It had been that way for most of their lives, probably one of the reasons the pair were so close. That they had been such was fortunate for Bellaydin – he hadn't really had any other friends, and his friendship with his sister was possibly the only thing that kept him grounded. That, and of course, his foster mother.

Bellaydin knew that the Eldara of Aderilund only tolerated him because of Saegralanna. He could see it in their collective gaze. He could hear it in their voices. Whether through the accusing stare, the haughty poise, or that certain tone of voice, Bellaydin knew when he was being patronised.

The Eldara had ruled their civilisation for six thousand years. They knew more about arrogance than humans could ever hope to learn, and they believed their achievements more than warranted such self-assurance.

"We gave the gift of civilisation to humans," the Eldara were known to say, "only to see them squander it."

Saegralanna was different. She had always been different. Bellaydin had heard stories, mostly in hushed whispers, from mouths that disapproved. Stories of Saegralanna's youth, of her travels, her affair, and the outcome of that affair – Polnygar.

If anything, the inhabitants of Aderilund disliked Polnygar's presence as much as Bellaydin's. In some ways, the resentment towards Polnygar was even more palpable. While Bellaydin was merely a foreign, alien element, sticking out like a sore thumb in the tranquil, serene Eldara society, Polnygar was a symbol of something the elves wished never happened and to be reminded of it daily truly rankled them. For all their scorn, the Eldara only wished Bellaydin lived somewhere else. With Polnygar, they'd rather she didn't exist at all.

Saegralanna had spoken many times of Bellaydin and Polnygar's father, but had not frequently discussed the circumstances under which they met, or parted, for that matter. From what he remembered, it had to do with Saegralanna's father – Polnygar's Eldara grandfather.

As befitting such a long and dedicated service to his liege and nation, towards the end of Saegras' life the Eldara was appointed ambassador to the Emparian court, to negotiate on Aderilund's behalf with that faraway kingdom for various trade concessions. With the crowning of a new king in that land, Saegras, accompanied by his young daughter Saegralanna, was among the first representatives to journey to Emparia to greet him.

Some years later, Saegras and his daughter returned with an infant child, which Saegras freely admitted was his own grandchild. The father's name was not given, at least, not to the general public. The child, Polnygar, was soon sent to live with her father, and was not heard from for more than a decade. By then, Saegras had passed on, and rumours had begun to circulate that so too had Polnygar's own father. One morning, a ship arrived carrying the young girl, and a few years later, a boy. That boy, of course, had been Bellaydin himself.

By then Saegralanna, despite the protest of others, had ascended to the leadership of House Aelsar, and there was little anyone else could do about it. Even Saegras' still living brothers agreed to the decision when their noisy protests came to naught. Despite their bigotry, the Eldara of Aderilund were loath to interfere with the lives of others. They felt it better to snipe away in private, Bellaydin noted grimly.

"Bellaydin," Polnygar said. "If you've finished daydreaming? Mother's just arrived home. Perhaps we should see how her day went?"

"Uh oh," said Bellaydin.

"What?"

"I know that look," said Bellaydin. "You're going to ask her again, aren't you?"

Polnygar feigned innocence. "I don't know what you mean, dear brother."

It didn't take long for Bellaydin to find out how his foster mother's day had been. As she entered the estate, Saegralanna's annoyance was plain to see.

"I take it things didn't go well then?" Bellaydin said.

"Oh, hello Bela, dear," said Saegralanna. "No. No it didn't."

"What happened?" asked Polnygar.

"That bigot Ivellios is still trying to taunt me for his own amusement. The fool is obsessed with us."

"What did he say?" said Bellaydin.

Saegralanna looked at him, smiled and shook her head. "Never you mind, Bela. It's not that important."

"So it was about me, then?" said Bellaydin.

"I didn't say that."

"Polnygar then?"

"I didn't say that either." Saegralanna put a hand on each of her children's shoulders. "Enough of that. Put him out of your minds. There's someone here I want you to meet."

Saegralanna pointed to the doorway, as a stranger walked in. Bellaydin found himself standing face to face with a tall human male, of middle years, his brown hair greying at the temples.

"Polnygar and Bellaydin Ap'Lydin", said Saegralanna. "Meet Augustin Bauer."

"It's good to meet you, young Master Ap'Lydin," said Bauer, extending a palm.

Bellaydin grasped the man's hand tentatively, and shook it.

"Ah, a good firm handshake. That I like to see." Bauer turned slightly, and, seeing Polnygar, his smile widened. "And Polnygar, wasn't it? We met in the marketplace, yes?"

"Yes," Polnygar hesitated. "That's right. What are you doing in our house?"

"Baron Augustin Bauer is due to meet the High Council tomorrow," Saegralanna said. "I offered to show him some of the things Aderilund has to offer."

"Yes," Bauer said. "But I'm mainly interested in this meal you've been talking about."

"Augustin will be joining us for dinner, my dears."

"I've heard your mother's kitchen serves the best food this side of Mokeria," Augustin chuckled. "So I thought it would be best if I find out why."

"That's no secret," said Polnygar. "It's the cook she stole from Lord Ivellios three years ago."

Saegralanna smiled. "Stole? I merely offered him a slightly higher wage than that stuffy spellweaver."

"Triple pay, Mother," Polnygar grinned from ear to ear.

Augustin guffawed. "Oh, I think I'm going to enjoy tonight."

The meal was, as expected, delicious. Saegralanna's cook was one of the Hsien people from the far southeast, renowned for their culinary talents.

The cook had long worked for the family of Lord Ivellios, though not particularly eagerly, and jumped at the chance to switch to House Aelsar. In truth, the payment had hardly been a factor at all. Ivellios had always been a rather unpleasant individual, especially to non-Eldara, so it was no surprise that his cook had left for a more congenial master.

"This is superb, my lady," said Augustin. "I've never tasted anything like it." He paused, "But then again, we Emparians aren't known for our cuisine."

Saegralanna smiled. "Let me see if I remember," she said. "Ah yes. *The Emparians will not eat anything they cannot put in a pie.*"

The table erupted into laughter.

"Now, I know that is not at all true, my lady," said Augustin, pursing his lips. "Sometimes we put our food between two slices of bread."

He smiled, resting his elbows on the table as the rest of the diners guffawed again.

"So tell me," said Saegralanna, "We haven't had much of a chance to speak. What concessions is King Henry hoping to get from the High Council?"

"King Henry?" Augustin said tersely, raising an eyebrow."Very little, I'd expect. The King, may Kytilas guard his soul, died four years ago."

"Oh," said Saegralanna, looking somewhat embarrassed. "I am sorry."

Bellaydin looked up from his meal. "As you can see, we don't get much news from the outside world here. We are somewhat isolated."

Augustin frowned, and then waved a hand dismissively. "Pay it no heed. I took no offence." He went on, "You can't be expected to know everything that happens in our kingdom, not from this far away. Though I thought the embassy might send word."

"Generally, news from the foreign lands comes to the High Council first," said Polnygar. "The Council is currently led by Lord Ivellios and he and Mother don't exactly see eye to eye."

"I was under the impression that the Speaker headed the Council," said Augustin.

Saegralanna coughed slightly. "Well, he does, officially. But he defers to Ivellios in most matters, making Ivellios Speaker in all but name. Ivellios, for his part, wouldn't defer to anyone except for the king or queen. And, even then, it would be somewhat reluctantly," she said.

"I see," Augustin sighed, putting down his knife. "And I thought politics back home were confusing." He shook his head. "Now, where were we? Ah yes. His Majesty King Henry died some years ago. His only surviving child has ascended to the throne, Her Majesty Queen Amaryllis. The Emparian Civil Wars are finally over, and attention has now returned to the process of rebuilding. I've been sent to see if the government of Aderilund can help us in that regard."

"Of course, you want the Council to honour the agreements my father made, don't you?" Saegralanna said.

Bellaydin had no doubt she was referring to the accords forged by Lord Saegras during his years as a diplomat.

"Well, yes, mainly that," said Augustin, tearing off a piece of bread and dipping it in some sauce. He chewed on it absent-mindedly. "There's a fragile sort of peace in Emparia at the moment. Yet, we dare not show any weakness in front of the Goriinchians. Don't want them getting any ideas, you know?"

"The Goriinchians? I sometimes hear Polnygar mention them," said Bellaydin.

"Oh, is that so?" Augustin said, "How much do you know?"

"Not much," said Bellaydin. "Well, a little. Some sort of human culture that exists near Emparia. She tells me there's been some wars between the

Emparians and the Goriinchians."

"I've only told him the basics, I don't know much more myself," Polnygar said.

"There's not much more too it. The Goriinchians are a bunch of savages who live to Emparia's south. Goriinchia is ruled by a brute of a king, Ygarak, who claims to be a prophet of some sort. The Goriinchians are aggressive by nature and constantly pose a threat to our southern border. They've been quiet for the past few decades though. Thankfully."

Polnygar cleared her throat and spoke up. "Will you be returning home after your meeting with the High Council?"

"No, I'm off to Carurlonia. There's much more to be done."

"Carurlonia?" said Polnygar.

"Macrodonia to be precise." Augustin rubbed his chin. "Yes, the Crown is keeping me quite busy these days. I'm going to meet with the young king of Macrodonia. There is work needed between ourselves and the Macrodonians. Mining rights, military alliances, that sort of thing."

"And from there?" Polnygar persisted.

Augustin shrugged. "I don't know yet. I go where I'm needed. Why do you ask?"

"She's asking because she wants you to take her with you," Bellaydin blurted out.

"Bela!" scolded Saegralanna.

"It's true," said Bellaydin. "She'd try anything to get out of this place."

"Well, can you blame me?" yelled Polnygar.

"Pol!" scolded Saegralanna again.

Polnygar rolled her eyes, Saegralanna glared at her while Augustin looked embarrassed and Bellaydin stifled a chuckle.

Bellaydin had lost count of the number of times they had had this conversation. Saegralanna and Polnygar had this argument at least once a week. It always followed the same pattern. Polnygar would mention a ship or caravan leaving Aderilund for distant lands, and express a desire to go with it. Saegralanna would then argue it was too dangerous and decide Polnygar was too young, and Polnygar would counter with earnest pleas as to her ability to deal with any dangers. The discussion would end with Polnygar loudly and passionately denying that her mother had any authority over her.

Invariably, the argument was never satisfactorily resolved to either participant's taste, since it would be brought up again, and again, and again. If nothing else, it was testament to both his sister's desperate desire to leave Aderilund, and her mother's patient insistence that she remained.

"Polnygar, we've been through this," Saegralanna pleaded gently.

"Oh, really, Mother?" said Polnygar. "Have we? This is the bit where you tell me it's too dangerous for me to leave Aderilund, isn't it? And then not bother with any follow up explanation?"

Saegralanna flushed, and there was a stony silence around the table.

"Uh…" Augustin Bauer started. He looked uncomfortable.

"Pol," Saegralanna said, "I'm only trying to protect you."

"I can look after myself," Polnygar said.

Saegralanna frowned.

"If I may," began Augustin. "I have no doubt, young lady, that you are perfectly capable of taking care of yourself, but the point is somewhat moot. I could not possibly take you anywhere without your mother's permission, and secondly –"

"I don't need her permission," said Polnygar, folding her arms across her chest.

" —and secondly," Augustin continued, "my travels are almost always on official business for the Royal Court of Emparia. They would be unlikely to permit me to take on extra followers."

Polnygar sat still, her brow furrowed and eyes prickling with frustration. Saegralanna glanced at her daughter, and gently placed her own hand on Polnygar's. Polnygar scowled, and yanked her hand from underneath her mother's.

"If you'll excuse me," said Polnygar, "I think I've lost my appetite." She stood up, and, leaving her plate and the remnants of her food on the table, turned and left the room. The three that remained glanced at each other. There were no words.

It was Augustin who broke the awkward silence. "I should be going. I don't want to intrude any further."

Saegralanna shook her head. "Please, stay for a little longer. I am sorry you had to be witness to that. You are a guest in our house, and we should not have subjected you to our squabbles. We are better than that."

"Think nothing of it, my lady," said Augustin, "My brother and I used to fight all the time, in front of dukes and earls, no less."

***

Much later, Bellaydin sat on the edge of his bed, idly reading one of Saegralanna's books. It had been one of her childhood favourites, a tale entitled *The Mage Lord's Daughter*. It was a tender, though tragic, story of the doomed romance between a human barbarian and the daughter of an Eldara spellweaver. Bellaydin had always wondered if the similarity between the young Saegralanna and the heroine of the book was mere coincidence.

"Here's my little brother with his nose in a book," said Polnygar. "Can't say I'm surprised."

Bellaydin looked up and frowned, "I must say, I was somewhat disappointed. Tonight was one of your less theatrical exits."

"Oh?" Polnygar said quizzically.

"Yes. Don't you remember, three months ago? You were as red as these bed sheets. You looked like you were nearly about to explode. Do you remember?"

"No," Polnygar said, somewhat tersely.

"Oh, come on," Bellaydin grinned, becoming quite animated. "You were yelling so hard your voice was going hoarse."

"Alright, alright." conceded Polnygar.

"And you say I have a temper," said Bellaydin.

Polnygar smirked. "Oh, you do. But you're always trying to pretend otherwise, suppressing it, keeping it simmering away. That can't be healthy." She sighed and tried to change the subject. "So, did I miss anything?"

"Not really," said Bellaydin, closing the book. "Mother simply kept our guest occupied with more chatter about the Council… you know, politics, gossip, that sort of thing. He left about half an hour ago."

Polnygar looked at Bellaydin.

"So do you believe me now?" she said, "Does it look like she'll ever let either of us leave? Sometimes it seems she still thinks of us as children."

"Well," said Bellaydin, "She is over a hundred years old. It's been quite a few decades since she was our age."

Eldara were incredibly long-lived, with their lifespan ten times that of the average human. As a result, Eldara tended to look down upon the young and untried, which from their perspective, was anyone under a century in age. With Saegralanna, this sometimes manifested itself as a gentle, but persistent, form of patronising, which drove Bellaydin and Polnygar mad.

"Maybe she'll let us go when we're a hundred or so, you know?"

Bellaydin smiled and nodded, as if making some profound point. By the look on her face, Polnygar didn't think he had. "Oh, come on Polnygar."

"What?"

"Smile."

CHAPTER 3

A voice echoed through the chamber.

"Honoured Lords and Ladies of the High Council, revered Speaker, please rise for their Majesties, High King Talan li'Karn-Raka and High Queen Talina li'Aderias."

Saegralanna rose to her feet, noting the haughty gaze of Lord Ivellios as the spellweaver did likewise.

"So pleasing to see there are still a few Eldara courtesies that you honour, Lady Saegralanna," Ivellios said under his breath. Saegralanna ignored his comment, and kept her eyes forward.

The Eldara monarchs had reigned over their people for almost two and a half centuries. They were joint monarchs, having both come from noble bloodlines, but their upbringings shared little in common. Talina's youth had been conventional; the eldest daughter of a Lord-Protector of Aderilund, raised with the expectation that she would one day ascend to a position of leadership in Eldara society.

Her husband, despite his bloodline, had been born in exile and into poverty. His parents had been murdered while he was still young and his home destroyed. It was only later he had discovered his true heritage. It was said that such a brutal set of circumstances had made Talan wise beyond his years, and laid the foundation for what was to become a successful reign.

"Your Majesties," said Speaker Quarion, bowing before the two monarchs.

"We recognise our most loyal subject, Quarion li'Ailynu," said Talan, "And we commend him for his wise and judicious stewardship of our kingdom."

One after the other, Talan and Talina each gently laid a hand on Quarion's head, speaking a quiet word of thanks.

"We also recognise the Lords of the Great Houses of Aderilund," said Talina. "We greet our brethren in the name of the Aspen Throne."

"Step forward, Lords and Ladies of the Council," said Talan.

The assembled members of the council took three steps forward and, one after the other, genuflected towards their king and queen.

"The Aspen Kingdom is prosperous and at peace. Our borders have never been more secure, and the strength and power of the Eldara have never been greater," Talan began. "But with prosperity and power come great responsibility. We must look to our friends abroad, and help them through their trials, as they helped us through ours."

Talan turned to his wife, and smiled.

"Some twenty years ago, the Emparian Civil Wars ended, and a new king ascended to the throne of Emparia, ending the strife that had endured there for so many generations," Talina said. "We, the Eldara of Aderilund, were amongst the first to greet the new king of those lands. We were amongst the first to forge a pact with the new regime. We honour those who spoke in our name. We honour the great spellweavers who served their nation. Vaerath, Polaeras, Aarden, Ivellios, Saegras…"

As the names were recited, Saegralanna noted that, like her own father, most of the spellweavers named were now dead. Ivellios was one of the few that still lived.

Upon hearing his name, the spellweaver glanced at Saegralanna, smiling smugly. "Ah," Ivellios said, with an exaggerated lilt in his voice. "It is truly such an honour to be named by the king and queen. If only your father was alive today. Such a shame he died so young. Perhaps it was the disappointment he felt."

Saegralanna restrained the urge to reach over and slap the spellweaver. That would have been undignified, especially in front of the king and queen.

"Emparia offered us generous trade concessions and, as a consequence, we have prospered. Now it is time for us to return the favour," Talina finished and nodded to the Speaker Quarion, who raised his hands.

"Lords and Ladies of the Council, please rise for the Emparian ambassador, Baron Augustin Bauer," the speaker said.

"Time for you to earn your keep, my lady," whispered Ivellios.

***

Augustin fidgeted with his sleeves, looking with disdain at the lace and silk. "Pah. Elven fashion. I look like a dandy and feel like a fool."

Earlier in the day, when Augustin had faced several elven diplomats dressed in his finest clothes, he had received several interesting reactions, ranging from quizzical frowns to muffled gasps. One elven woman had even fainted. It was later explained to him that what passed for "finery" in Emparia was something even the most modest of middle-class elves would refuse to wear. To face a royal audience in such garb was, to say the least, unthinkable.

"Fops," he said. "The lot of them. Saegralanna and her family are the only sane elves I've met here in my entire bloody stay. Small wonder she's considered strange by the rest of them."

A stiff, proud-looking elven functionary entered the antechamber. "You. Human. You've been called. The king and queen, and the Council, await you."

Augustin nodded, ignoring the elf's brusqueness. It was time for him to plead Emparia's case.

"Good people of Aderilund," said Augustin Bauer. "I come to you in the spirit of friendship and goodwill." He stood in the centre of the audience chamber, the elves seated in a semi-circle around him, just below the royal podium. "Your Majesties," he dropped to one knee in front of the monarchs, "you honour me with your presence."

"Please, rise. We are pleased to meet our friends from across the sea," said Talina. "Our Emparian friends are always welcome in the Aspen Kingdom."

Saegralanna glanced at Ivellios, but the spellweaver's face was without expression.

"The Emparian Civil Wars are over," said Augustin. "Yet we still face many threats, the greatest of which are the Goriinchians that press on our southern borders. While we fought amongst ourselves, they watched... waited... and regrouped."

"And what do you ask of the Eldara?" said Talan, frowning.

"We ask only that you live up to the promise you made our late King, your Majesties," Augustin said. "We are sorely in need of skilled soldiers, and the war has greatly taxed our manpower."

Ivellios curled his lip.

"Of course," said Talina. "We would be more than happy to assist you in any way."

Ivellios snorted. Saegralanna raised a finger to her lips. "Shhh."

"The Emparian Crown knows that elven archers are the finest in the known world, and cordially requests at least one battalion to assist in the protection of Emparia's borders."

The assembled aristocrats began to mutter amongst themselves. Ivellios looked disgruntled, a sneer upon his face.

"Quiet!" demanded Quarion. "The ambassador has the floor."

"It would be for only a short period, just enough to train our own…"

"Bah," shouted Ivellios.

The spellweaver rose, his face contorted with rage. "What is this nonsense?" he yelled. "We are not mercenaries. It is not our way to fight the wars of others. The squabbles of the lesser races are not our concern."

"Control yourself, Lord Ivellios." said Quarion.

"Control myself? I will not. This is outrageous. You all bow and scrape to this human as if he were someone of importance. Since when do the Eldara do the bidding of the Mal-halyth?"

There were assorted gasps from the assembled.

"If any of you value the traditions and history of our people you will send this buffoon on his way, and have no partnership with his nation of barbarians."

"Sit down, Ivellios," said Quarion.

"I will not sit down. I will not be silenced. Least of all by you."

"Sit down!"

"Send this man away from our land, never to return, and I will sit down, Speaker." said Ivellios.

"Spellweaver, SIT DOWN!" a voice boomed. It was not the voice of Speaker Quarion . This time it was High King Talan himself. The spellweaver had gone one word too far. "You will control yourself, Ivellios, or you will be removed from this chamber, and from my favour."

"I… apologise, Your Majesty," Ivellios stuttered. Apparently chastened, he resumed his seat.

Talan sat down, holding his fingers against his lips in silent contemplation. Augustin looked at the king expectantly. Eventually, Talan spoke. "Baron Augustin Bauer. We shall consider your proposal. You will have our answer in three days."

"Thank you, Your Majesty," Bauer bowed to the king with a slightly embarrassed smile before bowing to the queen as well. "And Your Majesty, too."

Out of the corner of her eye, Saegralanna noticed Ivellios fuming, his face a mask of barely restrained rage. She smiled.

***

Like most of the cities of the Aspen Kingdom, the centre of Aderial was dominated by magnificent gardens. The Eldara had long been recognised as gifted gardeners, able to coax lush plant growth from even the most barren of soils. In fertile lands such as Aderilund, the result was unsurprisingly even more impressive.

It was midday, and several elven children played amongst the parkland, laughing as they ran here and there. Bellaydin sat nearby, idly watching the scene in front of him, but his mind was elsewhere.

He had never really had any close friends in his youth. The Eldara were, by their nature, a rather conservative people, and Bellaydin had simply been far too different for most of them to accept. It had been the same for his sister. This was yet another reason the pair of them had been so close. They both knew that the other was the only one they could relate to.

"Bela."

Bellaydin snapped to attention at the sound of his sister's voice.

"Polnygar. as Mother returned from her meeting with the Council?"

"I'm not sure… I haven't been at home. I think the meeting has ended though."

Bellaydin frowned. His sister's response was vague and oddly evasive. "Are you feeling alright, Polnygar?"

Polnygar looked distant, but only for a moment. She shook her head and focused on her brother. "I'm fine Bela, really."

"It's just…" said Bellaydin. "You seem a little distant. That's all."

Polnygar gave a nervous cough. "Bela, I need a favour."

"A favour? What?"

Polnygar reached into her tunic, and fished out a sealed envelope. "I need you to give this to Mother."

Bellaydin took the envelope and turned it over with his hand, looking at each side. "Can't you give it to her yourself?"

Polnygar frowned, and chewed the edge of her lip. "I won't be around."

"What? What are you talking about?"

"Bela. Listen. I'm leaving forever. Today."

Bellaydin tried to respond, but his tongue stuck to the back of his throat. No words came to him.

"It's become obvious that Mother won't let me leave… let either of us leave. She's smothering both of us and you know it."

"I know she can be a little over protective, but gods, Polnygar. Have you really thought about this? Where are you going?"

"Anywhere I can," she said. "Far away from here, that's for sure. I'll stow away on a merchant's vessel if I have to."

Bellaydin shook his head in disbelief. "Do you realise how ridiculous

41

this sounds? You can't leave."

"Why not?" said Polnygar, her eyes set.

"Well… you…" Bellaydin struggled for words. "Do you realise how this is going to affect Mother? She'll be devastated."

Polnygar closed her eyes and gently laid a hand on her brother's shoulder. "She'll get over this in time. This is something I must do… for myself."

"But what about us, Polnygar?"

"Bela, you have to promise to say nothing to Mother before you give her this letter. Don't do it today. Wait until I'm too far away for her to chase me."

Bellaydin smiled weakly. "You know she'd chase you to the end of the world and back, Polnygar."

Polnygar nodded. "Can you promise me, Bela?"

Bellaydin struggled with his emotions, each tugging him in one way or the other. Then he saw his sister's expression, pleading with him. He nodded slowly. "Very well Polnygar, I promise. I just hope you know what you're doing."

They embraced. "Stay safe, Pol. Come back and visit us."

Polnygar squeezed her brother. "I will, you can count on that." She smiled gently. "Bela, are you crying?"

Bellaydin broke the embrace, and rubbed his eyes self-consciously. "What? No… No. I think I have a bit of dirt in my eye, that's all."

"Oh, Bela," Polnygar laughed affectionately. "I'm going to miss you. Come here."

She crushed him with another hug.

CHAPTER 4

As Lord Ivellios harangued Augustin Bauer in front of the High Council of Aderial, another noble, far away, addressed his own peers in the Great Hall of Castle Emparia.

Castle Emparia had stood for centuries, built by the legendary first king of the Tyron dynasty, Alarion, to celebrate the unification of the petty kingdoms of Emparia. Alarion's successors had built additions to the original fortress, reflecting the rise of Emparia as a world power. For years the castle had been the seat of power for the monarchs of Emparia, and in that time many famous feet had trod its stone floors. Indeed, such was its association with royal power, that the capital city of Emparia had itself become known as "Emperor's Palace", the original name having long since disappeared into history.

A herald, dressed in the livery of the Royal House of Morcor, announced the entrance of a newcomer, "Your Majesty, Your Graces, my Lords… May I present, His Lordship the Earl of Genio, William Caradoc Ap'Lydin."

Earl William Ap'Lydin strode to the centre of the chamber, glancing at each of the assembled nobles in turn. Four Dukes and two other earls made up the Council, and they were clustered around the queen. Behind them was a myriad of lesser nobles and knights.

"Your Majesty, Your Graces," said William, bowing to the figure seated on the throne before acknowledging the assembled dukes. "My lords," he said nonchalantly to the rest. "I will skip any further formalities and get straight to the heart of the matter. I have received some rather disturbing news from the Goriinchian border. We must act on it now, or the consequences could be dire for us all."

"Then please, your Lordship," said the Duke of Georgeton, "share with us what this 'disturbing news' entails. Or is this another one of your fantasies involving hordes of rampaging Goriinchians swarming over our borders and killing all those we hold dear?"

"This is no fantasy, Georgeton." William yelled furiously. "As we speak, the Goriinchian Prophet-King Ygarak is gathering together an army the likes of which Emparia has not seen for centuries. I fear he plans to strike soon, while we are still unprepared."

It was the Duke of Emperor's Palace who spoke next. "Even if what you are saying is true –"

"My spies have confirmed it," William cut in.

The Duke of Emperor's Palace brushed over the interruption. "Even if we were to take your word on this, there is little reason for you or any of us to be concerned. The scattered tribes of Goriinchia pose little real threat to the borders of Emparia. After all, they have made numerous attempts to invade us in the past, and on every occasion have crumbled before the might of Emparian arms. Some of us here are even old enough to remember their previous attempt. And how it was ended."

He gave William an almost reproachful look, as if to subtly remind him of the legacy of his grandfather. William had, after all, been named for him.

Sir William Ap'Lydin was the foremost knight of the realm, hero – and martyr – of the Second Goriinchian War. On the eve of victory against the Goriinchians, he had been struck down in battle. But it did not avail the Goriinchians, for, inspired by Ap'Lydin's example, the Emparian army struck back, and routed the Goriinchians, sending them fleeing to the safety of the mountains.

"Yes… ended. At the cost of my grandfather's own life," William responded. "I warn you, Your Graces, the Goriinchians are on the move –"

A voice interrupted William. "The Goriinchians are not our primary concern here, friends." It was the Duke of Alariat who had cut into the conversation.

The room fell silent. Even though Duke Haakon de Morcor was not technically the highest-ranked noble there, he was the queen's cousin, and as a consequence, highly respected at court.

"If I may," he began. "I believe the Duke of Oldharbour wishes to speak. He has been quite insistent of late and I would consider it a personal favour if you would take his words to heart."

The Duke of Oldharbour was a tall, sombre and austere man named Wulfric Highcrown. He had been a prominent advisor of the crown for decades. "Your Graces, from my own region some unsettling information regarding a certain religious group has emerged."

"Yes, Oldharbour, I know of them. The Cult of The Horned God, yes?" said the Duke of Georgeton.

Wulfric nodded. "I trust the Earl of Genio knows of the threat they pose. After all, your Lordship," he said, looking pointedly at William, "let us not forget the circumstances of your uncle's untimely death."

William shut his eyes and spoke, "I am aware of this group's existence. However, I believe it was an isolated incident and…"

"You'd like that to think that, wouldn't you?" Wulfric said. "But they are more dangerous than you accept. Enlim was not some lone malcontent, and his followers represent more than a few disaffected individuals seeking some kind of a spiritual fulfilment. They represent a threat to our way of life."

The Duke of Georgeton rolled his eyes. "Your Grace, with all due respect, the Church of Emparia has at its beck and call the power of the great Sun King, chief of the gods. Our soldiers fight in the name of the blessed Divine Martyr. We are favoured by the gods, any man knows that. How could an insignificant cult worshipping a false god pose any threat to our security?"

"The Cult does *not* worship a false god, Your Graces," Haakon de Morcor cut in, shaking a finger to emphasise his point. "Their patron, the so-called Horned God, may be mysterious and inscrutable, but he is real. As real as any god."

"Oh, and what makes you so sure of this, Your Grace?" the Duke of Georgeton asked. "Have you perhaps converted?"

"I have certain *contacts*." Haakon pursed his lips but would say no more.

"It would be wise if I were given the authority to investigate their activities, as I have requested before," said Highcrown.

"Yes, yes," said the Duke of Georgeton. "Perhaps if you hadn't badgered us, we might have agreed to this."

"If none here will take the threat seriously, then I will do what I must to protect these lands. Suffice to say, I will speak more of this when the time comes. Rest assured, they do pose a threat, whether you wish to accept it or not."

The Duke of Georgeton laughed loudly. "Hah, Oldharbour, you are getting paranoid in your old age."

The assembled lords chuckled to themselves, enjoying the levity of what was usually a rather dull affair. Despite the mirth, however, the figure that sat on the throne watched the proceedings with disinterest, her attention seemingly elsewhere.

"I trust we are not boring you, Your Majesty?" Haakon said.

"We, Alariat?" the Duke of Emperor's Palace inquired.

Haakon only smiled, and looked towards the throne. Queen Amaryllis was the sovereign ruler of Emparia, ordained of the gods, apparently born to rule, though many wondered if there had not been some sort of a divine mistake. She was utterly bored at state meetings, and William knew that many expected better of their monarchs. Perhaps it was just youth – after all, she was younger even than William. Barely twenty-five years of age, she ruled over a land that was, for the most part, peaceful and prosperous. Perhaps she just had to grow into the role. In time she would become more comfortable with the affairs of state and meetings with her advisors. From all William had heard, her father had loved such minutia.

The queen's late father, King Henry of Emparia, was the first monarch of the Morcor dynasty. He had taken the throne by force, defeating the last members of the corrupt Tyron dynasty. Up until the very end of his thirty year reign he knew no peace, sending troops from one end of Emparia to the other, seeking out ever more elusive pockets of resistance among the die-hard Tyron loyalists. Towards the end of his life, his victory was finally complete, but at great cost. The fighting had cost the lives of his three sons, and with no other heirs, Henry had married again. His second wife had died bringing Amaryllis into the world, and it was Amaryllis that the crown was eventually passed to.

The nobles of Emparia looked at her, awaiting her response.

"No, Haakon, please continue," Amaryllis said, fidgeting with the edge of her gown.

"Thank you, Your Majesty," said Haakon, a self-confident smile spreading across his lips. "And thank you, Genio." He motioned to William, who still stood in the centre of the hall. "While I find no real reason to place undue importance on this supposed gathering of the

Goriinchian host, I thank you for the information nonetheless. We will put it to good use, I can assure you."

The other Dukes nodded in agreement.

Earl William folded his arms and scowled. "By that I assume you mean that you will totally ignore the warning I have given and then mock me behind my back."

Haakon de Morcor raised an eyebrow, but the Duke of Emperor's Palace simply guffawed uproariously. "By the gods, you take after your grandfather. We couldn't get a thing past him either."

"But not for want of trying, I am sure, Your Graces," William said, smiling.

The Duke of Emperor's Palace winked at William while Haakon de Morcor narrowed his eyes. He looked as if he might say something, but he did not. The meeting ended shortly thereafter, when the young queen rose from her seat and announced she was retiring to her chambers.

It was much later when William left the outskirts of Castle Emparia, scowling.

"Blasted fools," William spat. "If this is what passes for leadership in Emparia we deserve our fate."

"My lord?" said the armoured knight who rode next to him.

William scowled. "Oh, nothing, Geoffrey."

Sir Geoffrey Keslin was a tall, broad-shouldered knight of thirty summers, ten of those served with the Earl of Genio as his foremost retainer and man-at-arms. With a handsome shock of blond hair and ice-blue eyes, Geoffrey was quite a contrast to the dark, glowering noble he rode alongside.

William Ap'Lydin was just shy of thirty-six years old, but his lined, careworn features made him appear much older. His black hair was cut short, shaved at the sides, and a shabby dark beard covered the lower half of his face.

"I take it your meeting with the Privy Council did not go well then," said Geoffrey, moving his horse up next to William's.

"No, it didn't," William said, sighing.

"Ah."

William glanced at the knight. "You don't think I'm being paranoid, do you?"

Geoffrey pursed his lips. "If I may, my Lord, perhaps when seen from their perspective – the perspective of one who has not seen the things you have – perhaps your warnings do seem a little alarmist."

William did not respond, but rode on in silence, deep in thought. *Five years on the frontier. Five years watching the Goriinchians, analysing their strengths and weaknesses. And, if no one would take him seriously, five years wasted.*

"My lord, I heard something from one of the pages. He overheard the Duke of Alariat. Is it true, is that Goriinchian cult once again infesting Emparia?" Geoffrey ventured.

"Hmm?" William sounded distracted. "What?".

"The Cult of the Horned God, my Lord," Geoffrey said.

"What about it?" William said, somewhat testily.

"Well I wondered if you agreed with the Duke that…"

"In Emparia the Cult of The Horned God is no more, Geoffrey," William said pointedly. "It disappeared shortly after the death of my uncle. King Henry outlawed it."

"Then you don't –"

"A passing madness infecting the people of the area. Nothing more, Geoffrey. Except in the lands of the Goriinchians, there is no organised worship of the Horned God existing anywhere."

Geoffrey took in a sharp breath. "My lord, I must say I find it a little odd that you can see threats massing from outside our borders yet refuse to acknowledge any coming from within."

William bristled at the comment. "I refuse to give credence to this mumbo-jumbo when we have an army of flesh and bone to fear."

"But even so, my Lord, with all due respect –"

"Enough, Geoffrey," said William. "Enough. I appreciate your efforts to persuade me. However, you must see my point. If the Goriinchians invade –"

"Then we will beat them back, as we always do, and they will stumble back to their lands bloodied and bruised," said Sir Geoffrey. "King Ygarak doesn't have a single man under arms who could match Emparia's finest."

William smiled. "I wish I shared your confidence, Geoffrey."

Geoffrey looked back at his liege lord and smiled in return. "I wish you did too, my Lord."

William laughed. "Come on, Geoffrey, let's get on our way."

"Yes, my Lord."

The days passed languidly by as they made their way towards Genio at a leisurely pace. As the pair of them travelled across the well-maintained cobblestone highways that were the arteries of Emparia, they took the time to drink in the rich pastoral landscapes.

For his part, Geoffrey did not bring up the matter of the Goriinchians again, but he knew the topic occupied his liege lord's mind. It always did. There were some people – usually disgruntled nobles from other areas of the realm – who considered Earl William Ap'Lydin obsessed.

"It's a vendetta," they would say. "There's nothing strategic about it at all."

Others would argue, "I very much doubt that a few unwashed barbarians pose any threat to the dominant power of this world."

"Of course, I agree... this whole issue that Earl Ap'Lydin has with the Goriinchians... it goes back to the death of his grandfather and uncle at their hands. He has *convinced* himself that the tribes to the south pose a threat so he can finally achieve some sort of justice for his family. It's pathetic."

And so on and so forth.

Aware of the silence that had descended on them, Geoffrey made an attempt at idle conversation. "It's been dry here this summer, has it not?"

"Aye."

"The farmers will be hoping for some rain, no doubt."

"Aye."

"Still, I suspect the harvest will still be as expected. No one will go hungry."

"Aye."

Geoffrey turned towards the earl. "Maybe we should encourage them to start herding dragons instead."

"Aye." There was a pause and William turned around suddenly. "Wait, what?"

"You seem to be a bit lost in thought, my lord," said Geoffrey. "Preoccupied, perhaps?"

William glanced at Geoffrey and grinned. "Enough of that, you sly dog. You know exactly what I'm thinking about."

"The Goriinchians," said Geoffrey, sighing.

"The Goriinchians," William echoed in assent.

"My lord, if you would just – "

"Here we are, Geoffrey," William interrupted the knight as he spied Hotar Citadel. "Home. Perhaps we should continue this discussion later?"

"Discussion?" Geoffrey smiled, despite his frustration. "Is that what you call a conversation where only one person is actually taking part?"

William chuckled. "Geoffrey, you are one of my oldest and most loyal retainers, but if you ever bring this up again, I swear, I'm going to have to kill you."

Geoffrey laughed. "Of course, my lord. That's what you said last time, and the time before, and the time before that…"

"Yes, yes."

"And," Geoffrey said, patting his chest, "here I am. Still as hale and hearty as ever."

William laughed, shaking his head. "That's enough now, I think I get the picture."

Much later, the pair sat in the earl's drawing room. Geoffrey watched as William paced up and down the room. "My lord, please. Sit. You haven't even touched your coffee."

"Geoffrey, you know I damn well can't stand that Qardleean sludge," William said. "Yet you had the kitchen staff make me one anyway."

"Yes, I know, but you seem so agitated. I thought it might do you some good."

"I have reason to be agitated. Look at this."

Geoffrey looked at the parchment that William had thrust in front of his eyes. He made a ploy of patting down his clothes. "I seem to have left my reading glass at home."

"We have no time for your jokes, Geoffrey, just read this," said William testily.

"Oh, fine," said Geoffrey, sounding somewhat exasperated. He scanned the words on the page. "Goriinchian, William? I thought you said – "

"Read it."

"My Goriinchian's only so good, you know. And this is written in that elvish script, to boot. Alright, alright. Let's see now…" Geoffrey pursed his lips and began to read aloud. "'I am a soldier of the great Ygarak, Long May He Reign. The Horned God is great. The Horned God is great. The Horned God and his Prophet are one. The Horned God is great. The Horned God is great'."

Geoffrey paused. "Bit of a one track mind, these Goriinchians, yes? Almost takes me back to my days with the Crusaders of Ralom…" With a sigh, he continued, "'We are the Suns of Truth, the Stars of Greatness. Our hearts are speaking the words of the prophecy. We are the awakening destiny of the world.' Oh, gods, this is tiresome."

"Keep reading," said William.

"Very well, my lord," said Geoffrey. "But you do know there's only so much I can take of this *Praise the Holy, the Good, the Merciful, the All-Knowing* rubbish." He gave a heavy sigh before continuing, "'The time is coming, the great reckoning. The mongrel dogs of the north will be vanquished, and Karlicia will once again be whole. The Horned God shall spread his blessings upon the land and bring forth the one whose coming was foretold by the seers. The Heir of Lydin.'"

William nodded at him.

"Oh, my lord, you don't think that…"

"Mighty strange coincidence, don't you think, Geoffrey?" asked William.

"Well, I don't know, my lord. I mean, yes, your name is Goriinchian, but for all we know one of your ancestors migrated from the south. And if so, so what? It might be a common name in Goriinchia."

"Is it?"

"I don't know. But that's the thing. Every second Goriinchian could be called Ap'Lydin, for all we know. I mean, my lord, you don't actually believe that this might be – "

"Of course not," snapped William. "But I don't need to. All that matters is whether the Goriinchians believe it."

"Oh, who knows with that lot? I'm not going to predict the labyrinthine workings of their minds. They and their little prophet-king are stuck in the frozen mountains of the south. Let them stay there, for all I care."

"Something tells me that Ygarak isn't quite satisfied with his mountain kingdom, Geoffrey."

"Well, who would be? The place is a bloody iced up wilderness, full of raging barbarians and mad cultists. You know, they have that bloody Horned God." He narrowed his eyes. "Tell me, my lord. In the time you spent in Goriinchia, what did you see? Some soldiers, they say... they say the cult's everywhere there."

William nodded. "Indeed. For once, the camp talk is accurate. In the last two and a half centuries, the worshippers of the so-called Horned God have insinuated themselves into every level of Goriinchian society. The cult is omnipresent throughout the lands of the Goriinch tribes and it has had a lasting effect on even the tiniest portion of their culture."

"Amazing... but where are the religion's roots? Where did it first begin? How did it come to be the faith of the Goriinchians?" Geoffrey said.

William sighed. "No one knows for sure. It appeared out of nowhere, shortly after the warlord Ygarak united the tribes all those years ago."

"This Ygarak, he seems to have ruled for centuries," said Geoffrey. "Is it also true what they say about him? That's he's immortal?"

William swallowed. "That, I doubt. The tales circulated by soldiers are not always true. Remember, they used to say the same thing about the Ran Tyron line of kings. No, I think what is more likely is that Ygarak is less of a name, and more of a title, given to successive Goriinchian rulers to maintain the illusion of an undying monarch with divine power. We need not fear this Ygarak. Indeed, I believe he no longer has any real power in Goriinchia at all."

"Then who?"

"Over the last few generations, the Cult of the Horned God has come to wield more and more power in the royal court of Goriinchia. It's now at the point where Ygarak's inner circle consists almost entirely of members of the faith. It has become quite clear to me that the cult itself wields the true power in Goriinchia."

"They rule through this Ygarak then? He is their puppet?" said Geoffrey.

"Not exactly."

"Then?"

"It is difficult to explain. There are many forces at work here, Geoffrey, mark my words."

"Of course my lord, but with all due respect, did you not say that the cult was of no concern?"

William waved his hand in a dismissive gesture. "In a way, it isn't. Its only true support base is the Goriinchian royal court and the warlords of the nation. When that collapses, the cult is sure to follow soon after."

"And their god, the Horned God?" ventured Geoffrey.

"Doesn't exist," replied William.

"You seem so sure of that, my lord."

"He's a figment of their imagination, no doubt about that," said William. "Unfortunately, belief is all that is required for fanaticism."

"Undoubtedly," Geoffrey said. "So they are dangerous?"

"They're nothing we can't handle, Geoffrey," said William. "The Goriinchian warriors they control, on the other hand…"

"How grave is the threat they pose?" Geoffrey asked.

"Come with me," said William.

The earl led his knight to a desk in the study, on which was a worn map covered in notations. "This is the border Emparia shares with Goriinchia," William said, circling a portion of the map with his fingers. "Fifty years ago, the garrisons along the line would be filled with thousands of troops, all ready to combat any threat – whenever such a threat would arise – but no more. The thirty year civil war against the Tyron pretenders has sapped our borders of resources." He pointed to a black mark. "Fort Victory, here, is emblematic of this problem. In the days of my grandfather, the fortress held a thousand men even at the worst of times. Now? Barely a tenth of that number. We simply don't have the troops to ward off a full-scale assault."

"But this is all speculation," Geoffrey said. "The Goriinchians have been quiet for half a century, my lord. What makes you think that they are planning an attack?"

"The warlords are restless, Geoffrey, that much is clear. The one I fear most is one Aonghus Culainn. He is the son of the former Warchief Padraig Culainn –"

"–who led the Goriinchians against your grandfather during the Second Goriinch War," said Geoffrey.

"And perished at my grandfather's hand," said William. "Yes, the very same. Intelligence has concluded that Culainn has been recently made Warchief by Ygarak himself. Something is definitely afoot."

"But what do they hope to achieve?" said Geoffrey. "Yes, they could invade, catch us unaware and wreak terrible damage, but surely the Goriinchians know what would happen in any situation of extended hostilities. Our industrial capacity alone would ensure that when we *do* strike back, we will crush them without pity. It doesn't make sense. None of this does."

William nodded in assent. "All the more reason to believe there are other forces at work here. There is something we are missing here. Something has led the Goriinchians to believe that they need not fear any reprisals from Emparia."

"But what could it be, my lord?" asked Geoffrey.

"I don't know," William sighed and collapsed into a nearby chair, clearly exhausted. "Geoffrey, I can't shake the feeling that we are in serious trouble. We just don't know what that trouble is."

"My lord," Geoffrey ventured. "You have been under a lot of pressure lately —"

"Here it comes," said William, rolling his eyes.

"— what with your wife's death and all," Geoffrey concluded.

"There," said William.

Six months ago a plague had struck the city of Genio. Among the victims was the Countess Margaret Ap'Lydin, William's wife. Many noted that, although William had loved his wife dearly, he never seemed to grieve for her. Instead, he maintained a stoic countenance at all times. When his wife's passing was raised in conversation, William would always change the subject.

Frowning, William stood and walked towards Geoffrey. "How old are your boys now, Geoffrey?"

"My eldest, Garret, is ten, while Günther, my youngest, is but eighteen months of age." He paused. "Why do you ask me this, my lord?"

"My Maria is twelve this year. Unfortunately, she cannot inherit my title. I have no heir, Geoffrey."

"You could always remarry, you know. I'm sure there are plenty of young women who'd be quite happy with a widower earl," Geoffrey said. "Even if he does have a tendency to be overly-melodramatic."

"Well, perhaps, but –"

"You have seen the youngest daughter of the Earl of Warding, yes?" said Geoffrey. "Beatrice, if I remember correctly. I think you might like her. She's – how shall I put this – quite a generous young girl."

"Well, thank you Geoffrey," said William. "Your concern is touching."

Geoffrey grinned. "Why, my lord. I think I saw the sarcasm practically drip off your tongue there. And to think, I was beginning to think you were without a sense of humour."

William snorted.

"So, where's this musing on your succession leading to? Getting another sense of your own mortality? I keep telling you that the solution is to drink more," said Geoffrey.

William rolled his eyes. "That's your solution to everything."

"If it works…" Geoffrey said, shrugging slightly. The joviality disappeared and Geoffrey's face became serious. "Look, my lord William. The Ap'Lydin name does not die with you. Your grandfather's heroism, and, indeed, even your own, will ensure that it survives long after our bodies decay into dust. And your bloodline is far from extinct. Why, you yourself ensured that, those dozen years ago."

William stared at Geoffrey blankly, and the knight took it as a sign that his lord required something to prompt his memory.

"I'm talking about your cousins, my lord," said Geoffrey, "Bellaydin and Polnygar."

"Yes, Geoffrey," nodded William. "I do remember that, you know, I'm not that old."

"Look, I'm headed off to Mokeria soon. Aderilund is on the way."

William smiled knowingly. "Ah, so I take it that you were approached for this secret mission as well?"

"They asked you first?" Geoffrey said.

"Of course. You are my sworn sword after all. I told them that you were your own man, and that they best ask you in person."

"What I don't understand was the need for all the damn secrecy," Geoffrey grumbled.

"Who was it who gave you this message?"

"An unknown benefactor on the Privy Council. He contacted me through an intermediary while you nobles were in session. He wants to help you."

"They're sending you to round up a few mercenaries and hired swords to make me feel better?" said William.

"Something like that, my lord," said Geoffrey, grinning. "They are trying, my lord, not trying very hard, granted, but trying nonetheless." There was a somewhat awkward pause. "As I was saying my lord, I could perhaps drop into Aderilund on my way back. If there's a letter, or something you want delivered to your cousins…"

"Give me some time to think about it, Geoffrey."

"Very well, my lord. I shall speak to you tomorrow." Geoffrey gave a short bow.

"Yes, Geoffrey, it's time for you to go have a few drinks about now, isn't it?"

Geoffrey blinked, and feigned a look of innocence. "Why my lord, I'm sure I don't know what you mean. You know that drunkenness is against the chivalric code."

William chuckled in spite of himself. "Just go, Geoffrey," he said. "And pour me one while you're down there."

"You're coming to drink with the troops, my lord?"

"It's my damn mess hall, isn't it? Besides, I think I'm going to need it."

"Of course, my lord," Geoffrey said, grinning.

CHAPTER 5

By dawn the next day, Geoffrey was already preparing his horse for the journey ahead of him. Hotar Citadel was a few hours outside of the city of Genio proper, and Geoffrey needed to reach the port by midday.

William had decided after all to pen a letter to his cousins for Geoffrey to deliver if he passed through Aderilund. A simple missive of familial greetings, the letter also invited either of the two younger Ap'Lydins to come visit their elder cousin in Genio.

Geoffrey wondered if either would give up the peaceful life in Aderilund to come to a land which, by all accounts, was sliding very close to armed conflict.

"Not bloody likely," he snorted to himself.

Try as he might, Geoffrey could not muster up the same level of concern his liege lord had over the Goriinchians. Skilled fighters though they were, they were little more than barbarians, and given favourable terrain and advance warning, Emparian armies had been known to defeat Goriinchian hordes that outnumbered them five to one.

"Willy always was a bit paranoid," Geoffrey muttered to himself.

Geoffrey was always very careful to make sure he never used the troops' nickname for William Ap'Lydin in front of the earl himself. While William was by nature a calm, even gentle individual, he took himself very seriously. Perhaps overly so – one of the reasons Geoffrey was always so jovial around him. He thought William needed to laugh a bit more.

As he fastened his travelling cloak around his neck, Geoffrey ran through in his mind what he expected to occur in Genio. His contact had promised to assist Geoffrey and William in gathering skilled mercenaries to bolster their small pool of levies and conscripts. The idea was that these professionals would be able to train the recruits as well as supplement them when the time came. At least that was what his anonymous contact had led him to believe. No real promises had been made, merely a few vague assurances.

A few hours later, Geoffrey stood expectantly at the dockyards of Genio. Sailors and labourers walked here and there, going about their duties. The smell of seawater and rank fish assailed his senses. Geoffrey wrinkled his nose in distaste.

"Oh, Genio, how I have missed your pleasing scent."

He looked around warily, hoping to find his mysterious contact quickly. Whoever they were, they certainly were not making themselves easy to spot. Nearby, at least one individual seemed to be taking an interest in Geoffrey. A tall, green-skinned humanoid with reptilian features regarded him with a cold, baleful glare. Geoffrey tried to avoid his gaze, but found his eyes returning to rest on the creature.

Geoffrey had heard of the Ahktarran Lizardmen a few times before. They were said to be a fierce warrior race from the scorching lands of Qarld, far to the west. Expert sailors and superb fighters, they were not often seen in the colder climes, particularly in so distant a place as Emparia. He wondered idly what this one was doing here.

The Lizardman, seemingly sensing Geoffrey's thoughts, began to walk towards the knight with great purpose. "You are Sir Geoffrey Keslin, are you not?"

"And you are?" said Geoffrey.

The Lizardman narrowed his eyes. "I am Kahlaf el'Lahn. Are you Geoffrey Keslin or not?"

"I am."

"Hrrm," the Lizardman grunted. "My lord has been expecting you. Please follow me."

Geoffrey was still hesitant. He was not sure if he could trust this Ahktarran.

"Why do you hesitate, human?" said Kahlaf. "Does my appearance distress you?"

The creature attempted a smile, baring his fangs in what ended up to be a more unsettling expression than was there before.

Geoffrey shook his head nervously.

"Then come," Kahlaf said.

Kahlaf led Geoffrey into a nearby tavern, *the Drunken Angel*, according to the sign above the door. Inside, the establishment was relatively quiet, with only a few sullen patrons drinking by themselves.

"Over there," said Kahlaf, pointing to a cloaked and cowled figure sitting alone at a table in the corner.

Geoffrey walked towards the stranger, with Kahlaf trailing close behind. He touched a chair cautiously, and seeing the figure indicate his assent, took a seat.

"Geoffrey Keslin," the figure said. "I am pleased that you have made the effort to arrive as I requested. I apologise for my aide's brusqueness. He is like that, but he has his uses."

"No apologies necessary, my lord," Geoffrey said.

"You recognise my voice then, Sir Knight?" the figure said.

"Somewhat. You mentioned you were a member of the Privy Council. I have been in attendance with my own liege lord the Earl of Genio on more than one occasion, and your voice is familiar."

The figure raised his arm and motioned to the barkeep, and ale was brought to the table quickly. Geoffrey assumed any costs must have been handled earlier, as he did not see coins pass hands.

"So, Sir Geoffrey," said the figure, taking a quaff of his drink. "You said you recognised my voice?" He reached up and lowered his hood, revealing an aged and weathered face.

"Wulfric Highcrown." Geoffrey exclaimed, before realising his gaffe. Slightly embarrassed at his lack of protocol, Geoffrey downed his ale in one gulp. There was an uncomfortable silence as Geoffrey regained his composure. No one really expected to see one of the most important and respected nobles in a common tavern, least of all to be summoned to meet with them. "That is to say... Your Grace, Duke of Oldharbour."

Wulfric Highcrown was unperturbed. "We shall ignore your – "He shot Geoffrey a look, "– familiarity in favour of getting to the task at hand."

"Yes, please," said Geoffrey, gulping down the last of his ale.

"Very well. I am sending you on a journey to Orspederia to recruit soldiers. Hopefully the previous envoy, Baron Augustin Bauer, has had some success with the elves and your task will be a little easier."

"Why me? Surely you have knights of your own."

"Indeed I do," said Wulfric. "But none are as suited to this task as you are. You also share a friendship with your own liege lord, the Earl of Genio. For now, my interests coincide with his. You shall best serve him by serving me, do you understand?"

"I think so," Geoffrey said. "When do you want me to leave?"

"As soon as possible. My ship is waiting for you. As you can imagine, I cannot go myself, so I will send Kahlaf to accompany you."

"That won't be necessary," said Geoffrey.

"This is for my own benefit, Geoffrey, not yours," said Highcrown. "Suffice to say I have a lot invested in this. More than you realise."

"Why the secrecy? You could have approached Earl William yourself during the Council."

"There are other players here, Geoffrey, whose motives are still unclear. I do not wish to play my hand in the open. Not yet."

"Well, I'll keep this all secret, don't you worry."

"I doubt that," Wulfric said. "But you have not been chosen for your ability to keep secrets. If you do reveal this, no one will believe you. I have covered my tracks."

"So you agree with Earl William then, about the Goriinchian threat?"

"William's concerns are valid, but not for the reasons he imagines."

"Meaning?"

Highcrown shook his head. "Even if it was explained to you, you would still not understand. Suffice to say there are other forces at work here than the Goriinchians."

"I see. And what does this mean to me?"

"Nothing. Gather your troops, train your men, and assist your liege lord against the Goriinchians. That is all you need to know, that is all you need to do. I will take care of the rest."

"I don't think I understand," said Geoffrey, shaking his head.

"As I said, Geoffrey, that is of no consequence." Highcrown reached into his cloak, and withdrew a small hemispherical piece of glass, placing it on the table.

"What's this? A magnifying glass? A lens?"

The Duke leaned forward. "Of sorts. You will find it will allow you to see further than you could otherwise. Simply hold it against your own eye and things will become clearer."

Geoffrey was sceptical. "And why give it to me?"

"Consider it a gift."

"Well, thanks, I guess," said Geoffrey, placing the lens back in his clothing. "What is it for? Why do I need such a thing?"

"You will have need of it, trust me. And do take care of it," Wulfric said. "I expect to see it returned to me eventually."

Highcrown rose from his seat, placing his hood once more over his head. "I will take my leave. The supplies and funds you will require for this trip have already been taken care of. We have arranged for you to stay here tonight. Tomorrow morning Kahlaf will find you, and the pair of you will leave for Orspederia. I will inform Earl William of your whereabouts. Good luck, Sir Knight." The Duke looked towards the Lizardman and nodded. "Come Kahlaf."

As the pair left the tavern, Geoffrey remained at the table, staring into the empty ale mug. What had he got himself into this time?

"Ah well," he said. "There's nothing else to do but wait." He yelled for more ale. "Oh, and something to eat, barkeep."

***

Augustin Bauer stood at the bow of the ship and brooded. Even now, days after leaving Aderilund, he was still unsure whether his mission had been a success.

The elven lords had come to an agreement to assist Emparia, but Augustin knew that it was more due to the influence of High King Talan rather than any real affection or interest the Aderilund High Council held for humans and their affairs. Indeed, Augustin noted, the words of encouragement that they had given him seemed to be just that – words. He was leaving Aderilund with little more than he had arrived there with. He tried to be optimistic. Another Emparian delegate was due to arrive in the area shortly after Augustin's own departure, so perhaps he would receive the mercenaries promised, but Augustin did not put too much faith in that.

Words are cheap. No wonder the elves use them as currency.

Augustin sighed and gazed over at the horizon. *Now, Macrodonia.* He was to take up the position as Emparian ambassador in the Macrodonian court. A chill sea breeze wafted over the ship. He rubbed his arms, and wrapped his cloak around himself for warmth. He muttered under his breath, "Everyone keeps telling me how unbearably hot the Macrodonian climate is. As far as I'm concerned, it'll be a welcome change."

The ship suddenly hit a large wave, and lurched to one side, nearly toppling Augustin from his feet. It righted itself soon enough, but Augustin was left scowling as he leant on the guard-rail, trying to regain his balance.

Ocean travel always required careful planning, due to the volatility of the waves. Sailing when the moons were out of alignment and the sea was placid was no trouble, but a trip coinciding with an alignment of any of the four moons or, heavens forefend, all four of them at once – well, suffice to say, Augustin knew no sailor mad enough to take that risk.

"My lord."

Augustin turned around, and noticed the approach of the ship's captain. "Ah yes, Captain, what news? How long 'til we arrive in Jagoncoilis?"

"A few more days yet, my lord." The captain paused, and looked a little uncomfortable.

"Is there something else you want to tell me?" said Augustin.

"Yes, milord,"

"Well?

"We've… we've got a stowaway, milord."

"A what?" shouted Augustin. "How?"

"Not sure, milord. She must have hidden aboard shortly before we set sail. At least it explains the mysterious thefts from the cooks, I guess."

"Oh, no," said Augustin. "I did not need this. Not now." Weary, he rubbed his face with his hands. "Wait, did you say 'she'?"

"Yes, milord."

A sudden sense of realisation hit Augustin Bauer. There was only one "she" who could possibly have had the opportunity and inclination to stow away on this ship.

"The men are bringing her up here now, sir."

Sure enough, two soldiers came up on deck, dragging between them a young woman who kicked and screamed the whole way. Despite the attempted disguise, her identity was patently clear, and the obviously elven ears did nothing to suggest otherwise.

Polnygar Ap'Lydin.

Augustin groaned. "Oh gods no, please tell me this isn't happening."

"Your call, milord. We could throw her overboard if you want."

"It's certainly tempting," Augustin said gruffly.

"You're joking," shouted Polnygar. "You wouldn't."

"Done worse things, my dear, especially to uninvited guests."

"But I had to. I knew you wouldn't mind. You merely had to pretend otherwise in front of my mother."

"What?" said Augustin. He laughed. "What in the Sun King's name gave you that idea?"

Polnygar blushed. "Well, I thought…"

"You seriously thought that you could stowaway here on the ship, and no one here would mind? Or better yet, that'd we all celebrate your little attempt at subterfuge?"

Polnygar chewed her lip, but did not answer.

"I've never been in a position to take on guests, girl," Augustin said, his face hard. "And I don't intend to start making a habit of it." He paused a few moments and stroked the stubble on his chin. "However, we're not in a position to turn around and take you back to Aderilund either. We're only a few days out from Jagoncoilis. You can stay until we reach there, then we'll see about contacting your mother. Until then keep your mouth shut and do exactly as I say. Is that clear?"

Polnygar nodded.

"Now let's see about finding you some quarters. I'll probably have to move some of the crew. They won't be happy, you know, but that's how things are."

"She can have my quarters, sir," the captain said. "I'll bunk down with the rest of the crew for the next few days."

"Thank you, captain," said Augustin. He breathed a sigh of relief and noticed Polnygar watching him expectantly. "Guess I won't be throwing you overboard, after all."

***

Earl William Ap'Lydin sat in his study, deep in thought, a Goriinchian manuscript in his hands. A knock came from the door.

"Blast. Carfel, I thought I asked for no interruptions," William said. The knocking persisted. "Carfel, I said I was not to be disturbed, no visitors."

The door creaked open and a familiar voice said, "No visitors at all? I was wondering, perhaps, if you had time for an old friend."

William looked up, and at the sight of the newcomer, broke into a wide grin. "Haakon."

"Willy," said Haakon, smiling.

William embraced the older man warmly.

"Oh, I forgot. You don't like that nickname do you?" Haakon said, grinning.

"For some people, I'm willing to make an exception. It's not often the Duke of Alariat himself comes knocking, after all. How are you?"

"I'm fine, my boy." Haakon eased himself into a nearby chair. "Affairs of state are keeping me busy, as always. I have no doubt the same is true for you."

"You might say that," William said, shooting a quick glance to the papers scattered on his desk.

"The Goriinchians?" Haakon said.

William nodded.

Haakon smiled. "Of course. The Privy Council, they're all worried about you, you know? Your... focus... on the Goriinchians concerns them. Some say it is distracting you from more important issues."

"I know," said William. "Are you worried about me too, Haakon?"

"William," he said, "I have known you since you were a small child. I have watched you grow, learn and mature into a finer man than I could ever hope to be. I know that you will always do the right thing in the end, even if you have to exhaust every other option first."

William smiled, despite himself.

"I'm teasing, Willy my boy," Haakon said. "You know I've always supported you in royal court, no matter the consequences. I owe your uncle that much, at the very least. So does Wulfric."

William nodded. Decades ago, as young men, Haakon de Morcor, Wulfric Highcrown and Alusine Ap'Lydin had been nigh inseparable. Even into their middle years, that bond remained, and they were as close as they had ever been. Then, twelve years ago, Alusine Ap'Lydin was brutally murdered, struck down by the man known as Simon Enlim. William had not been there when it happened, but he had heard the tale from Haakon many times. Wulfric Highcrown, too late to stop the killing, had given chase. The assassin, however, had taken his own life, and with it any way of finding out the reasons behind the whole plot. Only the symbol of the feared Cult of the Horned God upon the killer's corpse gave any clue as to those ultimately responsible.

"I think Wulfric still blames himself, even after all these years," Haakon said. "He feels if he'd been quicker, stronger, faster, then maybe, just maybe, he'd have caught the assassin."

"I was told the assassin never intended to escape," said William. "He always planned to take his own life after the deed was done."

"Aye, but I don't think that's much of a consolation to Wulfric. He's never been the same since that day. He was open, happy and light-hearted as a young man, not the cold, emotionless loner we see today. It's almost as if he's a totally different person."

"Does he ever speak about it?" said William. "I've never been close to him, so I've never had the courage to ask."

"He barely mentions it. I used to ask him what exactly happened, but after too many of those cold stares, I gave up. I can't help thinking that maybe that assassin told him something before dying – something disturbing." Haakon chewed his lip and furrowed his brow.

"What do you mean by that?" pressed William.

"Nothing – merely an idle thought," said Haakon.

"I guess the pursuit of the remnants of the cult is his way of coming to terms with his perceived failures."

Haakon nodded. "Well, yes. Even after King Henry banned and disbanded all chapters of the organisation, Wulfric was still not convinced. He always believed it still lurked beneath the surface of Emparian society. He's quite single-minded about it. A few years back there was a movement to decriminalise the worship of the Horned God, with some nobles arguing that the whole religion as it originally existed was long dead, and that any criminal elements had long since disappeared. Wulfric would have none of it, however, and demanded the ban remain in place."

"So Wulfric still believes the cultists are operating? Even over a decade after their last appearance?"

"That's what he thinks."

"And you, Haakon?"

"The Cult is dead. No doubt of it in my mind. There may be some people who pretend to worship the Horned God, but they're simply harmless eccentrics with no connection to the earlier group. They pose no threat, not in my mind. The delusions of lunatics are not our business. Let them be, I say."

Haakon settled back in his chair, and clapped his hands together, as if to punctuate an end to the discussion. William smiled obligingly.

"Now, if we may turn to other matters," said Haakon. "Perhaps I could indulge you with my company for supper tonight? Or will I have to take advantage of my position as liege lord and demand it?"

"We wouldn't want that now, would we?" William laughed. "I'll inform the cook." He affected an exaggerated bow. "Your Grace."

***

Half a day's journey away, Geoffrey Keslin was at death's door. Or at least he felt like it.

He was grateful that the ceiling continued to spin above him. It distracted him from the throbbing pain in his head. With a valiant effort, Keslin lifted his aching head from the pillow and groaned. "Ugh... one too many ales, I think." He wiped his hand over his face and winced, "Either that or I was unlucky enough to get myself in another damn bar brawl."

It was then that Geoffrey heard the pounding on the door.

"Go away." Geoffrey yelled. "I'm trying to die here."

"Sir Keslin." The voice that came through the door was scarcely more than a low growl. "This is Kahlaf el'Lahn. It is time for us to leave."

"I haven't finished my slow, horrible demise yet," Geoffrey protested.

"It is the agreed hour."

"Can we at least wait until dawn?"

"Now."

Geoffrey groaned again and rose, ever so carefully, from his bed. "Bloody hell. Let me put some clothes on then."

Geoffrey picked up the mug next to his bed and drained the last few mouthfuls of ale. "Back to work, it seems."

After the board was settled, Geoffrey joined the Ahktarran outside. "So, am I to assume we've been allocated some sort of vessel for this little voyage? We aren't going to walk to Orspederia, are we?" Geoffrey said.

"Of course not." The Lizardman motioned with a clawed hand towards a ship moored in the harbour.

Geoffrey glanced towards the docks with a wary eye. "It doesn't look like much." The ship in front of him looked unimpressive. Privately, Geoffrey had been expecting some sort of galleon, with luxurious quarters fit for a Duke. The ship he saw was barely a carrack, and in rather poor repair. "Not exactly what I had in mind for a ducal vessel, Kahlaf."

"This is the *Dusk Voyager,* and it will suffice for our purposes."

Geoffrey rubbed his chin. "This *will* make it across the sea to Orspederia, won't it?"

"I told you that it would suffice. I promised my master that I would see you safely to your destination, and back to Emparia. Are you questioning my knowledge in these matters? Or do you think I am lying to you, knight?" The Lizardman stared at Geoffrey menacingly, a slow growl coming from his throat.

"No, no, of course not," Geoffrey said, somewhat nervously.

"I will do what I have promised. No more, no less. That should be enough for you," said Kahlaf.

"Well, what more can one ask for?" Geoffrey said.

Kahlaf merely stared at him for a few seconds, frowned then turned away. As the Lizardman barked orders to the crewmen loading the ship, Geoffrey breathed heavily. He wondered what had he got himself into.

CHAPTER 6

It was raining again.

Bellaydin looked up into the sky, wondering how the grey clouds always managed to catch him by surprise. This was the fourth time in a month that he had been caught in a downpour during his trek home. For a while he had tried to shield himself from the shower using his travel knapsack, but when this proved mostly futile, he gave it up and allowed the rain to soak him.

It had been four weeks since Polnygar had left Aderilund, yet it seemed like barely a day had passed. Bellaydin fell back into his usual routine: spending the days alone on the bluffs, before returning home each evening. He felt a tug at his heart as he thought of his sister; Polnygar had been the closest thing he had to a friend. Aderilund seemed so lifeless and lonely without her.

Saegralanna was still coming to terms with her daughter's sudden departure. Despite Bellaydin's reassurances, she still appeared to blame herself for Polnygar leaving. For the first week afterwards, Saegralanna was in tears almost every day.

Bellaydin felt guilty. It was partly his fault, after all. He could have at least tried to persuade Polnygar to stay in Aderilund. Instead he had been unwilling to get into a confrontation – as usual - and simply let her go.

He had always been like that, foolishly trying to straddle both sides of the divide, only to end up looking, well, foolish. He had always wanted to leave Aderilund as much as, if not more so, than his sister. But he lacked the courage to say so, leaving Polnygar to repeatedly broach the subject with her mother while he'd kept his mouth shut. At the time he had convinced himself that he was doing it out of concern for Saegralanna's feelings. He did not want to upset the woman who had raised him. Now he wasn't so sure. Something gnawed at him inside. He wondered if Saegralanna would ever let him leave after this experience.

"Probably not," he mused as he arrived on the outskirts of Aelsar Estate.

Bellaydin stopped in his tracks. For whatever reason, he felt uncannily like he was being watched.

"Good evening, young master," a voice said. From the shadows, a cloaked figure emerged. Thin and lightly-built, the newcomer was sized like any other Eldara, but his face was invisible, hidden in the recesses of his hood.

"Good evening to you too, friend," Bellaydin nodded, and started on his way. The stranger called out to him as he turned.

"Wait, young master, a moment of your time. Do you know the way to Aelsar Estate?"

Bellaydin stopped, and turned to face the stranger. "Perhaps. But first, who are you?"

"A messenger," said the figure. "They call me Keras. You are Bellaydin Ap'Lydin, are you not?"

Bellaydin did not respond.

"A remarkable name you have, to be sure," said Keras. "Qardleean, if I am not mistaken. Your father or mother must have been an avid reader."

"What?"

"*The Tragedy of Belial'ad-Dīn*, the story of a man cursed by his lineage. Quite a famous work, and, appropriate, if I may say so myself."

Bellaydin began to back away from the man.

"Come now Bellaydin, I mean you no harm."

"How do you know me? Show me your face."

"I… cannot show my face. There are others watching me." He reached into his robes, fumbling for something. "As for your other question, I am an acquaintance of your foster mother, the Lady Saegralanna." He produced a rolled up scroll from his robes and handed it to Bellaydin. "This is a message for the Heir of Lydin."

Bellaydin looked at the scroll in his hands sceptically. He did not know what this was all about. "The who?"

The Eldara drew close and grabbed his wrist. Bellaydin winced as Keras' words hit him with dire urgency. "You are in great danger, Heir of Lydin. There are dark forces moving against you, forces you aren't even aware of." The Eldara's face was scarred, but his eyes blazed with fervour. Bellaydin tried to escape Keras' grip, but the Eldara held him in place.

"Your sister has been wise. If you wish to survive you must follow her example. You must leave Aderilund as soon as you can."

"Leave? And go where?"

"Just leave. It is for your own good. The destiny others would have for you is not one you would want to pursue."

Bellaydin's eyes went back to the scroll in his hands. "What are you talking about?" He looked up, expecting a response but the figure had vanished.

"What in the name of –?" Bellaydin glanced around. The man, Keras, was nowhere to be seen.

Bellaydin unfurled the scroll, smoothing out the parchment to take a closer look. There was no writing on it – merely a single symbol – a stylized image of a bestial face, horned and foreboding. His brow furrowed in thought, Bellaydin stared at the symbol quizzically, trying to ascertain its meaning. He had never seen such an image before but, curiously, in some way it seemed *familiar.*

Confused, he stuffed the scroll in his clothes and continued on his way home.

By the time he reached Aelsar Estate, the skies had cleared. Saegranna met him at the door. "Bela! Where have you been? You know how I feel about you being away so late."

"Sorry, Mother," Bellaydin said. His voice was distant.

Saegralanna's expression changed. "Bela, is there something wrong?" she said.

Frowning, Bellaydin thrust the piece of parchment into his foster mother's hands.

"What's this?" Saegralanna said. She opened the note and took in its contents. As she did, the colour drained from her face. "Bela, where did you get this?"

"A man gave it to me, he called himself Keras. Does any of this mean something to you?" asked Bellaydin.

"Keras? I don't…" she said slowly. "And this symbol… it's…"

"It's what?" Bellaydin said. "Is it bad?"

Saegralanna did not respond.

"He also mentioned something like the 'Heir of Lydin' and a destiny."

Saegralanna gasped. "Bela, are you absolutely sure that's what he said?"

"Yes, quite sure. What's wrong? What does this all mean?"

"I think… I think we need to have a talk."

As Bellaydin looked into Saegralanna's eyes, he noticed something in them he had never seen there before – fear.

"I think you need to be told, Bellaydin," Saegralanna said, as the pair of them sat in the drawing room.

"Told what? Is it about this symbol? This so-called Heir of Lydin? What? I want to know what's going on."

"Yes, it's about that symbol. It's also… it's also about your parents."

"What about them?" Bellaydin asked. He had an idea he wasn't going to like what he was about to hear.

"Bela, I've never told you how your parents died, have I?"

"No," he said. "And when I do ask, you try and change the subject."

Saegralanna nodded, and smiled self-consciously. "There's no easy way to tell you this, Bela, so I'm just going to come out and say it. Your parents were murdered."

"Murdered?" Bellaydin's eyes widened in shock. "How? By who?"

"This symbol," Saegralanna said, gesturing at the parchment. "It represents the Horned God, a terrible entity worshipped by the men of Goriinchia and mad cultists elsewhere. It was a cultist of the Horned God who killed your father and mother, Bela."

"What? And you choose now as the time to tell me this? Why in the Sun King's name couldn't I know beforehand? Perhaps before someone from this cult decides to pass me a threatening note?"

"I knew Keras when I was a girl. I never believed he could…" She trailed off. "I thought I could protect you, Bela – you and Polnygar. It's why I brought you both to Aderilund. I didn't think the Horned God's followers would ever come here, that they would dare show their faces in the Aspen Kingdom."

"Yes, well, scratch that theory," said Bellaydin testily. "Polnygar's lucky she already left. What am I supposed to do?"

Bellaydin knew it was a mistake to bring up Polnygar, but the words had left his lips before he knew what he was doing.

"Bela," said Saegralanna, tears welling in her eyes. The topic of her wayward daughter was still a sore point, but she managed to keep her poise. "I promised that I would keep you safe – both of you – and I intend to keep that promise."

Bellaydin sighed. "Look, I'm sorry Mother, I didn't mean..."

"It's fine, Bela, it's fine," said Saegralanna, wiping tears away from her eyes. "I should have told you this long ago."

"Who was it?" said Bellaydin.

"What?"

"The cultist who killed my parents. Who was he?"

"Bela, please."

"Tell me."

"As you wish," Saegralanna said. "His name was Simon Enlim. He called himself the Snake. Little else is known about him, but it is said he was Goriinchian born."

"And who exactly said that?"

"Your father's friends, Haakon de Morcor and Wulfric Highcrown. They heard Enlim speak. They witnessed the murder. Highcrown gave chase to the cultist, with Haakon following quickly after."

"And?"

"By the time Haakon had caught up, the cultist was dead and Highcrown unconscious, with no apparent memory of what had transpired except for vague recollections of a scuffle."

"So Enlim is dead then?"

"Yes Bela," Saegralanna said softly. "He is dead."

"The deaths of my parents have been avenged."

Saegralanna frowned. "In a manner of speaking, yes," she said. "But, as Wulfric warned me all those years ago, the remnants of the cult still exist, and there are those who seek to do you harm. I just thought, *hoped*, that they would never find you here, so far away from Emparia."

"And the Heir of Lydin? What in the name of the Underworld is the Heir of Lydin?"

"That was a person."

"A person?"

"Yes," said Saegralanna. "Your father."

"My father? What do you mean? What did my father stand to inherit? Some kingdom?" Bellaydin demanded.

"Calm down, Bela, please." Saegralanna said.

"Calm down?" Bellaydin asked incredulously. "You've kept this all secret for a decade and now you expect me to take it calmly?"

"I know this isn't easy, Bela —"

"You're damn right it isn't easy," he shouted.

"I understand, Bela." She placed a consoling hand on his shoulder. "Nobody knows what the cultist meant, Bela. But he, and every other one they captured after the murder, kept babbling about how Alusine, your father, was the 'prophesised one', the 'Heir of Lydin'."

Bellaydin frowned. "Yes, but what does that mean?"

"Bela," Saegralanna said gently. "They were crazed fanatics. It was some wild belief of their cult. It could have meant anything. But whatever it was, for some reason they marked your parents for death. They probably would have killed you as well, were it not for your cousin."

"William," Bellaydin murmured. He had never met his only cousin, William Ap'Lydin, but from what he had heard, the man was well established as an important noble in Emparia.

"Your cousin protected you with his life, Bela," said Saegralanna, "and ensured that you were brought here safely, far from the reach of the cultists of the Horned God."

"Or so you thought," said Bellaydin.

"Yes Bela, so we thought."

"I'm sorry."

Saegralanna smiled faintly, placing her hands on Bellaydin's. Bellaydin, for his part, flinched slightly. The silence was uncomfortable, and lasted for several minutes before it was interrupted by a fierce banging on the door.

"Lady Saegralanna! Lady Saegralanna!"

Saegralanna walked swiftly to the door, opening it with haste.

"Lady Saegralanna, thank the Great Mother you are here. It's terrible. I can't believe it myself. The Hall of the Ancients is in an uproar. You must come now."

"Calm yourself, Velthen," Saegralanna said, trying to sound reassuring.

"My dear Lady, it is simply unspeakable. The Speaker... he's dead. Murdered!"

"Oh, Goddess," Saegralanna gasped, placing a hand over her mouth in shock.

"Quarion has been murdered?" said Bellaydin from behind Saegralanna.

"How? Why? By who?"

"My dear lady," said the Eldara messenger, pointedly ignoring Bellaydin. "You must come at once. The other Lords are awaiting you. Ivellios has called a full session."

Saegralanna nodded.

***

As the messenger had said, things were chaotic at the Halls of the Ancients. A tall, thin spellweaver greeted Saegralanna as she arrived.

"My lady, thank goodness you have arrived. I am sure you have heard the news."

"Yes, Lord Vaerath," said Saegralanna. "Quarion…"

Vaerath nodded. "It did not happen that long ago, a few hours at the most. A guard stumbled across the body and raised the alarm. Come, they are waiting for us in the main hall." The spellweaver noticed Bellaydin standing near Saegralanna. "Can I help you, young human?" he said.

Bellaydin froze. "Uh…"

"It's alright, Vaerath. He's with me," Saegralanna said.

Vaerath stood still, mouth open. "But Lord Ivellios —"

"If Lord Ivellios has a problem, he can tell it to me, can he not?" she said.

Vaerath frowned and gave a shrug. "Very well, my lady. Come this way, then. You too, Master Ap'Lydin."

Vaerath led Saegralanna and Bellaydin to the main hall, where the other lords were assembled. In the centre, on a marble plinth, the body of Quarion li'Ailynu lay in state. The wound that had killed him had been cleaned, and in death, Quarion seemed almost tranquil, as if he were asleep. A white sheet covered the rest of his body.

At the head of the plinth stood Lord Ivellios, clad in robes of state. The spellweaver wore an odd expression on his face. "Lady Saegralanna, you have arrived. As you can see, a truly tragic event has taken place this evening. Quarion was a dear friend to us all."

Saegralanna looked the spellweaver up and down. "Wearing his robes already, Ivellios? A little presumptuous, is it not?"

"Not at all, my dear," Ivellios said with feigned courtesy. "As Lord Spellweaver, it is my prerogative to act as Speaker until the Council elects a new representative."

Bellaydin noticed Saegralanna's mouth twitch. She always did that when she was angry.

"So, what happened here, Ivellios? Do you know, or is this just another excuse for you to hear the sound of your own voice?" Saegralanna snapped.

"Temper, temper, my dear lady," said Ivellios. "These are the facts, here for all of us to see. Our revered Speaker, Quarion li'Ailynu, was murdered. A loyal guard discovered his body. The murderer must have escaped. We do not know his name. We do not know his face. But there is one thing that we do know."

Ivellios nodded to a nearby guard. Grimacing, the guard pulled back the sheet covering Quarion's corpse, exposing the dead Eldara's chest. There were gasps from the assembled lords and functionaries, and from Bellaydin and Saegralanna. Carved into the flesh of the now-deceased Speaker Quarion was the unmistakeable symbol of the Horned God.

"As you can see, my lords and ladies, the killer has left his mark on our beloved Speaker's form. The killer has violated Quarion's body, just as he has violated all of Aderilund."

There were murmurs and a few scattered cries of agreement amongst Ivellios' audience. As if sensing blood, the spellweaver continued, raising his voice in anger, shouting louder with each progressive sentence.

"The sanctity of our homeland has been forever desecrated, friends. If even the best, the wisest and most honoured of the Eldara are not safe, what of the rest of us?" Ivellios pointed theatrically to Quarion's body. "This is the symbol of the Horned God, a demonic presence worshipped by barbaric Mal-halyth. Some would have you believe that we here, in sacred Aderilund, under the protection of the Great Mother, are protected from such things."

People began to nod their heads and mutter in agreement.

"Some would have you believe that we are safe," Ivellios shouted.

Jeers erupted from the crowd.

"I say NO!" Ivellios was met with a roar of approval. "We are *not* safe! And why are we not safe? Because of this… *thing.*" With a sneer, Ivellios pointed directly at Bellaydin.

There were more mutters and murmurs from the crowd, with quite a few heads nodding in agreement.

"Ivellios!" Saegralanna yelled in disapproval.

"It is too late, my lady. We know," said Vaerath.

"Know what?" Saegralanna said.

"Everything," said Ivellios.

"What conspiracy is this?" Saegralanna said.

"You have seen this symbol somewhere else today, haven't you?" asked Ivellios.

"What is the meaning of this?" demanded Saegralanna.

"Saegralanna, please." Vaerath's voice was calm.

"Answer the question, my lady," said Ivellios coolly.

"Why should I? I'm not on trial here. Or am I being accused of murder now, Ivellios?" said Saegralanna.

"Have you, or have you not seen this symbol somewhere else?" said Ivellios. "Answer us."

Before Saegralanna could speak, Bellaydin did. "Yes." He produced the piece of paper with the mark, and showed it to the assembly. "There was a man... Keras, I think. That's what he said his name was. He gave me this."

"Keras, you say? An old friend of yours, isn't he Lady Saegralanna?" Vaerath asked.

Without so much as a word, Ivellios snatched the paper from Bellaydin's hand and held it up for all to see.

"Here is the proof of my allegations. See the symbol of the Horned God, brought here by one of Lady Saegralanna's associates. He must have come here for the Mal-halyths she keeps in her house. See the danger that Lady Saegralanna has brought upon us."

The Eldara Lords had been worked into a frenzy, and the muttering had now reached a crescendo, with cries of "No!" and "Shame!" echoing from the assembled.

"I say, no more." Ivellios shouted, "This cannot, and will not stand."

Some of the lords looked as if they disagreed but the majority nodded their head in assent.

"So what is it, Ivellios?" Saegralanna said acidly. "You will just toss Bellaydin out of Aderilund?"

"He should have never been brought here in the first place. You know that, my lady."

"And where is he to go?"

Ivellios blinked. "He has family elsewhere, does he not? His human family? Let them take him in. He is not our concern, and never was."

"You can't do that, Ivellios. Aderilund is the only home he's ever known,"

Saegralanna said.

"So? He is a danger to us. All of us."

"Then let us protect him. Don't forget, he is in danger as well – more so than we are."

"He is not our concern. He is not Eldara. HE IS NOTHING!"

At that, Bellaydin ran.

He did not know where he was going. In truth, he did not care. As long as it was far away. Far from the Hall of Ancients, far from the Lords Quarter, far from Aderial, and, if he could, far from Aderilund itself. As far away as possible.

At that moment, 'as far away as possible' happened to be the woods outside Aderial. That was fine by him. He needed to escape. Again.

This was what it was like to be Bellaydin Ap'Lydin. This was how it felt to be a stranger in your own homeland, to be something that others thought of as not quite right. A pollutant. Perhaps, just perhaps, Ivellios was right. He did not belong here. He should have never been brought here.

"Aargh," screamed Bellaydin in frustration. "What a mess."

He felt moisture on his head. "What… is it raining again?" Bellaydin said, touching his hair. He looked at his fingers. It was blood. Bellaydin looked up.

Hanging in the trees was a corpse, dismembered, and almost unrecognisable. Blood was dripping steadily from the body, forming a small pool on the forest floor. There was an unmistakeable stench surrounding the corpse, which Bellaydin was surprised he had not noticed before.

The body was swinging slowly, on the edge of a length of rope, but quite obviously, strangulation had not been the sole cause of death. The individual, whoever it was, had been killed in a gruesome fashion –

garrotted, disembowelled, then strung up in the wilderness.

Bellaydin felt sick to his stomach, and started to back away from the scene. It was then, however, that he realised he was staring at a familiar face. It was the man who had accosted him the night before, the one named Keras. But that was impossible, thought Bellaydin, didn't the Council say that this man had murdered the Speaker?

Suddenly, Bellaydin glimpsed movement out of the corner of his eye. The corpse's arm twitched. Keras was not yet dead. A slow, guttural groaning came from his mouth.

"H-H-eir o-o-f Lyyyy-din," he croaked. "Run…"

Bellaydin fainted.

CHAPTER 7

Polnygar felt as if she was being baked.

The heat was the first thing she had noticed about Macrodonia; the desert sands radiated it. The city streets and buildings were covered with an undulating haze. If Aderilund was a mix of pleasant blues and greens, Macrodonia was a land of reds, yellows and browns.

"How is it so hot here?" she asked Augustin as they strolled through the streets, shortly after disembarking the ship. "We're north of Aderilund, aren't we? Away from the equator?"

"Hmh," Augustin mumbled. "Something to do with the currents around Aderilund, from what the sailors tell me. They're always saying how those elves don't know how blessed they are. You go down to Port Hanon, girl, then you'll know what hot is." He paused. "That and what it's like to contract Feng-Hu fever."

Polnygar looked at Augustin quizzically.

"You don't want to know. Trust me," Augustin said. "It's three months of my life I'll never get back. Anyway, the merchant's quarter is this way, and the bazaar, is right over…" Augustin glanced from left to right, and then pointed, "here."

"What's that smell?" said Polnygar.

"Lentils."

"Lentils?"

"And mutton, by the smell of it. Let's go eat. This way, girl." Augustin set off in the direction of the bazaar and motioned for Polnygar to follow.

"Look, those people… are they Hsien?" Polnygar said, referring to the pygmy travellers who came from the lands south of Aderilund.

"Where?"

Polnygar pointed to several short, stocky, bald men who hurried past them.

"Oh, them? No, the people here call them the *Nemoi*. They're natives to Macrodonia. They work as scholars, scribes, that sort of thing."

"I've never seen one before," said Polnygar, clearly fascinated. "They look so strange…"

"Careful. I think they can hear you," Augustin said.

One of the Nemoi turned its head sharply, stared at Polnygar, and muttered something in a foreign tongue.

"I'm sorry," said Polnygar hurriedly. Luckily, the Nemoi seemed hardly concerned. He merely turned back around, increased his pace, and attempted to catch up with his comrades.

"I wouldn't worry. They're fairly harmless. Probably should keep your mouth shut though, girl."

Polnygar did not like being told what to do, and was about to protest, but thought better of it. After all, there was still a chance that Augustin might throw her overboard, even if he had to take her back on board the ship to do it.

Besides, she had to admit that Augustin was not quite the same as the hectoring and self-important nobility of Aderilund. He spoke with confidence, but without the arrogance that typified those that she had rebelled against most her life. He carried himself differently as well, and though on first impressions she had found him coarse and unrefined compared to the serene and elegant lordlings she was used to, she now was beginning to see a sort of rugged charm in his weathered features. He did not have the beauty of the Eldara, but there was something else – an unvarnished honesty to his features – that she found appealing.

A brief while later, Augustin and Polnygar were seated at one of the stalls in the bazaar, eating and talking.

"Mm, I'd forgotten how good the food was here," Augustin said, his mouth full.

Polnygar nodded in agreement.

"Now, we have to talk, girl."

"What about?"

"You know very well."

Polnygar said nothing.

"You shouldn't be here," Augustin said. "Look, I can organise your passage home, girl. Next ship leaving from Jagoncoilis. You'll be back in Aderilund by winter."

"I don't want to go home."

"It's not really a matter of what you want. In fact, I –" Augustin stopped mid-sentence, and looked around warily.

"What is it?" Polnygar said.

"We're being watched," Augustin said.

"What? By who? Where?" Polnygar said, suddenly alarmed.

August glared at her. "Shh. Keep your voice down, girl. They're over there, in the alley. No, don't look straight at them. Keep your eyes forward. Pretend we haven't noticed."

Polnygar nodded slowly, and kept her eyes fixed on Augustin. For a moment, she saw nothing amiss but then, out of the corner of her eye, she noticed several robed and cowled figures emerging from one of the bazaar's many alleyways.

"Who are they?" Polnygar whispered to Augustin from across the table. "What could they possibly want with either of us?"

His eyes set into a cold stare, Augustin gritted his teeth. "I don't know. And I don't intend to find out." He pointed to their right. "Come on, this way, girl."

"What?"

"It's time to leave. But let's do it casually, without letting on that we know they're following us. Maybe we can lose them somewhere along the way."

They rose slowly, both pretending to be oblivious to the approaching strangers.

"This is serious. Don't overdo it," Augustin whispered as the pair of them moved towards their escape route, pretending all the while to be chatting normally.

"Me?" said Polnygar. "I'm not the one overact – "

She stopped short as they turned the corner. In front of them, stood another three cloaked figures, blocking Augustin and Polnygar's escape. The remaining strangers were still coming towards them from the other side of the bazaar. Only one word passed Augustin's lips.

"Damn."

One of the cloaked figures closed in on him. "Excuse me, Emparian, but you seem a little lost."

Augustin did not respond. The other robed men were beginning to assemble behind Augustin and Polnygar.

"Who is your companion here? Aderilund is a long way away from here, isn't it?" The men were speaking Emparian, but with a peculiar lilt.

"I wouldn't know," said Augustin. "We just arrived from Caruillin."

"A lie. How quaint."

"Why would we lie about that?" Augustin said slowly.

"Why indeed? But the truth of the matter is, you and your young companion have just arrived from Aderilund."

"And what makes you say that?" Augustin said.

The man smiled, revealing gleaming white teeth. "We have friends in high places."

"Oh yes?" said Augustin. He reached towards his belt, inching towards his sword.

"I would advise against that," the other man said. "The results could be quite unfortunate, mainly for you."

Augustin looked around. The other figures silently cocked previously concealed crossbows. However hidden the weapons were before, his assailants certainly wanted him to see them now.

"I see," Augustin said, moving his hand away from the sword.

The other man nodded slowly.

"Who are you?" Augustin demanded.

The man smiled again. Augustin found the smile deeply unsettling.

"Our names are of no importance. Our identities are of no interest. We are simply the servants of the Horned God. The Lord of All has taken great interest in you, or to be more specific, *you.*" The man looked directly at Polnygar.

"*Me?*" she said, her voice hesitant. "But I'm not anybody important."

"Perhaps not yet," the man said. "But we speak of things to come. Events that we cannot let come to pass."

The man nodded to his associates, who lifted their weapons and aimed at Polnygar. She looked stunned, unable to say anything, whereas Augustin was furious.

"What in the name of the Underworld are you talking about? Leave her alone, she's just a girl." he yelled.

One of the other men spoke, "Your Eminence, is she the Heir of Lydin?"

"Perhaps, perhaps not. But one cannot be too careful. Take her in."

Polnygar stepped backwards, but there was nowhere to run or hide. Her back to the alley wall, she could do nothing but watch the events unfolding before her.

"I don't believe you," Augustin snarled. "You're lying. How would you even know that she was coming here? She's a stowaway, for the Sun King's sake. I ask you again, gods damn you, what do you want from me?"

"We have no interest in you," the man said to Augustin. "But it would be best if you did not interfere. Kill him, take the girl."

"No!" Augustin shouted.

Polnygar looked on in shock and horror as Augustin, sword in hand, leapt between her and the cultists. The crossbowmen opened fire. Augustin took a bolt in his left arm as he charged at the nearest cultist. As two of them fell to his blade, another cultist fumbled with his weapon, sending his bolt through Augustin's thigh. Clutching his leg, Augustin tried to ignore the pain. Pivoting on his wounded leg, he lunged at another cultist, taking off the man's arm. Another bolt struck Augustin in the leg, and he fell to the ground in agony. The surviving cultists surrounded the badly wounded Augustin, frantically reloading their weapons.

"I warned you," their leader said, "that it would be best if you did not interfere."

Augustin lay on the ground, his breath coming in ragged gasps. "Gods damn you, you honourless bastards," he said. He turned towards Polnygar. "Girl… run! Get out of here!"

Polnygar blinked and, after a moment's hesitation, turned quickly and attempted to flee. At the sound of her feet scraping the cobblestones, some of the cultists turned to pursue, while others frantically reloaded.

"Oh… no… you… don't." Augustin said between gasps, and with his remaining strength, grabbed the ankles of the closest cultist, yanking the man to the ground. The cultist's crossbow discharged, and Augustin took another bolt for his efforts, this time in the shoulder. Some of the cultists swivelled back around, preparing to finish off Augustin.

"Forget him, you fools, get the girl." their leader yelled.

But Polnygar was already gone.

"After her!"

Polnygar didn't stop running. Pushing through startled crowds, she thought of nothing except escaping the men who still pursued her.

"Guards! Guards! Help!" she screamed.

But there were no guardsmen to be seen, only shocked merchants, looking with terror at the black-clad men who were chasing her, shouting strange oaths as they did.

"Someone… please… help…" Polnygar said.

She was alone once again, close to collapsing as she stumbled down a different alleyway. Tears streamed down her face and her breathing was punctuated with loud sobs. She slumped to the ground. She knew that fleeing had probably saved her life, but she hated herself for it. Hated the way she had left Augustin there to die, merely to save her own wretched life. They had barely known each other, and he was not exactly pleased with the way Polnygar had stowed away, yet he had sacrificed his life to give her a chance to escape. His life for hers, was that a fair trade? Shadows loomed over her, and she heard a low, ominous chuckle. It was too late.

"Poor little girl," said the cultist. Nearby, his two compatriots blocked the only escape routes.

One of them grabbed her roughly, pinning her arms to her back. She struggled to escape, but to no avail. As his hand gripped her tightly, Polnygar noticed a tattoo on his skin, a stylized image of a horned and terrible face.

"This will hurt. But only for a moment," the cultist said. "It will be just like falling asleep."

Polnygar closed her eyes, sobbing. The crossbow clicked as the cultist methodically reloaded it. Fear overwhelmed Polnygar; Fear and something else. In the stillness of her thoughts, a white-hot ember of vengeance smouldered, and erupted forth into a righteous fire, bursting from the recesses of her mind. And the sky burned.

"What the –"

Polnygar heard the cultist shout in astonishment.

"Aargh, my hands!" screamed another.

"She's a sorceress! We've got to – "

"Fire!"

"It's burning!"

"There's no escape!"

Screams filled the darkness, screams so horrific that Polnygar kept her eyes tightly shut. They increased in volume, filled with such agony and pain. The smell of flesh sizzling and blistering assailed Polnygar's senses.

An agonized voice called out, "I'm burning!"

There was the roar of what sounded like a furnace or a ball of flame. It bellowed past Polnygar's ears. Then there was nothing but silence. Time passed before Polnygar dared to open her eyes. When she did, it was tentatively, and to great surprise.

The entire alleyway was blackened with soot and ash. Metal girders had twisted and deformed, as if from great heat. All around Polnygar were unmistakable signs of an immense inferno yet she – her clothes and her belongings – was completely unharmed. In fact, it was as if Polnygar had been totally protected by whatever had scorched the area.

Her assailants were not so lucky. All that remained of them were a few charred pieces of bone and cloth. Everything else was gone, consumed by the flames.

"What in the Sun King's name..." said a voice. The guards had arrived. "What happened here? What is this?"

The lead guardsman, a tall, angular man, pointed at Polnygar. "Witchcraft! In the name of Great Pharaoh, you are under arrest. Seize her!"

Stunned, delirious, and still not comprehending the situation, Polnygar offered no resistance.

***

Bellaydin heard voices.

"I think he's coming around," said a deep male voice.

"Good. He took quite a fall," a female voice responded.

The woman's voice belonged to Saegralanna, Bellaydin realised, even in his groggy state. The male's voice was unknown to him.

Bellaydin opened his eyes.

"Oh, Bela, thank goodness, I was so worried." said Saegralanna, tightly embracing him.

"Oww. I think I'm a bit tender," said Bellaydin. Pausing for a moment, he waited for the throbbing in his head to subside. "What happened?"

"You ran off, dear, into the forest. Then we found you unconscious. What happened? Was it something you saw?"

Bellaydin felt a cold chill go through him as he remembered the corpse of the strange man, the one named Keras. "It was Keras, the one who killed the Speaker. I found the murderer, but someone else had got to him first."

"We know, Bela, we know. The Council has been informed, and they're going to get to the bottom of it. Ivellios has promised a full, proper investigation."

From the tone of her voice, Bellaydin did not think that Saegralanna believed her own words.

"He wasn't dead. I don't think so."

"Now, now, Bela, dear. You're hurt, stressed. You were probably imagining things. It's not possible someone in that condition would still be alive."

Bellaydin groaned, and placed a hand to his head. "I think I must've hit my head on something as I fell," he said.

Saegralanna smiled gently, and applied a wet cloth to his bruised head.

"How did you find me? How did you know where I was?"

"Well," said Saegralanna. "It was Geoffrey who found you."

"Geoffrey? Who?"

"That would be me, young man."

The voice was the same one Bellaydin had heard moments before. In front of Bellaydin stood a tall, muscular man, his most notable feature a handsome head of blond hair and a crooked grin. The man extended his hand.

"Sir Geoffrey Keslin, Knight of Emparia, in service to the Earl of Genio. It's a pleasure to meet you, Master Ap'Lydin."

Saegralanna smiled, and added, "Sir Keslin only recently arrived. He was on his way to visit us and, when he heard you were missing, he volunteered to find you."

Geoffrey nodded. "To tell you the truth, it was Kahlaf that found you. I just tagged along." He winked at Bellaydin.

"Who is Kahlaf?"

Geoffrey laughed. "Oh, this should be interesting. Let's just say that he's my, uh, retainer or man-at-arms, that sort of thing."

"Well," Bellaydin said weakly, "you can thank him for me."

"Oh, I think you'll get the chance to thank him yourself. Just don't look at his fangs."

"Fangs?" Bellaydin said.

"Yes, he's a bit particular about people staring at them." Geoffrey came closer to Bellaydin and whispered in the young man's ear, "And be careful shaking his hand. Those claws of his can hurt." Geoffrey winked at Bellaydin again.

Saegralanna smiled. "You know, Bela, you're the reason Geoffrey is here in Aderilund."

"Me?"

"Well, you and your sister. But Saegralanna says I've missed the other Ap'Lydin, so I guess I'll just give the letter to you."

"A letter. Who is it from?"

Geoffrey fished inside his tunic, and withdrew a yellowed piece of parchment, sealed with wax. He handed it to Bellaydin. "It's from your cousin."

"You mean William? William's sent me a letter?" said Bellaydin, sitting up in his bed and breaking the seal on the letter.

"Well, most people call him 'my lord' or, 'the Earl of Genio', but yes, that cousin," Geoffrey chuckled as Bellaydin eagerly opened the letter.

"Dear Polnygar and Bellaydin,

I hope this letter finds the both of you in good health. It has been quite some time since we last met. You may not even remember me, and I would most likely not recognise you now."

Bellaydin skimmed through a few paragraphs of introductory greetings.

"And so I would like to extend an invitation to both of you. If it pleases you, I would very much like the pair of you to visit me for a period in Emparia. You may partake of whatever opportunities Emparia offers while here, and rest assured that, as my kinsmen, you will be accommodated with the level of luxury your heritage demands.

This offer stands for as long as you need, and you are free to take it up at any time you wish. There are no preconditions.

William Caradoc Ap'Lydin

Earl of Genio"

Bellaydin finished the letter, refolding the piece of parchment and placing it on the table beside the bed.

"The offer is there, Bellaydin, if you wish it. Polnygar may have already left, but I can still take you with me, if that's what you want."

Bellaydin looked at Geoffrey, and then at Saegralanna. "I do want it," he said. "But I can't." Bellaydin continued, "Gods know sometimes I hate this

100

place, and dream of Emparia, and wish, hope and pray for a chance to escape, but... but I can't. Aderilund is my home... even... even if the Eldara do not like it. I've never seen Emparia. I wouldn't belong there anymore than I belong here. What links it to me?"

"You have family there, Bellaydin," said Geoffrey. "Your cousin would always look out for you. It is the land of your ancestors, your parents. They – "

"My parents? I never knew them. Who are they to me but strangers?"

"There is another matter, Bellaydin. It is your cousin, William. He doesn't speak of it, but he has no heir. Upon his death, the Ap'Lydin line ceases. He cannot pass on his title, you see, and –"

"You think I could be his heir? What do I know of being an earl? I've not been there since I was a child. I know nothing of Emparia, and now you're asking me to join its nobility?"

"It would just be a precaution. William might still remarry, have a son, and –"

The discussion was cut short with a loud rapping on the exterior door. "Just a moment," said Saegralanna. She nodded to one of the house servants, who went to check on the commotion.

In a few moments, the servant returned, somewhat anxiously, with another figure in tow. Bellaydin stared in silent wonder at the strange creature in front of him. The figure, for all intents and purposes, was some strange amalgam between man and reptile. A forked tongue flitted intermittently between the creature's wicked, pointed teeth.

"Ah, Bellaydin Ap'Lydin. Allow me to introduce my, uh, associate – Kahlaf el'Lahn. I'm sure he's as happy to meet you as you are to meet him."

The creature glanced at Bellaydin and grunted, seemingly unimpressed.

"I think he likes you," said Geoffrey.

"My lady," said the servant anxiously. "I have just received word from the Council. They claim to have examined the body and made their decision."

"And? What is it the Council claims to have made up their mind on? Or should I say, Ivellios, for he *is* the Council now, is he not?"

Saegralanna's servant blushed, and looked slightly uncomfortable, but continued, "I have the message with me, if you would, Lady Saegralanna." He passed the scroll to her.

Unfurling it, Saegralanna read swiftly, her brow furrowing as her eyes scanned over the text. "Oh, he didn't... he couldn't... he..."

"What? What is it?" asked Bellaydin.

Saegralanna read out the proclamation: "It has been determined that the deceased individual was a member of the Cult of the Horned God, and the murderer of Speaker Quarion. The true target, however, was the human known as Bellaydin Tyron Ap'Lydin, a guest of House Aelsar. As a guest, rather than a trueborn Eldara son of Aderilund, Ap'Lydin has no inherent right to residency in Aderilund, and may only remain at the sufferance of the Crown and its duly appointed representatives."

Bellaydin felt a sinking sensation in his stomach. He was pretty sure he knew what the rest of this letter was.

"In order to ensure the stability, security and harmony of the Aspen Kingdom, the Council of Ancients hereby decrees that the right of residency for Bellaydin Ap'Lydin is revoked, indefinitely. He must leave the territories of the Kingdom in two weeks, after which he will be considered an outlaw."

"Outlaw?" said Geoffrey.

"By authority of Acting Lord-Speaker Ivellios, dated this year 5868 AF," Saegralanna said, finishing the letter. There was silence as most took in the contents of the letter.

"Well, I guess that's that then," said Bellaydin. "He's finally got rid of me, hasn't he?"

"Bela…"

"It's what he's always wanted, isn't it? For the last decade or so. And now it looks like he's got his dream." Wincing, Bellaydin threw back the blankets, and got out of the bed.

"Bela, please, don't over exert yourself. You need to rest," Saegralanna said.

"Didn't you hear, Mother?" said Bellaydin. "They're throwing me out of the country. I'd better go pack."

"Nothing's decided yet. I can appeal. We can get the decision overturned," Saegralanna said.

"Can we? I really doubt it. Only the king or queen can overturn the decision of the Council, and if I recall correctly, they just left for Liderial, and so are unlikely to return within two weeks. By then, I'll probably have every red-blooded elf from here to Talerial on my tail, hoping to drag my carcass back to Lord Ivellios for some sort of reward. Yes, I can see it now – kill the slimy Mal-halyth, get a hundred silver for your troubles."

"Bela," Saegralanna scolded. "You know that isn't the Eldara way."

"Isn't it?" said Bellaydin tersely. His shoulders slumped. "Oh gods, Mother, I'm sorry. But if you'll forgive me, I'm not feeling very charitable to Eldara at the moment."

"Nor should you," growled Kahlaf. The Ahktarran had stayed silent up until now. "They are honourless curs who would throw out a defenceless youth, merely to save their own worthless hides."

"Ahh… yes, thank you Kahlaf," said Geoffrey, looking rather embarrassed at his companion's forthrightness. He placed a hand on the Ahktarran shoulder. "Best let me talk from now on, all right?"

Kahlaf just glared at him.

"I apologise for that, my lady. When's he hungry, he does get tetchy…" Geoffrey emphasised his words with a brotherly pat on Kahlaf's shoulder – a gesture the Ahktarran didn't seem to appreciate. Geoffrey for his part just grinned, perhaps enjoying some sort of private joke. "You should have seen him deal with those two mercenaries from Huò."

Bellaydin looked pained.

"Bellaydin," said Geoffrey. "The offer is still there, if you'd like to take it. There's no pressure, but there will always be a place for you in Emparia."

Saegralanna interjected. "'Bela, you don't have to. You can stay, you know that? We can work something out. The king and queen will be informed. We could wait just outside the border."

Geoffrey looked at Saegralanna, then back at Bellaydin. "It is your choice, young master."

Bellaydin's mind swirled. His life, or at least the last twelve years, came rushing back through a torrent of joy and pain – of the good and the bad. Feelings surrounded him – the safety and security of Saegralanna's household, and then… and then the longing, the longing for the place of his birth.

With all eyes in the room fixed on him, he made his choice.

"I will go to Emparia."

CHAPTER 8

"You there," The guard barked. "You've got a visitor."

The guard was Macrodonian like the rest in the guardhouse, but was the only one to be bilingual, and had been chosen when it was discovered that Polnygar could neither speak nor understand the Macrodonian language. The guard's accent was thick, he spoke Emparian haltingly, and his pronunciation was sometimes incomprehensible but, for the most part, Polnygar did not have too much trouble with the general gist of his words.

"A visitor?" Polnygar said.

She had no idea who would visit her. After all, the only person she even vaguely knew in Emparia was Augustin, and he was most likely in a shallow grave somewhere at this point. Still, after two days in the prison, Polnygar was grateful for the chance of any company, friendly or otherwise.

"He's a very important one too, so don't you be putting your grubby little fingers on him, witch."

By now the tale of her "sorcery" near the bazaar had spread, and nearly every guard was convinced that Polnygar was some fireball-flinging witch. As a result, they tended to stay as far away from her as possible. The soldier who served her meals would often try to throw the bread and gruel through the bars.

"Who is he?" said Polnygar.

"Oh, like you don't know, witch," the guard said, spitting on the ground in contempt.

Walking towards the outer door, the guard opened it, speaking in hushed tones to a robed and cowled figure. The guard mumbled something in Macrodonian to the robed figure, who raised a hand in response, dismissing the guard. Muttering again, the guard swiftly left the room, closing the door behind him and leaving the robed man alone with Polnygar.

"Um," Polnygar said nervously. "Hello?"

A voice, warm and rich yet tinged with age, answered her. "Hello to you, my dear." The man drew back his hood, revealing a face that was unmistakeably Eldara – long silver-grey hair, pointed upswept ears, and green almond-shaped eyes under arched brows. "I must apologise. My Eldaric is a little rusty, after all."

"No, no, it's fine," said Polnygar, her eyes wide with wonder.

"Ah, you are too kind. You are Polnygar, is that not correct?" said the man.

Polnygar nodded.

"Now then, what happened? Why are you in here?"

Polnygar found herself stumbling over her own words. "They were chasing me. They had crossbows. They were going to kill me. And then…I don't know. Look, I can't even understand it myself, I don't expect you would."

The man smiled and held out a hand. Polnygar gasped as two small blue spheres of flame materialised within his open palm.

"Actually my dear," he said, as he casually juggled the little fireballs, "I rather think I might."

Polnygar watched him with awe, too stunned to offer anything more than a smile.

"I am Aelzandar li'Geihnos," he gently closed his palms and opened them again. The flames were gone. "Royal Wizard of Macrodonia, Chair of the Council of Nine and Lord Archmage."

" What are you doing here then?" said Polnygar. Aelzandar smiled warmly.

"Why, my dear, I'm here to set you free."

"How do you know my name?" said Polnygar. "Is that magic?"

Aelzandar chuckled gently. "Connections, my dear. You're quite the new flavour around here at the moment, especially at the Royal Court. I've heard strange stories, you know, of sorcery, of witchcraft, and of fireballs exploding in the Shnefren Bazaar. Then, of all things, the guards discover the missing Emparian ambassador, near death, abandoned in an alleyway. He's only just regained consciousness, and yours was the first name he said."

"You mean… Augustin Bauer?" said Polnygar. Aelzandar nodded.

"He's alive?"

"Yes," Aelzandar said.

"Oh, gods, he's alive. Will you take me to him?" Polnygar said, relief washing over her.

"Of course, my dear. We'll go straight to the Royal Palace from here. Just let me settle matters with the guard."

Aelzandar walked towards the door, and rapped firmly but politely on its wooden frame. With the sound of jangling keys, sliding bars and turning mechanisms, the door swung open. The jailer re-entered the room, looking upon Polnygar with a sneer.

"I hope this witch hasn't been too much trouble for you, your Lordship. I can beat her, if you'd like." The guard was speaking in Emparian again, most likely in a deliberate attempt to intimidate Polnygar.

"That won't be necessary, my good fellow," said Aelzandar. "But you will surrender her into my custody without delay. If you do not, there may be consequences. Do I make myself clear?"

Aelzandar was firm and pointed, but did not raise his voice. Even so the jailer's face twisted in abject fear.

"Of course, your Lordship." The guard stuttered. He stumbled towards Polnygar's cell and, fumbling with the keys on his belt, eventually found the right one to unlock her cell door. With a groan of its rusted hinges, the door swung open, and Polnygar stepped through.

"This way, Mistress Polnygar," said Aelzandar.

As they made a brisk pace towards the Royal Palace, Aelzandar gave Polnygar an impromptu lecture on the lands of Macrodonia. "As you can see, my dear, the lands of Macrodonia are rather devoid of trees, hence timber is an incredibly valuable resource here. As a result, every structure you see around you is constructed of stone, like the temples, necropolises, and palaces, or mud brick, like the simpler dwellings of the lower classes. It makes for a rather different architectural style to that of Aderilund, does it not?"

Polnygar, lost in the spectacular view of the city, was not really listening. The sun was almost at its highest point for the day, and its rays were giving the whole city a burnt, orange glow. The streets were much quieter here, without the chaos and commotion of the Merchant's Quarter.

"It's beautiful," Polnygar said in awe.

"Ah, then you should see Anacoilis, my dear — twice as beautiful as Jagoncoilis, and four times as ancient. There's nothing quite like the Great

Pyramid of Arnû-Kaliz, particularly at sunset. Ah, here we are, straight ahead."

A magnificent concourse spread out in front of them, lined with an alternating pattern of statues and obelisks. Fountains and various types of greenery broke up the monotony of stone. At the end of the open area, a few thousand feet away, was the Royal Palace, a magnificent edifice of stone and marble.

"And there it is. The Royal Palace. Look lively, my dear. You're about to meet Pharaoh."

The antechamber was crowded. Despite its immense size, the way to the throne room was packed with a mass of people. Even so, the gigantic columns that supported the ceiling of the long hall impressed Polnygar with their height and magnificence.

Polnygar looked around in wonder at the throng of people from all stations and all walks of life. Peasant rubbed up against noble, scribe up against guardsman, priest with merchant.

"What are all these people waiting here for?" Polnygar asked Aelzandar.

"An audience with Pharaoh," said Aelzandar. "One of the privileges of being a Macrodonian - speaking face to face with a living god. Now, that's something to line up for."

"God?"

"The Macrodonians consider their ruler to be a living deity, a son of the Sun King, and with maternal descent from Mysanas, legendary first ruler of Macrodonia." Aelzandar stopped. "It's all rather complicated. But that's religion for you."

"Not all these people look like they're Macrodonian," Polnygar said, surveying the crowd. She spied a few pale skinned, fair haired gentlemen clad in tunics and hose, standing next to a gaggle of jewelled, swarthy and turbaned individuals.

"Ambassadors from many lands, Polnygar. They, too, must await Pharaoh's pleasure. Those tall, blond men are from Skurj, and the darker ones next to them are Qardleean."

"Excuse me," came a voice. "Do you have an appointment, young mistress?"

Polnygar looked down in astonishment. A small, bald man, dressed as a scribe, and with a stylus in his hand, looked at Polnygar with impatience. He appeared to be one of the Nemoi pointed out to her by Augustin shortly after their arrival.

"I'm not really here to – "

Aelzandar cut her off. "Hebu, do not pester her."

The small man looked up suspiciously. "My Lord Aelzandar. She is your guest, then?"

"That is correct, my good man," said Aelzandar. "I am sure you can trust me to handle things according to protocol."

"Of course. I will leave her in your capable hands then, my Lord."

Muttering something under his breath, Hebu disappeared off into the crowd. His voice was heard intermittently as he questioned the other supplicants.

"The Nemoi are a very particular people, Polnygar," said Aelzandar, "and sticklers for proper procedure. They do, however, construct some very elegant and structured poetry. You must read it sometime. Ah, here we go. We may go in."

Polnygar stepped for the entrance.

"Wait just a moment, my dear," said Aelzandar.

"What?"

"You do not speak Macrodonian, is that correct?"

"Well, no, but…"

"Of course. I suspect there wouldn't be much call for it."

"Is it going to be a problem?"

"Well, it may make it difficult for you to understand anything that will be said in there."

"I could just follow your lead, I guess," said Polnygar.

"Well, you could. Yes, you could. But I have something better in mind." He grabbed Polnygar's hand very gently and then, removing one of the bracelets he wore, he slowly placed it over her arm.

"Jewellery?" said Polnygar. "Why are you giving me this?"

"This bracelet is attuned to the Art. It will enable you to speak and understand Macrodonian as if you had been fluent in it your entire life."

"And you're giving it to me?"

"Consider it a loan, Polnygar. I'm hoping that eventually you become fluent enough on your own that I can have it back." He smiled gently and gestured with a hand. "After you, my dear."

The throne room was as magnificent as she had expected, perhaps more so. A long hallway, lined with potted date palms, led to a raised dais where a glorious throne stood, inlaid with gold and precious jewels. On the throne, surrounded by his guards, attendants, and high priests, sat Pharaoh.

At first, Polnygar was shocked at how young he was. The man who sat before her, a somewhat bored expression on his face, seemed to be barely in his twenties. He was handsome, with dark eyes, accentuated by the black kohl that lined them. A finely made crown of Macrodonian design sat atop his shaven head, and he carried himself with a slightly arrogant air.

"Great Pharaoh," said Aelzandar, prostrating himself before the young man. "Your loyal and humble servant has returned."

"You do not visit court as often as you should, Aelzandar," Pharaoh said, "I miss our games of Shatranj. In your absence I have been forced to play those of lesser skill." The man standing next to Pharaoh turned a shade of crimson.

"Your Majesty, Arhotep is still learning," the archmage replied, with a hint of condescension. "Give him time."

Just as Aelzandar had promised, Polnygar understood every word he had said, despite knowing that he had said them in the Macrodonian tongue. She rubbed the bracelet in awe, not paying attention to her surroundings. The men standing with Pharaoh glared at Polnygar and, realising her unintentional break with protocol, she too dropped herself to the ground.

"Who is this, Aelzandar?" said the man standing next to Pharaoh. "Another stray you picked off the streets? Is it really necessary for you to bring every street urchin into this palace?"

"When I see potential in them, yes." Aelzandar said, "I make no apologies for that."

"Oh? Just like the beggar you brought in last month? Tell me, has his flea problem cleared up yet?"

"That beggar is now a loyal and honest member of the royal guard," Aelzandar said.

"He barely knows the right way to hold a sword. Within a month he'll be dead, with any luck. Where do you find all these hopeless cases, Aelzandar?"

"I see potential wherever I go, Arhotep. You might too, if you frequented anywhere outside of the brothels of Low Town."

Pharaoh laughed as Arhotep turned bright red. "He has you there, Arhotep."

"Your Majesty," the vizier said, "This is outrageous. Aelzandar is not treating my questions with the respect they deserve."

"Oh, I think I am." Aelzandar said with a smile.

Arhotep's face was bright red. "You are making a mockery of your king, archmage."

"Pharaoh…" Aelzandar said, seeking to avoid the vizier's question.

Pharaoh raised a hand dismissively, which Polnygar took as an indication that Aelzandar was to answer the other man.

"Very well, vizier Arhotep," said Aelzandar. "If you must know, this young lady here is something special, I think. I assume news of an incident in the bazaar has reached the attention of the royal court?"

Arhotep looked sceptical. "Is this girl the instigator of the incident in question?"

The vizier looked Polnygar up and down and then, leaning down to Pharaoh, whispered something into his liege's ears. Pharaoh's expression hardly changed. He waved dismissively at the vizier.

"Let the archmage have his toy, Arhotep, will you?" Pharaoh said. "It will entertain him for a while. Keep him out of trouble."

The vizier bowed. "As you wish, Your Majesty."

"Thank you, Pharaoh," Aelzandar said, bowing.

"You will be responsible for the girl in that case, Aelzandar," said the vizier. "She will stay in your quarters. Keep her out of trouble. We don't want another disturbance like the incident in the bazaar."

"Of course, my lord," said Aelzandar. "If there is nothing else, Your Majesty…"

Pharaoh waved dismissively, and Aelzandar bowed in thanks.

"Thank you, Your Majesty – this way Polnygar."

***

"These, Polnygar, are my quarters," Aelzandar said, showing Polnygar down one of the many sections of the vast, sprawling complex.

"There are sleeping quarters, studies, libraries and dining areas. I think these will suffice."

He parted a curtained covered archway. "Here, through here, this shall be your room."

Polnygar furrowed her brow. "I don't recall saying I was going to stay. Where is Augustin?"

Aelzandar closed his eyes, gently reprimanding Polnygar. "My dear, please, he is not yet conscious. There will be ample time later."

"Then what am I supposed to do until then?" Polnygar said. "Am I suddenly your prisoner? Is that what you told Pharaoh?"

Aelzandar looked hurt at the accusation. "No, not prisoner," said Aelzandar. "Guest, and, if you are interested, student."

"Student? What are you going to teach me?"

He placed a hand on Polnygar's shoulder, and kept his voice low.

"Polnygar, that incident in the bazaar was no miracle. You have a talent. A raw, unfocused talent, yes, but a talent nonetheless. I can help you tame that skill. Refine it, control it, even."

"What are you saying?" Polnygar said. "I'm no spellweaver…"

"Not yet," said Aelzandar. "But just as much of the Art runs through your veins as in those of any of the Eldara King's spellweavers. You have the makings of a great mage, that is for certain. You just need tutoring."

It seemed incredible to Polnygar. What on earth did she know about magic? She had never shown so much as a hint of any magic powers until the bazaar. Back in Aderilund, her mixed birth precluded her from even

114

dreaming of learning the ways of a spellweaver. But here…

"Let's say I'm interested," said Polnygar. "What would happen next? What would I give you in return? And just how long would it take?"

"We can start right away, if you'd like. By the time Augustin is well enough to travel, I'm sure you will have at least picked up the fundamentals."

Polnygar looked at him expectantly.

"Oh, and there is no charge, my dear. I teach for enjoyment these days. I have as much wealth as I could ever want. Do we have a deal then?" Aelzandar asked.

After a moment's hesitation, Polnygar nodded slowly.

"Excellent." Aelzandar motioned towards a nearby archway. "This way, my dear. Take a seat at the table. If you are ready, we shall begin."

Aelzandar placed a few sheets of paper down on the table, along with a quill and ink jar. "A few pages of papyrus should be enough to start with," said Aelzandar, "until you are more experienced."

"What spell am I going to learn?" Polnygar asked.

Aelzandar smiled. "The journey of a thousand miles begins with a few scant steps, my dear. In other words, like all prospective magi, you must start at the beginning - just as I once did."

With a force that almost visibly rattled Polnygar, the archmage slammed a thick, heavy book down on the table next to her.

"This spellbook is the very same one that I read when I was but a callow young pupil. It was given to me by my late master Cassian. And now, I pass it on to you."

"What do I do with it?" said Polnygar.

"You read it, understand its contents and copy it, every word, every line, and every page. Normally such a task is done in Draconic, but since I don't think you are familiar with that language yet, Eldaric will suffice for now."

"Where do I start?" said a somewhat plaintive Polnygar.

"Why, just as I said," said Aelzandar, opening the book to its first page. He traced a finger over the sentence at the top of the page. "At the beginning."

With a grimace, Polnygar dipped the quill into the inkwell, and began to write.

"See if you can get to *Cassian's Credulous Curfew* before you stop for lunch," Aelzandar winked.

"*Cassian's Credulous…* what? What kind of a name is that?" Polnygar said as she began to copy down the writing.

"Wizards are known to be fond of alliterative and somewhat bombastic names for our creations. Shameless self-promoters, the lot of us," Aelzandar said, a smile across his features.

A trumpet blared. Startled by the sound, Polnygar dropped the quill, knocking over the ink well and spilling ink all over her first draft.

"What's that?" she asked Aelzandar.

The archmage frowned. "It seems that Pharaoh is requesting my presence." He sighed deeply. "Make sure you continue with your writing, my dear. I will speak with you later, Polnygar."

***

Bellaydin felt the urge to vomit. He'd never travelled by sea before, and if this was how it usually went, he wasn't upset that he hadn't.

"Ah, there's my little landlubber," Geoffrey said, slapping Bellaydin on the back affectionately. He leaned in close. "You know, I wasn't sure if it was you or Kahlaf standing here. The green skin confused me."

Geoffrey was amused by his joke but Bellaydin found it difficult to laugh, particularly when it his stomach contents were attempting to leap from his throat at any minute.

"Hey, never mind," said Geoffrey. "No need to feel glum, Ap'Lydin. You might be sharing a cabin with me, but you never know, could be worse. You could be stuck down in the hold with all those soldiers. How do you think they're feeling right now?"

"Dead," Bellaydin said. "Either that or… or – "

A wave of nausea washed over him. Looking at the young man's face, Geoffrey grabbed Bellaydin by his shirt, and lifted him so that his head was well over the side of the ship. "Better out than in," Geoffrey said.

After it was done, Geoffrey helped Bellaydin back on to the deck. "Feeling better then?"

"A little, yes," said Bellaydin.

Geoffrey patted him on the back reassuringly. "Don't worry," he said. "You'll get used to it eventually. You should've seen me on my first boat trip. About three minutes after we cast off, I ran to the railing, dispensed of my lunch, and spent the rest of the afternoon there feeling sorry for myself." He shook his head at the memory. "Enough talk about our poor sea-legs. You're probably wondering why we've got a hold full of soldiers and mercenaries, correct?"

"Is there some sort of war going on in Emparia?" Bellaydin said.

"No. But we're not far from it," Geoffrey said. "Have you heard of the Goriinchians?"

Bellaydin tried to act nonchalant. "I know the name," said Bellaydin. "They're another nation to the south of Emparia, aren't they?"

Geoffrey chuckled. "Well, to a point, yes. But to call them a nation would be somewhat charitable. In truth, they are a group of clans, held together by various warchiefs, all under the guidance of a single leader. A man they call a god."

"They think their leader is a god?" Bellaydin said, somewhat incredulously.

"Well, the chosen prophet of a god, to be precise. They worship a Horned God, a nasty sort of thing, from what I've heard." Geoffrey looked at Bellaydin strangely. "Are you sure you've never been told this before?" he said.

Bellaydin's words caught in his throat. "My... mother... Saegralanna... she told me some things."

"And what did she tell you?"

"That it was Goriinchians who killed my grandfather."

Geoffrey, eyes downcast, looked over the side of the ship, his fingernails idly scratching off the veneer of the rail.

"Sir William Ap'Lydin – your grandfather – was killed during the Third Goriinch War. He died during the defence of Genio."

"The man who killed my parents," Bellaydin swallowed. "He was Goriinchian too. Simon Enlim."

Geoffrey avoided the younger man's gaze. "That is more complicated. Alusine and Eleanor had taken Enlim into their own home. He betrayed them. This was twelve years ago. I was new to your cousin's service. William was deeply affected by your parents' deaths. There were rumours, you see, of conspiracies and murky plots, and that the betrayal went further than just Enlim. Most people never believed in such rumours, but your cousin –"

Geoffrey paused. " – well, I don't know, not really. He barely speaks of it. He spends most of his days preparing for what he sees as the inevitable invasion from Goriinchia – the Third Goriinch War."

"Where did you find the Lizardman?" Bellaydin asked.

"Shhh," Geoffrey said, quickly covering Bellaydin's mouth with his hand. "Don't refer to him as that."

"Mmfmrmrffrm," Bellaydin mumbled. Geoffrey took his hand off Bellaydin's mouth.

"What should I call him then?"

"Kahlaf, probably," said Geoffrey. "And Ahktarran, if you must." He shook his head. "He's bad-tempered at the best of times, you know? No need to give him any reason to lose that sunny disposition now, is there? And to answer your question, I didn't so much find him. He's more a gift."

"A gift? Who in the name of the Underworld would give you that as a gift?" said Bellaydin.

"Someone who doesn't like me very much," said Geoffrey.

Bellaydin looked at him.

"Don't ask," said Geoffrey.

The months passed as the ship continued its voyage. Just as Geoffrey had promised, Bellaydin found the bouts of seasickness getting less frequent and less potent, until he could finally march up and down the deck of the ship and barely notice it lurching from side to side as it crested the waves. As they continued their sea voyage, Geoffrey regaled Bellaydin with tales of Emparia, from its geography and important cities to its recent history.

"The whole country's only just settled down now," he said. "Last five years are the first peaceful ones we've had for decades. When the de Morcors overthrew the Tyron dynasty, we ended up with thirty years of civil war, as the two families fought one another. It only ended when the Tyrons were extinct, and the de Morcors not far from it."

"Did you fight in the wars?" Bellaydin asked.

"Pretty much the formative experience of my youth." He frowned and added. "Hmm… that would probably explain a fair bit."

Kahlaf emerged from the cabin, and approached Geoffrey and Bellaydin. "The Captain has sighted Gorin," the Ahktarran said. "He says we should make landfall by tomorrow."

"Very good, Kahlaf," said Geoffrey. "Instruct the captain to take down the flag, and raise the neutral colours."

Grunting, Kahlaf turned and left.

"Why are we taking down the flag?" Bellaydin asked.

"I'm trying not to get us all killed while we stop for supplies in Gorin."

"And why would they do that?"

Geoffrey looked at him. "Don't you know? Gorin is the major port of Goriinchia."

"We're stopping in Goriinchia?" Bellaydin said.

Noting the young man's disbelief, Geoffrey adopted a more conciliatory tone. "We pretty much have to, Ap'Lydin. We don't have the supplies to make the rest of the journey. This is the only suitable port between here and Emparia."

"Besides," he added. "From what I've heard, Gorin is a much more relaxed place than elsewhere in Goriinchia. They don't take their religion as seriously as the lunatics up in the mountains. Just follow my lead, and you'll be fine."

Bellaydin nodded.

"Now, that didn't seem very confident," Geoffrey said, with a smile.

Bellaydin nodded again, this time more vigorously.

"That's better," Geoffrey said.

Gorin was larger than Bellaydin had anticipated, but its ramshackle nature did little else to impress him. Still, its streets teemed with all manner of people despite the late hour.

The Goriinchians, Bellaydin noticed, were a fair, if downtrodden people. Ginger hair seemed to be quite common amongst the men, who often wore tremendous beards. The hair of the women he was unable to comment on, since every female Goriinchian seemed to wear the same grey hooded cloak, which showed little of them except for small glimpses of their eyes. Intermittently, they passed the priests of the Goriinchian religion – sombre figures clad in robes of black who favoured long grey hair and tangled beards of the same shade. The emblem of the Horned God dangled on chains around their necks. Every time one passed him, Bellaydin could not help but shudder, as if a great chill had gone through him.

Before they had disembarked, Geoffrey had told Bellaydin to keep quiet the whole way, since speaking to each other in Emparian would only give the game away. Geoffrey knew Goriinchian to a reasonable extent, so he at least could get by. Bellaydin found the language mostly unfamiliar, except for a few curious similarities to the language of the Eldara.

Kahlaf, of course, stayed with the ship. His appearance alone would send most of the city into panicked screams. If the Ahktarran was bothered by this, he certainly didn't show it. His reaction to being told to remain onboard was a simple shrug of the shoulders. He did not even growl once.

It did not take them too long to purchase the supplies they needed. Though they may have seemed unusual, their gold was as good as any, and Geoffrey's command of the language helped ensure they did not accidentally give away their true identities. As they purchased the last of them, Geoffrey sent the supplies back to the ship with one of the crewmembers.

"Now just a little something before we leave," Geoffrey whispered in Emparian to Bellaydin.

"What?" Bellaydin looked towards where Geoffrey was pointing. A

121

rather rundown looking tavern loomed before him.

"Just for a few, you know?" said Geoffrey.

"Shouldn't we be getting back to the ship?"

"Fine, you can stay outside. I'll come and fetch you when I'm done."

"But…"

"I'll only be a few minutes."

"Wait…"

Geoffrey was already striding up the hill and disappeared into the tavern, leaving Bellaydin alone outside. Somewhat glumly, Bellaydin sat down on a nearby log and prepared to wait.

***

"Careful girl," said Augustin, wincing. "Leg still hurts a bit."

Over the past few weeks, Augustin had been on the mend, albeit slowly. Polnygar visited him daily, in between her studies with Aelzandar.

"Sorry," said Polnygar. "I thought it had healed."

"It's getting there," Augustin said, "but I'm still not one hundred per cent." He absentmindedly rubbed his bruised ribs."They've got good physicians here, I'll give them that. I would've thought wounds like these would be the end of me." He reached for the crutches against the bed. "Help me up, would you?"

"I don't think you should be walking around," Polnygar said. "You need to rest."

"Don't tell me what to do, girl," Augustin said coldly. "I'm the ambassador. I have a job to do, and an appointment with Pharaoh to keep."

"You can always get another appointment."

Augustin shook his head. "Either help me up, or leave me be," he said tersely.

Polnygar extended her arm and Augustin used it to lever himself upright, grabbing the crutches with his other hand. Shuffling about, he managed to position the crutches in a manner that would allow him to move himself down the hallways, albeit clumsily. Polnygar followed, offering the Baron her shoulder to lean on, as they made their way towards the throne room.

A familiar figure loomed before them, one which Polnygar was incredibly surprised to see here, of all places. "My sympathies for your injury, Baron," said Lord Ivellios. The Eldara Lord, as serene and cold as ever, stood with three of his fellows, all similarly attired in robes of state.

"Ivellios," Augustin panted. "What are you doing here?"

"Why, my dear man," Ivellios said in Emparian. "I am here as a representative of the Aspen Throne. An ambassador to the Court of the Pharaoh, just like yourself." He turned his gaze to Polnygar. "And you, young Polnygar," said Ivellios. "What a pleasant surprise to be seeing you again. I did not expect to see you here, though. I wonder how you managed to leave Aderilund without breaking your poor mother's heart."

Polnygar frowned, and did not respond.

"That's none of your damn business, elf," said Augustin.

"Temper, temper, temper," Ivellios said, waving a finger at the Baron. "Although, I suppose with humans, it is to be expected." He pointed at Polnygar. "You, Polnygar, should be wary of that. Your father's blood could flare up at any moment."

"Considering what you seem to think of us, why are you prancing around the palace of a human king, elf?" Augustin said.

"Humans have their uses," said Ivellios, shrugging. "As I'm sure you do. Good day." With a feigned gesture of farewell, Ivellios and his entourage disappeared down the hallway.

"Don't worry," said Polnygar. "He's always been an ass."

"I figured as much," said Augustin.

They continued on their way towards the throne room where, a short distance later, they encountered the vizier Arhotep.

"Can I help you?" said Arhotep.

"Yes, yes," said Augustin, replying in serviceable, but stilted Macrodonian. "I need to speak to Pharaoh."

"Of course," said Arhotep. "Do you have an appointment?"

"I'm the Emparian ambassador, Baron Augustin Edward Bauer."

"Do you have documentation, Baron Bauer?" the vizier said. He looked somewhat sceptical.

"Damn it, yes," Augustin said.

Leaning on Polnygar for support, Augustin reached inside his clothing, and fished out a sealed envelope. "This should be sufficient," he said, passing them to the vizier.

"Very good, just one moment." The vizier disappeared through the door to the throne room. It was quite some time later before the vizier returned.

"I must apologise," said Arhotep, "but there is no chance of you seeing the Pharaoh."

"Is he too busy today? What of tomorrow?"

"No, my lord, you do not understand. You will not be seeing him, not today, not tomorrow – not ever."

"What? Why not?" Augustin said.

Vizier Arhotep passed a scroll to Augustin and then departed without a word. With trepidation, Augustin unfurled it and read the scroll.

"What on… what is going on here?" Augustin yelled.

"Is there a problem, Baron Bauer?" Aelzandar stood nearby, his hands resting on his cane, a questioning look on his eyes.

"Ah… sorry… Lord Archmage…"

"Augustin, I told you to call me Aelzandar," the archmage said.

"Aelzandar. Sorry."

"What seems to be the matter?"

Augustin took a deep breath. "The Crown has removed me from the position of Ambassador, citing 'embarrassment perpetuated in the Kingdom of Aderilund'. They believe I deliberately insulted one of the highest-ranking of those elven mages. Namely Ivellios."

Aelzandar raised an eyebrow.

"Gods damn it," Augustin yelled again. "I bet that worm Ivellios is behind it. Those gods-damned elves and their tricks." Polnygar coughed. Augustin, realising what he had said, looked up at Aelzandar rather sheepishly. "Uh… no offence intended, my Lord."

"None taken," Aelzandar said with a smile.

"You are probably correct in your suspicions, Augustin," said Aelzandar. "But I would warn against airing them so openly. Ivellios holds a great deal of power, even outside of the Eldara Kingdoms. That being said, do not concern yourself too much with these events. You are both still my guests, and I insist you remain here until, at the very least, you are well enough again to travel."

"Why would you do this for me?" said Augustin, sceptical of the archmage's intentions.

"Ivellios and I have never seen eye to eye, let me put it like that. And I like to tweak his nose wherever possible. I must take my leave now, but I will meet the pair of you in my dining area for an evening meal. Until then, farewell."

CHAPTER 9

The minutes Geoffrey had spoken of stretched into hours, Bellaydin thought, as he sat in the middle of Gorin, with no idea of the direction or the distance to their ship.

"Hurry up, damn it," Bellaydin said to no one in particular.

The night air was chill and damp. The throng of people had thinned out, and now only the odd individual walked past, usually a guardsman replacing the blazing torches that provided illumination for the more important areas of the town.

"Wait a minute," said Bellaydin, noticing more flickering torches. "Those aren't guardsmen…"

A large group of men was moving down the streets to the docks. Each man held a blazing torch in their hand. Squinting in the darkness, Bellaydin could have sworn they looked familiar. Then it hit him.

"Oh no, oh no!" He jumped to his feet, and scrambled up the hill, yelling out Geoffrey's name. Hearing no response, he pushed on the tavern doors and entered the building.

Inside, the tavern was plainly furnished and poorly illuminated. A few Goriinchians sat inside while a surly man tended the bar. In the centre of the tavern, Geoffrey staggered about looking dishevelled, a mug in his hand, its contents splashing on the floor.

Bellaydin came towards Geoffrey, and the knight looked at him with a grin.

"Geoffrey, I think we're in trouble," Bellaydin said. Geoffrey laughed.

"Nonsense. Barkeep, a drink for my friend here." Geoffrey threw an arm around Bellaydin, taking him to the bar. He threw some coins at the bartender, and pulled Bellaydin to the side.

"Bela, I know," Geoffrey said, his voice quiet. Bellaydin was surprised by how clear and lucid suddenly sounded. "These men here," Geoffrey continued, "They've been watching me for quite a while. None of them have even touched their drinks. I don't think these men are here for the social life."

Bellaydin looked around, and then quickly turned back to Geoffrey. "They have the Horned God's symbol on their foreheads. Are they cultists?"

"Bela, this is Goriinchia. Everyone has that symbol tattooed on their skin. But these men are not simple farmers or labourers. They're well-armed, and they have that look about them."

"What do you mean?"

"They have eyes like wolves."

"What do you mean? Hungry?"

"No," Geoffrey hissed. "Like they're hunting prey."

Bellaydin felt his mouth go dry. He suddenly became very aware that he and Geoffrey were in the only non-Goriinchians in the tavern. "I saw more outside," he whispered, "They're headed to the docks."

Geoffrey nodded. "Someone knew we were coming. We need to get back to the ship and find Kahlaf." He held his mug up and raised his voice. "Well my friends, it's been great, but I'm afraid I must be leaving you all."

The men in the tavern said nothing, but rose from their seats and brandished weapons.

Geoffrey turned to Bellaydin, "What did I tell you?"

One of the men came at them, screaming in Goriinchian but Geoffrey sideswiped him easily, and the man collapsed to the ground. Bellaydin grabbed the dead man's sword, ready to fight.

"No, Bellaydin. Get out of here, find Kahlaf – I'll meet you at the ship." Bellaydin hesitated. "What are you waiting for? Go!"

As Geoffrey skilfully engaged the others, Bellaydin clutched his newfound weapon and dashed out of the tavern.

Bellaydin ran through the darkness until he reached the docks, hoping to see either the ship or Kahlaf. Instead, he was greeted with the sounds of battle. A violent melee was underway, as cloaked men battled with the ship's crew. It was not going well for Geoffrey's men – they were heavily outnumbered, and had been caught unawares.

Bellaydin lifted his sword gingerly. It was certainly a lot heavier than the swords he had sparred with in Aderilund. Just holding the thing made his wrist ache. Taking a few practice swings, Bellaydin looked again towards the battle raging at the ship. It seemed foolish, yet he could not let the men on the ship die in front of his eyes. He knew he was probably charging into death, and, while a good part of him was scared witless about it, there was another part that urged him on.

He crept towards the docks, trying to stay out of sight. As he moved, he heard the sounds of battle – not from the docks, but from a nearby alleyway. Following the sounds, he came across a frenzied scuffle between three combatants. Two were the same cloaked figures as before. The third was Kahlaf el'Lahn, who wielded a pair of scimitars against his opponents, grunting and roaring with each swing and thrust.

Kahlaf swung around and noticed Bellaydin staring at the fight. "Run Bellaydin, this is not your battle. I can handle –"

He ducked and weaved as one of his enemies made a stab towards his shoulder, showing surprising agility for his size. Wheeling about, Kahlaf caught the other adversary in the side, his scimitar slicing through flesh and bone. Within a few short minutes, Kahlaf had dispatched the other Goriinchian as well, letting the corpse lay where it fell. Panting and grunting, Kahlaf wiped the blades of his weapons clean on the robes of his dead enemies, and sheathed the scimitars before approaching Bellaydin.

"What are you doing with that sword, young human?" the Ahktarran growled.

"What's going on here? Are we under attack?" Bellaydin said.

"It would seem so," Kahlaf said. He put out his hand. "Give me the sword."

"What? No! Why?"

"A sword is dangerous in the hands of the untrained," said Kahlaf. "You wouldn't want to hurt yourself."

"I know how to use a sword."

"Is that so?" Kahlaf said. "You may have sparred with elves, human, but this is the real world now. Your enemies won't stop to observe proper technique. Nor will they wait for you to catch your breath." The Ahktarran glanced around. "Where is Geoffrey?"

"What about the ship?" said Bellaydin.

"There is nothing we can do for them now."

"But we can't let them..."

"If we go and help them, we will achieve nothing except adding our own corpses to the pile. I ask you again: where is Geoffrey?"

"Um… he's… indisposed."

"What do you mean?"

"He's at the tavern."

Kahlaf grunted, and indicated to Bellaydin that he should lead the way. As they reached the tavern, Bellaydin heard a commotion from inside the building. Kahlaf shook his head before pushing open the doors.

Inside Geoffrey Keslin stood alone, his sword pointed towards the heap of Goriinchians who lay at his feet. "Anyone else?" Geoffrey asked. "No?"

With his free hand he reached towards the mug of ale on the bar and drained it in one gulp. "I think we're done here." Geoffrey said. He bent down and took one of the dead men's coin purses, tossing it to the cowering bartender.

"Sorry about the mess."

***

Polnygar gazed at the painting.

The frieze took up most of the western wall of the room. It was incredibly detailed and probably of inestimable value. It depicted two men dressed in traditional wizard's robes that the artist had likely invented for the stylized scene. The two men were engaging in combat with a ferocious and massive dragon against a backdrop of what a typical Macrodonian landscape. The creature was truly awesome. It took up half of the artwork and was depicted in broad, bold brushstrokes. Between its deep, obsidian-black scales and its burning red eyes, the dragon seemed almost alive.

There was a label just below the picture, containing a few words in Emparian.

The Archmages Cassian and Aelzandar battle the Night Dragon.

"I see you have noticed my little collection of artwork, Polnygar?"

Polnygar turned around and saw Aelzandar looking at her with some interest. "Ah yes, archmage. Your art is very impressive."

"It is that," said Aelzandar. "But the artist has taken certain liberties with the subject matter, let me tell you."

"You mean the Night Dragon wasn't that big?" Polnygar said.

"Oh no, he certainly was huge. Probably even larger than depicted here." Aelzandar chuckled to himself as he watched Polnygar's eyes widen in awe. "No, I was actually referring to the depiction of myself. I can assure you I never wore my hair like that, dear girl." Aelzandar winked at her. "Additionally, at this time I most certainly was not an archmage. I was still a pupil, a mere student of the great wizard Cassian, who you can see next to me in that frieze."

"I know," said Polnygar. "I read the plaque."

"Interesting. I was not aware you were literate in Emparian. It is not common for elves of Aderilund to bother with such a supposedly unremarkable human tongue."

"I was born in Emparia, and, even when I came to Aderilund, my mother taught me."

"Then she was certainly a remarkable woman."

Polnygar asked another question. "Who was Cassian?"

"Ah, now that is a story," said Aelzandar. "You might like to take a seat." Polnygar took Aelzandar's advice, and sat down on one of the many cushions while the archmage did the same.

"In my youth, Cassian was the greatest wizard in the world - the great Lord Archmage of his time. I was fortunate enough to be chosen as one of his apprentices. I studied at his feet in the great Tower of the Magi, in Emparia. That was, until the tower was attacked by a rival wizard. In the ensuing battle, the structure was razed, and most inside killed in cold blood. I had assumed Cassian was one of the dead – certainly, there was no trace of him after the attack. I spent decades drifting, until, surprisingly, we were reunited."

"He had survived?" Polnygar said.

"Indeed, but he was reluctant to speak of the details of his miraculous escape. Regardless, two years later he died as we fought the Night Dragon – an event which is, as you know, rather imaginatively depicted in that artwork."

"Did you win the battle? I mean, it's obvious that you survived, but Cassian…"

Aelzandar nodded. "His death ensured victory, Polnygar. It is as simple as that. He sacrificed his life to be sure the Night Dragon was defeated. The last time I saw my master, he was still locked in combat with the beast as the pair of them tumbled into the great chasm. Neither was ever seen again. That was nearly two hundred years ago. Strange… doesn't seem nearly that long ago…"

Polnygar was silent as Aelzandar gazed upon the frieze somewhat wistfully, seemingly lost in memories of his past. "Master…" said Polnygar.

"Please, my dear, we have no need of formality here," Aelzandar said gently.

She smiled. "Is it not unusual for an Eldara to study under a human? I mean, the way Lord Ivellios and the other spellweavers talk…"

Aelzandar chuckled to himself. "The Eldara spellweavers and I rarely see eye to eye. They have their ideas on humans, and I have mine. It is one of the reasons I find it somewhat difficult to live in the Aspen Kingdom these days. But I'm sure you know this, it couldn't have been easy for someone of your parentage to grow up in Aderilund."

Polnygar nodded.

"Yes, yes," said Aelzandar. "I know of this obsession with racial purity that some of the Eldara lords have become enamoured with. Ivellios is merely the latest case." He frowned. "In fact, I find the whole thing a little curious, and perhaps even a little hypocritical, considering our own heritage."

"What do you mean?" asked Polnygar.

"My dear girl. I am an Eldara. So is Lord Ivellios, so is High King Talan and Queen Talina, and so is your mother, but the blood of the Eldara people is not as pure as zealots like Ivellios would have you believe."

"It isn't?"

"Not to one who studies the past unburdened by a desire to twist it to fit one's own ideology. No, a neutral reading of our own history reveals some quite interesting points." He raised a finger to his lips and drew in a breath. "Perhaps I could interest you in a short history lesson, Polnygar?"

"By all means," said Polnygar.

"Tens of thousands of years ago, the Eldara race was one – a primitive people living in the warm forests just north of what is now the border between Macrodonia and the Empire of Caruillin. In those days, we lived in a semi-nomadic state, and had little contact with the other races of the world. There were no great Eldara cities back then, Polnygar. Only warring tribes and a rustic form of nature worship. However, this would soon change."

Aelzandar coughed, then continued, "We Eldara claim to have been the first of the races to master the Art. This is not strictly true, for the mighty dragons were weaving spells of awesome power while we were struggling with the rudimentary task of developing a language. However, as with all folk tales, there is an element of truth in it, as the elves were the first race without an inborn propensity to the Art. In a sense, the first wizards were Eldara, although our people have never really used the term. We call them spellweavers, but I'm sure you already know that. Your grandfather was

134

one, after all.

"So, to return to the tale. The rise of the spellweavers would change Eldara society forever. About six thousand years ago, the Eldara people began a great migration north into the lands that were then held by giants. So began the ten-century long Foundation Wars, where the Eldara people carved out by force a homeland in the north. The wars had altered the Eldara people for good. They had come into contact with the other races of the world, and saw how they lived. In particular, the city-states of the giants, though in a steady decline, made a great impact on our people. Two main ideological groups appeared. On one side were those who believed that the elves should emulate the civilization of the giants, but improve on the idea and learn from their mistakes. This group was led by the Eldara warrior Lideros. The other faction held that civilization was inherently corrupt, and that the decadence to which the giants had slumped was an inevitable consequence of their decision to embrace civilized life. They followed the teachings of the forest ranger Selvaros."

"Lideros' faction won out in the end, I assume," Polnygar said.

"They did indeed, Polnygar. Lideros and his followers built Liderial, the first city of our people. Lideros was crowned King, and with that, Selvaros took his supporters and left forever, returning south, where they would take up the primitive life of their ancestors. They became known to us as the "Selvara", the elves of the wilds."

"So what does this have to do with the purity of Eldara blood?" Polnygar asked.

"I was just getting to that," said Aelzandar. "Now, as is well known, Eldara and humans, though seemingly two distinct species, can intermarry and produce fertile offspring. Of course, your own parentage attests to this, doesn't it?"

Polnygar nodded silently.

"There are those who would have you believe that such pairings are recent phenomena, no doubt linked to ongoing 'moral degradation' amongst the youth. They are, much as they might dislike hearing this, incorrect on this matter. Mixed-race children have existed for thousands of years among both our communities, ever since humans and elves first encountered each other. And here we come to the crux of the matter. All of us – every Eldara alive today has no doubt inherited human blood from his or her ancestors. Indeed, the much vaunted "purity" of the Eldara race is an illusion, something that hasn't been true for millennia."

"Why do you think this is denied by other elves?" Polnygar said.

"Who knows?" Aelzandar said. "Stubborn pride, I suspect. Anyway, the closest to pure-blood elves would be the long-forgotten Soldara, but few remember them these days."

"The Soldara? I've never heard of…"

"You probably haven't. They are a forgotten people. The Soldara split off from our ancestors around the same time as the followers of Selvaros, but for different reasons. The Soldara were comprised of the foremost ranks of the spellweavers, who by that time had formed an elite caste within the greater Eldara society. But the rise of Lideros and the warrior-nobles of his new kingdom began to diminish the power of the old magocracy. Eventually, the Soldara left Liderial forever, retreating through their mystic gates to a place where they could live away from the prying eyes of others. Their blood was considered the most pure of all, and supposedly it showed in their appearance – they towered over both humans and other elves, and had a serene, almost alien look. It was they who were the original guardians of our people, thanks to the automata – their metal soldiers. But now even the automata are gone, along with their Soldara creators."

"Do the Soldara still exist?" Polnygar said.

"Perhaps. Nobody knows for sure. The land they retreated to is now called Emparia, and, bar a few crumbling ruins, nothing else remains to attest to the lost magnificence of the Soldara lords. A few vague texts hint to the possibility that, knowing even their current home would eventually be overrun by the 'lesser' races, they used what remained of their power and removed themselves from our world forever, but beyond those tantalizing hints, nothing more is known."

"And so the ultimate irony is that those who preach racial purity today echo the words of their ancestors. However, such ancestors would no doubt have difficulty reconciling the apparent 'impurity' of the blood of their descendants with their creed."

Aelzandar smiled gently. "I believe that is perhaps enough, for now, my dear," he said. "If you would like to discuss history some more, I could always arrange another lesson. Until then, I must bid you farewell. Pharaoh is no doubt searching for me, and he does get anxious when he can't find me." The aged elf stood and bowed stiffly to the young woman. "May you find enlightenment, daughter of the Eldara."

Aelzandar picked up his cane from the corner, and left the room, leaving Polnygar alone.

"Huh," came a voice. "I thought I'd find you here."

"Augustin," Polnygar said, smiling.

"Yeah... well... what's left of me, that is." Augustin grimaced, and clutched the bandages on his side. "Healers say I should be right in a few weeks," he said. "Can't come soon enough."

He lowered himself on to a nearby bench, grunting slightly. "Me and my big mouth. I knew it was a mistake riling up that condescending oaf."

"I don't think you need to do much to rile up Ivellios," Polnygar said. "He never was the most sympathetic person."

Augustin moved his head in a show of resigned agreement. "Still, I guess I'm no longer acting as the Crown's little errand-boy."

"You seem to be taking it fairly well," Polnygar nodded.

"Well, it was never really my sort of thing anyway. I suspect it was just my father's way of getting rid of me."

"So, I suppose you'll be headed back to Emparia?" Polnygar asked.

Augustin shrugged. "I suppose so."

Polnygar looked at him for a moment and then, realizing Augustin had noticed, turned away quickly.

"Don't get any ideas," Augustin said with a chuckle, "I'm going to check the ship thoroughly before cast off this time."

Polnygar looked away so Augustin couldn't see her blush. "Don't flatter yourself," she said tersely. "I've been given the chance to learn the Art from the greatest spellweaver in the known world, I'm not going to give that up just to go to Emparia."

"Fair enough," said Augustin with a smile that Polnygar felt betrayed a bit of cheekiness.

Polnygar felt torn. Though she was enjoying the things she had learned under Aelzandar, Macrodonia would feel a lot less familiar without Augustin there. She found herself looking at Augustin without realizing it.

"It's going to be strange without you," said Polnygar wistfully.

"What?" said Augustin, "This place?"

"Just things…generally." Polnygar stumbled over her words.

"What are you talking about?" Augustin sounded confused.

Polnygar turned away. Her face felt hot.

"Polnygar?"

Polnygar did not respond. She just stood some distance away, no reaction on her face. The uncomfortable and somewhat awkward silence between the pair was broken by the return of Aelzandar.

"I am sorry, my dear," he said. "Pharaoh can be demanding at times. But I suppose that's the nature of the thing, wouldn't you say, Augustin?"

Augustin snorted. "Don't ask me. I've never met my queen. I get funnelled through whichever duke or earl is currently making my life difficult. Somewhere at the top there's a young woman wearing a crown, but I don't think she has any more idea of what's going on than I do."

Aelzandar smiled, an enigmatic expression on his face. "That too is the nature of things."

Augustin scoffed.

Aelzandar heard a noise behind him. "Ah, I see that you have discovered one of my treasures."

Polnygar was examining an exotic sword which was mounted above a table against one wall of the room. Suddenly aware of eyes upon her, she retracted her hand.

"No, it is perfectly fine," said Aelzandar. "You may touch it if you wish. You won't damage them."

Smiling, Polnygar reached out for the sword again, running her fingers across the finely made edge. "It's beautiful. Where did you get it?"

Augustin, too, was beginning to take an interest, struggling to his feet and hobbling over towards Aelzandar and Polnygar.

"That is the sword Sakkaru, also known as the Fire of Righteousness," said Aelzandar. "The curved blade is typical of what the locals here call a shamshir. I obtained it when I was a young man, travelling the world." He smiled. "Now that was a very long time ago, before you - before either of you - were born."

"And what of the rest of these things?" said Polnygar.

"Much the same," Aelzandar said. "Various items accumulated during my youth."

"That's putting it mildly," said Augustin. "That armour alone must be worth a small fortune. You've certainly lived an interesting life, archmage."

"I suppose I have," Aelzandar said. "Yet most of this happened to me when I was trying to live a rather un-interesting life."

"Which is your favourite piece, Aelzandar?" said Polnygar. "If you don't mind me asking, that is?"

"Not at all, my dear, not at all, but you won't find my most treasured possession hanging on this wall, I can tell you that much."

"No? What is it?" Polnygar asked.

"Don't pry, girl," Augustin said.

Aelzandar waved a hand. "No, no, there is no harm in asking. And I can show you it, if you would like." Aelzandar moved to the other side of the room, where a large, securely sealed chest stood. "Arcane locks are far more secure than regular ones," Aelzandar said to Polnygar as he raised a hand, his palm facing the lid of the chest.

He mumbled a few indistinct words and the chest swung open. Reaching inside, Aelzandar took out a smaller box and, after closing the chest, brought it to Polnygar and Augustin.

"What's that?" said Augustin.

"Just a moment, Augustin," said Aelzandar. The archmage tapped his fingers three times on the small box, again reciting the same words he had before. With a quick snap, the box opened.

Inside, carefully arranged on a cushion of silk, was what appeared to be a piece of ancient gold jewellery. From what Polnygar could see, it was an amulet, but it was only partially complete – a large section was missing.

"Behold," said Aelzandar, "the Tears of the Divine." He held up the jewellery so that both Augustin and Polnygar could see.

"It's beautiful," said Polnygar, "but it looks broken."

"Indeed it is," said Aelzandar. "And much to my shame. I found this when I was but an untempered youth, in the years I spent travelling the lands of Emparia. My two adventuring companions and I found the Tears and, being unable to decide who deserved the prize, broke it into three even pieces. These days, the wisdom that the decades have given me has allowed me to see the folly of my ways, and filled me with regret over the greed and destructive impulses of my younger self."

"Emparia, eh?" Augustin said, squinting at the jewellery. "Whereabouts?"

"There was a tomb somewhere in the southern highlands. My companions and I had heard the tales about the undead horror said to inhabit this tomb, guarding fabulous treasure. It was a fearsome battle, but we defeated the spectre and claimed this prize. I should mention, however, that the Tears were not whole even before we broke it further. The piece we found was but one half of the original amulet, and its purpose still remains a mystery to this day."

"You don't know what it does?" said Augustin, somewhat sceptically.

Aelzandar said, "I have spent much of my life trying to discover the powers of the Tears, but to no avail. I have poured over hundreds of tomes, most with only fragmentary references. Only one work, the so-called Tome of Divine Metaphysics, was of any real help, but I've never been able to find the original work, only shoddily produced translations and commentaries."

Polnygar was no longer listening to the words of the archmage. In fact, she seemed lost in a world of her own making, staring intently at the Tears of the Divine, which dangled from Aelzandar's fingers. As she stared at the Tears, she swore she could hear something. Soft, almost imperceptible, whispers echoed towards her ears. Strange promises seemed to emanate from the piece of jewellery, promises of power, and of wealth and glory.

Touch me, commanded a voice.

Polnygar obeyed. Reaching out a finger, she touched the Tears. A powerful jolt travelled between the Tears and herself, throwing Polnygar back several feet as sparks arced across the air.

"No!" yelled Aelzandar, dropping the Tears back inside the case and snapping it shut.

Polnygar felt as if she'd been hit by lightning.

"By the gods, Polnygar, are you alright?" Augustin said in shock.

"I think so," she said, her breath coming quickly.

Augustin went to help Polnygar up. "Just what in the name of the Underworld was that, archmage?"

Aelzandar looked troubled. "I must confess, I am not sure, but I do not think touching it was wise. This item has powers - powers far beyond even my ken. It is not to be trifled with."

"Lesson learned," said Augustin.

Polnygar nodded. "I think the Tears spoke to me."

Aelzandar's eyes widened. "I don't recall ever hearing a voice. Are you sure?"

"Absolutely."

He stroked his chin, deep in thought. "Interesting. Perhaps there is some sort of connection here."

"What do you mean by that?" demanded Augustin.

"I'm not certain. Not yet. For now, I think I will keep the Tears out of sight."Aelzandar went to place the small box back in the chest.

"Good idea," Polnygar agreed, but at the same time she felt that, deep down, the Tears were calling to her. It was almost as if there was something that they wanted her to know.

Perhaps Aelzandar was right. Perhaps she and the Tears were connected. But how? And, more importantly, what did this mean?

CHAPTER 10

Bellaydin and Geoffrey stood on the hill, the city of Gorin bathed in darkness beneath them.

Geoffrey turned to Bellaydin. "Where's Kahlaf?"

"He disappeared about twenty minutes ago, said he was going to get clothes."

"Clothes?" said Geoffrey. "Not really the time to play dress-up."

"I'm not sure that's what he has in mind," Bellaydin said.

Geoffrey drained the last drop from his flask and tossed it to the ground. "I sure hope he's bringing some food, too."

"So, what are we going to do?" Bellaydin asked. "We've lost our transport to Emparia, along with the rest of the crew, the soldiers you were bringing—"

"Alright, alright, don't remind me," Geoffrey said, rubbing the sides of his head. "Calm down, I'll think of something." He was silent for a few moments.

"Can we buy horses or something?" Bellaydin asked.

"Do you have any gold? I certainly don't. Don't get me wrong, I'm a knight. I dislike trudging around when I could be safely atop my horse. But I don't see it happening at the moment." He paused a moment, then lowered his voice. "Besides, the more conspicuous we are, the more likely we are to get into trouble."

"Trouble?"

"The followers of the Horned God, Ap'Lydin," said Geoffrey. "They destroyed our ship and murdered everyone on board. When they discover that didn't include us, they'll come looking for us."

"But why?" said Bellaydin. "What do they want with us?"

"Us?" said Geoffrey. "As I recall, it was you they seem to have an unusual interest in. After all, they did manage to find you all the way over there in Aderilund. Can't think it'll be too much more difficult to find you in their own homeland."

"And yet you brought me here," Bellaydin said.

"Calm down, it wasn't on purpose. Besides, I didn't expect we'd be marooned here. I thought we'd duck in quickly for supplies, then leave before any of the Jocky Goriinch knew we were here."

"Jocky Goriinch?"

"Old soldier's joke, Ap'Lydin," said Geoffrey. "As it is we're going to have to find some way north, whether that's along the coast, past Korfar, or through the mountain ranges. The coast way increases our chances of being caught and the mountains…"

As Geoffrey trailed off, Bellaydin saw a figure trudge towards them, moving through the shadows. His pulse quickened momentarily, until a familiar glint in the darkness revealed the figure's green skin.

"It's Kahlaf," said Bellaydin.

"Oh, he's back?" said Geoffrey. "I sure hope he's brought something to eat."

The Ahktarran lumbered towards them, his feet stamping the ground as he moved. In his arms he carried an assortment of clothes, mainly cloaks and robes. He tossed some of the clothes to Bellaydin and Geoffrey. "Here. Put these on," Kahlaf said brusquely.

"What? Why? What's wrong with what I'm wearing now?" said Geoffrey.

Kahlaf gave Geoffrey a withering look, as if he were dealing with a very simple child. "Your clothes are quite obviously the tailored garb of an Emparian knight, Sir Geoffrey," the Ahktarran said. "As a result you will stand out in Goriinchia as much as I would at a Nemoi poetry recital."

"Now that's something I'd like to see," Geoffrey said, grumbling as he examined the ragged cloak the Ahktarran had given him.

Bellaydin struggled with the rough clothes he had been given, and it was with a sense of regret that he discarded the finely made elven garments he had been wearing since he left Aderilund.

"One other thing, human," Kahlaf said to Bellaydin.

"What?"

Kahlaf removed one of his swords from his belt and beckoned to Bellaydin. "Your hair."

"What about it?"

"It's too long."

"What... why? Why does that matter?"

Kahlaf grunted. "Our appearances are known. Both of you should realise that."

With his other hand, Kahlaf withdrew a small, fine blade from a leather strap on his leg. He flung the blade to Geoffrey. "The beard has to go too."

"Alright, alright," Geoffrey sighed. He picked up the knife, stood up and walked towards the nearby stream.

Kahlaf, sword in hand, approached Bellaydin. He grabbed Bellaydin's hair, twisting it into one bundle and cut it off with a few quick slashes.

"Oww," Bellaydin complained.

"My apologies," said Kahlaf. "I must have pulled a few out by the roots." The Ahktarran threw the hair cuttings to the ground, and wiped the blade of his sword clean.

"Where did you get these?" said Geoffrey, smelling the clothes Kahlaf had given him. He took a deep whiff and then gagged. "Oh, gods, these reek."

"I am sorry that there wasn't a seamstress available, Sir Knight," Kahlaf growled in response.

Holding his nose, Geoffrey changed into the new clothes as Bellaydin did likewise. Kahlaf for his part donned a large, hooded cloak, wrapping it round his body and securing it with a length of rope. He pulled the hood over his face which went some way to obscuring his obviously non-human features. It would never fool anyone up close, but it looked like it would suffice for anyone looking at them from a distance.

"I knew it was a mistake coming here," said Geoffrey, looking with disdain at the wretched jerkin he was wearing.

"Then why did we?" asked Bellaydin.

"Seemed like a good idea at the time," said Geoffrey, shrugging, "Kahlaf, get the old clothes."

Kahlaf grabbed the bundle of old clothes and stuffed it into a sack. "We should probably burn them," said Geoffrey. "Though a fire may attract attention, so for now, you carry them." He tossed the sack to Kahlaf, who nodded silently.

"There is one other thing," said Kahlaf. "Bellaydin."

"Yes?" came the response.

The Ahktarran withdrew one of the scimitars from his back and passed it to Bellaydin. "You'll need this."

"But I thought you said a sword was dangerous in the hands of the untrained?" Bellaydin said.

"It is," Kahlaf said gruffly. "But in the event that we get separated, it would be even more dangerous for you to be alone and unarmed in hostile territory."

Bellaydin grabbed the hilt of the weapon tentatively.

"Besides, time permitting, I may find a few moments to teach you the basics as we travel," the Ahktarran said.

"So I guess the only question that remains is, did you find any food?" Geoffrey said.

"I managed to scavenge a little, but it won't last long. We will have to forage and hunt along the way."

Geoffrey scratched his head. "I can't be sure, but my recollections of Goriinchia do seem to be of plentiful game, but that was in the north." He sighed. "Well, we have little choice. We cannot return to Gorin. There are squads of soldiers looking for us. Even these disguises won't help us much. We're going to have to avoid the major towns and cities until we get to Emparia. We may be able to get some supplies from the smaller villages."

"Do we have coin?" Kahlaf asked.

"We'd have to haggle. I've only got a few silver on me, as it is. Most of it was on the ship," said Geoffrey.

"We will make do," said Kahlaf, securing the last of his straps.

"I guess that's that then," Geoffrey said. "We'd better get moving. It's nearly dawn."

"Let's hope we haven't been spotted yet," said Kahlaf, leading the way up the hill.

For the next few days, they made their way through the Goriinchian lowlands, the coast passing on their left and the rugged mountains on their right.

The first day was slow, with Geoffrey slowed by the aches from the night before. Within another day, however, he had apparently got over whatever pain he was feeling, and now led the group, several feet in front of either Kahlaf or Bellaydin.

The days turned into weeks.

As predicted, they rapidly ate through the little amount of food they had scavenged before leaving Gorin, but Geoffrey's comments on the game of the area proved to be sound, and they were soon able to supplement their supplies with what they caught, mainly birds and the occasional rabbit. Even so, between the three of them, their meals were never large, and, as the arduous trip continued, Bellaydin found himself losing the layers of fat he had left Aderilund with. Kahlaf too became progressively thinner, but the Ahktarran never complained. Bellaydin suspected that Kahlaf had experienced lean times on many other occasions in his life, and learned how to tolerate the hunger.

The days blurred into one another as they trekked through the wilds of the Goriinchian highlands. For the most part the land they passed was untamed wilderness, but on the fourth day they came across a small clearing beneath a set of cliffs. Half hidden in tangled vines and ancient oaks stood a few crumbling pieces of masonry and half toppled pillars.

"What is this? Ruins?" said Bellaydin.

Kahlaf grumbled. "This doesn't look like Goriinchian craftsmanship."

He ran a hand against a toppled statue.

Geoffrey glanced towards Bellaydin and Kahlaf with a half-hearted sort of interest. "I don't imagine it is," he said. "The Goriinchians themselves claim that some other sort of people once shared these lands with them, some sort of fey that they keep blaming all of their problems on."

"Fey?" said Bellaydin, looking again towards the ruins. "Elves?"

Geoffrey shrugged. "Anything's possible."

Bellaydin looked again at the ruins, appraising them with what Geoffrey had said firmly in mind. The columns did bear a resemblance to the architecture Bellaydin was familiar with in Aderilund, but there were a few distinctive differences. Something in the grass caught his eye.

"What's this?" he said. He bent down and picked up a broken piece of stone from the grass, dusting it free of dirt and grime.

"It's just a rock, I suspect," Geoffrey said, looking off in another direction.

Kahlaf grunted. "Idiot," he said under his breath, moving a clawed hand over the stone Bellaydin held and sweeping away the last layer of dirt. "It's not a rock. It is a mosaic."

"I see," said Geoffrey. "Very nice."

Kahlaf gave him a look.

"Kahlaf," said Geoffrey. "Pretend for a moment I don't know what a mosaic is."

Kahlaf snorted. "Pretend, indeed. It's a type of artwork, knight," the Ahktarran explained. "They get broken pieces of coloured rock and make pictures with it."

"And how do you know about art all of a sudden?" Geoffrey said.

"The temples of my homeland use mosaics as ornamentation. One tends to notice these things, knight, especially if one is not preoccupied with the distractions of a dissolute life."

Geoffrey rolled his eyes.

"I think I can make it out," said Bellaydin. He looked closely at the mosaic, wiping the last of the grime away so that he could see what the artwork depicted.

A curious scene appeared before his eyes. In the centre of the artwork stood a giant figure, robed and bedecked with all sorts of jewellery. The ears, though greatly exaggerated in size, were distinctly elven. On either side of the central figure two humans kneeled, their bodies in a submissive pose.

"What do you suppose this means?"

"Who can say?" said Kahlaf. "It is merely some sort of ancient religious icon, a long forgotten superstition. Interesting enough as a curiosity, but not much more than that."

Shrugging, Bellaydin placed the mosaic piece back on the ground.

"Well, if you two are quite finished, I figure we're about halfway to Korfar," said Geoffrey, resting against a fallen log. "I think we should probably make camp for the night."

Kahlaf nodded curtly, turning to Bellaydin. "This might be an opportunity for us to spar for a while, human. Come." He walked away some distance, out in the open. He drew the scimitar from behind his back and readied himself.

"Show me your technique."

With uncertainty showing on his face, Bellaydin drew his own scimitar. Once again, the sheer weight of the sword was what entered his mind as he held it. He swung it a few times, slashing through the air with what he hoped were reasonably authentic looking swings.

"Come on human," Kahlaf snarled, putting himself into a defensive stance. "Take your best shot."

Gritting his teeth, Bellaydin took a deep breath. Then, yelling at the top of his lungs, he charged at Kahlaf, holding the scimitar above his head, ready to strike at the Ahktarran as soon as he closed the gap between them. With a swiftness that astonished Bellaydin, Kahlaf leapt from where he stood, caught Bellaydin with the flat of his sword, and toppled him from his feet. Before Bellaydin could even open his eyes, the point of Kahlaf's blade was at Bellaydin's throat.

"Again!" Kahlaf shouted as he withdrew his sword arm and moved back.

Bellaydin scrambled to his feet, and brought his sword up again. This time, Kahlaf thundered towards Bellaydin with surprising speed. In desperation, Bellaydin raised his sword to defend himself. He managed to block a few blows from Kahlaf, though the force of the Ahktarran's swings nearly broke Bellaydin's wrists as they connected. He was not so lucky with Kahlaf's next attack, which met Bellaydin's rib cage, and was more than enough to wind him. Another assault soon toppled Bellaydin to the ground again.

"No more," Bellaydin wheezed.

"I was correct. We need to work on your technique," Kahlaf said.

Bellaydin groaned. He had hit his head on the way down, and in his blurred vision could barely see the Ahktarran before him.

"Stance was wrong, to start with. Your skill with a blade is lacking. And of course, you seem to have difficulty with the weight of the sword. All this will need improvement if you are to ever find yourself in battle."

"I guess so," Bellaydin said. He heard Geoffrey laughing behind him, the knight applauding his efforts, no doubt sarcastically.

"That was pretty good, boy," said Geoffrey. "Especially since you were fighting against a seven-foot tall scaled engine of destruction." The

Ahktarran didn't seem to be pleased at the statement, but Geoffrey only gave a wink in return. "It's a compliment, Kahlaf. Learn to accept them. Listen, Master Ap'Lydin, if you get tired of Kahlaf beating you up, just tell me. I'll be quite happy to take over."

"Uh… thanks, I guess," said Bellaydin, rubbing his head.

"Get up," said Kahlaf, extending a clawed hand. Bellaydin grabbed it firmly and Kahlaf pulled the youth up from the ground. "Have something to eat, then we will spar again, human," said Kahlaf, as Bellaydin limped towards the campfire.

"Here, try the stew," Geoffrey said, passing Bellaydin a bowl.

Bellaydin attacked the food greedily, the sparring match having only increased his hunger. As he ate, he found his thoughts drifting to how much things had changed in the last few months. With a pang, he realised that he was slightly homesick and, though he would never admit it, missed Aderilund. He particularly missed Saegralanna, and even more, his sister Polnygar.

He wondered how she was faring.

***

"And then I simply hold my hand up, like so," Polnygar said. "Add a bit of theatrics and then speak the right word… Ignis!"

A small flame erupted from Polnygar's hand, seemingly suspended an inch above her palm. It continued to burn despite the apparent absence of any sort of fuel.

Augustin looked on in wonder.

"Amazing," he said, shaking his head. He waved his hand above it. "It's hot. How is it you're not getting burnt?"

"It's part of the spell. I never feel the flame myself. Watch." Polnygar closed her palm, snuffing out the flame.

"Incredible, simply incredible."

"Surely you've seen magic before, Augustin?" Polnygar said.

"Not up this close, girl. Unlike elves, we humans don't have a noble class packed to the brim with spell casters."

"There must be a court wizard, or something?"

"Not in my lifetime," said Augustin. "So, tell me, what else have you been taught?"

She snapped her fingers and the door behind Augustin swung shut.

"Impressive," said Augustin, "for a parlour trick."

"What do you mean?" Polnygar said, her tone suggesting she was at least a little offended.

"Well, this is all well and good, and interesting to see, but I can't see how things like creating little fires and closing doors from a distance are going to help you in real life. I mean, unless you want to eke out an existence as an entertainer at town fairs."

"Now, now, Baron, will you leave my student alone?"

"Ah, archmage," said Augustin. "Didn't see you come in."

Aelzandar smiled gently as he approached Augustin. "Well, Baron, that is one of the advantages of one's own quarters. I don't need to knock."

Augustin chuckled. "You got me there, archmage," he said. "I'll leave you two in peace. My stomach is rumbling." Augustin departed, his limp barely showing.

"He seems to have made a remarkable recovery over the last few weeks," said Aelzandar. "Most remarkable."

"What do you mean?" asked Polnygar.

"Oh, I'm just thinking aloud, my dear. I encountered your countryman earlier on today."

"Who? Ivellios?"

"Yes. You didn't tell me that he'd been named Lord Speaker of Aderilund."

Polnygar looked surprised. "I... didn't... he's Lord Speaker? What happened to Quarion?"

"From what I hear, the former Lord Speaker met with a rather unfortunate fate."

"What?"

"He was murdered."

"Murdered, by whom?"

"I was not able to glean that from Ivellios. He muttered something about 'anti-Eldara terrorists' and offered up the usual human-orientated conspiracy theories. I think he believes that such a crime has vindicated his ideals for Eldara purity."

"But who could have murdered the Speaker? He didn't have any enemies, not that I remembered..."

"A random act of violence, it would appear. A great shame, too. I'd always got on fairly well with Quarion. We grew up together as children, we were friends then and we remained as such later, even though our lives eventually diverged and took vastly different paths."

"I'm so sorry," said Polnygar.

"It is fine. I am able to grieve in a fairly restrained manner these days. One of the side effects of living a life as long as mine is that you lose many, many friends over the course of it. You learn to grieve."

"Does it get easier?"

"No. But you get better at hiding it. And now Ivellios is both Lord Spellweaver and Lord Speaker of Aderilund. This bears watching."

"What?" Polnygar, smiling. "Don't you trust him?"

"Well, Ivellios can be devious, at the best of times. He has a rather… stringent definition on what is and what isn't moral." Aelzandar paused in thought. "Your brother's name is Bellaydin Tyron Ap'Lydin, is it not?"

Polnygar nodded. "Why do you ask?"

Aelzandar frowned. "Ivellios mentioned such a name during a discussion. He was boasting on how he had ensured the purity of Aderilund, and removed the last foreign elements – namely your brother."

"Oh no, Bela. What happened?" Polnygar said, the shock evident in her voice.

Aelzandar stroked his chin. "I'm not sure. Ivellios did not elaborate. He did, however, assure me that your mother saw fit to spirit Bellaydin out of the country."

"How can we trust what he says now?" said Polnygar.

"True, that is a concern," said Aelzandar. "But in this matter, at least, I believe Ivellios has no reason to lie. The grudge he bears against your family seems to be nothing personal, per se, merely what you represent."

"What do you mean by that?"

"Let me put it this way, Polnygar. Your mother is a little too… friendly… with humans for Ivellios' liking. You and your brother are constant reminders of that, and as a result, Ivellios would prefer that both of you be far from the Eldara lands." He paused. "And it would seem that, one way or another he has now achieved that goal." He shrugged. "Still, you are both safe. That is all that matters. And you are free of the Lord Spellweaver's malign influence."

"What do you mean by that?" said Polnygar. "'Malign influence'?"

"Ivellios and I do not get along, and we have different opinions on many subjects, let us leave it at that. Now," said Aelzandar, dusting his hands on his robes, "let us get back to your studies, shall we?"

"Yes master," said Polnygar.

Aelzandar gave her a look.

"Aelzandar. Sorry," Polnygar replied sheepishly.

"Have you finished with the spellbook I gave you?"

"Yes Aelzandar."

"Memorised each and every one of its incantations?"

"Yes Aelzandar."

"Good. Excellent. I look forward to you demonstrating each and every one to me."

Polnygar nodded but then suddenly felt pain in her hand. Aelzandar noticed her flinching. "My dear... is there something wrong?" said Aelzandar, concern evident in his voice.

"It's my hand," said Polnygar, showing the archmage her palm. "It still hurts."

Aelzandar placed his hand around Polnygar's wrist, and gently brought the hand up to his gaze. "Curious," Aelzandar said. "The scar shows no sign of healing."

It had been over a week since Polnygar touched the Tears of the Divine and the artefact burned her with its great power. Immediately after, a perfect imprint of the Tears had become visible in Polnygar's scalded flesh. Aelzandar had assured Polnygar that the scar would heal in time, and eventually fade. Yet it showed no signs of doing so.

"And the pain is still there?" He lightly traced a finger over the scar and Polnygar flinched.

"It seems so."

"Most curious."

"How long will I have to put up with it?" asked Polnygar.

Aelzandar paused in thought. "I'm not sure, my dear. As I told you, the Tears of the Divine and their power is a mystery to me. I know little about what they may have done to you, and even less on why they did it. There is…"

"Excuse me, Lord Archmage."

"Hmm? Oh, hello there Hebu. How can I help you?"

"Lord Archmage, your presence – and that of your apprentice – is requested in the great hall. The Pharaoh has need of you."

"Is that so?" said Aelzandar, raising an eyebrow. "Well, let's not keep him waiting."

Hebu bowed, and led the way.

***

"Great Pharaoh," said Aelzandar, bowing deeply. "You once again honour me with your favour."

Pharaoh recognised Aelzandar with a half-hearted gesture. "Arhotep," the monarch said, gesturing to his vizier.

"Yes, thank you, Your Majesty."

Aelzandar gave Polnygar a knowing smile, as if to indicate that he had correctly predicted that 'Pharaoh requests your presence' really meant, as it usually did, 'vizier Arhotep requests your presence'.

"Lord Archmage Aelzandar," Arhotep said. "You recall, do you not, that when you were first granted the position of Royal Mage of Macrodonia, it came with certain conditions?"

"I certainly do, your Eminence. I'm sure His Majesty agrees that my service here has been beyond reproach."

The Pharaoh simply nodded, then yawned.

"For the most part, yes," continued Arhotep. "Yet I have recently heard some troubling news."

"Arhotep, you know better than to listen to gossip," Aelzandar said.

"Then answer me this: have you, as requested, revealed to the Royal Court every dangerous magical artefact in your possession?"

Aelzandar blinked. "I have," he stated plainly.

"Is that so?" said the vizier.

"Are you calling me a liar, Arhotep?"

"Keep a civil tongue, archmage. I represent Great Pharaoh. I speak with his voice."

Polnygar smiled ruefully. She very much doubted that anyone was speaking with Great Pharaoh's voice, particularly as the young monarch was dozing on his throne at the moment.

"You there, girl," said Arhotep. "Show us your hand."

"Polnygar, don't," Aelzandar said.

"Do it," Arhotep ordered. "In the name of Pharaoh."

Polnygar hesitated.

"Don't listen to him, Polnygar. You are not Macrodonian. He has no authority over you."

"archmage, remember your oath," Arhotep said.

"My oath was to Pharaoh, not to any of his servants," Aelzandar said.

"I am his voice."

In front of Polnygar, Pharaoh stirred. "Arhotep... what is all this shouting in aid of?" the young man said.

Arhotep immediately dropped to the floor, kneeling next to his liege's ear. "Forgive me Your Majesty, but I believe that your archmage here is in possession of a dangerous artefact about which he has not informed the Royal Court."

Pharaoh looked about, disinterested. "Is this true, Aelzandar?"

"Your Majesty," said Aelzandar, smiling, "you know I would never knowingly keep a dangerous artefact without informing you of it."

"Then that is enough for me," Pharaoh replied, yawning again.

"But Your Majesty…"

"I said: enough, Arhotep."

"Look at the girl's hand –"

Pharaoh cut off his vizier with a wave of the hand. "I grow weary of this conversation. Lord Archmage, you and your apprentice are dismissed from my presence."

"Thank you, Your Majesty." Aelzandar said, bowing deeply. "Come Polnygar."

"Just what is with the rush?" said Polnygar, as she struggled to keep up with the departing archmage.

"Something is amiss, my dear. I can feel it."

"What do you mean? Is it what the vizier said?"

"The vizier is not a threat. He's merely an unimaginative bureaucrat, but he knows more than he should."

They turned the corner, arriving at the entrance to Aelzandar's quarters. Polnygar gasped. The door to the chambers was smashed in, and swung lazily from its hinges.

Frowning, Aelzandar moved the remnants of the door aside and entered his quarters, with Polnygar following close behind.

Polnygar looked with amazement at the chaos in Aelzandar's study. Furniture, books and artefacts lay scattered on the ground. Chests and footlockers were strewn on the floor, their contents littering the area. Bookshelves had been overturned, the books thrown halfway across the room. Surprisingly, it did not seem anything had been taken. Whoever had been in this room was looking for something specific, and had turned the place inside out trying to find it.

Then she saw it. Over in the corner, the footlocker that had once held the Tears of the Divine stood open, deep gouges on its face. The bands that had held it together had been almost completely torn off, along with, Polnygar surmised, the enchantments that had kept the chest sealed.

"No!" Aelzandar exclaimed.

He rushed to the footlocker, a look of abject terror on his face as he frantically searched its contents.

"Gone. The Tears – they're gone!"

Polnygar gasped.

"Gone," Aelzandar repeated.

With a speed that astonished Polnygar, the old archmage all but leaped from where he was standing to the opposite side of the room, picking up one of the toppled tables and rifling through the jumble of items nearby.

"Come on, come on," he said, frantically pawing through the mess.

"What are you looking for?"

Aelzandar ignored the question, merely furrowing his brow as he rummaged through the debris. "Here we are," he said, grabbing a clear, spherical object and bringing it up to the desk, where he affixed it to a small black stand. "Crystal ball," Aelzandar said, tapping the sphere. "This will show us our thief."

"How does it work?"

"It's tied to an enchantment fixed to the room," said Aelzandar. "Anything that transpires in these chambers is retained in the arcane matrix within this device. We can use the crystal ball to view such visions."

"You mean you can see the past with it? How is that possible?" Polnygar said. "I mean, the past is done with."

"The mysteries of the Art are great, my dear," Aelzandar said, seemingly distracted and therefore dismissive. "But I assure you, it is possible."

"How?"

Aelzandar looked a little annoyed. "Every action, every event, every consequence of such event, leaves an imprint on the fabric on the universe, an echo in time, if you will. This, my dear, is a device that allows us to view those echoes. Ah, there we are."

He caressed the crystal ball, slowly reciting a few mumbled incantations. Then, before Polnygar's eyes, the once cloudy surface of the crystal ball began to clear and, just as Aelzandar had promised, images began to appear in the clear surface.

"It looks like… it's this very room. Amazing."

"It is this room, my dear, but we are watching it a few hours ago. Now we shall see our culprit. Show me…" Aelzandar said, rubbing his hands over the sphere in slow circular motions.

Aelzandar and Polnygar peered into the crystal. And then they saw him.

"I don't believe it," Polnygar said.

"Careful, my dear, let's not jump to conclusions."

But the moving image in the crystal ball was as clear as day. It was Augustin Bauer, accompanied by a mysterious, heavily cloaked and cowled figure Polnygar did not recognise.

"But he couldn't…"

"Shh," said Aelzandar, raising a finger at Polnygar.

"It is here," came a voice from the vision, unmistakeably that of Augustin Bauer. "I saw him take it out."

The other figure nodded, and gestured in the direction Augustin indicated. The chest burst open with a loud bang, splinters flying through the air. The figure whispered something into Augustin's ear, and the Emparian nodded, stepping towards the shattered remnants of the chest.

"Something's wrong," said Polnygar. "He doesn't look like himself. Why would he do this?" Aelzandar gave her a look. "Alright, alright, I'll be quiet."

The vision of Augustin Bauer removed the small container from the now broken chest, and passed it to his companion.

"Thank you Augustin," said a distinctly familiar voice. "Now, come. There is work to be done."

"Yes, my lord Ivellios."

CHAPTER 11

"Left, right, feint, stab, swing... no, not like that... yes, that's better... now you are getting it!"

Kahlaf continued to yell at Bellaydin as the pair sparred. While he was still clumsy and had yet to land a blow on the Ahktarran, Bellaydin was getting noticeably better.

"That's right, yes, yes... good... Watch your footwork!"

Bellaydin nearly lost his balance and toppled backwards, but managed to right himself before he did.

"Sorry."

"Let us finish up here, I think," said Kahlaf, sheathing his weapon and patting Bellaydin on the back reassuringly. "You've made remarkable improvement but there's a lot more you still have to learn."

"There's still plenty of time for him to learn, Kahlaf," Geoffrey said from some distance away.

"Perhaps," Kahlaf said dismissively. "We are fugitives, if you recall? Goriinchian warriors surely pursue us even now."

Geoffrey stood, and walked towards the pair, shaking his head in exasperation. "Gods, Kahlaf, would you relax? Give the boy a break."

Kahlaf grunted. "Our enemies won't. Why should I?"

"Our enemies aren't here."

"Yet," said Kahlaf. "But I shall do as you wish." The Ahktarran shrugged.

Bellaydin listened to the two argue as if he wasn't even there. Exasperated, he decided to remove himself from the conversation.

"I'm going to go wash at the stream," Bellaydin said.

Geoffrey nodded, and waved him off.

Bellaydin left Geoffrey and Kahlaf alone to talk while he headed off towards the small stream he had seen earlier. Crouching on the bank, he plunged his hands into the water and splashed some on to his face. It felt cool and refreshing against his skin.

Cleanliness was something that the Eldara prized highly, and there had been no one in Aderilund who did not bathe at least daily. Bellaydin was accustomed to the fine white soap that the Eldara preferred, but here he would have to make do without such luxury.

Using each hand in turn, he washed some of the dirt off himself. It was then that he heard a noise.

It was coming from an area of bushes and shrubs not far away and sounded like some sort of animal, perhaps a rabbit. *No, bigger.* A large hare? He could not see much, especially in the late afternoon gloom. He rose from the ground slowly.

Despite his usual clumsiness, Bellaydin did have some skill in moving without making a sound. You did not spend most of your formative years in Aderilund without picking up some of the legendary Eldara talent for stealth. While he may have been considered a blundering oaf by their kind, Bellaydin was sure that it would be an entirely different matter outside their lands.

He carefully crept towards the noise, taking extra care to muffle the sounds of his own body. Barely half a foot from the bushes, Bellaydin carefully drew his sword, hoping to the Gods that the scraping of the blade against the scabbard would not scare off his prey.

"Gotcha!" Bellaydin yelled as he parted aside the bushes with his sword, ready to catch the rabbit when it tried to escape.

But there was no rabbit, no hare, nor any sort of animal at all. Instead, a rather startled girl stared at him with a mixture of shock and surprise, the wildflowers she had held in her hand now scattered at her feet. *She must be a Goriinchian*, Bellaydin thought, noting the flame red hair that could be glimpsed under the girl's hooded cloak. The girl stared at Bellaydin with alarm, acting as if she would run away at any moment. She was scared of him. Feeling rather foolish, Bellaydin put his sword away and raised his hands up, palms facing towards the girl.

"Look, I'm sorry, I didn't mean any harm. I didn't know you were there."

The girl looked at him blankly, before responding with a stream of impenetrable gibberish.

"Do you speak Emparian?" Bellaydin said. "Emparian? Speak?" He tried again in the elven tongue, but the reaction wasn't any different. "Look, let me help you." He bent down to pick up the wildflowers and passed them back to the girl, who shrank back from his gesture. "It's fine. I won't bite, I promise."

Tentatively she reached out towards him. Then with a start, she quickly snatched them from his hands, clasping them to her breast.

"There. That wasn't so painful, was it?" Bellaydin said.

"Bellaydin!" He heard Geoffrey call out to him.

The girl looked panicked.

"No, don't worry, it's just a friend," Bellaydin said, trying to calm her.

"Bellaydin!" came the yell again.

"Coming!" said Bellaydin, turning in the direction of Geoffrey's voice. "Give me a few moments."

He turned back to the girl, but she was no longer there. She had taken the opportunity to disappear into the forest while his back was turned.

"There you are," Geoffrey said. "What took you so long?" He had a stack of firewood in his arms.

"I was only gone for an hour or so," Bellaydin said. He looked around, searching one final time for the Goriinchian girl. Geoffrey looked at him quizzically.

"What are you looking for?"

"Nothing," lied Bellaydin. "Do you need help with that?"

"Here you go," Geoffrey said, giving half of the stack to Bellaydin. He topped it with a few more branches and kindling lying around.

"Well, come on then. Let's get this back to camp and get that damned fire going. I hope you're hungry."

When they reached the camp site, Geoffrey pointed to a spot nearby. "Just drop it there, Bellaydin," said Geoffrey. "I'll build the fire over here. Pass me that log there."

Before long, the pair had assembled a basic campfire that, courtesy of Geoffrey's flint and steel, burned contentedly before them. Kahlaf stood some distance away, surveying the horizon with his keen eyes. Bellaydin thought the Ahktarran looked like he was expecting trouble at any moment.

Geoffrey placed their iron pot over the fire and tossed the last pieces of their meat into it. "We're going to have to catch something tomorrow, that's for sure. We've still got a while before we reach Emparia, and we're not going to get there on an empty stomach."

"I sure hope the food is better there," Bellaydin said, looking in dismay at the black broth bubbling in the cook pot.

The last few months had been difficult for Bellaydin. Even the poorest of the Eldara ate fairly well, and Bellaydin's stepmother had been wealthy among her kind. The chefs of House Aelsar had been proficient in the preparation of all manner of dishes, some from distant and exotic locales. By comparison, since leaving Aderilund, the meals he had lived on barely qualified for the status of edible. Still, if anything, hunger quickly overcame all scruples and Bellaydin found that if he would not eat something today, then he would scoff it down tomorrow, barely pausing to chew.

"Tell me Geoffrey," said Bellaydin. "What precisely is going to happen to me once we reach Emparia?"

Geoffrey let out a chuckle. "We're more than halfway there, and now you think to ask?"

"Well, it didn't occur to me, really."

"Your cousin's the Earl of Genio. You'll be well looked after, trust me. No doubt he'll find somewhere useful to stick you in his household."

"If I might interrupt this fascinating conversation?"

"Yes, Kahlaf?" said Geoffrey. "You want something to eat?" Geoffrey held a spoon of the broth up near the Ahktarran's face, offering him some.

"Food will have to wait," said Kahlaf. "We are being watched."

"What? By who?" said Bellaydin, standing up in shock.

"There, on the cliff, over there," Kahlaf said, pointing. "I spotted him in the distance some time ago."

Bellaydin followed Kahlaf's finger, attempting to make out the blurry figure in the distance. "I can't really see anything."

"If only those elves had given you their sight, huh?" Geoffrey winked. "Not that I can see much more than a blur though. Unless…" Geoffrey patted down his clothing, eliciting a few glances from the others.

"What are you looking for?" asked Bellaydin.

"I was given something before I left Emparia. I wonder if… yes, here it is." Geoffrey withdrew his hands from his pockets, holding a lens before Bellaydin.

"A lens?"

"Yes," said Geoffrey. "But if I were to make a wager, I'd say it was no ordinary lens, wouldn't you say, Kahlaf?"

The Ahktarran just grunted.

"Let's just hope I'm not about to look incredibly stupid," Geoffrey said. Bellaydin watched as Geoffrey placed the lens over his eye and looked into the distance again. Slowly a smile crept across his face. "It must be magical. I can see everything perfectly. And I can see… oh no, oh my gods…" The smile quickly turned into a frown.

"What? What is it?"

"Saldarri," Geoffrey said.

Kahlaf growled, "Who or what are the Saldarri, knight?"

170

Geoffrey was frantically putting out the campfire, scattering the cooking equipment in an effort to put out the flames.

"We've got to leave now," Geoffrey said. "No time to explain."

"But…"

"Now! I just hope they haven't seen us," said Geoffrey, grabbing the last of his belongings.

"Why is that?" Bellaydin said, still unsure of what was going on.

"If they've seen us, then we're already dead. Come on, let's go."

"Our best path would be through the woods, knight; if we stay on the open plains we're sure to be seen," Kahlaf said as the trio quickly departed from their camp.

"If they haven't already seen us, you mean," said Geoffrey grimly.

"I don't understand," Bellaydin said. "Who are the Saldarri? Why are we running from them?"

Geoffrey stopped in his tracks, and wheeled around to face the youth. "Listen now, Bela, and listen well, because this is the only time you're getting it. The Saldarri are the elite trackers of Goriinchia. Strange, savage men who scorn civilisation and all it represents, yet know more about the wilds than any human ever could. The Goriinchian warlords use them to hunt fugitives and, as far as stories go, no one has ever, ever escaped a Saldarri tracker. If we're lucky, they'll catch us and hand us over to the Goriinchians. If we're not, well they'll keep us for themselves."

"What would they do to us?" Bellaydin said.

"Stories are that they wear the bones of their victims. So… use your imagination," Geoffrey said. Bellaydin shuddered.

"This way," said Kahlaf, pointing to the forests. "It's our only chance to evade pursuit."

"What's that sound?" Bellaydin said.

"What sound?" Geoffrey said testily.

"Listen."

Geoffrey did so. A low rumbling echoed from some distance away. He could hear the sound of hooves pounding the earth.

"Damn. Horsemen." Geoffrey said. "Into the forests. Quick!"

"Which way?" Bellaydin said.

"Doesn't matter, just run."

Bellaydin did as Geoffrey ordered, running full pelt into the woods, ignoring everything but the sound of his own feet thumping the ground, his breath coming in ragged gasps and the staccato of his beating heart. It was fear that drove him on. Fear of what the Goriinchians would do to him when they caught him. All around him was shouting and the sound of scuffling, but Bellaydin was unable to tell friend from foe. All he could concentrate on was the furious boiling heat in his head.

Then, suddenly, it all stopped. The forest around him was quiet. In every direction, tall, strong oaks blocked his view. He could not tell the way he came from the way he was going. He pulled himself up, panting as he leaned against a tree to catch his thoughts. Geoffrey and Kahlaf were nowhere to be seen, but there was also no sign of his pursuers.

No sooner had he thought that than he heard a soft, almost imperceptible noise behind him. He stiffened and slowly turned his head.

"Turn around and you are dead, Enparran," said a heavily accented voice. "Raise your hands and place them on your head."

"Are you a Saldarri?" said Bellaydin, obeying the voice.

There was no response, only the sounds of muffled footsteps

approaching him. Rough hands grabbed Bellaydin's wrists, and he felt the coarseness of the rope being used to bind his arms behind his back.

"Turn around," his captor ordered.

Bellaydin turned around, seeing the man for the first time. He was of medium height, with ragged grey – almost silver – hair, almond shaped eyes and skin decorated in elaborate tattoos. Stubble covered the warrior's cheeks, he wore a rugged outfit of leather and tartan, and carried a sturdy longbow by his side. Bellaydin had no doubt the warrior had other weapons with him, even if Bellaydin could not see where they were. This man must be a Saldarri.

There was one feature that intrigued Bellaydin more than anything else – the man's ears were, like those of Bellaydin's own sister, elongated, pointed at the ends, and lobe-less. Did this Saldarri have Eldara blood like Polnygar? Bellaydin pushed the thought aside. Even if the man was half-elf, he was unlikely to discuss it with a prisoner. Besides, as Geoffrey had said, the man also wore a necklace of apparently human bones. Bellaydin had no desire to add his to the warrior's collection. Only thing to do was to shut up and do as he was told.

"Walk," the Goriinchian said, poking Bellaydin in the back with a sharp object, most likely a knife or dagger. Bellaydin noted he had been correct about secret weapons.

As he and his captor walked through the forest, Bellaydin was astonished by how silently the Goriinchian moved. While Bellaydin's footsteps crunched through the undergrowth, the Goriinchian's barely made a whisper. He did not even seem to snap a single twig. It was no wonder that Bellaydin had not noticed him until it was already too late.

They emerged into the sunlight in short order. Unlike Bellaydin, the Goriinchian obviously knew exactly where they were, and how to navigate the forest. Grabbing Bellaydin by the hair, the Saldarri pulled him towards him with one hand. The Saldarri cupped his hand to his mouth, and let out

173

a loud ululation.

In a few short minutes, Bellaydin found himself surrounded by many more Goriinchians – some Saldarri scouts on foot, the others differently attired horsemen. Astride powerful looking steeds, the horsemen were also dressed in leather and tartans, but some wore chainmail shirts, and Bellaydin spotted the occasional tabard emblazoned with the emblem of the Horned God. Bellaydin's heart sunk when he noticed Geoffrey and Kahlaf struggling between two burly Saldarri warriors. One of the horsemen sidled towards Bellaydin, muttering something to his Saldarri captor. The Saldarri deferred to the horseman, responding with a salute and a few words of his own before pushing Bellaydin towards Geoffrey and Kahlaf.

"Together again," Geoffrey said dryly. "I wouldn't miss it for the world."

"You have led us on a quite a chase, Enparrans," said the lead horseman, his heavily accented Emparian sounding stilted to Bellaydin's ears. "But you are out of luck, it seems. The Horned God has smiled upon us this day."

Next to the speaker, another horseman laughed cruelly, "Where are your false gods now, Truth-Abhorrers?"

The lead rider motioned for the other to be silent. "Enough of your interruptions, brother, it serves no purpose at this time."

"They are heathens and idol worshippers, Aonghus," said the other horseman, spitting at the ground. "And your tolerance of them is a sign of weakness."

"I said enough, Cathan!"

"Aonghus," said Geoffrey. "That name sounds familiar."

"Do not be coy, Enparran dog, all heathens know and fear the name of

Warchief Aonghus Culainn," said the horseman named Cathan.

Geoffrey did not respond.

"Does this Goriinchian speak the truth, knight?" said Kahlaf. "Do you know this so-called Warchief? By name, if not by reputation?"

Geoffrey said nothing at first, his mind merely casting itself back many months to a conversation with Earl William in Genio.

"Oh yes," said Geoffrey slowly. "I would say that I know his name alright."

"And?" said Bellaydin expectantly.

"We are in very serious trouble," Geoffrey said quietly. He gulped, and took a breath. "Tell me," he said to Aonghus Culainn. "Why is a Warchief leading a band tracking a few lost Emparians? Surely there are more important matters at hand. We are nobody special."

Aonghus smiled. "Oh, I wouldn't say that, Sir Geoffrey of Genio."

Geoffrey flushed. "I'm sure I don't know who you mean."

"Come now," said Aonghus. Next to him Cathan Culainn laughed.

"You don't know what you're saying," fumed Geoffrey.

"Oh? Is that so? I know who you are. We would recognise the servant of the Heir of Lydin anywhere. You are not lost Enparrans of no apparent importance. You are something special indeed."

He yelled out to his assembled warriors. "Take the prisoners back to camp. We have a campaign to plan."

CHAPTER 12

William caught his breath. "Are you sure?"

"Yes, my lord. There's no sign of them. They seem to have disappeared shortly after making landfall in Gorin."

"Damn it, what are the Goriinchians telling us?"

"Nothing, my lord. They've barely told us anything. I've been hearing rumours, however."

"What sort of rumours? What do you mean?"

"Well, my lord, we still have sources in Goriinchia. Messages have been arriving – by runner, by tracking bird… some of them claim to have seen a burnt out husk of a ship in Gorin's harbour."

"And what of the crew and passengers? What of Geoffrey? My cousins?"

The emissary shook his head. "We've heard nothing. My lord, they may be dead."

"You think the Goriinchians have killed them?"

"It is possible."

"I don't believe that. They'd be fools to not demand a ransom."

"They're fanatics, my lord. They don't care about gold."

"Everyone cares about gold, Carfel," William gently scolded the man, who smiled in return.

"Ah, Willy, my boy. There you are," said a voice.

William turned his head. "Haakon, I hope you had a good journey," William said, extending a hand. He turned to his aide. "That will do for today, Carfel."

"Yes, my lord," the steward said, bowing before leaving William's presence.

Haakon de Morcor grabbed William's hand, giving it a firm shake as he smiled warmly at the younger man.

"Thanks for the favour," said William. "I never dreamed that my name would come up for a Ducal council. But with you speaking on my behalf..."

"Don't mention it, my boy," Haakon said, resting a hand on William's shoulder. "I'm always happy to bring you up at court and you are eminently suited to delivering the queen's justice You're a fine man, a credit to your family."

"And it was on such short notice, too," William mused.

"Yes, well," said Haakon, looking a little uncomfortable. "The illness of the Duke of Emperor's Palace was quite unexpected. One day he was fine, the next, totally bedridden."

"So I heard," said William.

"I wouldn't worry. I expect he'll make a full recovery. But in the meantime, this turn of events is good news for you." said Haakon, brightening, "You will be the first earl to sit on a Ducal council. Your grandfather would be proud, as proud as I am."

"Thank you, Haakon, but I would have preferred for it to happen in less unfortunate circumstances," said William. "What does the Duke of Oldharbour think of all this?"

"Wulfric is not pleased, as you might expect. Though I'm sure he will come around. You have that affect on people, my boy."

"Hah," said William. "Let's get seated, shall we?"

"So, how does this work?" William asked Haakon as they took their places at the table.

"It's quite simple really. The three of us will hold council here, and petitioners will come in one by one, asking for rulings on their situations. A majority vote from at least two of us will decide the matter."

William nodded. "I understand."

"Good. You know, it was very generous of you to host this, Willy," said Haakon.

"I didn't think I had a choice," the earl chuckled.

"Well, you know how the queen is. I'm glad you took the suggestion under consideration."

William shrugged. "I actually thought you would have preferred Genio to Wishapton. I didn't think you'd want to hold the Ducal Council anywhere this out of the way."

"I quite like Wishapton; it's a nice enough town. A little close to Goriinchia, perhaps, but one can't have everything. And I must say, the accommodation here is excellent."

William nodded. "It was the summer home of my aunt and uncle, when they wanted to get as far away from Genio as possible. They came here quite frequently, especially in their later years."

"Yes, I remember visiting Alusine here quite a few times," Haakon said. "There were some good times. We certainly enjoyed the hunting."

"Being this close to the border never bothered you?"

"Oh gods no. What Goriinchian alive could've outfought either of us? Besides, things were a lot quieter down south those days. I think the Goriinchians were scared of us."

"And now?"

Haakon raised an eyebrow in response.

"Enjoying yourself, my lords?" said Wulfric Highcrown, approaching the pair.

"At my age there's little enjoyment to be found, Your Grace," said Haakon, "so I tend to take advantage of any opportunity I get."

"Yes, well, enough of that. We have work to do. No time for nonsense." He turned to William. "If you get lost, Ap'Lydin, follow my lead," Wulfric said gruffly. "You will see how a Duke of Emparia dispenses justice."

"Oh, good," said William as Wulfric took the seat next to him.

Wulfric banged the ceremonial gavel on the table, and announced the beginning of the session. Nearby a scribe prepared to take notes.

"The Ducal council is now in session. Presiding are Wulfric Highcrown, Duke of Oldharbour; Haakon de Morcor, Duke of Alariat; and William Ap'Lydin, Earl of Genio." He shuffled the papers in front of him. "The Earl of Genio is standing in the stead of the Duke of Emperor's Palace, who is unfortunately ill. Right, let us get down to business. Who is the first supplicant today?"

"Dugald Ap'Morten, Your Graces," announced the page. "He wishes to petition the council on the matter of religious freedom."

"Send him in," said Wulfric.

"Very good, Your Grace." The page bowed, and did as ordered.

Dugald Ap'Morten was a thin, wiry man in his mid-fifties. He wore his hair long, with a thin, ragged beard and robes of grey and black. Around his neck hung a medallion bearing the symbol of the Horned God.

"Please state your name, birth place and occupation for the council," said Wulfric.

The man seemed nervous, stumbling over his words. "Dugald Ap'Morten, Your Graces. I was born here in Wishapton. I'm a priest."

"You have a Goriinchian name," said William.

"My parents emigrated from Goriinchia, milord."

"And you have never been there yourself?"

"No milord."

"Tell me then, pastor, which faith do you follow?" said Wulfric.

"I… I serve the Horned God, Your Grace." Dugald said, holding up the holy symbol for the nobles to see. William could not believe how bold the man was about his religious beliefs.

"You are, of course, aware," said Haakon, "that the worship of the Horned God has been illegal in the kingdom for over a decade."

"I understand, Your Graces."

"It says here," said Wulfric, perusing the documents in front of him, "that you were exposed by your neighbours as running an underground church for others of Goriinchian descent. Do you deny these charges?"

"No, milord."

"As a result you have been imprisoned for this past year. Is this correct?"

"It is, milord. But I have served my time."

"And according to this you now wish to petition the Crown to overturn the legislation banning the organised worship of the Horned God."

"Yes milord."

"You realise that the Church of the Horned God was implicated in many heinous acts, do you not? Plots, murders, conspiracies — all of which led to the decree from the king that prohibited the Horned God's worship. Do you agree that such acts amounted to treason against the crown?"

Dugald swallowed. "Yes, I do."

"You do?"

"Their actions were treasonous, Your Graces, yes. But they were the actions of men, not of a god. They were a select few, those who plotted against the King, and they do not represent the faithful as a whole. In its haste to deliver justice, the Crown delivered a verdict on the many for the crimes of the few."

Wulfric pursed his lips. "Is that so?"

Haakon stroked his chin in thought. "What is it you desire? What do you wish to have considered by this council, and by the Crown?"

"I ask for nothing more than the freedom to practice my faith, and for that same freedom to be granted to any of those who worship the Horned God. We are loyal citizens, Your Graces. We are not traitors. There shall be no plots against the Crown, no betrayals of Emparia to Goriinchia. We just wish to praise the one true God, and be allowed to do so in peace."

"Do you know who I am, Dugald?" said William.

"You are the Earl of Genio, my lord," said Dugald.

"I lost family to the worshippers of the Horned God," said William. "What do you say to that? How can we be sure that Emparian worshippers no longer wish to murder those who do not believe?"

"My lord, I and all those who truly follow the Horned God are sorry for your loss, and I will again say to you that those who committed the crime were no kin of mine. The Horned God teaches peace and brotherhood, not treachery and murder."

"Very well, I think we have heard enough," said Wulfric. "Leave us. We shall announce our decision in an hour."

***

An hour later, the council was re-convened, and the three nobles delivered their decision.

"We have reached a decision," said Wulfric. "But it is unlikely to be unanimous. We shall deliver our findings individually first. Haakon –"

"Thank you, Your Grace," Haakon said. "After carefully considering all the facts in this matter, I am of the opinion that our petitioner is correct when he claims there to be a strong separation between the criminal and non-criminal aspects of the organised worship of the Horned God. I would also argue that any such treacherous elements have since been rooted out and destroyed, and the Church, as it was over a decade ago, no longer exists. I agree that the Crown has been negligent in confusing the treasonous actions of a few with the wider religious community. Therefore I would recommend that the Crown rescind the decree banning the worship of the Horned God. Punish any criminal elements, not the faithful as a whole."

"I thank the Duke of Alariat for his decision. What follows is mine." Wulfric folded his hands as he delivered his decision. "The followers of the Horned God are known malcontents and traitors to the Crown. I see no evidence that the beliefs, nor the tenets, of the faith have changed substantially in the past ten years. I would remind their Graces of the links the religion has to Goriinchian nationalism, of the virulent anti-Emparian elements in religious texts, and the security threat that the Church of the Horned God would pose in any future conflict with Goriinchia. Furthermore the leaders of said church never fully divulged the reasons behind the murders of Lord and Lady Ap'Lydin. I see no reason to lift the ban at this time, or indeed, at any time in the future."

There was a protracted silence after Wulfric's address. William suddenly noticed all eyes were upon him. With Wulfric and Haakon both going different ways, the council was obviously waiting on him to deliver the final decision.

"I guess it's my ruling that will solve this deadlock," said William.

"That is correct, Lord Genio," said Wulfric. "I suggest you weigh all the options, and choose wisely."

"I am aware that I may seem conflicted on this case," said William, "and worshippers of the Horned God have caused me personal distress and family loss. However, I have also taken into account the words of our petitioner, along with the comments of the Dukes of Oldharbour and Alariat. It is true there are some tenets of this faith that trouble me, but I can say the same about many religions. We Emparians have always prided ourselves on the tolerance and pluralism in our nation, and I see no reason that such optimism is unfounded. I share Lord Oldharbour's concerns of a possible future conflict with Goriinchia, and the possible dual loyalty of Goriinchian-Emparian subjects. But does not the continued prohibition of open displays of their faith alienate them further? So it is with some reservation that I concur with the Duke of Alariat on this matter, and recommend that the Crown rescind its decision of a decade ago, and end the veto on the church of the Horned God."

As William finished his address, Haakon nodded approvingly at him. Wulfric looked somewhat pained, and leaned over to whisper in William's ears.

"You have signed our death warrants, Ap'Lydin."

"At least we'll die as honest men, Wulfric," William responded.

"Of course. Maybe they'll write it on our tombstones," Wulfric hissed.

***

"Aelzandar," Arhotep said with irritation. "This is most irregular."

"Well, I'm afraid there is no time for pleasantries, vizier. This is an emergency, and His Majesty needs to be informed."

Aelzandar had burst into the throne room, Polnygar in tow, with no prior warning. It was a rather serious breach of protocol.

"What do you mean, emergency?" the vizier demanded.

"A crime has been committed in this palace. A crime which had its origins in this very room."

"What? What are you accusing me of?" said the vizier.

The Pharaoh had begun to take an interest, and put down the goblet he was drinking from. "Yes, this should be interesting, archmage," said Pharaoh. "What are you accusing my vizier of?"

"The Tears of the Divine have been stolen. Curiously the theft occurred at precisely the same moment that I had been summoned here. Quite a coincidence, wouldn't you agree, Arhotep?"

"I… I don't think I like your tone, elf."

At that, Pharaoh himself interrupted. "You would have to admit Arhotep, it is quite a coincidence. You accuse my royal mage of withholding some sort of magical artefact, at the same time that said artefact disappears." Pharaoh fidgeted with his jewellery. "I wonder what it all means."

"Come Your Majesty, he wastes our time…" Arhotep said.

Pharaoh laughed. "Our time, Arhotep? I think you overestimate your importance."

"I'm terribly sorry, Your Majesty," the vizier spluttered.

Pharaoh yawned, "Think nothing of it. Now, archmage, tell me, what of this robbery? Who are these thieves that are roaming free in my palace?"

"They were not thieves, Your Majesty," said Aelzandar. "At least, not until they stole the Tears."

"And you know their names?"

Aelzandar took a deep breath. "The Eldara ambassador Lord Ivellios and the former ambassador of Emparia Augustin Bauer."

"But Augustin was enchanted or something. Ivellios must have cast some sort of spell on him," Polnygar blurted out.

Pharaoh raised an eyebrow.

"Are you certain of this, girl?" asked the vizier. "What evidence do you have of such enchantment?"

"Well… it's not like Augustin to do such a thing of his own free will," Polnygar said.

The vizier scoffed. "And how would you know him? From what I hear, you are only recently acquainted with the Ambassador yourself."

"Forgive me, Your Majesty, the dear girl has spoken in haste," Aelzandar said.

"But it's true, it must be. He wouldn't do such a thing," Polnygar insisted.

"I wonder how well you actually know him."

"Enough, Arhotep," Pharaoh said, seeming to have shaken off his lethargy. "Archmage, these are quite serious charges you bring against these ambassadors of mine. How can you be sure?"

"I have scried them through the use of the Art, Your Majesty. There is no doubt."

Pharaoh straightened up, leaning back against the throne. "Well, then there is no time to waste. Tell me, archmage, what do you suggest?"

"What? Your Majesty, I must protest. There is no real evidence."

"I said enough, Arhotep," Pharaoh said.

"Your Majesty," Aelzandar said. "I must retrieve the Tears. They are far too important and powerful to fall into the wrong hands."

"Of course. What do you need? Soldiers? How many?"

"It would be better, I think, for me to leave without soldiers, Your Majesty. I will travel much better in a smaller group."

"How small, precisely?" asked Pharaoh.

"Very small. Myself, and my pupil here, will suffice."

"If that is what you think is best," Pharaoh said.

"I will also need to know how Ivellios found out about the Tears. I believe the vizier might be able to help me there."

"What? I... don't know what you mean," the vizier said, visibly sweating.

"Oh, tell him, Arhotep," said Pharaoh. "In the meantime, I think I might have a bite to eat." Pharaoh rose from his throne and left the throne room, his leopard skin cloak trailing behind him.

"Take a seat, vizier," said Aelzandar. "This might take a while."

"He came to me," Arhotep admitted, his voice wavering. "Asking such questions..."

"Ivellios came to you?" said Aelzandar. "And what did you tell him?"

"Nothing... nothing of substance, I swear to you. Just my suspicions regarding you, the girl, and the Emparian. I said I thought you were hiding something. It was nothing. You have to believe me."

"But you didn't know about the Tears then, did you?"

"No, it was only later... Ivellios returned, and said he had learned of a

187

'great secret', and that you were hiding a thing of great and terrible power, one which could bring ruin to the kingdom."

"That snake!" said Polnygar.

Aelzandar shot a remonstrating glance towards the young woman.

"Oh, I'm sorry," she said.

"Do you always interrupt, girl?" Arhotep said, regaining some of his disdain.

"Quiet," said Aelzandar, no anger registering in his voice. "Tell me Arhotep, what precisely did Ivellios do to Augustin?"

"I don't know what you're talking about," Arhotep said.

"Tell me," the archmage said. His voice was quiet, barely a whisper, but he spoke with such authority that Arhotep's eyes widened in fear.

"Oh gods, you have to believe me, I had nothing to do with it. I didn't see it… but, yes, Ivellios left the palace shortly before you arrived. The Emparian was with him. He was… quiet. Almost servile. It seemed so much unlike him."

"Where were they going?"

"I don't know."

"TELL ME," Aelzandar thundered, lifting up the vizier by his jewelled collar.

"Ralom. They were going to the Holy City. I swear to you, it's the truth! May the Sun King damn me for all time if I lie."

Silence.

After a few tense moments, it was Aelzandar who spoke, his voice once again calm and controlled. As he spoke, he let go of Arhotep's collar, dropping the man back on to the throne.

"Very good, Arhotep. You have told me what I need. You may leave."

Normally the vizier would have bristled at the thought of the archmage giving him an order but, as Polnygar noted with a smile, now Arhotep leapt from the throne, and fled from the room as fast as his feet would carry him.

"Now my dear, we must make preparations. Time is of the essence," said Aelzandar. "They have a head start on us."

"You want me to come with you?" said Polnygar. "Why?"

"There are various reasons. You are still my pupil, and have much to learn. Hence you need to be at my side – I can continue to instruct you as we travel. Secondly, and most importantly, you and the Tears seem to have some sort of connection. We may need that connection to track our wayward friends. This way, my dear." Aelzandar placed a fatherly hand on Polnygar's shoulder and steered her back towards their quarters. "As I said, time is of the essence."

***

Bellaydin had never been a prisoner before, and he was not sure that he relished the experience. The Goriinchians had taken a distinct pleasure in subduing the captured trio, beating them into submission with cudgel, staff and whatever weapon was at hand. Geoffrey and Bellaydin had gone down quickly, whereas Kahlaf took a bit more "convincing". Quite a few Goriinchians ended up sorely bruised in the attempt. Now, like his two companions, Bellaydin found himself nursing a splitting headache in his new mobile prison cell. The pounding of his head only slightly distracted him from the sickening lurch of the jail as the oxen dragged it over the muddy paths of northern Goriinchia.

He did not know where they were going precisely. His guards did not tell him much, and in any case they knew little Emparian – only enough to throw taunts of 'infidel' and 'thrice-damned-son-of-a-whore' at him. The last one stung in particular, if only because it reminded him of a very similar insult that the elven children of Aderilund used to throw at Saegralanna.

"Hey Enparran," yelled a guard. "Where your many gods now? Eh? Why don't they save you? Oh mighty Kartilas, save me, save me."

Kytilas – who Goriinchians knew as Kartilas – was a warrior god favoured in Emparia, yet, due to his childhood in Aderilund, Bellaydin knew little about him, or indeed about anything at all to do with Emparian religion. He was more familiar with the Eldara religion – the "Transcendent Court" of Hydria, the Great Mother, and her Firstborn.

"Eh, Enparran, maybe he no hear you, eh?" the other guard mocked. "Maybe his Mummy and Daddy won't let him play. Ha-ha! He can't come out and play!"

Bellaydin found himself lost. An insult lost a lot of its effectiveness when it was so obscure as to be completely incomprehensible. The guards didn't seem to mind the lack of any reaction, though, as they were too busy laughing amongst themselves. A few moments later Bellaydin's cage was rocked as the prison lurched to a stop. He guessed that they were here - wherever 'here' was.

"Last stop, Enparran," yelled the guard. "Take him!"

The door to the cell was wrenched open and two burly Goriinchians grabbed Bellaydin, dragging him outside.

"Where are we?" Bellaydin said groggily. "Where are you taking me?"

The warriors did not reply, merely laughing and mocking Bellaydin with an insulting imitation of his voice. Half dragging, half shoving, the Goriinchians took their captive forward, over the crest of a hill that overlooked a large valley. In the gloom, Bellaydin noticed hundreds of tiny dots of light below, campfires, illuminating the darkness. As they got closer, other shapes began to come into focus.

"By the gods," Bellaydin breathed.

There, in the valley, was the largest military camp Bellaydin could have ever imagined. Soldiers, generals, camp-followers – there must have been over ten thousand there, easily. The logistics alone were mind-boggling. It was an invasion army, Bellaydin realised. The target, of course, could be none other than Emparia.

"Of all the things in the world, I never thought I'd say this," said a voice, "but Earl William was right."

Geoffrey, restrained by a few Goriinchians of his own, looked in wonder at the military base below them.

"Right about what?" grunted Kahlaf, as he was pulled towards the group by a whole gang of guards.

"This. It's an invasion army," Geoffrey said. "Ten, fifteen, maybe twenty thousand strong."

A Goriinchian struck Geoffrey across the face, sending him to the ground. "Hold your tongue, Enparran," the Goriinchian grunted, the Emparian words coming thick and slow. "Your kind is doomed. Pity you will not live to see it…"

Geoffrey tasted blood on his lip."Why are you trying your luck invading Emparia again, you kilted lunatics?" he said. "The pasting we gave you last time not enough for you?"

The guard's face turned furious, and he stamped down hard on Geoffrey's hand, causing the knight to cry out in agony. The other warriors had to restrain Kahlaf, as the Ahktarran tried to break free. "Heathen dog," the guard said. "There is no Emparia. It was built on lies and treachery. There is only Karlicia, and it will once again be whole."

The guard nodded to his companions, and they grabbed Geoffrey by the scruff of his neck, hauling the knight to his feet. Bundling the three prisoners together, the Goriinchians marched them down into the valley.

"An Tiarna Culainn," the lead warrior said, bowing to the figure in front of him. Aonghus Culainn, First Warchief of the Goriinchians, acknowledged the gesture with a slight flick of the wrist.

"Go mbeannaí Dia thú," Aonghus responded.

"What on earth are they saying?" Bellaydin whispered to Geoffrey.

"Nothing much," said Geoffrey. "My Goriinchian is a little rusty. I think that —"

"Ciúnas!" yelled the warrior.

"I think that was him telling us to be quiet," Geoffrey said.

"Yes it was, Enparran," Aonghus said, speaking Emparian. "I am curious. The pagans of the north rarely take the time to speak the holy tongue. How is it that you do?"

Geoffrey said nothing.

"Answer the Warchief!"

"My lord has an interest in your people."

Warchief Culainn grinned broadly. "William Ap'Lydin. A most worthy adversary," he said. "I look forward to the day when we meet. It will be a glorious battle. I can only hope that the Horned God will be with me against such a foe." The Warchief looked towards the prisoners. "And so the Heir of Lydin sends to me three spies... perhaps he is seeking to discover my weaknesses? Hmmm?"

The Warchief approached Bellaydin, and crouched down in front of him, bringing his own eyes level with Bellaydin's. "And who are you, boy, to travel with such company? William's knight I know, and the beast-man with him is of little consequence. You, however..."

Geoffrey shot a glance towards Bellaydin. The look in the knight's eyes told Bellaydin to exercise caution.

"I'm nobody. Just a squire."

Aonghus looked Bellaydin up and down. "You Enparrans and your squires!" he laughed. "Why don't you make your boys warriors straight up,

192

instead of prancing about teaching them poetry and skirt-chasing!" He stood. "You say you are nobody. Perhaps you are. But then, I don't fully believe that. There is something else. I can see it in your eyes."

"He's just a boy," said Geoffrey. "Leave him."

"And why does the Heir of Lydin send a mere boy with his finest soldier here? Tell me that, heathen knight."

Heir of Lydin. The Warchief kept using that phrase, the one Bellaydin had heard before, spoken to him by the assassin in Aderilund. But there it had referred to him, now the Warchief was using it to refer to Bellaydin's cousin William. Then there was Saegralanna, who had told him that the Heir of Lydin was Bellaydin's own father, Alusine. What did this mean? Were they both the Heir of Lydin? How many heirs were there?

"Struck dumb by the wrath of God," declared a nearby warrior, chuckling for good measure. The surrounding group laughed with him. Aonghus did not.

"I asked you a question, unbeliever," said Aonghus. "In the name of the Horned God, you will answer me."

Geoffrey remained silent for some time, before finally venturing a curt response. "I would never do anything in that name."

"Of course not," said Aonghus. "You Enparrans have not yet been exposed to His glory, but fear not. That time is approaching. Soon, the words of the prophet-king will be heard in all corners of Karlicia."

"You mean Emparia," Geoffrey said.

Aonghus narrowed his eyes and approached Geoffrey, standing so close to the knight that Geoffrey could feel the Warchief's rancid breath on his face. "There is no Emparia - only Karlicia, the portion which is free, and that which is still occupied."

Geoffrey did not respond.

"Take the three of them from my sight. Hang them in the morning."

Bellaydin found himself once again confined to a cell, or more specifically, a cramped iron cage, suspended from a metal pole in the centre of the camp. Similar cages hung nearby, two of which contained Geoffrey and Kahlaf respectively. Others were empty, or, more unsettlingly, contained desiccated corpses and half mouldering skeletons. He glanced towards Kahlaf. The small size of his own prison kept Bellaydin hunched over. He could not begin to imagine how uncomfortable the seven-foot Ahktarran was feeling.

"I knew it was a mistake getting out of bed this morning," said Geoffrey.

"This is no time for jokes, knight," said Kahlaf. "We are to die in the morning, have you forgotten?"

"On the contrary, Kahlaf. This is precisely the time for jokes. As you say, we are about to die. If we must face death, best to do it with a smile, to show that it holds no power over us."

Bellaydin sunk down in despair. It was easy for Geoffrey to say that. He was a knight. He'd been trained all his life to face danger. Death held no fear for him. Bellaydin had spent almost his entire life in Aderilund, where though he may not have felt like he belonged, he had always been safe.

He had dreamed of Emparia for so long. And now to have come so far, to come almost in sight of that dream, only to see it slip away from him? He wished things could have stayed the same. He wished he was home, with his sister, and his mother. Right now he would have done anything just to see their faces, to hear his sister laugh, to see his mother smile.

He curled into a ball, arms gripping his legs. Tears stained his eyes and his chest heaved with a strangled sob. *Was this how it must end?*

CHAPTER 13

"Do try to keep up, Hebu," Aelzandar said, as they made their way towards the barge that was to take them upriver.

"Sorry, Lord Archmage," said the Nemoi, struggling under the weight of books and papyrus scrolls. "I am somewhat confused though."

"Oh, really? About what?" Aelzandar asked.

"Why Pharaoh would send me with you," the Nemoi said, standing still while he tried to stop himself tumbling under the weight.

"To help me with all of this, of course," Aelzandar said. "And you are doing such a fine job too."

"This isn't in my job description," Hebu said, fumbling and dropping a scroll.

"Isn't your job to serve Pharaoh in any manner he deems fit?" Aelzandar said.

"But I am not a pack mule," Hebu said.

"No one said you were, my dear man," Aelzandar said soothingly. "For one, mules don't talk."

"Oh, my Lord, that is too much…"

Polnygar scraped to the ground and picked up the scroll. *"The Properties and Enchantments of Homunculi and Golemcraft,"* she read aloud. "What's this? A spell?"

"Just some minor research of my own I've been conducting recently. We can perhaps discuss it more when we next speak of the Soldara." Aelzandar stopped, and looked behind at Hebu, who had not moved, instead glaring at the archmage. "It was a joke, Hebu," Aelzandar said, smiling. "Here, let me help you with that."

He bent down to the Nemoi's height and grabbed the heaviest tome. "I think I'd prefer to carry this spellbook with me, anyway. It always helps to have one close at hand."

"You have my thanks, my Lord," said a visibly winded Hebu.

"Don't mention it, my good man. You just concentrate on keeping those scrolls from falling into the river."

"Yes, my Lord."

"Thank you Hebu, your assistance is most appreciated." Aelzandar turned to Polnygar, offering her a hand. "Here, my dear. Let me help you aboard."

"It's fine," said Polnygar. "I can manage."

"I'm sure you can, we do have a long trip ahead of us, though."

"How far is Ralom?" Polnygar asked, taking a seat on the barge.

"Oh, it's quite a few weeks from here, my dear," said Aelzandar, sitting down beside her.

Hebu scrambled over the side of the barge, his small stature making the task difficult.

"Aren't you going to help him?" Polnygar said.

"Don't mind me, my lord," Hebu said testily, cutting into the conversation. "I'm doing perfectly fine over here."

"You see, my dear?" Aelzandar said, with a smile. "He said he's fine. Nothing to worry about."

Despite feeling more than a little sympathetic for the overloaded Nemoi, Polnygar allowed herself a little chuckle.

"Oh, that's delightful," said Hebu, as he stuffed the scrolls and books into the sea chest nearby, and took a seat next to the pair.

"A week or so up the Jagontay River by barge, then onwards to the Holy City. Should be a pleasant enough trip for the most part," said Aelzandar, laying his staff down next to him.

"I don't understand. Can't you just… I don't know… use your magic to take us there instantly or something?"

"That would be nice," said Aelzandar. "But I'm afraid the requirements of arcane teleportation are a little more complicated than that. To use the Art to travel, one is required to have carefully prepared the arriving and departing locations by constructing special teleportation circles. While I have one prepared in Macrodonia, there is none in Ralom that suits our purposes."

"Oh," said Polnygar.

"So my dear," said Aelzandar, "I'm afraid this is the best I can do." He put a hand on her shoulder, and, with his other, reached for one of the spellbooks. "Look on the bright side… it gives you plenty of time to study."

"I was wondering why I had to bring all of these," said the Nemoi.

"Hebu," said Aelzandar. "You were a scribe. You understand the power that knowledge brings. Page three hundred and seventy six, Polnygar,"

"Yes, master."

Aelzandar waved a finger.

"Yes, Aelzandar."

"Being a scribe gave me the power to feed my family, my Lord. That was enough power for me. Now, do you really need me for this trip?"

"Of course."

Hebu's shoulders slumped. "I must have really offended Pharaoh, or Arhotep – much the same thing these days."

"I think not." Aelzandar leaned back as the barge made its gentle way up the river. "I wouldn't be surprised if Arhotep's long career is finally reaching its end," the archmage said knowingly. "Things may be different around the palace by the time we return."

Without turning his head, he added, "Keep writing, Polnygar, don't think I don't know you've stopped."

"Just my luck," said Hebu. "A position is about to come up, and I'm stuck out here."

Aelzandar raised an eyebrow.

"And there's no place I'd rather be, my Lord," Hebu said, with mocking sincerity.

"There's a good fellow," said Aelzandar. "It's a long trip, you know. Perhaps you could entertain us with some of that famous Nemoi verse."

"My Lord," said Hebu, aghast. "You know that the content of the Nemoinomicon is considered off-limits to those who are not Nemoi."

"The Nemoi – what?" Polnygar said.

"*Nemoi – nom –icon,*" said Hebu, enunciating the words slowly and deliberately, with more than a hint of sarcasm, "The great work of the Celestial Architects. Do you know nothing?"

"I've never heard of it," said Polnygar.

"The Nemoi are somewhat reluctant to share its wisdom with outsiders." Aelzandar said.

"There would be no point." Hebu adopted a superior tone. "It would be like casting pearls before swine. That is why it is forbidden."

"Ah, well, so it is. Even if it does seem a shame to let cultural prejudices get in the way of the sharing of knowledge."

"My lord, you of all people should understand the power of cultural prejudice," Hebu said tartly. "After all, when was the last time you visited the lands of the Eldara?"

Aelzandar smiled wanly. "Ah well. It was worth a try." The archmage turned to his pupil. "Have you finished Polnygar?"

"Nearly there," she said.

"Excellent."

Hebu looked towards Polnygar. "I wonder why you volunteered for this trip, girl."

"I didn't," Polnygar said, barely raising her head from the book.

Aelzandar smiled. "I thought it best for her continued education and wellbeing that she accompanies me."

Hebu stared at the archmage for a few seconds. "I'm not a fool, my Lord," the Nemoi said. "There's something you haven't told me and, perhaps, haven't told her. It's about that magical artefact, isn't it?"

"In a manner of speaking, yes," he said. "Polnygar and the Tears seem to have some sort of a connection. So we need to keep her close as we pursue the Tears."

"Ah, now I see," said the Nemoi. "You're using her as bait, aren't you?"

"What?" Polnygar said, slamming the spellbook shut, "Aelzandar, what is he talking about? Is it true? Am I just bait?"

"Absolutely not, my dear. I would never put you in danger. Your safety is of the highest priority."

"I don't like being lied to," Polnygar said, "Or being led around like a prize calf."

"I am doing no such thing."

Hebu spoke up. "For someone whose safety is paramount, you do seem to be leading her straight into the lion's den, so to speak. She's only just begun her training and you're dragging her halfway across Carurlonia with you."

"Don't be ridiculous, Hebu," Aelzandar said. "What would you know of such matters, anyway?"

"Enough to know that you're not telling her the whole story. "

"Nonsense," said Aelzandar, waving the Nemoi away dismissively.

"Aelzandar," said Polnygar. "I don't understand… what does he mean? What aren't you telling me?"

"There is nothing to fear Polnygar. Stay close to me and no harm will come to you. I have planned for all eventualities."

"More plans," Hebu scoffed, "And what if it doesn't work?"

"My plans have never failed," said Aelzandar, "And no one will come to harm."

"How do you know?" Hebu asked.

"I just know."

Polnygar listened to the archmage's words. His voice was full of self-confidence, as if failure was inconceivable in his mind. Despite this a small grain of doubt began to germinate in Polnygar's mind. For the first time since meeting Aelzandar she did not feel safe. She wondered what she had got herself into. She didn't like to admit it but she found herself missing the peace and tranquillity of her mother's house, and her thoughts went to her family. Memories and feelings weighed down on her as her heart ached for all she had left behind.

She corralled her thoughts. There was a reason she left home in the first place. There was no future for her there, not in a land of preening spellweavers and simpering lordlings. Ivellios and his ilk. Outside of her family no one in Aderilund ever wanted her for anything, but now here she was doing something important – apprentice to the greatest spellweaver of them all. The nobles back home would have been scandalised. The thought made her smile and she let out a small chuckle. She wish she could see their faces now.

***

In the cage, time ground to a halt. His apparent imminent death hanging over his thoughts, Bellaydin barely noticed his thirst, his hunger, or the great ache in his muscles.

"So this is what waiting for death is like," Bellaydin said aloud.

His cheeks were wet with tears, but he did not care. If crying on the way to the gallows was not appropriate, when else was it?

"Oh gods, how did this happen?" he cursed.

"Your false gods will not answer, Enparran."

Bellaydin raised his head, and noticed a small cloaked figure standing on the ground below his cage. "Is it true? You infidels have never heard the blessed voice of the Horned God?"

"Well... no... I don't hear any voices. Not usually." He paused. "Your voice is familiar, do I know you?"

"My name is Morgan, Enparran," the figure said. Her Emparian was spoken in a thick Goriinchian accent, but she was otherwise understandable. Though her choice of words were simple, her fluency still impressed Bellaydin.

"Wait, you're the girl I met in the forest, the Goriinchian."

"That is your name for us," the girl said.

"What should I call you then?"

"We are Karlicians, the true people of the holy land."

"The holy land?"

"Karlicia, the land Enparrans stole from us," Morgan said.

"Look, I didn't really steal anything from anyone," Bellaydin said, feeling more than a little frustrated. "This is the first time I've even set foot in these lands. I've never even been to Emparia."

"But you are Enparran, are you not?"

"Yes, I'm Emparian, um, Enparran. But I lived most of my life elsewhere, across the sea, in the Kingdom of Aderilund."

The girl, Morgan, looked at him sceptically, as if unsure whether to believe him or not. "Adara-Land?"

"You know, Aderilund. Have you heard of it? Land of the elves?"

At the mention of elves, the girl's eyes widened, and she said something in her own tongue.

"What did you say?" asked Bellaydin.

"You were raised by Fey, Enparran?" the girl said, her voice incredulous. "The fathers of the Saldarri?"

"I'm not sure I follow," said Bellaydin. "Is Fey what you call the elves?"

The girl ignored his question. "Why are you so far from home, Enparran —who – was –raised-by –Fey?" Morgan asked. "You are risking your life."

Bellaydin slumped in his prison. "You don't have to tell me that."

Looking around, he added, "But aren't you risking yours?"

"What do you mean?" Morgan said.

"Well, I can't imagine they'd like a girl chatting with prisoners by herself. You might get into trouble."

"Don't worry about me, Enparran," the girl said. "The others are too scared of my father."

Bellaydin felt a sudden sinking feeling in his stomach. He did not like where this conversation was going.

"Your father? Who is your father?" he asked.

"You met him, didn't you? He is the Warchief Aonghus Culainn."

Bellaydin moved his mouth to speak, but no words came out. Instead he made a few sounds that were little more than strangled gasps.

"Are you alright, Enparran?"

"I didn't know he was your father," Bellaydin said, when he finally got his voice back. "You won't tell him about this conversation, will you?"

"No, why would I?"

"No reason," said Bellaydin, somewhat relieved.

"You know my name, Enparran," said Morgan Culainn. "But I don't know yours. Will you tell me?"

"Why? Are you in charge of carving my tombstone or something?"

"I am curious. You seem familiar for some reason. It's like we've met... before the time in the forest."

Bellaydin sighed. "My name's Bellaydin Ap..." He stopped mid-sentence, remembering where he was. "Just Bellaydin."

"Pleased to meet you, Just Bellaydin," Morgan said. "You Enparrans have such strange names."

"No, no…" Bellaydin was about to correct Morgan, but then thought better of it. He was going to die tomorrow, his corpse dumped in some shallow grave. It really did not seem to matter if the name he went out with was: "Just Bellaydin."

"I've got to go now, Just Bellaydin," said Morgan, "before my father notices I am missing. It was nice to talk to you. I hope your death tomorrow is quick and relatively painless."

"Um, thanks," said Bellaydin.

"Here," said Morgan, fishing some sort of medallion from underneath her smock and passing it to him through the bars. "You should pray to the Horned God tonight. It is not too late to ask for his mercy."

Morgan disappeared into the night, her cloak trailing after her. As she left, a silence hung over the air for a few moments, until it was finally broken by a thundering, coughing bout of laughter. It was Kahlaf. The Ahktarran was actually laughing, or at least wheezing and coughing in a way that resembled laughter.

"So," came a nearby voice. "You've done what I never could Ap'Lydin." It was Geoffrey.

"What's that?" Bellaydin said, groaning.

"You made the big lizard actually laugh. Nice job… Just Bellaydin." Geoffrey barely managed to finish the sentence before he too joined the Ahktarran in the laughter. "Even if that is the last thing I'll laugh about in my life, it was still worth it," Geoffrey said. "Just Bellaydin… that's amazing."

With nothing to say in response, Bellaydin collapsed back against the wall of his cage, exhausted. "Maybe if I'm lucky I'll die in my sleep tonight," he said grimly.

"That's the spirit," said Geoffrey. "Cheat the noose. Hey, it's better than giving those bastards the satisfaction."

He's just joking, Bellaydin thought.

Or so he hoped.

"How's Wulfric?" asked William.

"The same," Haakon said.

"That bad, huh?" William said.

Haakon smiled gently. "Willy, my boy, listen to me. You can't blame yourself for Wulfric's reactions. You're like your grandfather, a clear thinker, and Wulfric is…"

"Trouble?"

"Wulfric is Wulfric. He's been like this since your uncle died. I think if he could, he'd stamp out every last sign of the Horned God. He'd even climb to the heavens itself if he had to."

"Knowing what Wulfric thinks about that religion, I don't think he'd go to the heavens looking for the Horned God."

"Well, just as well the Underworld is easier to find then, isn't it?"

Despite his worry, William smiled again. Haakon had always been good at cheering him up, even when William was a child.

"He'll come around in the end, my boy, I guarantee you," Haakon said, placing a hand on William's shoulder reassuringly.

William breathed in deeply. "So tell me, on the subject of my cousins, do you have news?"

Haakon looked about nervously. "Let's find somewhere private," he said to William, ushering the earl into one of the small rooms. "Take a seat, William," said Haakon, "and shut the door."

William did as Haakon asked, settling himself down into one of the chairs. "What have you learned, Haakon?"

Haakon took a seat, and leaned towards William. "Whether you are aware of it or not, I have contacts in the lands of the Goriinchians."

"Contacts?"

"It would be best if Wulfric did not hear about them. He and I do not see eye to eye on this matter."

"And what have you got from these contacts?" William asked.

"It seems the Goriinchians have captured three individuals they claim are Emparian spies – your spies, to be precise."

"My spies? I don't have any…"

"One of them is apparently named Sir Geoffrey Keslin," said Haakon.

"Oh." William rubbed his forehead. "What in the blazes is he doing in Goriinchia? Are my cousins with him?"

"The other two are described as a young Emparian male and an Ahktarran."

"Well, the first one could be Bellaydin, but I don't know what Geoffrey is doing travelling with an Ahktarran. So, no mention of anyone who matches Polnygar's description?"

"No, William," Haakon said quietly.

"Damn it," William said. "I can only hope she's safe. Maybe she didn't accept the invitation."

"It's quite possible," Haakon said, scratching his chin. "My contacts assure me that there was no one else in the party when the Goriinchians found them."

William nodded and noticed Haakon's gaze move away.

"Wait, Haakon, I know that look. There's something else you're not telling me."

Haakon rubbed his hands together, coughing. "Well, yes, William, there is," he said.

"What?"

"The last I heard, the so-called Emparian spies were scheduled for execution."

"What? Where are my soldiers? We must organise a force to go down and save them. We must…"

"We must what, William?" Haakon said gently. "What can we do? From what I hear they are held in the war camp of the largest force the Goriinchians have ever fielded. Any troops of our own we send down there will be simply slaughtered. Then there's the potential to open up war between Emparia and Goriinchia at a time when our defences are not yet primed."

William sunk back into his chair. "You're right. But to let them die, without – "

"There is nothing you can do," said Haakon. "Their fate is in the hands of the gods."

"Aren't all of ours?" mused William.

"There might be something *I* can do, however," Haakon said.

"What do you mean?"

"As I said, I have a few contacts within Goriinchia. I shall see if my influence is still worth anything. But I warn you, we may already be too late."

***

Bellaydin slept fitfully. His sleep was dreamless, except for the thought that lay in his subconsciousness – he was going to die. There was no escaping it.

Then, something woke him.

"Enparran… are you awake?" came Morgan's voice.

He opened his eyes slowly, shaking the remnants of sleep from his mind. Morgan stood outside of his cage, looking at him expectantly. It was still night. The only illumination was the stars and moons overhead.

"I heard the other prisoners talking to you," Morgan said. "They called you Ap'Lydin."

Bellaydin was silent.

"Is this your name? Are you an Ap'Lydin, Enparran?"

"What does it matter?" Bellaydin said.

"Are you or are you not?"

Bellaydin sighed. He was tired, exhausted both physically and mentally. There did not seem to be any point in continuing the charade. What could possibly happen? That they might kill him a few hours before schedule?

"Yes. My name is Bellaydin Ap'Lydin."

Morgan nodded. "Then you need to come with me. *Now.*"

Bellaydin blinked in surprise. "I'm sorry?" he said.

"You must come with me," Morgan repeated.

"What? Where?"

Morgan bit her lip. "I can't tell you right now. But you need to come with me."

Bellaydin was perplexed. What in the name of the gods was this girl on about? Where did she want to take him? Several scenarios ran through his mind, some pleasant, some not so. Quite a few ended with his messy death. Then again, staying in the cage was almost certain to lead to death, messy or otherwise.

"Look, I'd love to come with you but I'm sort of stuck here, in this prison, all the way up here." Bellaydin gripped the bars of his cage for emphasis.

"I can let you out, Enparran. I have the key," Morgan stated.

"Well then," Bellaydin said. "I'm all yours."

Morgan approached a nearby mechanism, and cranked the lever on it, causing Bellaydin's cage to suddenly shake, lurch, and then move shakily towards the ground, groaning as it did. It reached the ground with a shuddering clank, loud enough that Bellaydin was quick to look around to see if anyone else had noticed it. Remarkably, no one had.

"What of my friends?" Bellaydin asked while Morgan fumbled with the cage's lock.

"They must remain here," she said as the lock mechanism clicked.

Bellaydin did not say another word. He hoped he could escape when the time was right, and maybe find a way to free Geoffrey and Kahlaf.

"This way," said Morgan, leading him onwards. They were leaving the war camp.

"Where are we going?" Bellaydin asked, struggling to keep up. Morgan was setting a brisk pace.

"Do you Enparrans always ask questions?" Morgan said. "Especially when you won't get answers?"

"No, I think it's just me."

She continued to lead him from the camp, along a seemingly disused forest path that wove its way up a series of steep hills and bluffs. As they continued, the path got less and less distinct, until it was hardly visible at all. Eventually, after a few hours, Morgan stopped in front of a cave.

"We are here, Enparran," she said.

"This is it?"

"Yes," Morgan said simply, beckoning towards the cave's opening.

"You want me to go in first?" Bellaydin said.

"Yes," Morgan said again.

Shaking his head, Bellaydin entered the cave. The inside was cool and damp, and the gloom was only alleviated by the glow of luminescent moss. The steady drip of moisture and low chirping of insects was all Bellaydin could hear around him.

"What am I looking for here?" Bellaydin said.

"Keep walking," said Morgan.

Bellaydin did as Morgan told him, continuing through the cave system until the tunnel opened up into a large cavern, illuminated by candlelight. This cavern was furnished, if a little spartanly, with tables, chairs, bookshelves and a simple bed. At the table sat a hunched figure, their face obscured by a hooded cloak.

"Go," Morgan said, poking Bellaydin in the back.

Bellaydin approached the table slowly. The figure made no move to greet him. Indeed, the figure did not seem to move at all. "Um... hello?" Bellaydin said.

The figure suddenly bolted upright, throwing back the hood. Bellaydin could see that it was an old woman, her skin lined and wrinkled, her hair tangled and grey. A dull grey mask covered the upper half of her face, leaving only her eyes visible. She muttered something unintelligible in Goriinchian and then looked at Bellaydin expectantly.

"Seanmháthair," Morgan said. "He is Enparran. He does not know the Holy Tongue."

The old woman smiled, showing yellow, crooked teeth. "Ahh... So, you know nothing of the ways of your ancestors do you, child?" she said in seemingly flawless Emparian.

"You speak my language?" Bellaydin said, approaching her warily.

"She is the Seeress," Morgan said, taking down the hood of her own cloak. "She knows all the tongues of men and beast."

"The Seeress?" Bellaydin said.

"Yes, that is my name, child," the Seeress said. "Take a seat, won't you?"

She indicated a nearby chair and Bellaydin, still a little confused as to the whole situation, eagerly sat down.

"Morgan is of my line," the Seeress said. "She calls me her grandmother but, in truth, she is a few more generations removed."

Morgan took the chair on the other side of the Seeress. Now that her hood was down, Bellaydin noticed the girl's appearance for the first time. She was striking, rather than typically beautiful, with a full head of long red hair, fair, freckled skin and murky green eyes. Tattooed on her forehead was the symbol of the Horned God.

"And now the child of my own flesh brings this Enparran to me? Why is that so?" The Seeress reached out a hand to Bellaydin, seizing him by the chin, and roughly turning his face from side to side, her eyes narrowed as she scrutinised him.

"He is of the clan Ap'Lydin, Seanmháthair," Morgan said.

The Seeress' eyes opened wide. "Is that so? But I thought the Heir of Lydin was safely ensconced in his fortress in the Occupied Lands? This doesn't make sense."

There it was again. Heir of Lydin.

"Maybe there is more than one Heir of Lydin," Morgan mused.

"How do you know that he is of Ap'Lydin blood?" the Seeress demanded.

"I heard his companions say it," Morgan said. She sounded defensive.

The Seeress looked at Bellaydin sceptically. "You. Enparran. Is this true? Are you an Ap'Lydin?"

Bellaydin's head throbbed as thoughts swum around in his mind. While it was perhaps foolish of him to tell this stranger his name, this might be his only chance to discover what was going on. "Yes," he said. "My name is Bellaydin Ap'Lydin."

"So, my grandchild speaks the truth," said the Seeress. "You are an Ap'Lydin." She paused, looking him up and down. "Yet you speak the tongue of the Enparrans and your face is that of a Dafor…"

"He says he was raised by the Fey," Morgan added.

"You are the child of Fey? That, I did not see…" She turned to Morgan.

"What is it, Seanmháthair?"

"Gariníon. Leave us," the Seeress said. "Wait outside, if you must."

"Yes Seanmháthair," Morgan said, rising from the table and leaving the cavern.

After Morgan was out of sight, the Seeress turned back to Bellaydin. "So, young Ap'Lydin… what is it you seek here? Answers?"

"I just want to get back. My friends are in danger. We were captured by the Goriinchians and–"

"That is not what I asked, child," the Seeress said. "Why are you here?"

"Well," Bellaydin said. "It was your granddaughter who brought me here."

"So it was, so it was," the Seeress replied. "She thinks you may be the Heir of Lydin."

"She and a lot of other people," said Bellaydin. "And most of them seem to want to kill me."

The Seeress stared at him for a few moments before speaking again.

"That is to be expected. Do you know what the Heir of Lydin is?"

"No. I know I'm supposed to be him, that's all."

"No, you are not," said the Seeress. "But you could be, child. You could be."

"What do you mean?" asked Bellaydin.

"The Heir of Lydin is a figure of prophecy, my child. The question is… do you fit this prophecy?"

"What prophecy?"

"The Heir of Lydin is the third and final messenger of the Horned God – a prophet whose coming has been foretold for centuries."

"If the Heir of Lydin is supposed to be some sort of prophet for the Horned God, why in the name of the Underworld are his worshippers trying to kill me?"

"As I said, you are not the Heir. Not yet."

Bellaydin was confused and frustrated. The conversation was increasingly cryptic, and was going nowhere. Besides, it occurred to him that he had been here for quite a while, and Kahlaf and Geoffrey were still in danger – if they were alive at all. He had to get out of here. He started to stand, but the Seeress slammed a withered palm on his arm, holding his hand to the table.

"Where are you going, child?" the old woman said.

"Where am I going? Where do you think? My friends are about to die unless I do something," Bellaydin said.

The old woman laughed – a horrible, screeching sound, like that of a harpy. "Your friends will die regardless of what you do, child," the Seeress said. "Do you really think you can rescue them from the largest army ever seen in Goriinchia. Alone?"

Bellaydin's stomach sank. The Seeress was right. What on earth did he think he was going to do? Run into the camp and face thousands of heavily armed Goriinchian soldiers without so much as a weapon himself? Free his friends, and then the three of them would fight their way through an entire army and on to safety?

He scolded himself. *Don't be ridiculous*, he thought. *You'd only get yourself killed.* The Seeress seemed to notice his internal conflict. Perhaps she could read it on his face.

"Sometimes, child," she said, "we find discretion is the better part of valour. And cowardice is the best path. Do you not see?"

Bellaydin nodded slowly, even though somewhere, deep in the back of his mind, a voice cried out for him to say otherwise.

"So He –Who – Might –Be – Heir, is it answers you want?" the Seeress asked.

"Yes," Bellaydin said softly. "Tell me."

The old woman smiled again, her wide gap-toothed grin unsettling Bellaydin as much as it had the first time. With a gnarled hand she reached across the table and grabbed a curved, pointed piece of bone. She held it in front of her face, admiring it in the candlelight. Then, with barely a sound, she once again held Bellaydin's hand to the table.

"Wait, what are you –" Before Bellaydin could finish the Seeress rammed the bone straight through the middle of Bellaydin's palm. He yelped in pain as blood spurted from the wound, coating the bone in the Seeress' hands.

"Are you mad? What in the name of the Underworld are you doing?" Bellaydin said, ripping his injured hand from the Seeress' grip and staring with astonishment at the bloody wound. "Why did you do that to my hand?"

"You said you wanted answers, child. That is what pain brings," the

Seeress said.

Bellaydin stared in shock at the Seeress, still clutching his own hand. "If I'd known you were speaking of a metaphor, witch, then I'd…"

She ignored him, taking the bloodied bone and throwing it onto the saucer in front of her, covering it with various herbs and reagents. Then, reaching for the fire, she withdrew a stick, flaming at one end, and set the concoction in the saucer alight.

"What is this?" Bellaydin asked as the smoke began to rise from the saucer.

"Why, child, these are your answers."

Bellaydin blinked. He still did not understand. On the table, the saucer still smouldered, giving off smoke and ash. The fumes wafted around his head, making his vision hazy. He took a breath, and inadvertently inhaled some of the acrid smoke. His vision blurred and his head throbbed, suddenly feeling far too heavy for him to keep erect. Bellaydin slumped onto the table.

And all was darkness.

CHAPTER 14

"Awaken."

Bellaydin opened his eyes, expecting to see the cave where he had passed out, and the Seeress still in front of him. But he did not.

He was not there. He was not anywhere he recognised. He stood atop a mountain bluff, standing on the edge of a cliff. Mist swirled around him, obscuring his vision. He could not see what lay in front of him, behind him or below him.

"Where am I?" Bellaydin said aloud.

"You dream, child." It was the Seeress' voice. Not from outside, but from within Bellaydin's own mind.

Bellaydin turned his head from side to side. The mist had receded slightly, allowing Bellaydin to glimpse other figures. To his left stood a middle aged man, holding a young girl protectively and, despite the unfamiliarity, Bellaydin recognised the man. It was his cousin, William Ap'Lydin. The girl must be William's daughter. To Bellaydin's right stood a young woman, dark haired, with unmistakeable pointed ears.

Polnygar.

"Pol!" Bellaydin yelled out, waving to his sister.

But there was no response. Polnygar did not even move her head. "William!" Bellaydin yelled out to his cousin.

"They cannot hear you, child. They dream too. What you see are merely the images you hold in your own mind."

"But they seem so real. And my cousin, his daughter, I barely know them. How is it I dream of them?"

"A sending. Each of you here dreams this dream, all at the same time. But you cannot interact."

"We're all dreaming this?" Bellaydin said. "Why?"

"These are the last of the great bloodline, Bellaydin. These are the Heirs of Lydin."

"Great bloodline? What do you mean?"

"Ah, child. You, like the others, do not yet realise your significance, nor why you are important to the Horned God."

"And why is that?"

"These times were foretold, child."

"What? What does that mean?"

"If you seek answers, look into the valley below."

With those words the remaining fog melted away to reveal a vast, open plain miles below the cliff. In the valley swarmed a massive army – three, five, maybe ten thousand men strong. Bellaydin's vantage point allowed him to see the force's full extent. The great mass formed around a single focal point, a raised hill, upon which stood a massive tower, black as night, and radiating a pale light in the twilight.

"What is this? War? Where are we?"

"We are in Goriinchia, child," the Seeress said, *"But not as it is now. This is the Goriinchia that once was."*

"Karlicia," Bellaydin breathed.

"Yes, that is what they call it. What you see now is a vision of things that have passed. The Last Great War Against the Fey."

"The Fey… you mean elves?"

"The Lords of the Fey were the ancient rulers of Karlicia, until the men rose up against them. The Lords may have had great power, but humanity had numbers on its side and, one by one, the great citadels of the Fey were toppled until only one remained — this one before you. Even now, below, as you watch, the Fey Lords send their minions against the humans."

"What does this have to do with me?" asked Bellaydin. "This happened thousands of years ago, did it not?"

"The humans are led by one General Lydin, the greatest hero of Karlicia. You, your sister, your cousin… you are all his heirs."

"The Heir of Lydin," Bellaydin breathed.

He looked down into the valley, watching as battle raged below. The Seeress was right. The humans had the numbers, but the masters of the citadel had their own troops, but Bellaydin could not see what sort of soldier they might be. The masters also wielded potent magic, and as Bellaydin watched, a bolt of lightning exploded from one of the higher levels of the tower, wiping out hundreds of humans with a single arc.

"But what does it all mean?"

Bellaydin suddenly threw his head back and screamed out in agony. An intense pain had erupted in his head, forcing him to his feet. He huddled on the ground, his head in his hands, sweat glistening on his forehead.

"What is going on?" he asked, getting on to his feet as the pain ebbed.

"The End."

Below, a great hush suddenly descended on the valley. As Bellaydin watched, the pale light glowing in the tower expanded and brightened, enveloping the whole tower, the armies around it, and eventually the entire valley. A great rush of noise, like the whoosh of thunder, accompanied the spread of light. Then the valley exploded.

Bellaydin was thrown back by the impact of the explosion, landing on his back. A great cloud of smoke and vapour, shaped like a mushroom, wafted from the valley. Scrambling over to the edge of the cliff, Bellaydin looked over to the valley below, his eyes wide with shock. Nothing was left except the smoking ruins of the tower. Of the great armies that had clustered around them, there was no sign. The verdant grasslands on which they stood was black, burnt and devoid of life.

"And that, child, was the end of the Fey, and of General Lydin. But his line lives on."

"In me," Bellaydin added.

"Yes. You and your kin. But only one is the true Heir."

"And who is that?" Bellaydin asked.

From the Seeress there was no response. Instead, Bellaydin felt a slight tingling sensation, and a cool breeze brushing his ankles.

"What on –"

With a jolt, he found himself lifted into the air, levitating as if dangling from some unseen string. His body lurched forward, and, with little warning, whatever force that was controlling Bellaydin flung him head first over the edge of the cliff. Frantically flailing in the air, fear gripped him as he hurtled towards the valley below. The black ground, charred corpses and crumbling citadel all loomed larger as he fell towards them. He tried to scream, but no sound came out of his mouth.

The ground rushed to meet him.

***

When he awoke, Bellaydin was lying in the cool grass, completely unharmed. His forehead was still damp with sweat, a testament to how vivid the dream had been. A young woman stood above him, her eyes studying him with concern.

Morgan.

"What did you see, Enparran?" she asked.

"A lot… I'm… not sure what it all means," Bellaydin confessed. He rubbed his palm. The wound was no longer fresh. In fact, it had begun to heal. How long had he been dreaming?

Morgan seemed to read his thoughts. "You were out for three days, Enparran."

"Three days?" he said, incredulously. "No wonder I feel famished."

He stood up slowly, rubbing his head, still sore and muddled from the experience. As he did so, another realisation hit him. Three days ago, he was in the prison in the Goriinchian camp – with the others. "Oh no, oh no. Geoffrey… Kahlaf… I've been out three days. I don't even know if they're still alive."

"If they are dead, we can only hope they accepted the Horned God in their final moments, and have joined him in paradise," Morgan said quietly.

Somehow that didn't reassure Bellaydin.

"Come, we must return to camp."

"Wait, you're taking me back to that cage?" Bellaydin said, his eyes wide. "You can't do that."

She cocked her head. "Why not?"

"Well, they'll kill me."

"If it is the Horned God's will, then there is nothing we can do to

221

change it."

Bellaydin's frustration boiled over. "Damn the Horned God's will! I'm not prepared to die for someone else's god."

Morgan looked downcast, and her next words were very soft. "The Horned God is the lord of all creation. All humanity are his children, even those who have gone astray, or those who have never heard his voice."

Bellaydin grabbed Morgan's wrist and stared at her.

"Look, I don't know. Maybe you're right, maybe not. All I know is that if you take me back to that cage, I'll be killed. I'm not going to let that happen. I'm going to see if my friends are still alive. You can come with me, or you can stay here. But I'm telling you, there's no way I'm walking to the gallows without a fight."

"Your friends are probably already dead, Enparran," Morgan added softly.

"Maybe, but I don't know that for sure. And if there's any chance they're still alive, then it's worth the risk."

***

Polnygar awoke, shivering. The dream was so vivid, so real, and Bellaydin was there, just as she had remembered him, standing next to her. The visions still ran through her mind – an ancient battle in a faraway land, and a phrase, repeated over and over.

Heir of Lydin.

"My dear," Aelzandar said, his face obscured in the darkness. "You look a little startled. Is something the matter?"

"I had a dream… nightmare. I'm not sure," Polnygar said, rubbing her temples.

"A nightmare?" Aelzandar said. "It has been a long journey, my dear, and a stressful few weeks. I'm not surprised. Of what did you dream?"

"It was the strangest thing," said Polnygar. "I dreamt of a battle, an ancient battle. There was a citadel, I think. That story you told me, of the Soldara? I think it was one of their towers."

"A citadel of the Soldara?" said Aelzandar. "That is a curious thing to appear in your dreams, my dear. You must have listening to my ramblings fairly closely."

"I guess I was. There was something else."

"Oh?"

"I kept hearing three words, over and over again," Polnygar said. "Heir of Lydin."

Aelzandar gave a thoughtful look.

"The same thing those thugs called me who attacked me."

"Indeed. But those were not mere thugs," said Aelzandar. "They were the followers of the Horned God, the divine overlord of Goriinchia."

Polnygar nodded. "That's what they said." She paused. "Why would I dream of such things?"

Aelzandar was soothing. "As I said, it has been a trying couple of weeks."

"Yes, but," Polnygar said, leaning back, "it seemed so real. As if I was there. And Bela was there too."

"Your brother?" said Aelzandar.

"Yes, and my cousin, William, was in the dream as well."

The Nemoi laughed. "Doesn't sound like any of my dreams. Sounds more like a family reunion."

"Quiet, Hebu," Aelzandar said.

"Yes, master," Hebu said, grumbling to himself as he walked away.

223

"Do you know what any of it means?" Polnygar said.

"What it means?" said Aelzandar. "It was probably just a dream. They don't mean very much."

"But the words…"

"The words are significant on the face of it, in their own right, regardless of the dream. Perhaps we can discover something about that in Ralom."

"Why would there be anything about it there?"

"The Holy City is quite a cosmopolitan place, and has more religions in one street than you would find in all of Orspederia. If there's some ridiculous prophecy at work here, we'll be able to find something of interest there. But that can all wait. Ivellios is our first priority."

"And Augustin," Polnygar said.

"And Augustin," Aelzandar agreed.

He looked at Polnygar. "I want to believe you about him, my dear, I really do. But for now, I must assume his guilt, and proceed accordingly. To do otherwise, to presume that he is somehow controlled against his own will and can be safely ignored. That would endanger us both."

Polnygar nodded. She knew that Aelzandar spoke the truth. They could take nothing for granted. She walked to the edge of the barge, looking out. The river was still, the night sky reflected in the water. She shivered, anxiety washing over her. In a few days they would be in Ralom. What would face them when they finally arrived?

***

Bellaydin lifted his head tentatively, peering over the rocks.

"What do you see?" Morgan asked.

For nearly a minute, Bellaydin did not respond as he looked towards the camp site, squinting in the early morning sunlight. He saw Kahlaf and Geoffrey, still in their cages. They were both shifting about inside. "They're alive," Bellaydin said, breathing a sigh of relief.

Morgan frowned. "Are you sure? They were to be executed. The sentence is almost always carried out, especially with regards to infidels and spies."

"I don't know why, and I don't know how," Bellaydin said, "but they're both still alive. They're there… in chains, near those soldiers."

Morgan scrambled up the incline until she was next to Bellaydin, and looked towards the campsite, holding her head up for a better look.

"You are right," she said. "We should thank the Horned God for his grace and intervention."

Bellaydin pretended he did not hear. The Horned God was the last person he felt like thanking. Morgan was right about one thing, however. It did seem strange that the Goriinchians had put neither Geoffrey nor Kahlaf to death. He wondered what exactly was going on.

"We should go back. Surrender ourselves," Morgan said.

"No," said Bellaydin testily. "Don't you dare."

Morgan glanced his way briefly, then turned her head away and sat down beside him sullenly. "Then what is it you want, Enparran? I told you that your friends would have to remain here. I promised nothing."

"Still doesn't mean I'm not going to try and save them."

The girl looked at him quizzically, tilting her head as she regarded him. "You are strange, Enparran, very strange."

"I have a name," he said, as he continued to watch the camp.

"Sorry. You are strange, Bellaydin Ap'Lydin."

He was about to tell Morgan that "just Bellaydin was fine", but remembered the confusion it had caused before and decided to avoid the misunderstanding by not correcting her.

What should he do? What could he do? Charging straight in there would mean death, there was no doubt about that. He could not leave without Kahlaf and Geoffrey. Even discounting the moral question involved, he would never survive the trip to Emparia without their help. And then there was Morgan. Bellaydin had trouble figuring her out. On one hand, she wanted to hand him straight back to the Goriinchians but, on the other hand, she had made no real move to do so. What was really going on here? He turned to Morgan.

"Do you think it would be possible for us to get closer?" he said.

"Yes," Morgan said, standing up.

"No, no!" Bellaydin pulled her back down. "I meant, without them seeing us."

Morgan frowned. "It might be possible," she said. "Why do you want to get closer?"

"I want to be able to hear what they're saying."

"You don't speak the holy tongue, Enparran."

Bellaydin nodded in agreement, then said, "But you do."

***

Geoffrey scratched his chin idly, trying to make sense of his situation. This was doubly difficult, due to the combined effect of the chains on his wrists and the throbbing in his head.

He should be dead. That was what he had been told. The Goriinchian soldiers had jeered and yelled at him for hours over his impending gruesome fate, and then nothing. He was taken to his cage, along with Kahlaf, the pair of them chained together. Then they were left in the company of a few surly soldiers, who had done nothing except glare at them. To top it off, Bellaydin was nowhere to be seen. Had they already killed him? Had they transferred him to a different prison camp? Geoffrey did not know. He hoped for the best, but prepared himself for the worse.

"So, here are the mongrel dogs of the north," said an approaching Goriinchian, spitting out the words of Emparian as if the very act of saying them poisoned his tongue.

Kahlaf growled, but Geoffrey said nothing.

The Goriinchian turned to one of the guards and spoke a few words in his own language. The guard nodded and opened Geoffrey's cage, but kept his weapon pointed at the knight.

"I know you recognise me, Enparrans, as I recognise you," the Goriinchian said, clutching the holy symbol that hung around his neck.

"Cathan Culainn," Geoffrey said. "Brother to the Warchief."

The Goriinchian looked offended, and slapped Geoffrey across his face, snarling. "I am the High Priest of the Horned God. The right hand of the one true Lord! You should not address me in such familiar terms."

Cathan swung at Geoffrey again, landing another blow on the knight, and knocking him to the ground. Then the Goriinchian trampled Geoffrey's fingers with his boot, a satisfied look spreading across his face as Geoffrey's hands crunched beneath his foot. "Consider that a warning from on high, infidel," Cathan said. "Learn your place." Cathan turned to the soldiers. "It is time. Bring them."

The soldiers nodded, and hauled Geoffrey up from the dirt. Three of them grabbed Kahlaf as well, and they half-pushed, half-dragged the Ahktarran and Geoffrey across the camp, with Cathan leading the way.

"Where are you taking us?" Geoffrey spluttered.

Cathan stopped in his tracks, and turned around. "You are most fortunate, infidel. Despite your lack of faith and your heathen ways, the Horned God has smiled on you. The sentence of death has been commuted on the orders of King Ygarak himself. The Prophet-King demands your presence."

"Why?" Geoffrey said.

"That is not for us to know, infidel," Cathan said. "Perhaps you are to pay him homage."

They reached a large, ornate tent in the centre of the camp. It was much more lavish than the ones that surrounded it, so Geoffrey was not surprised when Cathan announced that this was the King's tent. The presence of the king with the army, however, was deeply troubling. This was no mere skirmish that the Goriinchians were planning to launch. Ygarak was obviously intent on an extensive campaign.

"Take them inside," said Cathan.

The interior of the tent was large, spacious, and well furnished. At one end rose a throne, atop which sat a figure who Geoffrey reasoned could only be the King of the Goriinchians, Ygarak himself.

Geoffrey had heard the descriptions of the Goriinchian King, but little could have prepared him for the sight that was before him. A giant of a man, eight inches over six feet, Ygarak wore a concealing suit of finely crafted armour, its metal plates decorated with Goriinchian symbols and patterns. A tattered tartan cloak completed the royal garb and a great horned helmet covered the Goriinchian king's head, giving nothing but the barest glimpse of Ygarak's eyes.

Geoffrey and Kahlaf were driven to their knees by a series of swift blows from the guards.

"It does not suit you to stand in the presence of greatness, infidel," hissed Cathan. He took a step forward before he too lowered himself to the ground. "Great King," Cathan said, prostrating himself before Ygarak. "Prophet of Prophets. Right Hand of the Horned God. The one true Lord of Karlicia."

There was a silence as Ygarak regarded the scene in front of him. Then the king spoke. "Rise Cathan Culainn, honoured servant. And you rise too, infidels."

Geoffrey was taken aback by the sound of the Goriinchian King's voice. Ygarak spoke with a commanding, almost impossibly deep bass. The sound of his voice sent shivers down the Emparian's spine.

"You tremble, infidel," said Ygarak, "and I know why. You are overawed by my presence. After so many years of following false prophets, you are surprised to find yourself face to face with a real one."

"Face?" said Kahlaf. "I see nothing but a mask. Show yourself, coward."

There was silence as no one spoke. Finally, after an agonisingly long wait, Ygarak laughed a deep, almost metallic chuckle that reverberated throughout the room.

"You are brave, beast," said Ygarak, "but mistaken as to your own importance. I am Ygarak, and you are nothing. To gaze upon my face would kill you. No infidel could gaze upon my holy form and live. I have been blessed by the Horned God, the One who reigns over all."

"He does not reign over me," Kahlaf said.

"Ah, but in time he will," said Ygarak, his voice growing deeper. "I, as foretold, will spread the true faith to the lands of the north, and one day the entire world will bow down to the Horned God."

"Never," Kahlaf murmured. But Geoffrey noticed the Ahktarran did not say that with confidence.

"There are many in the occupied lands who already sympathise with our cause, of course," Cathan cut in. "Despite the attempts of some to cover up the truth, to confound the innocent with dreams of false gods and depraved decadence."

"I don't believe you," said Geoffrey. "The last worshippers of the Horned God in Emparia disappeared years ago."

Cathan said nothing, but smiled. Ygarak began to laugh again.

"Delude yourself if you wish, Enparran," the Goriinchian king said. "But know that I have infiltrated every last inch of the occupied lands, and you are fortunate that I have for it has saved your wretched little lives."

"Wait... what?" said Geoffrey.

"I am sparing you. Consider it an act of mercy."

"You're sparing us? Why?" Geoffrey said.

"I am freeing you, infidels, so that you may run back to the occupied lands, and cry to your little queen that her reign will soon end," Ygarak said, leaning back into his throne. "Or do you wish me to reconsider?"

"Your Holiness..." stammered Cathan. "Are you sure about this? Mercy to these... infidels. It seems so strange."

With surprising speed, Ygarak stood, withdrew his sword and pointed it straight at the high priest's throat.

"Cathan," Ygarak said in a low voice, "you forget your place. I suggest you remember it, and quickly."

Cathan, humiliated, threw himself to the ground and, in between tears and moans, begged his king for forgiveness. "Great King, forgive me, I spoke ill... it was the presence of the infidels so close to your holy person. Such a thing has me unnerved."

Ygarak sat down on the throne, wrapping his cloak around him. "You are forgiven, High Priest. I know that you serve me in all things, and without question, unlike some of my followers."

It appeared to Geoffrey that Cathan knew who Ygarak referred to, as the High Priest nodded quietly, and made a sign to ward off evil.

"Cathan," said Ygarak, "you shall see to it that my will is done. The prisoners are to be taken to the outskirts of our camp and left there, stripped of their possessions. They have four days to reach their brethren in the north."

"What happens after four days?" asked Geoffrey.

Cathan smirked, and touched the weapon at his side.

"We follow, infidel. And my soldiers, the army of the Horned God, will destroy everything in its path," Ygarak said.

"You're going to attack Emparia in four days?"

"That is correct, infidel," said Cathan. "So you'd better hurry if you want to warn your lord. Guards!"

Hearing Cathan's voice, the guards once again grabbed Geoffrey and Kahlaf. As they were escorted from his presence, the pair heard the voice of King Ygarak mocking them as they departed.

"Soon you will run, little Enparran – you and your tame beast. Run back to your master and know that I follow."

***

"Enparran. I see them."

Snapping to attention, Bellaydin looked in the direction Morgan was pointing. Some distance away a group of Goriinchian soldiers was herding two blindfolded figures to the edge of the military camp. Bellaydin squinted. Even if he had not recognised Geoffrey, Kahlaf's form was unmistakable, even from this distance.

"That's them alright," he said. "What is happening? Are they being released?"

Morgan shrugged. "Perhaps the Horned God has heard our prayers, Enparran."

"You mean your prayers," he said.

Morgan looked at him and smiled. "I was praying enough for the both of us, you know."

"I don't doubt that. Looks like your God came through for us though. The soldiers are leaving."

Sure enough the soldiers escorted Geoffrey and Kahlaf to a distance outside the edge of the Goriinchian camp and then, making sure they were tightly bound with rope, abandoned them both, and returned to the camp.

Morgan stood.

"Wait," Bellaydin said. "I don't like this. It's strange. What in the gods name is going on here? First they want to kill us, now they're letting us go? Why?"

Morgan uttered her usual response. "It is the Horned God's will."

Bellaydin closed his eyes and said quietly, "I knew you were going to say that."

Morgan only smiled enigmatically in response, and, turning her back on Bellaydin, began to walk towards Geoffrey and Kahlaf. Bellaydin's eyes widened. They were still within the borders of the Goriinchian military camp and liable to be seen at any moment, yet here was Morgan, walking towards the prisoners without a care in the world.

"Gods damn it." Bellaydin whispered behind her, slipping on the wet grass as he tried to stand. "Come back Morgan, it's not safe."

But Morgan was already off, walking towards the slumped forms of Kahlaf and Geoffrey. Bellaydin ran after her.

"Careful, we're going to be seen," Bellaydin said, grabbing Morgan's arm.

"The Horned God will protect us," Morgan said. "He is guiding our path."

A few muffled sounds attracted his attention. A short distance from Bellaydin a blindfolded and gagged Geoffrey Keslin struggled against the rope that bound his hands.

"Oh, in the name of…" Bellaydin ripped off Geoffrey's blindfold.

Geoffrey's eyes widened as he looked around, and recognised Bellaydin. "Mwmewwadwin." Geoffrey mumbled through the gag. Chuckling, Bellaydin removed the gag from Geoffrey's mouth. "Bellaydin!" Geoffrey repeated.

"What is going on here? How did you escape?"

"I should ask you the same question," Geoffrey said. "But unfortunately, it's hard to talk when the ropes are cutting into my wrists."

"Oh, sorry," said Bellaydin.

As he struggled to untangle the knot on Geoffrey's wrists, Bellaydin turned to Morgan and said quietly, "While I'm doing this can you free the, uh, friend of ours over there?"

Morgan looked towards the growling, struggling Ahktarran snarling in the grass only a few feet away.

"He doesn't bite," said Geoffrey, "…much."

***

Much later, both Geoffrey and Kahlaf were free, and the group quickly brought each other up to speed on what had occurred. Bellaydin, however, decided to keep his experiences with the Seeress to himself. It did not seem right to relate the vision to Kahlaf and Geoffrey. He had no idea how they might react to the information. After the discussions had ended, Morgan, having stood out of hearing range at Kahlaf and Geoffrey's request, approached Bellaydin.

"Enparran," Morgan said. "You have found your friends, it is… it is time for me to leave."

Despite her words, from the tone of Morgan's voice and the look on her face, it was obvious to Bellaydin that the Goriinchian was somewhat reluctant to do so.

"You don't have to go, Morgan," Bellaydin said. "You can come with us, if you want, back to Emparia. My cousin is an important man. He can –"

"No, Enparran," Morgan said softly, cutting Bellaydin off mid-sentence. "I can't leave my father, or my grandmother. They're all I have in the world. I'm sorry. I must go back to them."

Bellaydin nodded. "What if they suspect that you helped me escape?" he said.

"Without any real proof, they wouldn't dare accuse me of anything. They fear my father. They know our family has the favour of both the Prophet and the Horned God."

She turned to the horizon, looking back towards the Goriinchian camp. "Oh, they may say things to themselves. They may curse my name under their breath, but they won't say anything to my face. They probably won't even ask where I've been." She turned to Bellaydin again. "Here," she said, pulling some sort of scroll from her belt, "take this."

"What is it?" Bellaydin said, accepting the gift from her.

"The Sayings of the Prophet," Morgan said. "The Holy Word of the Horned God."

"I can't accept this," Bellaydin said, handing it back to her. "It must be worth a lot."

"It is just a copy of the original, Enparran," Morgan said. "And I want you to have it. You don't believe in the Horned God. But maybe I can open your eyes. It is the least I can do for you."

Bellaydin's hand slackened, and he managed a smile. "Ah… thanks."

Morgan smiled. "Goodbye, Bellaydin Ap'Lydin. I don't know if you truly are the Heir of Lydin, but I am happy to have met you all the same."

With those words, Morgan Culainn disappeared into the night. Bellaydin stood still as she left, watching her figure until she finally vanished into the murky gloom.

"Don't feel too bad, Ap'Lydin," said a voice. "It would have never worked out."

Bellaydin turned around to see Geoffrey standing behind him.

"What?" Bellaydin said.

"I saw how you were looking at her."

"I wasn't looking at her like that," Bellaydin said, flushing.

"Uh huh," said Geoffrey, brushing down his filthy tunic. "You be careful around those Goriinchians girls, Bela. You let them sink their claws into you, and the next thing you know, you're face down in some Goriinchian temple slobbering before the Horned God."

"I'll try and remember your advice," Bellaydin said drily.

"We should get moving," grunted Kahlaf. "We have little time to spare."

Geoffrey nodded his assent. Patting himself down, Geoffrey took a look at their surroundings, and glanced at the horizon apprehensively.

"I figure we are about a day and a half south of the border. If I remember correctly, the closest town is Wishapton. It's a small settlement that lies in the very southern regions of the Earldom of Genio. If we can reach there, we can hopefully send a message to Earl William."

"A day and a half's journey," said Bellaydin. "That gives us, what? Two and a half days to get a message to Genio?"

"It's not long enough," grunted Kahlaf.

"Well, those are the cards we've been dealt," Geoffrey said.

"So it seems," said Kahlaf. "We'd better get moving."

***

William Ap'Lydin entered the study. "You asked for me, Your Grace?" he said.

"Yes, my boy," said Haakon, placing the book he was reading down on the table. He approached William, keeping his voice low. "I have some information that might interest you."

William looked interested. "What is it?"

Haakon moved his face closer. "They are alive."

William blinked in surprise. "Geoffrey is alive? My cousin too?"

Haakon nodded.

"How can you be sure?" William asked.

"I mentioned my contacts, didn't I? The message just arrived. The Goriinchians have released them. As we speak, your cousin and his companions are probably making their way north."

William exhaled. "They're alive. But by the gods, what is the game here?"

Haakon looked confused. "I'm sorry, William?"

"The Goriinchians. Why did they release Geoffrey and my cousin? For what purpose?"

Haakon looked nervous. "I'm not sure, William. I can only tell you what I know," he said.

"They're up to something, I can feel it. I wouldn't be surprised if it's tied in with some sort of attack upon Emparian territory. I should make preparations…"

William turned to leave, but Haakon grabbed his arm. "William. You must promise me. Not a word of this to Wulfric."

"You don't want me to tell the Duke of Oldharbour? Why not?"

"Wulfric and I do not see eye to eye on every issue. I've told you that before. He wouldn't approve of these... contacts... of mine in Goriinchia."

William raised an eyebrow. "I thought the word amongst court was that I was the single-issue anti-Goriinchian fanatic."

Haakon's face relaxed. "If you think that's bad, you should see what they say about me behind my back. Being the queen's cousin doesn't automatically endear you to everyone, my boy, let me tell you." He narrowed his eyes. "You don't approve of my contacts either, do you William?"

William hesitated, trying to find the right words.

"It's not my place to approve or disapprove, Your Grace. I'm sure you have your reasons and they do seem to have come in handy."

"But...?" said Haakon.

"But it does seem dangerous. I mean, how do you know you can trust them? How do you know they won't betray you to Ygarak or his generals?"

"That is always a danger, William," said Haakon. "But I trust these contacts implicitly. We both wish for a brighter future for our nations on this continent, and an end to the distrust and jingoism that brings war after war."

William sighed. "You may have a point. And for now it seems to have paid off. We need all the information on the Goriinchians we can get."

Haakon nodded.

"Now, how long until they reach Emparia?"

"What?" Haakon said suddenly.

"Geoffrey and my cousin, how long until they reach Emparia?" William looked at Haakon. The duke's face had gone quite pale.

"Haakon, are you feeling alright?"

Haakon rubbed his forehead. "Oh, sorry. Yes, I'm fine. Just tired, that's all." He paused to catch his breath. "Geoffrey's group, well, from what I've learned, they were probably less than two days on foot away."

"Good. I'll organise some of the guard to meet them and bring them here," William said, turning to leave. "Oh, Your Grace?"

"Yes, William?"

"Get some rest. You look terrible."

Haakon nodded, smiling weakly.

CHAPTER 15

"I see him, master," Polnygar said.

Aelzandar stopped, and looked across the plaza, to the crowd milling on the other side. "I see him too, my dear girl," Aelzandar said. "And what's more, I think he sees us."

"He's still got that Emparian on a leash, my lord," said Hebu.

"You mean Augustin," Polnygar corrected him.

"Augustin, right…" Hebu barely even glanced at the girl.

The journey to Ralom had been long and somewhat arduous, but, as soon as they reached the fabled holy city, Polnygar did not take long to decide it was well worth the trip. While not as large as other cities in the lands of Carurlonia, Ralom far surpassed any other in sheer magnificence. A grand and ancient metropolis bisected by the river and sheltered by the mountains, Ralom was set against the vivid backdrop of a great waterfall. One of the largest in the world, it was known in the Ralomish tongue as 'The Smoke that Thunders'. Its waters shrouded Ralom in almost permanent mist.

"The City of the Three Gods," Aelzandar had said as they entered. "The sacred triune of the western realms – the Sun King, the Silver Lady and the Divine Martyr – are all worshipped within these sacred walls."

"How melodramatic," Hebu responded, rolling his eyes. "Where's the dignity?"

"Quiet, Hebu. Ralom is one of the wonders of the world."

"It demonstrates how stupid humans can be, does it not? I mean, right in front of them they see the wondrous work of the Celestial Architects – consider the intricate inner workings of the dragon fly, for instance – yet humankind gets dewy-eyed over a bunch of rocks arranged in a semi-attractive fashion. Why, it reminds me of a particularly elegant piece of verse written during the reign of the fourth Emperor of ancient Davorea. If I recall correctly…"

Hebu droned on and on, and Polnygar found herself starting to tune out the Nemoi scholar's ramblings. Aelzandar was right. Ralom was a wonder. From its elegant, well-planned streets and boulevards, through the shrines and temples that crowded its suburbs, to, finally, the magnificent basilica that stood, tall and proud, in the exact centre of the city. Built from marble, whiter than any Polnygar had ever seen, it was a fitting testament to the strength and glory of the Church of Ralom. Atop the basilica, three elegant spires reached towards the sky, symbolising the triune of deities to whom Ralom was dedicated.

Polnygar suddenly became aware of the silence around her. Hebu had stopped talking, and now he and the archmage were both looking at Polnygar expectantly.

"Don't let the beauty of the holy city distract you, my dear," Aelzandar cautioned. "We have an important job to do, after all."

Polnygar nodded. Aelzandar did not have to say the name. They all knew who they were after – Ivellios. Somewhat surprisingly, the spellweaver hadn't been that difficult to track once they entered the city proper. Every citizen they passed had heard of the "elven lord" and his "loyal man at arms". Polnygar knew who the latter was: Augustin Bauer, the traitor. Or so it seemed. Polnygar herself was not sure. Hebu certainly seemed to think so, openly referring to Augustin as a "gods-cursed turncoat" whenever the opportunity arose. Aelzandar, for his part, was silent on the topic. Did he suspect something else?

Polnygar had privately decided long ago that it was impossible that Augustin was aiding Ivellios of his own free will. First of all, from what she had seen the Emparian and the spellweaver shared a mutual loathing. Secondly, the time she had spent with Bauer prior to the betrayal had convinced her that he was an honourable man, and not one to betray the trust of his friends and allies. So what had happened then? In Polnygar's mind, there was only one conclusion. Ivellios was a powerful spellweaver – one of the most powerful in all of Aderilund, in fact – so was it not possible, nay, likely, that he had used that power to ensnare Augustin into his service?

Of course, the one question that remained was why. Why Augustin? Perhaps Aelzandar was too powerful in his own right for Ivellios to control. Yet if that were so, Polnygar thought, why had the spellweaver made no attempt to enchant her? Was she really that strong-minded or resistant to such powers? Or was it merely a lack of opportunity? Or perhaps it was the opposite. Ivellios may have seen Augustin as the bigger danger and not have even considered her a threat.

"He's in the central plaza, master," Hebu said. "Almost everyone I've spoken to has confirmed it. They're saying the "great elven lord" is giving a speech to the masses, right in the shadow of the great basilica."

"Is that so?" Aelzandar said.

"What do you suppose he's giving a speech about?" said Polnygar.

"Nothing of great merit, I'd argue," said Aelzandar. "He always was a rather bombastic over-opinionated fool, even when I knew him in his youth. Age does not appear to have worked much improvement, either."

Polnygar turned her head towards Aelzandar. She was surprised at the force with which the normally gentle-minded archmage delivered the character assessment.

"How shall we proceed, my lord?" Hebu asked.

"Carefully," Aelzandar responded. "We don't know what tricks he might have up his sleeve, or how many additional minions he may have gathered since he left Macrodonia. We should be cautious."

"Right," Hebu nodded. The Nemoi turned to Polnygar. "I hope you're paying attention, girl," he said. "We don't want any sort of recklessness."

"What do you mean?" said Polnygar, sounding hurt.

"Your little stunt back in the streets of Macrodonia put you in prison, if you'll recall. I wouldn't try it here in Ralom. The crusader-knights here have a reputation for being quite zealous, and have a quite astonishing phobia of witches."

"I'll keep that in mind," Polnygar said. She did not really believe the little man. As far as Polnygar was concerned, he was just trying to scare her.

"You don't believe me, do you?" Hebu responded, as if reading the girl's thoughts. "Of all the papyri in Macrodonia…" Hebu let out a torrent of curses and swearing.

Aelzandar laid a hand on the Nemoi's shoulder. "That's enough, Hebu. Your point is well-taken. We shall all be cautious."

Hebu and Polnygar both nodded.

"Let's go," Aelzandar said, and with that, the trio made their way to the central plaza.

"People of the holy city," Ivellios proclaimed to the crowd that had gathered to listen. "I consider it a great honour to speak with you here today."

There were a few murmurs of appreciation from the assembled, and a scattering of perfunctory applause.

"Here in Ralom, you have seen many wonders in your time – many priests, many prophets, many gods. Perhaps you are a little jaded, no? Of course, you have every reason to be. Many are the charlatans who have stood in this spot. Many are the impostors who have mocked you with their impiety."

"Is he including himself there?" Hebu said to Aelzandar.

"Shh," the archmage responded.

"But now, good people of the holy city. Now you are going to see something different. I am going to give you something that the others did not. I am going to give you the truth."

Polnygar looked at Hebu, who gave her a sceptical look, and then towards Aelzandar, who stared ahead with a similar expression.

"A new era is about to dawn. This I tell you not as a warning or a threat, but as a piece of good counsel – a sign to prepare yourself, for the epoch awaits." Ivellios paused, presumably for dramatic effect. "What epoch is this, you ask? What great world-changing events are almost upon us?"

Ivellios turned his head to Augustin who had been standing next to him during the sermon, showing no reaction of any kind to the words being said. "Augustin, friend, the Tears," Ivellios said.

Augustin blinked, as if coming out of a stupor, and glanced towards Ivellios. The spellweaver nodded, and Augustin placed something in Ivellios' outstretched hand.

"Behold, people of Ralom. Once lost, now found again, and brought before you. This instrument through which the world, nay, the universe, shall be remade – the Tears of the Divine."

Dangling the Tears from his fingers, Ivellios held his arms high, so that the entire crowd could see the small object glistening in the afternoon light.

"What is he, stupid?" said Hebu.

"He certainly seems foolhardy," Aelzandar said. "Or incredibly arrogant."

"That is Ivellios, alright," said Polnygar. "He thinks he's invincible."

"You'd think he'd try to conceal that he was carrying such a thing," Hebu said. "Or maybe I'm misreading the situation."

"Ivellios is arrogant, as Polnygar has said, but he is also clever. He knows what he's doing, or at least he thinks he does," Aelzandar mused.

"Well," said Polnygar. "Are we going to get the Tears back?" She drew her sword from its scabbard.

"Wait," Aelzandar said, holding his hand in front of her. "Remember caution, Polnygar. That is what we said would use."

"Right," said Polnygar, gripping the hilt of her sword. "Caution."

Next to her, Hebu smirked. "Easy now, girl."

"People of the holy city, rejoice! The Tears herald the end of the old order of things. They shall wash away the flotsam and jetsam of the past, destroy all which has become stagnant."

The spellweaver continued with his speech, his words becoming more florid and overblown as he went on. The crowd became noisier. Though many scoffed and laughed at his words, there were enough who took him seriously, and cheered as he shouted out his denunciation of the "stagnant" forces that supposedly controlled the world.

"Now, both of you listen to me," Aelzandar said. "When we do this, we do it together, is that clear? Follow my lead, if you will."

Hebu nodded, and Polnygar did as well. "If possible, we would like to apprehend them alive. But if there is no other option…" Aelzandar trailed off, and noticed the look of alarm on the young woman's face. "Polnygar, my dear, I know this may be difficult, but we must proceed with the assumption that Augustin has freely chosen to side with Ivellios…"

"But he didn't. There's no way –" Polnygar cut in.

"Listen to me, Polnygar," Aelzandar said, grabbing her by the wrist. "We must assume this. To do otherwise could be fatal. It would be very dangerous to underestimate him."

Polnygar nodded slowly, fighting back the tears.

"I know you will do the right thing, my dear," Aelzandar said gently.

Polnygar smiled weakly, but, deep down, she thought that Aelzandar's faith might be misplaced. Truth be told, Polnygar did not in fact know what she would do when the crunch came. Would she be willing to kill Augustin? And, for another matter, would she be willing to spare Ivellios, particularly after all he had done? She did not know. But she was about to find out, one way or another.

"How should we do this?" asked Hebu.

"Carefully," Aelzandar said, "And together. He may not have seen us yet."

Polnygar returned her sword to its scabbard, and the three of them moved through the crowd, cautiously. Aelzandar walked on her left, Sakkaru still strapped to his back. Hebu moved on her other flank, seemingly unfazed about facing an opponent twice his size while armed with nothing more than a bunch of papyrus scrolls. Still, Polnygar was reasonably confident, if only because there were three of them. And Polnygar was certain that, even at his age, Aelzandar had the magical prowess to best Ivellios on his own, leaving Hebu and Polnygar to handle Augustin.

But there was something else that worried her. As they pushed their way through the throng, Augustin and Ivellios hardly reacted at all. Augustin stood there, still as a statue, and Ivellios continued with his preaching. A chill went down her spine when she realised that the spellweaver's gaze had come towards her. She might have thought, even briefly, he had still not spotted her, were it not for the way that Ivellios stared at her. His eyes focused on her, penetrating her soul, gazing at her with contempt and revulsion, as he had looked at her so many times in Aderilund. He knew that they were coming for him, and if so, Polnygar expected that the spellweaver was prepared.

"He's seen us," Polnygar said. "He's looking right at me."

"It seems stealth is no longer an option," said Hebu.

Aelzandar cursed. "To the Underworld with it then. This will not be as straight-forward as I had hoped. Follow my lead."

Polnygar swallowed her fear and steeled herself to continue. The crowd began to shout and yell as the group made their way, jostling Polnygar to and fro. Finally the trio reached the podium where the spellweaver stood and he stopped talking as they approached.

"You've led us on a merry chase, Ivellios," Aelzandar said, leaning on his staff, "but it is over now. There is nowhere left for you to run. Return what you have stolen from me and I shall let you go."

Ivellios looked from Aelzandar, to Hebu, to Polnygar and then back to Aelzandar, before breaking into a wide smile. "Ah, Aelzandar. Such a pleasure to meet again. What is this property of yours I have absconded with?"

Aelzandar stared at Ivellios, his eyes set and his teeth gritted. "You know very well of what I speak, spellweaver," the archmage said. "The Tears. Return them to me. Now."

Ivellios sniffed. "My, my. Such a serious tone. One which expects to be obeyed, I gather."

The crowd began to murmur and mutter. A few scattered individuals laughed.

"Stop playing games, Ivellios," Aelzandar said. "This is serious. The Tears are dangerous in the wrong hands."

"The wrong hands? And who decides which hands are wrong? You, Aelzandar?"

There was more laughter from the crowd, along with a few cheers and jeers.

"I will not ask again. Return the Tears to their rightful owner," Aelzandar said, his grip tightening on his staff. His voice was firm, unwavering.

"Rightful owner, Aelzandar? Is that how you see it? If I recall correctly, you stole the Tears in the first place. In fact, from what I hear, you are nothing but a common tomb robber."

With those words, Aelzandar blinked. From her own vantage point, Polnygar remembered what she had been told. Even she knew that there was one thing above all others that the people of Ralom would never tolerate. That was someone who defiled the sanctity of the afterlife – a grave robber.

The crowd erupted into a fury and swarmed Aelzandar and his companions, screaming, yelling, pushing and shoving. Polnygar watched in horror as men and women grabbed and tore at the sleeves and hem of Aelzandar's robes, seeking to pull him down into the fray.

"It appears, Aelzandar, that once again your arrogance and lack of foresight have brought you down," Ivellios said, laughing as the archmage disappeared under the throng. "But you will have to excuse me, I'm afraid. I have business to attend to elsewhere. Goodbye, my friend. I'm sure we shall meet again." He smiled greasily. "That is, if you survive."

He nodded to Augustin, and the two stepped down from the podium, avoiding the seething crowd, and disappeared down one of the many nearby alleyways.

Hebu fended off a man trying to pick him up. "We can't let the spellweaver get away."

"We have other problems to deal with, Hebu," said Aelzandar, putting up a mighty struggle against the crush of people. Every time the archmage pulled himself away from one person, he was immediately grabbed by another.

Polnygar had wrested her way free from the crowd, who were mostly focused on Aelzandar, and found herself on the edge of the plaza. She looked towards Aelzandar and Hebu who, despite the brawling crowd, seemed to be in no real physical danger, and then towards the alleyway, where she heard the faint, retreating footsteps of Ivellios and Augustin. Polnygar caught Aelzandar's attention with a wave, and then pointed to the alleyway.

"Ivellios went here, master," she said, straining her voice over the din of the crowd.

"I see, Polnygar," Aelzandar shouted back. "But as you can see, I'm a little busy right now."

Polnygar looked at the alleyway, back to the crowd, then back again to the alleyway. Then, with the impulsiveness that characterised many of her decisions, Polnygar decided to do what she thought had to be done.

Waving to Aelzandar, Polnygar disappeared down the alleyway.

"What is that girl doing, my lord?" Hebu said, panting.

"No, Polnygar. Stop, it's too dangerous!"

But it was too late. Polnygar was already gone.

***

The stars over Wishapton were clear and bright as Caric stood at his post. The job of night watchman had long been a quiet one. Little had happened in this remote town for quite some time, since the height of the civil war. Despite ominous rumours and often hysterical claims, the Goriinchians were no closer to launching an invasion than they were a decade again. At least, that was how Caric saw things. Nice and quiet. Nothing to worry about. Just a few hours of easy, light duties, then retire when his replacement came on. But that was when he saw the strangers.

"Hold there a moment," Caric called out into the night. "Let me come closer, so I can get a good look at you." Picking up the flaming torch, Caric walked towards the three shadowy figures, using the torch to guide his way in the darkness. Suddenly a grotesque monster loomed in the darkness, seven foot tall, all scales and fangs.

"Of all the gods in heaven," Caric exclaimed, dropping the torch in shock. It landed in the wet grass, sizzled for a moment, and snuffed out. The creature growled. Next to it, a middle-aged man held up his hands in a peace-making gesture.

"Calm down, Kahlaf, you can scare people sometimes with that face of yours," the man said. The monster, apparently named Kahlaf, simply grunted again. Next to the man was a dark-haired youth, bedraggled and dirty. The man extended a hand. "Sir Geoffrey Keslin. I need to get a message to the earl. It's of the utmost importance. When does the next courier leave?"

Caric eyed the man. In his current squalor, the man did not exactly seem like he was the foremost knight of the Earl of Genio, but Caric sensed some urgency in the man's request.

"You can tell 'im yourself, Sir Geoffrey," Caric said. "The earl's here."

"What? He's here?" Geoffrey said.

"Aye, Sir Geoffrey. He's been expectin' you."

Apparently surprised by this news, Geoffrey nodded, and whispered something to his companions. Then he turned back to Caric. "Then there isn't a moment to lose. Let us see his lordship at once."

249

"Right away," Caric nodded, picking up the torch and relighting it. "This way, Sir Geoffrey."

As Geoffrey, Kahlaf and Bellaydin walked the narrow streets of Wishapton, a few of the townsfolk, roused from their beds by footsteps the night watchman's blazing torch, came out to watch them. Most glanced at Geoffrey and Bellaydin only briefly, and reserved their staring for the tall and exotic Ahktarran. Some had heard stories of a race of walking lizards from distant lands, but until this day there were very few in Wishapton who had ever seen one.

"Why are they gawking at me?" Kahlaf hissed.

"Maybe they're in awe of your beautiful face," Geoffrey said. Kahlaf looked towards the knight, who was trying valiantly to maintain a straight face.

"Oh, gods…" Bellaydin said, struggling to stifle his laughter. Eventually it became too much, and he burst into laughter, joined shortly after by Geoffrey.

"Might I remind you two jesters," Kahlaf said, "that very shortly we are to be at war, with little chance of victory. Is there anything amusing about that, I wonder?"

The smile disappeared from Geoffrey's face. Bellaydin did not respond either, but now that it came to mind, Kahlaf was right. If what the Goriinchians had told them was true, they had, at bare maximum, less than a week before Ygarak's army, thousands strong, would be on their heels. By what he could see around him, Wishapton did not exactly strike him as a fortress capable of withstanding such an army. He shivered involuntarily as he came face to face with the fact that before the week was over, he may very well be seeing the end of his life hurtling towards him on the tip of a Goriinchian axe.

"I really should have stayed in Aderilund," Bellaydin said.

Geoffrey gave a thin-lipped smile, "What, and miss out on all the fun we're going to have?"

Before long, the group had arrived at their destination; Castle Wishapton, a decently sized and well-fortified citadel, dominated the centre of the town of Wishapton. As they came closer, Bellaydin noticed a small detachment of guards had come down to meet them, along with three other figures.

"By all the gods," Geoffrey said. "We finally made it, Kahlaf."

Kahlaf grumbled. "That may be so, sir Knight, but, if you recall correctly, we failed in our mission."

"Mission?" said Bellaydin.

Geoffrey let out a heavy sigh. "He means the soldiers we were supposed to bring."

Bellaydin noticed the frown on the usually jovial Geoffrey's face. From the sounds of it, this was going to be an uncomfortable reunion.

"Now there's a sight for sore eyes," said a voice.

Bellaydin looked and saw a man, about his height but a decade or so older, standing in front of them, two other men on either side of him.

"My lord," said Geoffrey, dropping to one knee in front of the man.

"Geoffrey, Geoffrey, Geoffrey," said the man. "Since when do we do this sort of formality?"

Geoffrey rose to his feet, and turned towards Bellaydin. Grabbing the young man's shoulder, Geoffrey directed him towards the other man. "Bellaydin Ap'Lydin, allow me to introduce you to His Lordship, William Ap'Lydin, Earl of Genio, and your –"

" – cousin," Bellaydin finished.

William smiled broadly. "It's been a long time, Bellaydin."

Bellaydin nodded, lost for words.

"Come here and give your cousin a hug," William said.

Before Bellaydin could protest, William embraced him in a near-suffocating embrace. It was only when Bellaydin began to cough and splutter that his cousin released him, still smiling wide. He ruffled his cousin's hair affectionately.

"When I last saw Bellaydin, he was just a child," William said to his companions wistfully. "And now, well, it's amazing the changes that can happen in twelve years."

Bellaydin smiled, a little self-conscious.

"Where is your sister? Where is Polnygar?" asked William.

"She didn't come. She'd already left Aderilund to go to Carurlonia by the time your letter arrived," Bellaydin said.

William's shoulders relaxed.

"Ah well, as long as she's safe. For a while I was beginning to think you'd lost her along the way."

These words stung Bellaydin, even though he knew they were nothing more than friendly banter. In truth, he did not know how Polnygar was – if she was safe, or even if she was still alive. It had been many, many months since he had last seen her, and, with all the things that had happened to him in that time, how could he be sure that she was alright? There was, however, nothing he could do about it. For now he decided to push such thoughts out of his mind.

"Bellaydin, this distinguished-looking gentleman on my left is Haakon de Morcor, Duke of Alariat," William said. "He knew your parents quite well."

"William, as always, you are the master of understatement. Eleanor was my cousin, and Alusine one of my dearest friends." Haakon took

Bellaydin's hand, and shook it firmly. "It is both a pleasure and an honour to meet you, Master Ap'Lydin. You know, you look just like your father when he was a young man. Quite incredible."

William grinned again, and then turned Bellaydin towards the other man. "And this is Wulfric Highcrown, Duke of Oldharbour," William said. "He —"

Before William could finish, Wulfric cut in.

"You're late, Keslin," Wulfric said.

Geoffrey's eyes widened. "I apologise, Your Grace, we ran into a few problems and…"

"So it would seem. And where are those soldiers you were supposed to fetch? Am I to take it that after I sent you halfway across the known world, you return with just one boy?"

"Well, no but, let me explain…"

"I have no time for excuses, knight," Wulfric said. He turned towards Kahlaf. "Come Kahlaf, we have things to discuss."

"Yes, master," the Ahktarran said, head bowed in apparent reverence.

With that, Wulfric left the group, and returned up the path to the gates of Castle Wishapton, Kahlaf trailing closely behind.

"Don't mind Wulfric," said William. "He has a lot of things on his mind lately."

"Well, he's about to have a great deal many more things on his mind, my lord," Geoffrey said.

"What do you mean, Sir Geoffrey?" asked Haakon.

"The Goriinchians are poised to invade Emparia."

"What?" William shouted in alarm.

Haakon's eyes widened. "That is incredible," Haakon said. "How can you be sure of this?"

"The three of us have escaped a number of harrowing days in a Goriinchian gaol. I assure you, I'm not making this up. Their army is only a few days behind us, and Wishapton is directly in their path."

"Oh gods," said William.

"My lord," said Geoffrey. "You were right."

William nodded. "Aye Geoffrey," he said, "but this is not exactly the way I would like to have been proved as such."

"William," said Haakon, "we'd best all get inside. We have much to discuss and many preparations to make."

***

"Gentlemen," said Wulfric Highcrown. "We face a grave crisis here. We are facing a battle of epic proportions."

The group had since moved to the Great Hall of Castle Wishapton, and the earl and the two dukes sat at opposing ends of the table. At William's side sat Bellaydin and Geoffrey, and to the left of Wulfric Highcrown stood the Ahktarran Kahlaf.

"Perhaps it is our doom we face, no?" said Haakon quietly.

"So it would seem," said William, barely glancing at Wulfric.

"You know this battle may break us, William, don't you?" Wulfric said. "How many soldiers do we have here?"

"In Wishapton? With the militia, we have about two hundred, two hundred fifty maybe."

"And what if we equipped every able man in the town?" Kahlaf said.

"Five hundred, maximum. And many of them wouldn't last long in battle," William added.

"And how many Goriinchians do we face?" Wulfric asked.

"At least ten times that," said Geoffrey, "maybe more."

"Gods..." said William.

"You can say that again," Geoffrey said, reaching for his drink. "Well, here's to a glorious death." He toasted and took a deep gulp from his tankard, savouring the taste of the beer.

Wulfric stood. "It seems the Goriinchians have been able to pinpoint the weak spots in our border," he said forcefully.

"There are many of those," William said gloomily.

"In fact, if I didn't know better, I'd say they had an inside source," Wulfric said.

"Are you accusing someone of being a spy, Your Grace?" Haakon said. "I'd be more discreet with your accusations."

"No one here, no," Wulfric said, glaring at Haakon. "I am simply reminding you and the Earl of Genio of a certain religious group. One that, if I am not mistaken, has many strong and unbroken ties with Goriinchia."

"What?" said Haakon, nearly leaping from his seat in anger. "This is outrageous. Where is your proof of this? William and I made a decision, and I would hope that you, of all people, would not second guess it."

"In case you have not noticed, Your Grace," said Wulfric. "We are at war!"

"Please, Your Graces. Peace." said William, attempting to come between the men, who were nearly at each other's throats. "This is not a productive argument."

Seemingly chastened, the two men resumed their seats.

"Let's not fight amongst ourselves," said William. "There will be plenty of fighting to come in a few days."

"Maybe," said Geoffrey, taking another swig of beer. "But maybe their Graces think it's a better idea that we kill each other now and get it over and done with."

Kahlaf grumbled. "If we are to have any chance, we need reinforcements."

Wulfric looked towards the Ahktarran. "Indeed. And that was precisely the mission I sent you and the knight on, was it not, Kahlaf?"

The Ahktarran mumbled something unintelligible.

"And yet you failed. Still, you both managed to save your own wretched lives, which is something. But it seems now that, if I want something to get done, I will have to do it myself." He stood again, looking at all those assembled. "I am going to leave as soon as possible, and take the fastest route north, to the capital. With luck, and enough fresh horses, I should arrive in only a few days. I intend to inform the Privy Council of this, and at the earliest opportunity, return with a sizeable force."

"But that will take weeks, Wulfric," said Haakon.

"Perhaps. It may take a little less and if Wishapton can withstand a siege, that may be enough time to turn things around. Regardless, I can do no good here by myself; you have ample battle commanders."

Having said his piece, Wulfric departed, with little more than a curt nod at both William and Haakon as any sort of farewell message. Only when he was long gone, did anyone say anything.

"Remember, Willy," Haakon said, "Wulfric is… Wulfric. Always."

William smiled at Haakon, chuckling to himself quietly. "Well," said William. "That seems to be that. There is not much else we can do at this stage. There will be plenty of things that need to be taken care of in the morning, but for now, we can push that out of our minds. Leave our worries until tomorrow. We should all try to get some rest tonight. It might be the last good sleep of our lives."

"What do we do with Geoffrey?" Bellaydin asked, poking the snoring knight.

"Oh, leave him," said William. "It won't be the first time he's fallen asleep in the Great Hall." William turned to the Ahktarran. "Kahlaf, I can trust you to take Sir Geoffrey to his room, can I not?"

The Ahktarran grunted and screwed up his face, but nodded anyway.

"Excellent," William said. "Don't be too rough, though." He turned to Haakon, and whispered something into the older man's ears. Haakon nodded, and said something to William in response. "Bellaydin," said William. "We have quarters that you can use near ours. Come, walk with us for a while."

"Yes, William," Bellaydin said.

Leaving Kahlaf to grapple with the comatose Geoffrey, William, Haakon and Bellaydin left the room.

"You may not remember it, Bellaydin," said William, as the three of them walked down the hallway, "but you spent a good deal of your formative years here."

"Really?" said Bellaydin.

"Yes," Haakon said, nodding. "Castle Wishapton is considered the summer residence of the Earl of Genio. During William's minority, when your father was acting in his stead, the Ap'Lydins divided their time between this residence and Hotar Citadel in Genio itself, some days to the north. Once William had reached his majority, he set up court in Hotar Citadel, and your father retired here to raise you and your sister."

"Was this where they were, um…"

Haakon shook his head sadly. "No, Bellaydin," he said. "That shocking crime took place in Hotar Citadel. There is no stain of treachery in Wishapton."

"At least not yet," said William.

"Ah, here we are," said Haakon. "Take at look at this, Bellaydin."

In front of them was a large oil painting, depicting a man and a woman and their two children – two boys, not too far apart in age.

"Who are they?" Bellaydin asked.

"That, Bellaydin," said William, pointing to the man in the picture, "is our grandfather, Sir William Ap'Lydin. Next to him is our grandmother, Maria Ap'Lydin and then, these two boys… well, the older one to the left is my father, Caradoc, and the one to the right is your father, Alusine."

Bellaydin examined the picture again. From what he could see, his grandfather had been a tall, strong figure, gruff and bearded. Even at this young age, Bellaydin's father had his trademark grin, while Caradoc Ap'Lydin was wearing a sullen frown.

"There is another portrait, however, which you may find more interesting," said Haakon. "It's just a few steps over… ah, right here."

This painting was obviously done by the same artist, or at least in imitation of the artist's style. It was another family scene, with a man, a woman and a boy and a girl. This time, however, Bellaydin did not need to be told who the painting depicted. He would recognise them anywhere.

"This painting, this is Polnygar and me!" he said.

"Indeed," said Haakon. "I was here when this was painted, in fact. It was quite some time ago, let me see… more than a dozen years now. I think you would have been around four years old."

Bellaydin nodded. The younger Bellaydin stood between his two parents in the portrait. Alusine, with his wide smile, dark features, curly black hair and bristling moustache. Eleanor Ap'Lydin, Bellaydin's mother, by contrast looked subdued, her red hair dimmed, her eyes a washed out, watery blue. To the left of the young Bellaydin and his parents stood an adolescent

258

Polnygar, showcasing the smirk on her lips and the twinkle in her eyes that Bellaydin knew so well. He noted that, at this age, Polnygar showed much more of her elven ancestry than she did now. As she aged, she had come to resemble the human side of her family more and more.

"What's that on my father's robes?" Bellaydin asked, pointing to a stylised cross.

"That?" said William. "That is the crest of the Ap'Lydin family. It's a design of Goriinchian origin, though you wouldn't see it much in that land anymore. It's the symbol of the god Kytilas."

"Your father was married in those robes," said Haakon. "I should know. I was there."

William laughed. "Why am I not surprised?"

Haakon turned to William. "Careful young man, you should show respect to your elders. After all, I was at your birth as well," he said, and then pointed to Bellaydin. "Yours too."

As they continued on their way to Bellaydin's quarters, the mention of Goriinchia sparked something in Bellaydin's memories. "William, I was wondering... what do you know of the Heir of Lydin?"

There was a brief, awkward silence.

"Now, where have you heard that, my boy?" Haakon said.

In the space of a few minutes, Bellaydin did his best to explain all that had happened since his departure from Aderilund – from his first meeting with the assassin in Aderilund to the vision he had received in the cave of the Seeress. As he mentioned the vision, William suddenly cut in.

"I'm sorry. This vision... are you sure that's what you dreamed?"

"Yes," said Bellaydin. "Why do you ask?"

"Strange... that is precisely the same dream that I had. And, from the sounds of it, I dreamed it at the exact same time." He stroked his beard, deep in thought. "Curious."

"And what of the Heir of Lydin?" said Bellaydin.

William shrugged. "It's an old Goriinchian superstition. A sort of 'sleeping king' myth, about the supposed long prophesised return of an ancient folk-hero. It's all tied up in their religion somehow. You know how these things are."

Bellaydin nodded.

"When we have time later, I can show you the research I have done into Goriinchian beliefs," William said and paused for a moment. "Do you speak the Goriinchian language?"

Bellaydin shook his head.

"Ah, well that's to be expected. I'd be surprised if you'd ever been exposed to it," William said.

"If you have the time, Bellaydin," said Haakon, "William and I could educate you on the basics. We are both fairly fluent speakers."

"I'd like that," said Bellaydin.

"Well, we'll see what we can do," said William. "In the meantime, you should get some sleep. I imagine it will be a busy day ahead of us tomorrow. Your room is over there, first door on the left. Have a good night."

"Thank you, William."

"Sleep well, master Ap'Lydin," said Haakon, nodding at Bellaydin as he left.

.

CHAPTER 16

Ivellios stared at Polnygar with contempt. "You should have stayed with your master and the gnome, girl. You have no idea who you are facing here."

Despite the fear that threatened to bubble up within her, Polnygar swallowed hard and held her head up defiantly. "I know who I am facing. A traitor, a thief and a murderer." she said.

Ivellios' lip curled in amusement. "Is that so? You've finally worked that out, have you? Pity then that none will ever believe the word of a mongrel half-breed like yourself over that of a spellweaver. You are nothing, girl – nothing but a mere Mal-halyth!" He spat on the ground.

"What did you do to Augustin?" Polnygar demanded, pointing to the diminished figure who stood, shoulders slumped, next to Ivellios.

"I've simply opened his eyes to a wider view of the world, that's all, girl. He no longer shares your petty concerns. Isn't that right, human?" Ivellios said to Augustin.

Augustin nodded slowly, his good eye glassy and unfocused.

"You see?" Ivellios said, a smug expression on his face.

Polnygar drew her sword. "Whatever you've done to him, take it back," she said, her voice wavering.

Ivellios laughed. "Or what? You can't hurt me, girl. I shall do what I please, take what I wish. I suggest you don't let your feelings for this man overwhelm your mind, little half-breed."

Polnygar suddenly felt uncomfortable, and tried to turn away from the spellweaver's gaze.

"Oh yes, I know. I've seen how you look at this human. I know how you burn for him. I know how your loins quivered with desire every time he came near."

Polnygar said nothing.

"You sicken me," Ivellios said, his eyes full of hatred and revulsion. "You're nothing but a whore, just like your mother."

Polnygar exploded in fury. "Don't you dare say that about my mother!" She felt the anger course through her body – she felt the heat in her head and the fire in her veins. A tingling sensation started at her chest, and then began to travel down her arms and legs. It was happening again, as it had happened in the streets of Jagoncoilis. The power within Polnygar wanted to get out again. But this time, Polnygar was ready for it. She had trained for this – all those weeks of study under Aelzandar, the hundreds of lessons, the reciting of arcane words, the mental exercises – she knew that now, unlike before, she could control this power. She knew that she could focus it.

Her fingertips ignited into flames and ever so carefully she moved her hands, bringing her fingers together and rolling the fire into a ball. Then, with all her strength and fury, she flung the flaming sphere towards Ivellios. The spellweaver was taken by surprise, but reacted quickly enough that, with a wave of a hand and a few words, Polnygar's fireball dissipated in a few puffs of smoke.

"Well, well, well," Ivellios said. "It seems you've learned some things in the past few months little girl. But," he held up a single hand, "two can play this game."

White-blue tendrils of flame erupted from his fingertips and, steadily growing longer, the flames coiled about each other until, as Polnygar's had, they combined into one sphere. Ivellios upturned his hand and lazily manipulated the fire until he held a solid ball of flame above the palm of his hand.

"Amazing, isn't it?" said Ivellios. "The powers of ether are simply astounding. As are the lengths to which they can be manipulated."

Ivellios brought up his right hand and, as if squeezing water from a sponge, drained tendrils of flame from his left. Then, as the fire wafted around his outstretched fingers, he directed it towards Polnygar.

"Augustin!" yelled Ivellios. "Deal with her."

Eyes wide with terror and any words of incantations quickly dying on her lips, Polnygar scrambled to the ground, rolling out of the way of the wreaths of fire that flew towards her. Augustin approached her, sword drawn and a murderous look in his eyes.

"Farewell, little mongrel girl," said Ivellios. "I go now, but I have no doubt we shall meet again. You can tell your master I have found that which he has hidden and go now to the north to claim my prize. I challenge you both to come and find me."

With a terrible cry, Augustin thrust his sword down towards the prone Polnygar. She barely rolled away in time, and the Emparian's sword smashed through the dirt instead.

"That is, if you survive," Ivellios noted.

In an instant, he was gone, disappearing up another one of the narrow streets of Ralom. Polnygar knew she had lost him. There was no point trying to track his escape route. The only important thing now on her mind was escaping alive.

Augustin tried to grab her leg. She struggled ferociously, kicking him hard in the face with her other foot. Grunting in pain, he let go, and she quickly wriggled out of his reach, grabbing her sword from the ground.

"Augustin, please, you have to wake up," Polnygar said. "Take a look at what you're doing."

But her pleading had no effect. Augustin grunted again, and lunged towards her, swinging clumsily at her. The blow was so lacking in finesse that even Polnygar, with her limited combat experience, was able to easily deflect it with her own sword. She felt sick to her stomach. She was going to die here, and at the hands of someone who, not long ago, she had called a friend and admired above all other men. Tears stung her eyes, and not just tears for herself. She also cried for Augustin.

"Just stop!" she sobbed. "It's me. Polnygar! You have to remember. I don't know what Ivellios did to you but you have to snap out of it."

If anything, this just enraged Augustin further. He charged at her, his eyes maddened with blood lust and his lips flecked with spittle. Polnygar parried another clumsy attack, and returned with a swing of her own, which he attempted to block.

Augustin roared in pain, dropping his sword. Now he appeared to have lost all remaining traces of humanity, and reaching out with his hands attempted to throttle the life out of Polnygar. She tried to yell out, but his grip was too strong and he tightened his fingers around her throat, slowly crushing her windpipe. As her breath left her, Polnygar kneed Augustin in the groin, causing him to shout in pain and release his grip. Polnygar moved back, grabbed her sword and brought it down with as much force as she could muster. The blade cut through flesh and bone, spattering Polnygar's face and chest with blood and completely severing Augustin's right hand from his wrist. Augustin screamed with a terrible fury, and dropped to his knees, clutching the bloody stump where his hand once was.

"I'm… I'm sorry Augustin. I had to do it," Polnygar's eyes were blurry with tears.

Augustin did not respond, he just sat stunned, clutching his arm, mumbling and grunting in agony while he stared at Polnygar, his eyes still devoid of thought or emotion. Blood streamed from his wound, and Polnygar knew she had to act quickly, lest he die from loss of blood. She steeled her mind, and focused enough to form flames at her fingertips and then, before Augustin could react, she directed the flame towards his bleeding limb. The baron cried out in agony, but Polnygar persisted, cauterising the wound and stopping the flow of blood.

"Polnygar!" came a voice, "Polnygar!"

Polnygar turned around. "Aelzandar? I'm here!"

Aelzandar and Hebu appeared from a nearby alleyway, their clothes ripped and torn. "What is going on? Where is Ivellios?" Aelzandar said.

"He escaped. I swear Aelzandar, I did all I could," Polnygar sobbed.

Aelzandar softened, and took the girl into his arms. "There, there, my dear, I know you did," he said, comforting her. "The important thing is that you are safe."

"What about him?" said Hebu, pointing towards Augustin, who was babbling and kneeling in a pool of his own blood.

"I'm sorry, I had no choice. Oh, gods, I'm sorry Augustin," The Emparian shrank away from her touch.

"I think, my dear," said Aelzandar, looking at Augustin with interest, "you may have been correct. This man's mind had been ensnared."

"Can you do anything to help him?" Polnygar asked urgently.

Aelzandar shrugged. "I will do what I can, I assure you." He approached Augustin carefully. "Hebu, Polnygar, I need you two to restrain him for me."

The Nemoi nodded, and gestured for Polnygar to grab Augustin's other side. Aelzandar lay his staff down on the ground carefully, and knelt down in front of Augustin.

"You can trust me, Augustin. Though you do not recognise me I am a friend." Gently, Aelzandar held Augustin's head in his hands. The Emparian said nothing, but continued to breathe heavily, staring wildly at the archmage in front of him. Aelzandar closed his eyes. "Yes… Ah… I see," he said.

"What?" said Polnygar. "What is it?"

"A simple charm, so amazingly straightforward, I wonder why he bothered."

"Can you get rid of it?" Polnygar said.

Aelzandar looked towards her. "Patience, my dear."

Aelzandar turned back to Augustin and, closing his eyes, began to chant. The words were strange, and guttural, but even without knowing what they meant, Polnygar could tell they were words of power and majesty.

"He speaks Draconic," Hebu said solemnly. "The language of wizards."

As he spoke, Aelzandar's words came quicker and quicker, until they became a stream of words directed straight at the terrified Augustin.

Augustin gagged, his chest heaving as if he was going to throw up. A small metal sphere, slightly bigger than a pebble, fell from his mouth and clattered to the ground. Aelzandar took his hands off the man's head. Augustin closed his eyes and collapsed, his head slumped against his shoulders. He had fallen unconscious.

"What in the name of the gods is this?" Hebu said, picking it off the ground and handing it to the archmage.

"I am not sure – a clue, perhaps. It will need reflection." He placed the small object within his robes and tore off one of his sleeves. "Bind his arm, Hebu," Aelzandar said, passing the Nemoi the strips of ripped cloth.

"Yes, my lord," said Hebu, "I think I have my poultice with me."

With practiced skill the Nemoi tended to Augustin's wounds, bandaging the man's arm and doing his best to tend to the scalded flesh. Polnygar's eyes went wide. It appeared the Nemoi was not just the simple scribe she believed him to be.

Hebu stood. "It is done. Lie him down on his back."

Aelzandar and Polnygar did so.

"Is he —"

"He will be alright when he wakes up," said Aelzandar. "The enchantment is gone."

"Yes, but we've lost Ivellios," Hebu said.

"It wasn't my fault," Polnygar protested.

Aelzandar placed a hand on Polnygar's shoulder. "My dear, no one is blaming you in the slightest. If anything, the failure is mine. Ivellios is gone, and the Tears with him. I am thankful that you have managed to escape the encounter alive."

"Ivellios said something to me as he ran, something about finding what you'd hidden. He said he was going to the north."

Aelzandar grabbed her tightly. "Are you sure that's what he said? The north?"

"Yes," said Polnygar. "Why, what does it matter? What's in the north?"

Aelzandar was silent for a few minutes until he finally uttered but two words. "He knows."

"Knows what?" said Hebu. "What's in the north?"

"Something that must never fall into the wrong hands," said Aelzandar.

"I don't know how Ivellios learned of it, and that troubles me greatly." He picked up his staff. "I must travel to Skurj."

"What about me?" asked Polnygar.

Aelzandar looked at Polnygar, his eyes weary. "I can't ask you to come with me to Skurj, my dear," he said. "I've put you in enough danger as it is."

"So, then what?"

"I think it's time we contacted your mother, and I send you back to Aderilund," Aelzandar said.

"You're going to send me back home, is that? Without another word?"

"My dear, it is for your own safety," Aelzandar said. "Please, you must—"

"I've come this far," she said, crossing her arms. "And I'm not turning back now. I'm going to Skurj. You'll need my help."

"Polnygar, I appreciate the offer but really…"

"Polnygar, my lord is feeling guilty," Hebu said. "He fears what he has brought you into. He knows you could very well have died today, and has grave concerns about what will happen in Skurj."

Aelzandar frowned. "I would ask you to keep a civil tongue, Hebu. You serve me, remember?"

"Yes, my lord, but I also serve truth. As you pledged to do, remember?" Hebu said quietly.

Aelzandar tried to turn away. "I have done what I thought was right. Now I must deal with the consequences. Alone."

"I'm not leaving," Polnygar said defiantly. "You can't force me to."

Aelzandar frowned. "No, you're right. I can't force you."

"You can force *me* to go home, if you'd like," Hebu said.

Aelzandar shot Hebu a look.

"Sorry," Hebu said.

The sound of footsteps heralded the arrival of a group of guardsmen. They were powerfully built, bearded, and dressed in burnished bronze breastplates and red cloaks. They carried shields and large axes and surrounded the group. "Hold, in the name of the Patriarch!"

"Guardsmen, we shall do as you ask," Aelzandar said, raising his hands up in a gesture of peace. Polnygar and the others did likewise,

"I am Captain Ragnar of the Skurjan Guard," one of the soldiers said, "We are investigating a disturbance at the central plaza."

"Of course, Captain," said Aelzandar, "I am the archmage Aelzandar. You have my assurances that the situation is under control, and the instigator has fled the city."

Ragnar nodded. "I have heard of you, Aelzandar, and know that your name is held in high esteem by the Patriarch."

Someone groaned.

"Oh gods. Augustin!" Polnygar said, running to the man's side.

Slowly, as if emerging from a long dream, Augustin Bauer raised his head. "Where am I?" he said. "What happened? My head... oh, it's killing me..."

He made to rub his face with his hands when he yelled out in terror, "My hand! My hand's been cut off! What in the name of all that is good and holy – "

"It's alright, Augustin, you're with friends," Polnygar said, stroking the man's face tenderly.

"What happened to my hand?"

"You need to relax, Augustin," Aelzandar said. He turned to the guardsmen. "Captain Ragnar, can you help us?"

The guard captain nodded, and turned to one of his fellows. "Fetch a litter. We will need to move him."

"What happened to my damn HAND?" Augustin screamed.

"I'm sorry, Augustin," Polnygar said, tears in her eyes. "There was a battle…"

"You've undergone a very traumatic experience, Augustin," said Aelzandar, standing over the Emparian. "Something which no one should have to go through."

"I don't remember much…" Augustin said, his voice still weak. "Only images, really, flashes of memory… where are we?"

"You are in the Holy City, human," said Hebu. "Ralom, just north of Macrodonia."

"Ralom?" Augustin spat, clutching his stump of an arm. "What in the name of the Underworld am I doing here? And who are you?" He looked directly at the Nemoi.

"I am called Hebu," the Nemoi said, bowing. "And I serve the great Pharaoh of Macrodonia and, through him, my Lord Aelzandar."

"Charmed," Augustin grunted. "Though that still doesn't tell me why I'm here."

"Ivellios," Polnygar said simply. "He did something to you. Cast a spell on you, made you do things against your will."

"Cast a spell on me? I don't remember that."

"I'm not surprised, Augustin," said Aelzandar, resting a hand against the man's forehead, checking his temperature. "It was a rather subtle enchantment, after all."

Augustin cursed under his breath. "Where is he? Let me at him. I'm going to kill that pointy-eared bastard!" He tried to stand but as he did, he suddenly doubled over in pain, and collapsed to the ground again.

Aelzandar tried to calm the man. "You need to rest, Augustin. You are in no state to fight anyone."

The guardsmen returned with a litter and Aelzandar and Polnygar assisted in carefully lifting Augustin and placing him on it. Two of the guardsmen lifted the litter, eliciting another groan from Augustin.

"Ivellios is long gone. He is travelling to the North." Aelzandar looked thoughtful. "He means to reach Skurj. I intend to follow, and deal with him once and for all."

"What do you mean by that, archmage?" said Augustin. "You're going to kill him?"

Aelzandar paused. "If it comes to that, then yes."

"Then gods be damned if I'm staying behind. I'm coming with you, too. I've got a few scores to settle with that whore-son."

Aelzandar shook his head. "No, you are terribly injured. You need rest."

Augustin gritted his teeth.

"Listen, I've had worse…" He paused, grasped the bandaged stump, and then said, "Well, maybe not worse, but I've been in wars. I've seen death and carnage. I'm not some perfumed courtier who doesn't know which end of a sword to stick into his enemy. And I'll be damned if you cheat me of my revenge!"

Aelzandar took a step back.

"Besides," Augustin said, softening somewhat, "I've still got one hand. That's enough for my sword." He waved with his left hand as if for emphasis.

"Well, my lord," Hebu said, "I don't think you get rid of either of them that easily."

Aelzandar closed his eyes. "No. I didn't expect that I would."

"Well, what now?" said Hebu. "Are we leaving for Skurj then?"

"I think," said Aelzandar, "before anyone leaves – for anywhere – we all need to get a good night's sleep. But first we need to see a proper healer for Augustin. Then, of course, we all need a good meal. I hope that during it, I can persuade this pair to change their minds about coming with me."

"Good luck," said Hebu.

***

Bellaydin rose early, refreshed after the first good night's sleep he had had in months. A servant came to his room shortly after Bellaydin had awoken to call him to breakfast in the Great Hall. The servant left clothes for Bellaydin to wear. The garments were well-made – especially compared to the rags Bellaydin had spent much of the previous weeks wearing – and were emblazoned with the Ap'Lydin crest. Looking at them, Bellaydin guessed that they were probably some of William's spare clothes. He dressed himself and, after a few minutes, left the room for the Great Hall. When Bellaydin arrived, he found William waiting for him. Next to him sat a young girl, perhaps thirteen years of age, who greatly resembled William.

"I hope you slept well, Bela," William said.

Bellaydin nodded. "First good sleep since I left Aderilund."

"Well," said William, "I don't know if I can quite match the renowned hospitality of the elves, but I will do my best."

Bellaydin smiled.

"This is my daughter, Maria," William said. "Maria, this is your Uncle Bela."

"Hello Maria," Bellaydin said, taking a seat at the table.

"Hello Uncle Bela," the girl said softly.

"She's a little shy," William said. "She doesn't meet a lot of strangers."

Bellaydin nodded.

"Are you going to be staying with us, Uncle Bela?" Maria asked.

"For a while, yes," said William. "I thought it might be nice for us to have family around Maria."

The girl smiled. "I've never met any of father's family. I hope you decide to stay for a long time."

"Me too, sweetheart," William said. "Now, let's eat, shall we? There's plenty of food, dig in."

William was not exaggerating. Bellaydin's mouth watered at the array of food laid on the table before him. There were a variety of breads and cheeses in addition to many types of meat – mutton, pork, beef and duck. As Bellaydin helped himself to an ample serving of each, a servant poured ale into his mug.

"You've certainly got some appetite there, Bela," William said, tearing off a piece of bread and eating it.

"I'm famished," Bellaydin protested between mouthfuls. "This is the first real food I've seen in months."

William chuckled. "Well then, enjoy it. We've got a long day ahead of us."

"Might I join you, gentlemen?" came a voice.

William looked up. "Haakon! Of course, of course."

"Thank you, my boy," said Haakon, taking a seat next to William. "Pass me some of that mutton, Bellaydin."

Bellaydin obliged, offering Haakon a piece of bread as well. Unlike Bellaydin, who devoured every morsel he could get his hands on, Haakon ate sparsely.

"We have much to do today, William. Wishapton is ill-prepared for a siege."

"I have already sent word out to the nearby villages for them to come to the protection of the castle, Haakon," said William. "They should begin arriving sometime today."

Haakon nodded, and took a gulp of ale. "Luckily it's been a good harvest this year and we have ample supplies for a siege."

William sighed. "With the forces we face it may not matter," he said. "We're going to have great trouble keeping a force that size out."

"Did you send word to Genio?" Haakon asked. "We're going to need those reinforcements."

"A scout should be on his way north now," said William. "I don't expect much. I wouldn't be surprised if Wulfric made it to the capital before word reached Genio."

Haakon shrugged.

"Where are Geoffrey and Kahlaf?" said Bellaydin, expecting to see them at breakfast.

"That pair is out getting the militia together," William said. "I thought it a good use of their skills. Plus, it might keep them out of trouble."

Haakon chuckled. "That I doubt."

"Father," said Maria, "may I be excused? I have my tutor waiting for me."

"Yes, yes, go on," said William, waving a hand.

Maria stood, bowed politely and left. William watched her the whole time. "I hardly see her these days," he said. "It's a busy thing, preparing a girl for her marriage."

"Who is she marrying?" Bellaydin asked.

William raised an eyebrow. "Haven't decided yet," he said. "I've only got the one daughter, so I better make the right choice. No sense rushing into it."

"Shouldn't she decide who she wants to marry?" Bellaydin asked.

William laughed. "Bela, you sound like Geoffrey. No one in the nobility gets to choose who they marry. Why leave something like that up to the vagaries of chance?" He sighed. "Ah, well, things to do, things to do. Where am I going to get the time?"

"What am I going to be doing?" said Bellaydin.

"Hmm?" William said, distracted.

"With the battle." Bellaydin said.

William grasped his hands together and leaned towards his cousin. "I will not let you come to harm, Bela, don't worry. I can send you to the north, to the capital. You should be safe there."

"You're sending me away?" Bellaydin asked. To leave William, after they had only just reunited, seemed craven, especially since he might never see his cousin again. Despite his fear of the impending attack and what it might entail, it didn't feel right to flee.

"I don't want to run while everyone else fights." Bellaydin declared.

William and Haakon exchanged a look.

"Bela," William said, "If you stay here, I cannot guarantee your safety."

"I'm not asking you to."

"Wulfric is only a day gone. I will send you and Maria with a few trusted men to catch up to him. You will be safe in Oldharbour."

"I want to stay here," Bellaydin insisted. He felt like the decision that was his to make was being taken away from him.

William tried to compromise. "If we survive this, I promise I will make you my squire."

"I want to stay and fight with Geoffrey and Kahlaf, and you." Bellaydin was insistent.

"That won't be happening," William said firmly, "It's too dangerous."

"All my life I've never felt I belonged. Now, for the first time, I feel like I'm somewhere that I do belong. I'm not going to leave."

"He is persistent, is he not?" Haakon said with a smile.

"Please William, don't send me away. People have always shifted me from one place to another, all in the name of my own safety. Once, just once, I want to decide something for myself. Enough running, it's time to fight."

William looked lost for words. Haakon turned his gaze towards him. "This all sounds very familiar, don't you think, William?"

William tried to suppress a smile. For a moment, he said nothing. When he did speak, his voice was warm with familial pride. "If that is what you want," he said. "I will be proud to have you fighting by my side."

"Just as I thought. A true Ap'Lydin," Haakon said.

"What do you mean?" Bellaydin said.

"He means you have greatness in your blood," William said.

Haakon laughed. "Perhaps," the older man said, "but also trouble. You forget, William, I've seen more Ap'Lydins come and go than you ever have."

The conversation between the two men continued, diminishing into a few good-natured taunts and ribbing until Bellaydin lost track, and turned back to his meal. He helped himself to another serving of pork while William and Haakon continued their banter.

He was not sure what he should think of William's offer to make him a squire. Indeed, Bellaydin only vaguely knew what a squire did. Such a rank, though common in human nations, never existed in Aderilund where most of the ranks of the aristocracy was comprised of the great spellweavers and their immediate families. If he remembered correctly, a squire was some sort of assistant to a knight or, more correctly, an apprentice that might be expected to become a full knight themselves once they became of age.

"My lord William!"

William cut short his conversation with Haakon as Carfel entered the room, panting for breath.

"What is it?" the earl asked testily.

"My lord, you must see this. Just outside the castle, there's a mob gathered."

"A mob?" William said, narrowing his eyes.

"I think there's been a lynching, my lord."

"A what?"

Breakfast was cut short and William, Haakon and Bellaydin followed the messenger outside where, sure enough, a small crowd had gathered outside the castle gates. They were yelling and hollering, chanting anti-Goriinchian slogans.

"What in the blazes is going on here?" asked William. "Who's the leader here?"

A large meaty man, bearded and burly, stepped forward. "I am, milord," he said. "Name's Edric."

"Very well Edric," William said. "Do you mind telling me what this is all about?"

"Well, milord," Edric began. "There's been a lot of talk since last night about the Goriinchians and all that."

"Go on," William said.

"Some people have been sayin' there's a traitor in our midst, milord. One of them stinkin' Horned God lovers giving away all our secrets, lying in wait to open the gates when the Goriinchians get him. Well, no need to worry about that. We got the bastard."

"What bastard?" demanded William.

As he spoke, Edric lowered his head, and the rest of the crowd parted to make way for William. Through the mass of people, Bellaydin saw that a rudimentary gallows had been constructed and, from the noose, swung a fresh corpse.

"Oh, gods, no…" William said. "Not him."

Bellaydin felt sick. The corpse stared at him, eyes bulging horribly and neck broken and askew. Bile threatened to come up his throat, as it had when he had seen the hanged man in Aderilund. He vomited on the ground before him.

"Dugald Ap'Morten," Haakon breathed.

"Gods damn it," William swore. "Our decision was that these people were to be left in peace. That was the law. Now because of rumour and innuendo, an innocent man is dead."

"But he's the enemy," the man named Edric protested. The crowd cheered him on.

"No, he was not. Soon thousands of Goriinchians will be coming here to face us, why are you fools looking for more enemies?"

The crowd looked slightly embarrassed. Many began to mutter amongst themselves.

"We need every able-bodied man we can get to work together if we are to have any chance at all. This one bit of… stupidity. It has jeopardised all of that!"

"We were only doin' what we thought was right, milord," Edric said.

William stopped in his tracks. "Aren't we all?" he muttered.

Haakon placed a hand on William's shoulder. "It's not your fault, William," he said.

"I know," William said. "But I can't help feeling maybe I should have handled things differently."

Haakon nodded. "You know you must enforce the law, William. These people must be punished."

William sighed. "I know. Fetch the guards."

"Of course, William," said Haakon. "I'll make sure they take care of this. I have a few other things that need taking care of as well, so if you don't mind, I'll take my leave now." Haakon nodded politely to William, and then disappeared up the path.

William turned to Bellaydin. "I'm sorry you had to see that," said William. "Are you alright?"

"I'm fine," Bellaydin said, coughing. "Just brought back a few bad memories." He told William of what had happened in Aderilund.

"Oh my gods, I had no idea," said William. "It's lucky you're here then, where we can protect you better than those in Aderilund."

It seemed to Bellaydin that William was disparaging Saegralanna, if ever so gently. "You misunderstand me, Mother was always looking out for my welfare," Bellaydin protested.

"I'm sure she was, Bela," William said, "but the rest of the elves would have had other priorities."

Bellaydin did not respond. Not only did he not want to prolong the argument, but he also believed that William had made a good point.

"Well, Bela," William said, changing the subject, "If you want to fight with us, I need to know that you are able to wield a sword. Let's see how you handle yourself."

"I'll do my best," said Bellaydin. He tried to sound confident. In truth he was a little nervous.

"First things first, though," William said. "We need to get you equipped."

"I have the sword that Kahlaf lent me," Bellaydin said.

William raised an eyebrow and let out a chuckle. "You're an Ap'Lydin, Bela – a nobleman. You need something better than an Ahktarran's cast-off. Come. Let's go back to the castle. I'll show you what I have in mind."

The trip back into the castle took about a quarter of an hour. William led Bellaydin into some sort of armoury. The walls were festooned with all manner of weaponry, and various sets of armour hung on racks about the room.

"Sorry about the mess," William said. "One of the side effects of a decade or so of peace. Things get a bit disorganised."

Bellaydin smiled. "That's alright, I've never been in an armoury before anyway."

"Ah, then I could have just said this was how they were supposed to look, eh?" He smiled briefly, rubbing his chin as he looked around at the weapons. "Now, let me see, what would be suitable." William picked up a sword from its rack and passed it to Bellaydin. The sword was about thirty-five inches or so in length, thirty of those inches being the blade. Unlike Kahlaf's weapon, this sword was light, and exceptionally well-balanced.

"It feels good," Bellaydin said, moving his arm about.

"Take a few practice swings," William suggested.

"Right," said Bellaydin.

William moved out of the way, and Bellaydin slashed and thrust in the air a few times with the sword, marvelling at how much easier it was to wield than the others he had used.

"It's a fine sword, isn't it?" said William. "Amazing how the right size and weight can make all the difference."

"Kahlaf's sword nearly broke my wrist." Bellaydin said.

"I'm not surprised. His is balanced for a seven-foot tall heavily muscled killing machine."

Bellaydin had to chuckle at that.

"Now, let's see about finding some armour," William said. He turned to Bellaydin. "Have you much experience wearing any?"

"None at all," said Bellaydin, shaking his head.

"Of course. I can't imagine you ever needed to. Still, it's never too late to learn. Of course there's no point saddling you with anything too heavy."

"No? Why not?"

"In battle you have to be able to move, swing your sword and dodge blows, that sort of thing. If you're not used to the heavy armour then you'll basically be a sitting duck. Doesn't matter how much metal you're wearing. In your case, we'll need something light, yet durable. In fact…"

William stopped mid-sentence, then rushed over to a chest in the corner of the room. "Well, I guess it's better this goes to you than anyone else," William said, lifting the lid.

"What is it?" Bellaydin asked.

William reached into the chest and withdrew a shining mail shirt. "Here," he said. "Take it, it's only right that you have it."

Bellaydin looked puzzled, but nonetheless accepted the gift. "Why should I have it?" he said, feeling the shirt with his fingers. The chains in it were amazingly fine and well-crafted.

"It belonged to your father, Bela," William said. "I'd nearly forgotten that I still had it. Go on, try it on."

Bellaydin removed his outer tunic, and slipped the mail shirt on over his undergarments. It fit well and was surprisingly light.

"It's of elven design," said William. "That's why you can't feel it. They enchant their forges, I think. I don't know for sure. Whatever it is, they know how to make comfortable armour."

"Where did my father get this?" Bellaydin said. "It must have cost a fortune."

William looked uncomfortable, and tried to look the other way. "The story is, he was given it as a love token by that elf woman he was enamoured of. The one he... lay with."

"You mean Saegralanna," Bellaydin said.

William nodded, but turned away. It seemed he wanted to talk of something else – anything else.

"She's Polnygar's mother, William," Bellaydin said. "Why can't you say her name?"

William ignored the question. "Enough of this. I need to see your skills. Let's go to the sparring room, shall we?" William marched out of the room at surprising speed, leaving Bellaydin to hurry after him. The earl continued up a hallway and, after turning a corridor or two, led Bellaydin to another room. This room was wide and mainly empty, except for a few practice dummies and, in one corner, a water-filled washbasin with a few bloody towels next to it. "Right," said William, "show me your footwork."

Bellaydin did as asked and, swinging the sword, arranged himself in a fighting stance.

William chuckled.

"Oh, gods no, you'll fall over if you tried to fight like that," he said. "Let me help you." He grabbed Bellaydin's feet, one after the other, and shifted them into different positions. "There, try that."

Bellaydin pivoted on his feet, then, swinging his sword, advanced several steps, taking care to shield his body as he did.

"See? Much better," said William. He drew his sword from his belt. Immediately, Bellaydin was taken aback. William's blade was unlike any he had seen. It glowed with a blue-white light and, as Bellaydin looked closer, he swore he could see frost on the blade.

"This is Kaltban, Bela," said William. "The great blade of the Ap'Lydins. Our grandfather recovered it when he was fighting in the battles for the holy city of Ralom. That would have been… oh, seventy years ago now."

"Why does it have ice on it?" Bellaydin said.

"Go ahead and touch it," said William.

Bellaydin did so. "Ouch. It's freezing."

"Indeed," said William. "It is part of the sword's enchantment. There was probably some reason behind it, but since its original owner is long since gone, we'll never find out." He swung it in the air a few times in a dazzling demonstration of swordplay. "Still, as you can see, it is a magnificent weapon. The cold of the blade adds an extra surprise for anyone unfortunate enough to be on the receiving end."

"There's some writing on it. Looks like Eldara script," Bellaydin said.

"Yes, some sort of elven proverb," William said offhandedly.

Bellaydin read it out loud, as William looked impressed at the young man's fluency in the foreign tongue.

"What does it mean?" William said.

"The Gods Weep - And Heaven is overthrown," Bellaydin said.

"See, just as I told you, some sort of proverb," William said. He turned to Bellaydin. "Now, little cousin. The moment of the truth. Time to show me what you've got."

Bellaydin looked from Kaltban, and then to his own weapon. "Isn't this a bit of an unfair fight?" said Bellaydin. "You're using a magic sword."

William pulled back his tunic to reveal bare skin. "Well, unlike you, I'm not wearing any armour."

"I didn't think we were going to try and hurt each other!" Bellaydin said.

William chuckled. "Calm down Bela," he said. "I'll go easy on you." He paused. "For starters."

Bellaydin nodded, and held his sword in the starting position, saluting his cousin. William did likewise. Then, with a cry, the sparring session began. William advanced on Bellaydin, his sword held high. With a grunt, he brought it down, only to have Bellaydin block it before twisting his body to the left, and following up with a feint to the right, and a swing to the left.

"Good," said William, parrying the blow. "But let's try for the unorthodox."

William yelled a war cry and charged towards Bellaydin, knocking him to the ground with his shoulder, before once again bringing the sword down. Bellaydin parried this blow just in time. The swords rang as both Ap'Lydins pushed against the other.

"Almost lost a nose there, cousin!" William said, grinning.

"Keyword," Bellaydin said, "is almost."

With a roar he pushed back at William, propelling the elder Ap'Lydin into the air and back a few steps. Once again their swords clashed, but this time it was William retreating backwards across the room.

"Yes, yes," he said. "Not bad at all."

Their swords continued to clash as Bellaydin advanced. Occasionally, William or Bellaydin would let their guard down, and their opponent would manage to draw blood. The wounds were never too serious, but were enough to cause a gasp or grunt. Soon William found his back against the wall, with little room to move.

"Yield," Bellaydin said, grinning.

William laughed. "Well done. There's one other thing you have to learn."

"What's that?" Bellaydin said, his sword pointed at William's chest.

"Anticipation!" William punctuated his comment with a swift kick to Bellaydin's nether regions.

"Oww…" Bellaydin said, dropping his weapon, and slumping to the ground.

"I think that's enough," William said.

"Why did you do that? That was hardly fair." Bellaydin winced.

"Bela," said William. "This is war, not a jousting carnival. Your opponent's not going to stop to observe all the rules of chivalry. You should use every dirty trick at your disposal. Bite, kick, punch, attack your enemy's weak spots any time you get the opportunity."

"You could have just told me that," Bellaydin groaned.

"I thought it needed to be shown," William said. "Come on, let's get cleaned up." He tossed Bellaydin a towel.

"Here, wipe yourself down. You're bleeding on your chin as well, by the way."

Bellaydin rubbed down his face, getting rid of as much of the sweat and grime as he could.

"You're not bad, Bela, not bad at all," William said, rubbing himself down. "Those elves must have taught you something about sword fighting, after all."

"My moth… uh… Saegralanna taught both Polnygar and I from the age of twelve onwards," he said. "Although elven swords are a fair bit lighter than these."

William rolled his eyes. "No doubt." As he was wiping away blood, William took a sharp intake of breath and, grunting, looked at his arm.

"Hey, you got me pretty good here," he said.

"Sorry, William," Bellaydin said.

"Ah, don't worry, Bela," William said, dismissing his cousin's concern. "Just as long as you do as well against the enemy, I think you'll do fine."

"Thanks," Bellaydin said, smiling. "But I think you let me win."

William slapped his cousin on the back, chuckling. "Oh, can't you just accept you beat me, Bela? Humility does not become you."

Bellaydin smiled in response.

"My lord!"

William turned his head. "Geoffrey?" he said, looking out the doorway.

A hurried Geoffrey Keslin pelted down the hallway at breakneck speed.

"What's going on?" said William.

"Scout has arrived, my lord, from the frontier outposts."

"And?" William said, with a tone of urgency.

"My lord, they're here," Geoffrey said between gasps. "Oh, gods, they're coming."

"Slow down," William said. "The Goriinchians are coming, is that what you're saying? They've been spotted?"

Geoffrey paused for a few minutes, trying to catch his breath. "Yes my lord, and, just as I told you, they've brought every damn warrior from here to Korfar."

"Then it is as we feared," William said, "We have less time than we thought." He cursed under his breath. "Maria will have to remain here. It's too dangerous to try and get her away with the Goriinchians so close." He placed a hand on Bellaydin's shoulder. "It looks like you got your wish, Bela. You'll be fighting here with us, just as you wanted." Urging Bellaydin along he said, "Let's go."

"Make way for the Earl of Genio," announced Geoffrey as William's party descended from the castle. Soldiers and townsfolk moved out of the way as they approached.

"Where is the scout?" said William. "Show him to me."

Leading the way, Geoffrey took William and Bellaydin to the castle gates where, next to a detachment of soldiers, a haggard man leant against an exhausted horse.

"My lord," the scout said weakly, "I came as quickly as I could. I bring word of the Goriinchians."

"Tell me what you saw," William said. "Then you can rest."

"Thank you, my lord," the scout said. He took a deep intake of breath. "I was stationed at Fort Victory, right on the border. At first we thought it was some sort of mirage, or trick of the light, the haze we saw on the horizon. It was only when it got closer we realised that this was no delusion. It was real. An army of thousands – painted warriors, Saldarri archers, black-cloaked cultists. All were there. Not to mention the great leaders, Warchief Culainn and, most of all, the Goriinchian Prophet-King himself, Ygarak. The army dragged with them great siege weapons. I didn't think those barbarians knew how to build them, but somehow they've got them."

As the scout told his story, the soldiers' faces paled. William, out of all of them, tried to mask his fear but even *his* voice began to stutter.

"Go on," he said quietly.

"We drew lots to determine who would go to warn Wishapton. That was why I ended up being the one riding north as my brothers fought and died."

"And Fort Victory?"

"It is nothing but a smoking ruin, my lord. I saw it, as I looked behind me for one last glimpse. Completely obliterated. The defenders were butchered to the last man."

"What is your name, soldier?" William asked.

"Jakeb," he said, "Jakeb Smith." The scout paused. "They are coming, my lord," he coughed. "Nothing will stop them."

William blinked, but said nothing.

"We need a bloody miracle," said Geoffrey, "and we need it right this damn minute."

"Miracles may be a little short on the ground, knight," growled Kahlaf , "but I have some news that may raise your spirits. This scout was not the only one to arrive in the last hour. Come with me."

Kahlaf led William, Bellaydin and Geoffrey towards the gates of the city. The streets of Wishapton were oddly quiet, Bellaydin noticed. Most of the townsfolk must have already headed for the safety of the castle.

"What is it that you mean, Ahktarran?" said William. "Who else has arrived?"

"My lord William," said Kahlaf. "Sir Geoffrey and I were given a task by the Duke of Oldharbour. He wished for us to find for you reinforcements against the Goriinchians. Up until now, we had assumed that our disastrous encounter with the enemy in Gorin had meant that mission had failed completely."

He came to a halt in front of a small group of soldiers. At first Bellaydin wondered for what reason. There were soldiers all over Wishapton at the moment, why did these ones hold significance?

Then he noticed something. These soldiers were not all humans. Half of them – the archers – were Eldara. Bellaydin's heart skipped a beat. These were not ordinary militia, these were mercenaries – some of the very same mercenaries they had thought killed in Gorin.

"These troops we did find were more resilient than even we had hoped. Though this is barely a quarter of them, they have escaped the clutches of the Goriinchians, found their way north and rejoined us here. That is, if not a miracle, then, at the very least, an incredibly fortunate turn of events," Kahlaf said.

"Indeed it is," William said excitedly. "We need every soldier we can get."

One of the soldiers, a tall, lean elf with a scarred face, stepped forward. "It will be a pleasure to fight by your side, William of Emparia," the elf said, his Emparian heavily accented.

"What is your name, archer of Aderilund?" William said. He was careful to avoid using the term 'elf', which he knew their kind found offensive.

"I am Neriaos," the elf said. "I serve the Great Houses and the Aspen Throne."

Another soldier, a human with tan skin, spoke up. "I am Firouz of Mokeria, great lord," he said. "I lead the infantry. We shall fight together and we shall win together."

"Either that or we'll die together," Geoffrey said.

"Be quiet Geoffrey," William said out of the corner of his mouth.

"All of us are tired and hungry, great lord," Firouz said, "and we would greatly appreciate if you would give us time to rest and recuperate."

"Certainly, certainly," William said.

Both Firouz and Neriaos nodded in acknowledgement of William's hospitality.

"Thank you," said Neriaos.

William nodded, and grasped the man's hand. "Welcome to Wishapton," he said. "Geoffrey, take these men to the castle. Get them some food, and find a place for them to rest."

"Not a problem, my lord," the knight said. "Come on chaps, this way."

As Geoffrey and the mercenaries disappeared up the path, Kahlaf turned to William.

"You know that this doesn't change much," Kahlaf said. "We are still massively outnumbered. In a few days, we will all be dead, mercenaries, nobles, peasants, all."

"I won't give up hope, Ahktarran," William said.

"Hope. Huh," Kahlaf scoffed. "Hope is merely the denial of reality." With one last look over his shoulder, Kahlaf left William and Bellaydin to themselves. "Delude yourself if you wish. The truth approaches, whether you accept it or not," the Ahktarran said as he departed.

"Charming fellow," William said plainly once Kahlaf was out of earshot.

Bellaydin grinned. "You haven't spent months with him yet."

"Yes," William said. "He doesn't seem to be the most pleasant travel companion."

"Where did the duke find him?" Bellaydin asked. "I've never seen one of the Lizardmen before."

"An Ahktarran? Oh, they pop up every now and then, usually as hired muscle by some merchant. They come from a desert land, far from here — many months across the sea to the east. Where Wulfric found Kahlaf, I can't say. He showed up one day and there the Ahktarran was, shadowing him at every turn."

"Sounds more than a little creepy," Bellaydin said.

"You're not wrong there, Bela," William said.

"Lord William!" came a voice. "Lord William!"

"I think someone's calling for you, William," Bellaydin said.

"Well, no rest for the wicked," said William. "Bela, I'll see you at supper."

CHAPTER 17

"Easy," Polnygar said, as she tenderly guided Augustin's hand. "There you are. Now you've got it."

"It's going to take me a damned long time to get used to this," Augustin said grumpily as he dipped the spoon into the soup bowl.

"You have to try," Polnygar said gently.

"Bah," Augustin said. His left hand trembling, he brought the spoon up to his mouth and nosily slurped the contents. When he was finished he placed the spoon back in the bowl.

"I just wish you'd chosen the left hand, girl," he said, smiling slightly.

"I didn't really intend to cut off either," Polnygar said.

He moved both his shoulders, flexing both limbs. "Damn," he said, "Sometimes it almost feels like it's still there."

"I'm really sorry, Augustin," Polnygar said.

Augustin shrugged. "What for?" he said. "It was nothing more than self-defence. I would have done the exact same thing in your situation. In fact, you probably saved my life."

Polnygar looked confused. "Um, how?"

He pushed the bowl aside. "Suppose for a second that I had seriously wounded you, or, worse yet, killed you. Now imagine what would have happened had the archmage found us seconds after I did that. He'd take one look at your corpse and disintegrate me in an instant."

"I don't think –"

"You don't see it, do you girl?" Augustin said, shaking his head. "It's the way he looks at you, the way he speaks to you."

"What do you mean?"

"He treats you as if you were his own daughter, Polnygar," Augustin said, "and a father's rage is one of the most terrifying forces known to man."

"And what about you?" Polnygar said. "What do you see me as?"

Augustin looked uncomfortable. "I…" The words died on his lips, and he turned his face from her gaze. "It's not important what I think," he said, frowning.

"Yes, it is," Polnygar said.

Augustin did not respond, but regarded her with interest.

A voice interrupted them. "Ah, I knew I would find the both of you here."

"What is it, Hebu?" said Augustin testily.

"Aelzandar wishes for both of you to join him in his lodgings. He says we have plans to make."

"Very well," said Augustin, groaning as he stood. "Damn that elf."

***

294

A few minutes later, Augustin, Hebu and Polnygar had arrived at Aelzandar's quarters.

"Ah, Augustin, Polnygar," the archmage said, rising from his seat. "I hope Hebu wasn't too brusque."

"No, it's fine, we were just eating," Polnygar said.

"Humph," Augustin said, "if you can call it that." He rubbed his stump self-consciously.

"Augustin," said Aelzandar. "I am sure that, with time, you will learn to overcome this newfound disability. From what I have seen you are a man who thrives on challenges."

"I'd thrive a lot better with two hands," Augustin said.

"Of course," Aelzandar said gently.

"Hebu," he said, "fetch Augustin and Polnygar some chairs. I'm sure they don't want to stand up the whole time they are here."

Hebu nodded, and pulled two chairs towards the guests.

"Thank you," said Polnygar, taking the chair from Hebu. Augustin did likewise, but groaned as he did so.

"I have found us passage with a caravan heading north to Selvarial," said Aelzandar. "This should offer us increased protection and safety on our journey. We want to avoid any further... incidents." He glanced at Augustin, frowned, then continued. "We leave in three days."

"Not a moment too soon," said Augustin. "And when I finally get my hands – hand – on Ivellios, he's going to miss much more than just a limb, let me tell you."

"I have no doubt, Baron," said Aelzandar. "But for now, put those thoughts out of mind. We have a long trip ahead of us. And Polnygar, there are few other things you need to know. You remember that I promised to do some research on the Heir of Lydin while we were here?"

"You've found something?" Polnygar said.

"That is correct. While we have been resting and recuperating, I had Hebu fetch me various tomes and scrolls from the great libraries of Ralom."

"Just like that, huh?" Augustin said. "Seems odd for the scholars to have gone out their way to help a stranger."

"My dear Baron," Aelzandar said, "I have some influence here and I would hardly classify myself as a stranger. The Patriarch Alimero is a friend of mine."

"Is he now?" said Augustin. "I'm sure there's a story behind that."

Aelzandar paused. "Yes, but now is not the time to tell it."

Augustin shrugged.

"What did you find out?" said Polnygar, trying to steer the conversation back to the original topic.

"I have much information on it, which I will make copies of and take with us to peruse while we travel north. For the moment, however, I can give you a brief summary, my dear."

Polnygar nodded. "Tell me," she said.

"Very well," said Aelzandar. "This is what I have learned. The Heir of Lydin is a rather complicated element of the theology of the Church of the Horned God, the state religion of Goriinchia. This Heir is believed to be a long-prophesised messianic figure who will spread the faith of the Horned God over the entire world or, in some alternate readings, destroy such faith instead."

"How can that be right?" Augustin said. "Save the religion, or destroy it? That's two completely different things."

Aelzandar fixed the Emparian with a knowing glance. "My dear Baron, are you truly saying that you've never heard of a self-contradicting piece of religious dogma in your entire life?"

Augustin remarked, "You've got me there, archmage. So, what's this got to do with Polnygar?"

Aelzandar looked at Polnygar thoughtfully, stroking his chin. "It would seem that they are under the impression that Polnygar is this Heir of which we speak."

"Just because of my name?" Polnygar said. "But there must be dozens of people with the name Ap'Lydin - hundreds, even."

"Perhaps," said Aelzandar. "Perhaps not."

"And if I am this Heir," Polnygar said, becoming more animated in her speech, "why in the name of the Underworld are they trying to kill me? If I'm some sort of prophet, surely that should mean they wouldn't harm me."

"That would be my thoughts as well, my dear," Aelzandar said. "Unfortunately such thinking is reliant on our assailants being perfectly rational figures. That in itself may be wishful thinking. Whether you are or are not this prophesised figure is irrelevant for now, we must proceed under the impression that they believe you to be so, and they are willing to cause you great harm." He turned his gaze to Augustin. "And great harm to those who travel with you."

"Huh," said Augustin. "Let them try. As long as they don't cut off my other hand, I think I can handle whatever they throw at me."

"Oh, I have no doubt," Aelzandar said. "No doubt at all."

***

Bellaydin splashed himself with water, washing the grime and sweat off his hands and face. As he did so, he caught a glimpse of himself in the water's reflection and noted the changes that had occurred in the months since he had left Aderilund. Gone was the plump, smooth cheeks of his adolescence. The time in Goriinchia had thinned him out, and his once clean-shaven cheeks were covered with a ragged and adolescent beard. The

Eldara were fastidious about facial hair – few of them could grow any. They saw it as unclean, and regarded anyone who sported a beard or moustache as repugnant. In Aderilund, Bellaydin had taken a razor to his face every day of his life since he was fourteen, but since he had left, he had not shaved once.

In his head, Bellaydin counted the months since he had left home and realised, with a start, that his birthday was fast approaching. *I will be eighteen in a week*, Bellaydin thought. Then another thought came to him, one less encouraging than the last. He was about to participate in a battle that they had virtually no hope of winning. In truth, he was unlikely to live to see his eighteenth birthday. The thought of that tore at him, gnawed at him deep inside.

"You look troubled, Squire," came a voice. It was Kahlaf.

"Just thinking about the battle," Bellaydin said.

The Ahktarran's expression changed. "It would be best not to think too much about that, human," he said. "Keep your mind clear, and on the task at hand."

Bellaydin nodded. "We're all going to die, aren't we?" he said. Bellaydin wasn't sure what he was expecting from the Ahktarran. Sympathy? Consolation? Did he want Kahlaf to pat him on the back and say it would be all right in the end?

"Perhaps," came the brief response from Kahlaf. "Perhaps not. I've been in many battles in my life, and I have often faced fearful odds. I have survived situations worse than this."

"We have a chance then?" Bellaydin said.

"Oh yes," Kahlaf said, his tail lashing. "A small one, but a chance nonetheless. If we can hold the keep, we might last long enough for reinforcements to arrive."

As the Ahktarran flexed an arm, Bellaydin noticed a mark on Kahlaf's shoulder that he had not seen before. It appeared to be some sort of bisected oval, branded into the flesh.

"What is that brand on your shoulder?" Bellaydin said.

Kahlaf turned to Bellaydin sharply, eyes cold. "Do you always pry into the personal affairs of others?"

Bellaydin shrank back. "Uh, no, no… I'm sorry."

Kahlaf stood quietly for a moment, his reptilian face twisting into a sneer but, after a few moments, his eyes softened and his face relaxed. "However, since we all may be dead and gone soon…"

Kahlaf took a seat on a nearby bench and signalled for Bellaydin to join him. His head bowed, Bellaydin did so. "You asked about this mark," Kahlaf said, tapping his shoulder. "It is a slave brand."

Bellaydin's eyes widened in surprise. "You were a slave?"

The Ahktarran nodded. "I have told you I was a warrior, but those days ended long ago," Kahlaf said. His voice was low, almost tinged with sadness. "In my youth I fought for the great lords of Har Ahktar – the Hakeems – in many of the savage conflicts that flared in the lands of Qarld. For a decade I served loyally until one day we faced an enemy we could not overcome – the Sultan of Qar Udel. I was captured, stripped of my weapons and armour, and sold into slavery. I spent fifteen years drifting from taskmaster to taskmaster, performing all manner of menial labour. Every day I longed for death, to be released from such humiliation."

"How did you meet up with Wulfric?" Bellaydin asked.

"The duke found me working as a common labourer in the city of Oldharbour," Kahlaf said. "As was his prerogative, he took ownership from my current owner. I have served the duke faithfully ever since."

"He didn't free you?" said Bellaydin.

Kahlaf eyes locked on to Bellaydin's gaze. "No. He did not. Why would he? He had need of my skill at arms. For the duke, it was far more convenient for the bond of ownership to remain," Kahlaf said.

"Don't you want to be free?"

"What I want is irrelevant," Kahlaf said. He breathed in heavily, his nostrils flaring. "Tell me, is being a squire your fondest desire?"

Bellaydin flushed. "Well, I wouldn't say that."

"Yet you will do it. You will not refuse your cousin," said Kahlaf. "That is how it is with my own duties." He stretched his neck, blinking. "And what of you, Bellaydin Ap'Lydin? How is it that someone so pale bears a name from my own country?"

"What?" Bellaydin said.

"You are named Bellaydin, are you not? A most unusual name for someone of your ancestry, but most recognisable for any man in Qarld."

"My name is Qardleean?" Bellaydin said.

"But of course," Kahlaf said, frowning. "Have you never heard of the Tragedy of Belial'ad-Dīn?"

Bellaydin shook his head. "Who or what is Belial'ad-Dīn?" he asked.

The Ahktarran looked at him suspiciously, but continued. "It is an old folk tale, from my country. He was the descendant of jinn."

"And who or what is jinn?"

"You mean what *are* jinn. They are demons of smoke and fire," Kahlaf said. "This man, despite his ancestry, tried to live an honourable and virtuous life. And, for a time, he did. But eventually his true nature – that bequeathed to him by his father – came to the fore, and he transformed into the very sort of monster he had once fought. In my country, the name Belial'ad-Dīn alludes to someone cursed by their heritage." He turned to Bellaydin. "What about you, pale Belial'ad-Dīn. Are you similarly cursed by your fathers?"

"I don't think so." Bellaydin found himself unable to deny it with confidence. After all, he knew so little about his own parents, and indeed why they even gave him such a name. "I hope not," Bellaydin said quietly.

From Kahlaf there was no response. After a few minutes of silence, the Ahktarran muttered to himself, and rose from his seat. "The hour grows late, Ap'Lydin," Kahlaf said. "I am needed with the soldiers, and I am sure that your cousin awaits you for the evening meal in the Great Hall."

Without another word, Kahlaf departed, leaving Bellaydin alone with his thoughts. Bellaydin sat for a few moments more, his mind running over the events of the day, and the few weeks before. By this time tomorrow he very well could be fighting for his life. The thought chilled him to the bones. A few moments later he had arrived in the Great Hall. William, Geoffrey and Haakon were already there, discussing the defensive preparations over the evening meal. William was too engrossed in his conversation with the other men to have noticed Bellaydin's arrival.

"How are the mercenaries settling in, Geoffrey?" William asked, in between mouthfuls of venison.

"As well as can be expected," Geoffrey replied. "The Mokerian foot soldiers don't speak any Emparian, so they tend to keep to themselves. They're incredibly skilled though. They'll do well in battle. Those elven archers, well, we've all heard about the things elves can do with a bow, but I've got to tell you, those pointy-ears can get so gods-damned haughty."

"We need every man we can get, Geoffrey," William said, sawing a small loaf of bread and placing half of it on his plate.

"Indeed," Haakon said. "Let's hope this isn't a last meal we're eating here."

"No word from any of the nearby lords or knights yet?" asked William.

Geoffrey shook his head. "Not yet."

"Damn," said William.

"We must hope and pray that the Duke of Oldharbour arrives in time with reinforcements," said Haakon.

William paused, looked up, and noticed Bellaydin. "Ah – Bela. Please, sit down. Eat." he said.

"Thank you, William," said Bellaydin.

"Have some of the venison," said William. "It's quite good, especially with the wine."

Bellaydin did so. William was right. The venison was delicious.

"On another note," said Geoffrey. "The last of the peasants arrived today from the surrounding villages. Congratulations my lord, you are now the proud protector of three and a half thousand civilians."

"I want every able-bodied man to be given a weapon and put in the militia," William said.

"Already done," Geoffrey said.

"And the gates are sealed?"

"As tight as the bloody gates of the Underworld, my lord," said Geoffrey. He raised an ale mug. "Now we've just got to wait for our friends to arrive. Don't worry, I'm sure they'll be here before we know it." He drained the mug in one gulp. "I don't know about you, my lord, but when we get to the Realms of Righteousness, I'll miss the ale."

"There won't be any in the afterlife then, Geoffrey?" said William, his eyes twinkling.

"Well, you know what the priests say. After death we have to look forward to an eternity of purity and simplicity. So, from the sounds of it, no grog."

"I can see why you're not looking forward to it, Geoffrey," said Haakon.

"It's why I thought I'd drain the castle dry before hand, just to be on the safe side. Bellaydin, pass me that jug would you?"

"Careful, Geoffrey," said William as Bellaydin passed the wine jug towards the knight. "You're supposed to be leading my troops into battle."

"Against thousands of Goriinchians? Well, in that case, I'd better drink some more."

Despite himself, Bellaydin could not help but laugh, and William and Haakon joined in. Their laughter was only cut short when a deep, reverberating sound echoed through the dining hall.

"What was that?" said Bellaydin.

"The signal horn," said William, dropping his spoon. "The Goriinchians have been sighted."

***

"Stay close to me, Bela," said William, as they climbed the steps leading to the rampart. Bellaydin nodded, and did as asked.

"Shouldn't we go back and put on some armour?" he asked William, feeling a little exposed and vulnerable in the loose tunic and trousers he wore. "I feel almost naked."

William chuckled. "Bela, relax," he said. "We're not going into battle yet. First the Goriinchians arrive. Then they send over someone to offer us terms of surrender. We naturally refuse, and then they settle in to try and starve us out."

Bellaydin was confused. "When does the battle happen?"

"When they realise we've got enough food and water to last months and that reinforcements are on the way. Before that, however, they'll probably catapult a few corpses over the walls."

"Why?"

"To try and get us to die of disease first," William said nonchalantly.

Bellaydin shuddered. His stomach was churning with nervous anticipation. He did not understand how William could be acting so calmly with the knowledge of the carnage that awaited them.

"Don't worry, we'll get to fight them soon enough," William said. His face turned suddenly grim. "None of us are in a rush to get to the bloodshed, I assure you."

They reached the top of the walls, passing a few militia who stood guard along with a few of the Eldara mercenaries.

"I can see them, my lord," said Geoffrey, peering through the spyglass. "They're coming towards us at a fairly steady march."

William looked to the horizon uneasily, and Bellaydin did likewise, noting a blot on the horizon that grew larger every minute.

"I can't see much myself," William said.

"Here," said Geoffrey. "Try this." The knight passed to William the same spyglass which Bellaydin remembered him using when they were in Goriinchia.

"What is this?" said William. "Where did you get it?"

Geoffrey shrugged. "The Duke of Oldharbour gave it to me. It has some sort of enchantment bound to it that enhances vision. I didn't ask the duke where he obtained it from."

William rubbed the spyglass with his fingers, a sceptical look on his face, and then held it up to his eye, gazing towards the horizon.

"Do you see them?" Bellaydin asked eagerly.

"Oh yes," said William. "And it's just as the scout said. Thousands of them. Infantry, archers, cavalry, siege weapons, the lot."

"Here, you take it," William said, passing the spyglass to Bellaydin.

"Thank you, William."

"Geoffrey," William said. "Assemble the honour guard. Raise the standards. I want to put on a show for their diplomat."

"Right away, my lord," Geoffrey said.

As William commanded, the standards were raised – the cross of the Ap'Lydins representing William, and the black stallion of the de Morcor family standing for Haakon. Under these standards both William and Haakon's bodyguards stood mounted in full armour. William and Haakon were in full regalia, mounted upon their steeds, while Bellaydin stood next to his cousin's horse, holding its reins.

As they assembled, the Goriinchian army inched closer and closer, drums banging, men shouting and the long mournful sound of bagpipes filling the air. Within a short period, the army was large enough to be seen clearly, and as it reached the outskirts of Wishapton, it halted in its tracks, waiting for the siege equipment to catch up.

"Here we go," said William quietly as, in the distance, he heard Goriinchian officers shouting orders to their men.

"Here comes the emissary, my lord," said the lookout.

From the horizon rode a small group of horsemen, galloping towards Wishapton.

"Open the gates for them," William called out. "Bring them straight here."

"Yes, my lord," responded the lookout. He passed on the instructions.

Four riders entered the city. Three of them were quite obviously Saldarri rangers, armed with longbows. The fourth rider, the leader, was cloaked in black. At full pelt they drove their horses up the streets of Wishapton not stopping until they were a few scant feet in front of William. The horses whinnied as the riders yanked them to a stop and dismounted. The Saldarri stood close by their leader's side as he stepped towards William.

"Greetings to you, infidel Lord," the cloaked figure said, drawing back his hood. "I am Cathan Culainn, High Priest of the Horned God. I am here to offer you a generous settlement – a chance to surrender."

Neither William nor any of the other Emparians spoke. They only eyed the emissary warily. Bellaydin swallowed hard, remembering his last encounter with Cathan Culainn. He hoped the High Priest did not recognise him.

"These are our terms, as brought down to you from the Horned God himself. You will surrender the city to the magnificence of the Prophet-King Ygarak. You shall hand yourself personally into his custody, Heir of Lydin. The remainder of your people will be accepted into the Horned God's faith and reunified with Karlicia, but otherwise allowed to live freely," Cathan said, his lips twisted into a sneer.

"Why do you call me Heir of Lydin?" William demanded.

"That is what you are, infidel Lord. You are and always were intended to be a slave of the Horned God. It is your one true purpose," Cathan replied.

"You are mistaken. I am not this Heir you speak of."

Cathan gave a sinister smile. "Oh, we shall see, lord of infidels. We shall see. What is your answer?"

William nodded to Bellaydin, who stepped aside. Tugging the reins of his horses, William urged his horse forward, and rode it until he was so close to Cathan that the Goriinchian could feel the horse's breath on his face.

"This is my answer, Goriinchian filth. We are freeborn men, men of Emparia. We shall never grovel and kiss the ground in the name of your weak and pitiful god." William spat at the ground.

The Goriinchian frowned. His words were cold, devoid of emotion or feeling. "You should reconsider, infidel lord. The whole might of the nation of Goriinchia is arrayed at your doorstep. Warchief Aonghus Culainn, unbeaten in battle, leads our forces. The great Prophet-King himself is here, providing inspiration to his troops. You are outnumbered ten to one. You have no chance, only death awaits you." His lips twisted into a sneer. "Think of your men."

"Leave," William said, his words dripping with hatred.

"Our Prophet-King has conquered all those who stood in his way. Even Mael the Apostate, last and greatest of the unbelievers, wilted before the might of the Horned God's chosen one. Do you wish to share his fate?"

William moved his face closer to the emissary. "Are you deaf? I said leave!" he snarled.

The Goriinchian emissary took a step back. "I can see my words are wasted on faithless fools such as yourself, Heir of Lydin," Cathan said. "You should know that since you have refused our offer, we are obliged to kill you, and all the people within these walls."

"Get out!" roared William.

"So be it. Know that it is death now that comes for you." The Goriinchian nodded to his fellows, and they mounted their horses. "Hiyah!" Cathan yelled, lashing the reins of his horse. The Goriinchian party galloped out of Wishapton almost as quickly as they had entered.

"How long do you think we've got before they attack?" said Bellaydin, watching Cathan and his men depart.

"Not long," William said. "Not long at all."

***

Bellaydin waited.

The minutes turned into hours, and the hours into days. Still, the Goriinchians did not attack. Their siege engineers made token efforts to damage the walls, but were easily driven off. Then they started to catapult fresh corpses over the walls, hoping that disease would spread. In all of this, Wishapton's defenders stood firm.

But, after three days, Bellaydin knew this would all change. William had said that Ygarak was getting impatient, and he demanded results from his generals. It would not be long until they abandoned the tactic of trying to starve out Wishapton's defenders. No, now they would drive them out with fire and steel.

***

The drumming, the endless drumming. It was all he could hear. It filled his thoughts, pounded in his skull. The noise had been going on for over an hour, driving Bellaydin mad. The only other sound was the wail of the Goriinchian bagpipes – an almost funeral dirge which, Bellaydin thought glumly, was perhaps rather appropriately heralding their own impending deaths.

"Don't worry, it'll be over soon," said Geoffrey. "They've got to sleep some time."

"Oh gods, I hope so," Bellaydin said. "I can't take much more of this."

"They're trying to destroy our morale," William said. "I think their captains know that we'll outlast them in any siege, so they're hoping they can trick us into surrendering without a fight."

Geoffrey nodded, then, suddenly, his eyes widened in shock. "Incoming!" he yelled. "Take cover!"

Bellaydin watched as men rushed about all around him, moving out the way of whatever was hurtling towards them.

"Over here, Bela," William pulled the squire towards him. As he did so, a huge flaming projectile soared overhead, colliding with a nearby building. The house erupted into flames, and the fire quickly spread. "I want men out there to put out those flames," yelled William. "Right this instant."

"Yes, milord," shouted a soldier, before barking a few orders to other men. Within a few minutes, men were dashing to the well with buckets.

"Here comes another one," yelled Geoffrey.

Another fireball exploded near them, feeding the scorching inferno that was quickly devouring the houses of Wishapton. It was lucky that women and children were already evacuated into the castle. For now, it was only militia and other soldiers who remained in the village proper. The Goriinchian mangonels continued to fire into Wishapton relentlessly, destroying all that they hit. Regardless of how the battle turned out, Wishapton would be nothing more than ashes by the time any reinforcements arrived.

"They're moving their catapults," Geoffrey said, looking over the walls "They're changing their targets."

Below, on the ground, William signalled for the men to reassemble. "There's nothing we can do about the fire. We need to save the water."

"Incoming!" yelled Geoffrey again.

This time, the Goriinchian catapults fired ordinary rocks, but they had readjusted the trajectory so that rather than targeting the village of Wishapton, they went for the castle atop the hill. Luckily the increased distance played havoc with the accuracy of the catapults, and most shots veered far off target, either flying straight over the walls or past the castle. A few, however, were well aimed enough that they smashed into the walls of the keep. Fortunately the building was strong enough to withstand most of the blows without any noticeable damage.

"They're not going to get us that easily," said William. He turned to Bela. "Wait here for a moment."

William ran to the walls, climbing the steps quickly and reaching the top of the wall in no time at all. With a tremendous cry, he leaned over the edge, so the Goriinchians could see him and waved his sword defiantly. "Come and get me, you kilted maniacs."

Bellaydin was surprised. Such bravado was unusual coming from his usually sedate cousin. He froze where he was, unsure as to whether to join

William on the walls. Eventually, after some hesitation, he dashed up to join his cousin.

"Are you mad? Get down, my lord!" said Geoffrey, trying to pull the earl back from the walls.

"I'm alright, Geoffrey. I'm fine," William said.

"Here, Bellaydin, take your cousin aside. The heat's affecting his mind," Geoffrey said.

"Would you stop it?" William said, angrily. "I said I am fine." He stood up uneasily, rubbing his head. "Ah, those bloody drums," he said. "They've... stopped?"

He looked around anxiously. Just as he spoke, the great noise from the Goriinchians ceased. An eerie silence descended upon the battle field. A voice cut through the still.

"Heir of Lydin!" High Priest Cathan shouted. "The great Ygarak, Prophet of Prophets and Eternal King of Karlicia wishes to offer you one last chance to save your people. Simply surrender yourself, and the others shall be allowed to live."

The High Priest sat atop his steed, moving back and forth in front of the Goriinchian armies, seemingly waiting for the Emparian response. "My brother is the greatest general in the known world, infidels," Cathan said. "Even now, he discusses strategy with our great king. There will be no escape for any of you. That I can assure you. What is your answer? Wisdom or folly?"

There was a whooshing noise, then the sound of something skewering flesh. The High Priest yelled in pain. Embedded into his arm was a single arrow.

"Does that answer your question?" William said. He turned to the elven archer next to him. "Damn fine shot," he said.

The Eldara archer nodded and quietly thanked William.

The High Priest yanked the arrow from his arm, screaming in pain as he did so. "So be it!" Cathan said, his voice punctuated with ragged gasps. "You have chosen folly. And that folly will be your death." Cathan drew his sword, waving it above his head threateningly as he reared his horse.

"What is that all about?" said William.

"They always try to scare you with this sort of dramatics," said Geoffrey.

"It's working," said Bellaydin quietly. His palms were cold and sweaty and his heartbeat rapid.

"Bela," said William. "That was the easy part. The next bit is terrible."

"Oh gods," Bellaydin said.

"Here it comes," Geoffrey said. "They're bringing up the ram."

"Reinforce the gate!" yelled William. "Archers to the walls!"

The elven mercenaries, led by Neriaos, took their positions as foot soldiers scrambled below, propping up the gate with whatever was at hand.

"Back, back!" Geoffrey yelled, as men rushed about him, reforming their lines. On top of the walls, a mixture of militia and elven mercenaries formed the line of archers. Below, behind the town gate, militiamen were supplemented by Mokerian mercenaries and the dismounted cavalry from William's bodyguard.

"Archers – aim!" said Neriaos, leading both his own mercenaries and the militia bowmen. He held his hand up, waiting as the Goriinchians moved the ram closer, and closer, and…

"Loose arrows!" Neriaos said. A rain of arrows landed on the Goriinchians, skewering dozens. The archers reloaded and let loose another volley. More Goriinchians keeled over into the dirt, arrows sticking from their bodies. Goriinchian reinforcements rushed in to replace their fallen comrades, pushing against the ram with all their might. With a shuddering lurch, it moved towards the gate.

"Here they come," Geoffrey yelled.

"Hold the gate!" William said.

There was a loud groan and bang as the ram slammed against the gate. Bellaydin heard a loud, pain-filled scream behind him. As William struggled with Geoffrey and the other soldiers in reinforcing the gate, Bellaydin rushed to the assistance of Haakon de Morcor. He grabbed the older man's arm, and slung it over his neck, propping him up.

"I'm… fine," Haakon's voice sounded irritable. "It's just… the excitement." He winced, cursing in pain. Beads of sweat appeared on his forehead, despite the chill of the air. He clutched his chest again.

Bellaydin was hesitant. "Are you sure?"

"Yes," Haakon said, almost out of breath. "Take my sword. Place it in my hand."

Bellaydin reached around the man's waist, grabbed the sword by its hilt, and carefully drew it from its scabbard. Then, turning the hilt towards Haakon, he passed the sword to him.

"Thank you," he said. He paused for breath, and held his sword up in the air. His arm trembled and he stumbled a bit, but, after a few moments, his breathing eased. "Now go," Haakon said.

"Yes, Your Grace," Bellaydin said, bowing. Without a backward glance he left Haakon, running back to William and the others who were still trying to reinforce the gate.

"The oil!" yelled William to the soldiers on the wall. Bellaydin watched as three soldiers heaved a large cauldron over to the edge of the wall, tipping its contents on to the Goriinchians below. The screams of agony that followed were horrific.

"This is no time for squeamishness, Bela," William said, noticing

Bellaydin's expression. "Better them than us. Don't stop now, men." William yelled to the walls.

There was a loud bang and the sound of splintering timbers.

"The gate's giving, my lord!" Geoffrey yelled.

"Hold!" yelled William. "Hold!"

Bellaydin did his best to help, assisting soldiers in propping up the gate and, when there was a spare space, holding his own body against it. Time moved agonisingly slowly, and each shout and yell added to the strain Bellaydin felt on his muscles. The ram continued to slam the gate time and time again, each blow rattling the insides of Bellaydin's skull, and bruising his shoulders. Behind the gates, the Goriinchians groaned and strained, and every so often, one screamed, his skin burning from the oil or his chest skewered by an elven arrow.

Then, all of a sudden, the banging stopped. Bellaydin heard cheering from upon the wall.

William looked about. "What in the name of – "

A voice came from the wall. "My lord! We've done it. The ram's on fire. The Goriinchians have dropped it and the stragglers are running back to their lines." The gate defenders joined in the cheers.

"Praise be to the gods," William said.

Geoffrey patted William on the back. "No offence, but I didn't see Kytilas down here with us in the mud, my lord."

The stress of the past hour or so gave in to temporary relief and William laughed out loud. "You rascal," he said. "I'll forgive that blasphemy for now, as long as you get up on that wall and watch those Goriinchians like a hawk."

Geoffrey nodded. "Right away, my lord," he said, putting his sword back in its scabbard. "A knight's work is never done."

"We're not out of this yet," a gruff voice said from behind.

Turning to Kahlaf, William placed his hand on the Ahktarran's shoulder. "No, we aren't. But the men fought well, and they deserve their accolades."

"Save your cheers, William," Kahlaf warned. "Tomorrow we may all be dead."

Nodding curtly to Bellaydin, Geoffrey went to join the archers and other soldiers atop the walls.

"Did we win?" said Bellaydin.

"For now," said William. "But that won't be the end of it. The Goriinchians are toying with us. After that farcical attempt, they're going to throw everything they have at us."

"Everything?" said Bellaydin, his heart sinking.

"Well, their generals and king are probably going to sit on their backsides up on the hills back there, but don't worry, there will be plenty of Goriinchians for all of us, even without the leaders charging at us."

"You've done well so far, William," panted Haakon, "but now comes the real challenge." He paused, clutching his chest again.

William's eyes flashed. "Your grace, you are in no condition to fight. Come. While we have some breathing space, let me have the men escort you to the safety of the castle."

"Gods damn you both," said Haakon. "Willy, you are as much a damn fool as that cousin of yours. I am fine. I will fight, as I always have."

William seemed taken aback. Bellaydin guessed that his cousin did not often see such a temper from Haakon.

"I'm sorry, I'm sorry," Haakon said, seemingly contrite. "Battle stress, you know how it is. I am truly grateful for both of you fussing over me, but please, I insist, no special treatment. I will not have it said that Haakon de Morcor cowered in a castle while others fought in his name."

"There's no shame in it, Haakon. You've proved your valour, time and time again. You need not prove it here."

"Perhaps," said Haakon, moving his sword arm. "But I will do so anyway."

William bowed. "If that is your wish, Your Grace," he said, formally addressing Haakon. "It will be an honour to fight alongside you."

"More formality, Willy? You really must be worried," said Haakon, a twinkle in his eyes.

"Well, since we might not survive this, I thought it was about time I started addressing you properly," he said smiling.

"Oh? So says the little boy who used to throw his food at me when I visited his uncle."

Bellaydin looked at his cousin. "What did he say?"

"Ignore him," said William. "He always does this." The sky above them thundered. "Rain," William observed, as drops began to fall on to his face, increasing with frequency.

"At least it will put out the fires," Bellaydin said as the shower quickly became a downpour. William nodded.

"Oh, William."

William turned around, looking towards the wall, where Geoffrey stood, waving to him. "What is it?"

"You might want to get back here," he said, drawing his sword. "Now."

Looking alarmed, William drew his own sword and walked towards the walls, motioning for Bellaydin, Haakon, and all the other soldiers on the ground to follow. "What do you see, Geoffrey?" William asked as he hurriedly mounted the steps.

"Oh," he said, "nothing much, just my horrible, imminent, bloody death approaching me."

"No time for this," said William, approaching with Bellaydin. "What is it you see?"

"Take a look, my lord," said Geoffrey, motioning to the horizon.

The Goriinchian army was advancing again, and this time they were going to hit with their full force. Vast lines of soldiers marched towards the walls of Wishapton, bringing with them siege towers and ladders for scaling the walls. As the great machines rumbled towards the walls, the soldiers cheered and banged their weapons together, bringing a percussive accompaniment to the wailing bagpipes.

"Here we go," William nodded towards Neriaos.

"Archers, ho!" the Eldara said, ordering the bowmen to follow.

"Aim!"

"Loose arrows!"

A stream of arrows flew across the air, cutting a swathe through the Goriinchian line. Out of nowhere, swift Saldarri rangers appeared, and responded to the Emparian barrage.

"Shoot at will!" Neriaos yelled as some of the Goriinchian arrows hit true, militia falling off the wall, dead. Another swarm of arrows shot towards the enemy, but the Goriinchians hardly slowed in their pace. A whizzing arrow flew towards William, and he raised his shield just as a single arrow penetrated an inch into the shield's front.

"They've reached the walls. This is it, everyone," said William. "Spread out, cover every attack."

Bellaydin moved, but William grabbed his arm. "You stay here Bela, where I can see you."

Bellaydin's heart was thumping wildly as he looked towards the approaching Goriinchians.

The bowmen fired again, felling dozens more Goriinchians, but the dead were insignificant compared to the mass of soldiers that continued to march. The Saldarri rangers had pulled back, not wanting to put their own soldiers in the crossfire.

"Positions!" yelled William. Nearby, Kahlaf followed the earl's lead, and barked orders to the militia around him. Most of the defenders were on the walls with their liege lord. Haakon and his troops stood below, on the ground, ready in case the Goriinchians made another attempt on the gate.

"Fire at will!" yelled Neriaos. The archers abandoned any attempt at symmetry and began to fire whenever ready. More Goriinchians died, their bodies falling into the mud, but the enemy advance was not slowed.

"You alright down there, Haakon?" William yelled, without turning his head.

"Not a problem Willy," Haakon said, his voice sounding strained. "Concentrate on the task at hand."

William looked towards Kahlaf, and nodded.

"Draw steel!" William yelled. There was the sound of steel scraping as the militia and mercenaries did as commanded.

The siege towers were right in Bellaydin's vision now, inching forward with menacing consistency.

"Steady!" yelled William, adopting his fighting stance.

The archers changed targets, firing at the men in the siege towers as best they could, before switching back to the Goriinchians below, specifically those attempting to plant the huge siege ladders into the dirt below. Atop the towers, Goriinchian archers fired back at the defenders but were quickly dispatched by the Eldara bowmen.

"Here they come," said Geoffrey.

With a loud bang the siege towers came to a stop, their gangplanks crashing down on the wall. From inside the towers came a mixture of shouts and screams as the Goriinchians charged out, attacking the defenders.

The first wave was cut down swiftly, William and Geoffrey killing two apiece. The other mercenaries made short work of the rest, though two militia were cut down during the melee. Standing beside his cousin, Bellaydin's heart raced but, as yet, he had not crossed swords with an enemy. Though he knew it would be not be long until he did.

He did not turn his head to look further down the wall, but he could hear Kahlaf roaring in triumph, and had no doubt the Ahktarran had smashed any Goriinchian foolish enough to challenge him.

"Second wave. Get ready!" William said as another group of Goriinchians charged over the gangplank.

A giant brute of a man loomed before Bellaydin, eyes aflame with hatred. He lunged at Bellaydin, swinging the axe towards the young man's chest. Frantically, Bellaydin tried to remember what he had been taught of swordplay, but in the heat of battle all memory of posture, proper technique or style fled his mind. He twisted his body, barely avoiding a disembowelling blow from the Goriinchian and then, his expression tightening with fear, counterattacked, thrusting the sword into his assailant. The Goriinchian's eyes widened, rolling in their sockets as Bellaydin's sword cut through flesh and bone. Dropping the axe, the Goriinchian tried to pull back, blood gushing from the embedded sword. With a startled cry, Bellaydin pulled on his sword, tearing it from the man and sending an arc of blood spattering in the air. The Goriinchian staggered back, and toppled from the wall, his life spent before he hit the ground.

Bellaydin had never dwelled on what it would feel like to take a man's life, and now that he had done so, he was not sure if he was thrilled with the experience. The rush of adrenalin and thrill of battle was small satisfaction when compared to the horrid expression on the man's face as Bellaydin's sword had pierced his flesh, skewering him like a stuck pig.

Then there was the blood. Bellaydin had never seen so much of it. He felt disgusted with himself, repulsed by the death he had dealt out against a fellow human being. His stomach lurched, threatening to expel its contents.

"Bellaydin, watch out," yelled William.

Bellaydin blinked, suddenly becoming aware of his surroundings and ducked narrowly avoiding the wide sweep of a Goriinchian's sword. His cousin finished off the Goriinchian with a single sword thrust, and kicked the body from the ramparts.

"Keep a clear head," William said. "We're not out of this yet!"

Another Goriinchian bellowed a challenge to Bellaydin, but his moves were sluggish and tortured, no doubt due to the arrow stuck in his side. Still, he brought his weapon down towards Bellaydin's, but the blow was easily parried. Without thinking, Bellaydin pulled his sword arm back and swung again cutting a deep, wounding gash across the man's chest, and sending him tumbling to his death.

His second kill was somehow easier than the first. The same cold feeling was there, deep in his heart, but this time it seemed almost muted. His heart still pounded, and his throat was dry, but the queasiness of before was gone, replaced with a new feeling, one that felt like exhilaration.

"Another wave," yelled William, as the surviving defenders reorganised themselves.

"There's too many," shouted Geoffrey. "We're being overrun!"

Bellaydin looked as more and more Goriinchians swarmed out of the siege towers, slowly overwhelming the defences. The militiamen were the first to be cut down, not skilled enough to hold off multiple assailants. The mercenaries lasted longer, often taking down half a dozen enemies before they themselves fell to Goriinchian blades. The tide of the battle was turning against the defenders, even Bellaydin could see that.

"Fall back!" William said. "Fall back to the keep!" His call was echoed by the surviving defenders, and, fighting off their attackers, they began to make a fighting retreat to the keep. "Back, back!" William ordered, dispatching a few more Goriinchians as he and Bellaydin retreated down the stairs.

"Grab the horses!" Geoffrey yelled, leaping on to his mount.

Men scattered, trying to get on the horses that were whinnying with fright. Haakon was already on his, looking through the mass of fleeing soldiers.

"William," he called out. "William!"

"I'm here!" William called out, his hand still gripped around Bellaydin's wrist.

"Get to your horse!" Haakon yelled, pointing his sword to the other side of the path.

"On my way!" William yelled, his hand slipping from Bellaydin's. "You'll have to get on mine as well, Bela," William said as he ran as fast as he could through the field, now rapidly becoming mud from the heavy rain. Behind them Goriinchians splashed and skidded in an attempt to catch up. Bellaydin heard the sounds of battle, and that of the dead and dying. He slipped, nearly losing his footing.

"Hurry my lord," Geoffrey said, as lightning flashed overhead. Eldara archers ran past the soldiers, providing cover.

"Come on, Bellaydin," William yelled, as he grabbed the reins of his horse.

Bellaydin scrambled up the hill but his feet, already slick from the mud and blood, slipped and he tumbled over backwards, sliding back down the slope towards the approaching Goriinchians.

"Bela!" William called out.

Bellaydin heard the coarse laughter of the Goriinchians and muttered words in their language as they tramped towards him, sensing an easy kill. A Goriinchian brought down his sword in a killing blow and Bellaydin rolled out of the way, leaving the blade to pierce the ground and spatter him with mud. He heard more Goriinchians approaching, yelling and laughing as they came.

"Hiyah!"

Bellaydin heard the sound of galloping hooves. He looked up. Haakon rode toward him, sword aloft, trampling any enemy that got in his way. The duke's sword glittered in the afternoon light as it felled foe after foe and soon Haakon was upon Bellaydin, slaying the Goriinchian who menaced Bela with a single blow. Haakon turned his horse and extended a hand to Bellaydin, barely stopping to do so. Bellaydin levered himself up from the mud and grabbed Haakon's hand. The duke, grunting with exertion, pulled Bellaydin up on the horse, and then, with a triumphant yell, galloped away from the ditch, towards the castle.

Seeing the successful rescue, William spurred his own horse into action, taking one final look for any surviving soldiers, before joining the rest in the frantic gallop to the safety of the castle.

"Open the gate! Open the gate!" yelled Geoffrey as they galloped over the drawbridge.

The portcullis groaned as it slowly lifted up, allowing the fleeing soldiers to enter the castle. Archers fired from the castle at pursuing Goriinchians, trying to give the surviving Emparian troops enough time to reach safety.

"In, in!" said William, waving the troops into the castle.

"There are a few stragglers," Geoffrey said, pointing outside the gates where the Goriinchians were pursuing a few mercenaries and militiamen.

"They'll never make it in time," said Haakon.

William pulled on his reins, turning the horse around. "Then we must give them time. Come Geoffrey," William said, drawing his sword.

"Again and again," the knight said, doing likewise.

"Haakon, get Bellaydin and the others inside. Now!"

Haakon nodded as Geoffrey and William charged the Goriinchians coming towards the castle.

"Inside, now, while we have the chance!" Haakon said to Bellaydin.

"What about William?" Bellaydin said, looking back towards them.

"He knows what he's doing," said Haakon.

Against Bellaydin's will, Haakon urged his horse on and the pair of them rode into Castle Wishapton.

.

CHAPTER 18

Bellaydin shivered.

How long have we been holed up in here? Minutes? Hours? Days?

Outside, the sounds of battle were unrelenting: the shouts of the enemy, the clash of steel on steel, the rumbling of drums and wail of bagpipes, the smashing of timber and brick. One noise stood out over all – the screams of both friend and foe as they took one another's lives. Bellaydin shuddered. He would never forget that sound as long as he lived.

His stomach growled. Hunger gnawed at him as his parched throat thirsted for a drink of water or ale, wine… anything. People huddled around him. He could smell the stink of their sweat and fear. Over the din of the battle, something sounded out.

"What's that?" said Haakon. In the torchlight, Bellaydin could see the duke's face was thin and pallid, like parchment stretched too thin. His grey hair lay flat against his skull, wet with sweat and grime. His cheeks were fuzzy with grey and black stubble.

The noise came again – the sound of a signal horn being blown.

"Open the gate! Open the gate!" There were more noises and some scuffling, followed by the ringing of steel.

"What's going on?" Haakon said, drawing his sword and running to the gate. He pushed his way to the front of the group of soldiers, despite their efforts to hold him back.

The sentry called out again. "Close the gate!" Bellaydin heard the portcullis tumble down but only a lone horse came through before the gate was shut. The soldier on the horse was badly injured, slumped in the saddle. He was bleeding from many wounds, but there was no mistaking him.

"Geoffrey!" Bellaydin called out.

Haakon stared at the wounded knight. "Of all the – Get the healers. Now! Take him, go, go!"

Geoffrey moaned as the horse stumbled through the crowd. As he passed Bellaydin, the knight suddenly grabbed the younger man's hand. "Bela…" he said, burbling through blood covered lips. "Bela…"

"Geoffrey!"

"They've taken him."

"Who?" Bellaydin asked.

"William. They've taken William." The knight's head slumped and he fell back in his saddle.

Haakon grabbed the attendant's hand. "I told you to get him to the hospice."

"Right away, Your Grace," said the attendant.

As Geoffrey was led away, Bellaydin approached Haakon. "They've taken William. We've got to rescue him."

"No," said Haakon. "It is too risky. The Goriinchians have surrounded the castle. Besides, we don't know if he's still alive. Not for sure."

"But we can't just leave him to die," Bellaydin said, his voice breaking.

"I said no!" Haakon roared, turning around. Bellaydin stepped back, shocked at Haakon's fury. The duke looked at Bellaydin for a moment, and his expression softened. "Look, I am sorry Bellaydin," he said gently. "But there's nothing we can do for your cousin. William is dead. And, unless something changes, in a few hours we will be, too."

"Lord Alariat." It was Neriaos, the Eldara mercenary leader. An ugly gash cut his face from his eyebrow to his upper lip.

"Yes, elf," Haakon said. "What are our losses?"

Neriaos shook his head. "Earl Genio is lost, captured. Firouz of Mokeria is dead, his skull split in two. Sir Geoffrey is grievously injured, and no one has seen the Ahktarran. We've lost half our fighting force."

"Damn!" said Haakon. He frowned, and looked towards Bellaydin, who was still standing nearby hesitantly. "Go help the surgeon," Haakon said.

"But I – you need me, I can fight."

"There will be time enough for us all to fight again," Haakon said. "I wouldn't will that moment upon us. To the surgeon with you, Bellaydin. See what you can do."

Bellaydin did not move.

"Bellaydin," Haakon said. "With your cousin missing, you answer to the highest ranking noble still here - me. That's an order. Go."

Bellaydin didn't respond. Haakon turned to the younger man, eyes hardened.

"Yes, Your Grace," came Bellaydin's eventual answer. "You might want this." He passed the spyglass to Haakon.

"Go," Haakon repeated as he took it.

Bellaydin did not waste another moment. Leaving Haakon, he followed the anguished moans of pain echoing amongst the halls until he reached the surgeon's ward. He grimaced as he entered, his eyes passing quickly over the wounded, all of whom were suffering in pain, be it light or great. While some men sobbed quietly, others screamed out, their agony stabbing Bellaydin in the chest.

"Ap'Lydin, isn't it?" said an attendant, approaching Bellaydin.

Bellaydin nodded.

"Aren't you the nephew of the Earl of Genio?" he said.

"Cousin," Bellaydin said.

"Right, cousin." The man tossed a bloodstained rag at Bellaydin. "Make yourself useful, won't you?" he said.

Bellaydin held the cloth gingerly, trying not to get his hands covered in blood. "What do you want me to do?"

"What are you, feebleminded?" said the man testily, motioning to the injured soldiers. "Help us! Staunch some of those wounds."

"Oh, I see, sorry," Bellaydin said.

The other man tended to a patient, shaking his head in disbelief. Bellaydin went to minister to one of the injured. As he looked at the individual's face, he recognised him immediately. "Geoffrey, how do you feel?"

Sir Geoffrey Keslin moved his body slightly, turning his head towards Bellaydin. For a moment there was no recognition in the knight's eyes, but then his blood-caked lips cracked into a weak smile.

"Bela…" Geoffrey murmured.

He moved a hand and felt his ribs. He winced as he ran his fingers along the bandage on his side.

"I feel like a mountain fell on me," he said softly. "How do I look?"

Bellaydin frowned.

"Be honest," Geoffrey said.

"Alive," Bellaydin said.

Geoffrey grinned, the pain still evident on his face. "That's good enough, I guess."

He rolled over, staring at the ceiling, and coughed.

"What happened?" Bellaydin asked. "What happened to William?"

"They took him," Geoffrey said. "The Goriinchians pulled him from his horse, dragged him through the mud. I tried to give chase, but there were too many. I was attacked from all directions." He breathed out, his voice wavering. "So I fled. And, shame of it all, was not even conscious when I reached the safety of the castle." With a suddenness that made Bellaydin jump, Geoffrey grabbed the younger man's hand, gripping it tightly as he looked into Bellaydin's eyes. "Bela, you must understand. William was still alive when they took him. They didn't kill him, and I think that they still haven't."

"What do they want with him?"

Geoffrey coughed, his breath coming in wheezing gasps. "I don't know, but it won't be anything pleasant." He groaned, clutching his wound.

"Sir Geoffrey," an attendant said. "You need to lie still."

"Damn you!" Geoffrey spat, trying to get up. "I'll lie still when I'm dead."

The attendant grabbed him, and carefully lay him back down on the mat. "If you don't stop moving, you will be dead."

Geoffrey grunted, and turned away. Bellaydin watched the knight stubbornly refuse to do as instructed and felt a deep sense of guilt and shame.

"Is my father here?"

Bellaydin turned around and saw Maria, looking around plaintively at the wounded men.

"Maria, I'm sorry, your father is not here." Bellaydin crouched down to look her in the eyes. "He didn't come back."

"Is he alright, Uncle Bela?" Maria's eyes shone with tears.

"I don't know, Maria, I don't know."

Maria sobbed and grabbed tightly on to Bellaydin's waist.

Bellaydin's mind was in turmoil. His cousin was in real danger, and there was nothing that could seemingly be done about it. Haakon had earlier refused to send out soldiers to rescue William, and Bellaydin thought it unlikely that he would change his mind. Geoffrey was badly wounded, and would need all his strength to pull through the night. Kahlaf was nowhere to be seen, probably dead as well. The reinforcements promised by Wulfric Highcrown had still not arrived, and by the looks of it, would come too late for William.

Bellaydin knew that the only way he would ever see his cousin alive again was if *he* ensured that it happened. But doubt nagged at him. How would he succeed where more experienced warriors had failed? He could just be throwing his life away on a cause that was already lost, but William had risked his life to save others. A commander, putting himself in danger's way for his men. Perhaps it was right that someone risked themselves to save William, and who better to do it than Bellaydin? In the short time that he had known William, his cousin had done so much for him. It was time for Bellaydin to do something in return.

Still, the fear was there. The fear of what exactly he would have to do, and of the fate that likely awaited him. The Goriinchians were outside, baying for Emparian blood, each one of those warriors a battle-hardened veteran of countless wars, any of them more than capable of tearing

328

Bellaydin to shreds, especially if he tried to take them on without any assistance. Visions of his own brutal, bloody death hovered over him. He felt a sickening sensation in his stomach, and a cold clammy chill travelled up his back.

He shook his head, swallowed his doubts, and steeled himself. He had to find courage. His cousin's life depended on it. He turned his thoughts outward, and tried to formulate a plan on how to proceed. The first thing he had to figure out was how to get outside. There was no way that Haakon would open the gate and let Bellaydin leave, but there were other options, perhaps. He just needed to find them.

"Please Uncle Bela, please, find my father and bring him home."

Maria was still crying, and Bellaydin stroked the girl's hair, comforting her.

He looked at Geoffrey – the knight having now fallen asleep – muttering and twitching through pain-filled dreams. "Now it's my turn," Bellaydin said to himself, quietly. Then he left, filled with purpose.

***

William awoke to laughter. He tried to open his eyes, but could only manage one. The other was too bruised and swollen, and he could barely move the eyelid. William's feet and hands were bound, his weapons and armour taken from him. All around him Goriinchian warriors pointed and jeered, some spitting at him, the others mocking him in their language. When they had first captured him, killing his horse from beneath him, the Goriinchians had beaten him mercilessly with the blunt ends of their weapons, bruising his body all over and breaking bones in his arms and legs. When it was clear he was no longer able to fight back, he was dragged through the mud back to the Goriinchian lines. There he had been beaten again, this time until he was unconscious.

"William of Wishapton," said a deep voice.

William recognised the man who stood before him – Aonghus Culainn,

Goriinchian Warchief.

"My men are enthusiastic. I hope they didn't hurt you too much," Aonghus said.

William tried to answer, but only a gurgle came from his cracked, bloody lips.

"I know you speak the holy tongue, Enparran," said Aonghus, "so I know you understand me. Whether you speak back is entirely up to you. Regardless, you are our prisoner. To do with as we please."

"It will not avail you," William croaked. "I am replaceable, my men will fight without me."

Aonghus smiled. "Perhaps they will, but I suspect their hearts will not be long in it. Especially once your corpse is returned to them."

"You can kill me – " said William.

"We intend to," said Aonghus.

" – but it won't win your war," William finished.

Aonghus crouched to the ground, bringing his face level with William's. "Listen, William," he said. "You and I are soldiers. This is nothing personal. It's just war. Would you not do the same to me, were I in your mercy?" William just stared.

"Of course you would," the Warchief said.

"Aonghus. I am here."

The Warchief turned his head towards the approaching figure and, seeing who it was, turned back to William.

"Brother," Aonghus said, his eyes still on William. "So nice of you to join us."

"Don't be snide, Aonghus," said Cathan. "Remember, the Horned God sees all."

Aonghus stood, and turned to Cathan. "Of course," he said. "I am, as always, his humble slave."

"That is good news for both of us," Cathan said. He turned towards William. "So this is the great and mighty Heir of Lydin then? Humbled before the Horned God, just as we all are?" His eyes roamed over William, critically. The earl struggled in his bonds.

"You are not to move in the presence of the High Priest, infidel," a Goriinchian soldier snarled, and smashed William in the back of the head with his club.

Cathan stepped towards the still figure of William, who lay sprawled on the ground, dazed. "I had expected something more, I must admit," Cathan said. "Still, if you are the one for whom we have been waiting…"

"I am not so sure, my lord," a soldier said, grabbing William's hand and twisting the palm towards Cathan. "Look. He does not have the mark."

"Without the mark, he is no one, is he not?" Aonghus asked Cathan.

"Perhaps," Cathan said. "Or perhaps it's not yet time. It is said that the mark would show itself in the presence of the Horned God's power."

"So, then, he *is* the one we want?" Aonghus said.

Cathan took another look at William. "So it would seem," the high priest said. "Aonghus, you may now pull your troops back to the perimeter of the town."

"What? Madness! The battle is nearly ours. We need to press the attack."

"The attack is of no importance, brother," Cathan said. "It was merely a distraction to draw out the Heir."

"You have sent hundreds of my warriors to their death for one man?" Aonghus was furious.

"We are all but slaves of the Horned God, brother," Cathan said coolly, "and our lives are of little import except where they further his will. The

Heir is all that matters. He is all that we require."

"I don't believe you," William said.

"Oh, believe me, infidel, that it is true. And you must live with the fact that hundreds of people will die because of you. Their blood is on your hands, Enparran."

"Cathan," said Aonghus. "The day is almost ours. Give me a few hours more, and the fortress will fall. Please, we must press our advantage, or the infidels will regroup."

"The infidels can rot in their keep, brother," Cathan said. "The Horned God will deal with them in time. Now that the Heir is in our possession, we are already victorious."

"But the battle – "

"These are the words of the Horned God, Aonghus. Do you dare defy him?"

"No, but surely there is–"

"You may petition His Majesty if you wish, Aonghus, but the decision has been made."

"I will prove you wrong, Cathan," said Aonghus. "I will speak with King Ygarak."

"See that you do, brother. Now, go. Leave me with the Heir."

Aonghus swore under his breath, and left in a huff, muttering as he disappeared into the throng of soldiers.

"Now, infidel, we shall speak," said Cathan. "There is much we have to discuss."

"There is nothing I wish to say to you," William said, ignoring the pain that sapped his strength and made his voice waver.

"Oh, but I think there is, Heir of Lydin. It may very well save your life."

Cathan brought his face down towards William again and sniffed the air in front of him contemptuously. "You stink of the heathen ways of the north, Enparran," Cathan said. "Soaked in wine and piss, and infested with lice. Is it true your kind sleeps with their dogs?"

William said nothing. "You stay silent in the presence of your betters, infidel. That is encouraging."

"What do you want with me?" William demanded.

"You are more important than you realise, Enparran," said Cathan. "But you will never find true fulfilment in the company of infidels and truth-abhorrers. You are the Heir of Lydin, the most favoured of the slaves of the Horned God."

William spat in Cathan's face. The priest wiped off the spit and then slapped William across the face. "Faithless fool, do you even comprehend the situation you are in? I hold your life in my hands. The power I have been given over you is absolute."

"Then kill me already." William said.

Cathan chuckled. "Not yet. I have something else in mind." He stood, raising his arms. "You are an infidel, marked for death by the Horned God himself, but our great lord wishes to tell you that he is not completely without mercy. He offers you a choice."

"Choice? What choice?"

"You can live, Heir of Lydin. Become that which you were always meant to be. You refused me once, but I ask again. Join us."

"Join you?" William said.

"Yes, Heir of Lydin. Become a slave of the Horned God. Find greatness."

Cathan looked at William expectantly. William, however, simply laughed. "Why do you laugh, infidel?" the Goriinchian said. "Do you mock the

333

Horned God?"

William stopped his laughter, and fixed Cathan with a cold stare. "Do you believe for even a single moment that I would be a slave to your god? Even to save my own life?"

"Are you refusing?" said Cathan. The tone of his voice suggested he was genuinely surprised and shocked.

"Damn you and your blasted god, barbarian! Not in a thousand years will I bow and scrape like a slave to the horned thug."

Cathan looked stunned, as if he'd been hit with a thunderbolt.

"Does that answer your question?" William said.

Cathan screamed in anger, and struck William across the face with his fist.

"That's for the blasphemy, infidel. You have decided your own fate."

A sharp pain shot through William's jaw as he was struck again. Groaning, he spat out a tooth and a mouthful of blood on to the ground. Another blow knocked him into unconsciousness.

***

Bellaydin wiped the filth from his clothes. After a long search, he had eventually found the only route that could get him out of the building unnoticed – the latrine. Bracing himself he climbed into the foul pit only to slip and find himself unceremoniously dumped in the moat below. Gasping and spluttering for breath, he scrambled up the shore. Surprisingly, there were no Goriinchians anywhere to be seen. Bellaydin wondered what was going on. Had they lifted the siege? A foul stench hung in the air, mostly due to the corpses lying all around – Emparian and Goriinchian alike – left to rot where they fell. Bellaydin bit back the urge to vomit. Now that he had made it outside, he was not sure how exactly he should proceed. How was he going to find William, let alone rescue him? He would be spotted immediately.

Unless, he thought

He rushed to a nearby Goriinchian, lying dead near the moat. Holding his breath to avoid the horrid smell, Bellaydin carefully stripped the body of the tartan cloak wrapped around its chest. It smelt horrible, but was mostly free of blood. He knew it was also likely infested with lice, but, justifying this with the knowledge that he would not have to wear it for long, he dusted it off, and wrapped it around himself.

The helmet was next. Luckily, the Goriinchian had died with a sword thrust to the stomach, so the helmet was in relatively good condition. He carefully took it off the dead man, and placed it on his own head. It did not fit that well, but at least it stayed on, and it obscured his facial features. It would do. Bellaydin picked up the warrior's axe, took a few practice swings, and carried the weapon with him.

As Bellaydin walked through Wishapton, the signs of battle were everywhere – burnt out buildings, crumbling stone and hundreds of corpses littering the streets and thoroughfares. But of the living, there was no one to be seen. He continued towards the walls of the town, marvelling at the apparent serenity. The muddy ground was covered with footprints, and it was obvious that large numbers of men had very recently marched through the area. Carrion birds wheeled around in the sky above him, biding their time before they descended to feast. And still, through all of this, Bellaydin did not see a single Goriinchian soldier. What was the cause of this?

When he finally reached the city gates he saw the portcullis was raised, and the mechanism had been broken, jamming the gate open. Clearly, even though they had left, the Goriinchians had wanted to make sure that they could quickly re-enter if needed. Bellaydin idly wondered if they had done the same to the gates on the other side of the city wall. He stepped through the gate, crossing the ground that separated Wishapton from the outside world. Once he did so, the sight that met his eyes caused his throat to go dry, and a cold tingling to run down his spine. In front of him stood the entire Goriinchian force, just outside Wishapton, and seemingly surrounding the city's walls in a vast circular formation.

He was easily spotted, several warriors approaching him curiously. They came right towards him, and, poking him aggressively, said a few words in Goriinchian to him. Bellaydin froze. He had no idea what the men were saying. He knew nothing of the Goriinchian language. The warriors, however, looked at him expectantly, expecting some sort of answer. Bellaydin knew he would have to think fast. He placed his hand on his throat, and gurgled something incomprehensible. He hoped that the warriors would think that his throat had been wounded in battle and that he had lost the ability to speak. The fact he had the piece of tartan wrapped around his neck might go some way to making the deception seem plausible.

Evidently, the ploy worked. The warriors looked at him for a few more moments and laughed loudly, babbling some more words of Goriinchian. One of them slapped Bellaydin on the back and pointed towards a mass of warriors camped nearby. Bellaydin gathered the warrior was telling him to go join them and, bowing his head in gratitude, Bellaydin headed off towards the group.

Despite his nerves, Bellaydin tried to assume a nonchalant pace, hoping it would allow him to blend into the mass of soldiers. A few Goriinchians glanced at him fleetingly, before looking away, apparently satisfied that he was nothing but a lost soldier. Underneath all the armour, Bellaydin was sweating, and not just from the heat. He had no idea what he had got himself into. It was an impulsive decision to leave Castle Wishapton in the first place. What was he doing now, trying to infiltrate the Goriinchian army? Rescuing his cousin? Just how would he find him? And if he did find William, how would the pair of them escape? He didn't know the answer to any of the questions. It was times like this that Bellaydin wished he was religious, a devout follower of the gods. Even one god would probably do it. He wished he had the unswerving faith of the Goriinchian Morgan

Culainn, for instance.

Just as those thoughts ran through his mind, Bellaydin stepped over the crest of a hill, and came across a group of Goriinchian women washing clothes in the river. Amazingly, the very name he had pondered three minutes before now sprang to his lips as he noticed one of the women in particular. "Morgan," Bellaydin breathed.

Trying to stay out of sight of any soldiers, Bellaydin approached the girl. His armour clanked every step of the way. "Morgan! Morgan!"

Morgan dropped the cloak she was washing, and turned her head. She muttered something in Goriinchian – from the tone, it was obviously a question.

Bellaydin shook his head. He did not understand her. He would have to take a risk. He took off the helmet. Morgan's eyes widened. She gasped, placing a hand in front of her mouth.

"I need your help," Bellaydin whispered.

Morgan looked unsure.

"Please."

She seemed to be weighing up the idea in her mind. Then, after a few minutes, she turned to the other women, muttering some words in Goriinchian. Nodding, they gathered up the washing, and went on their way. As soon as the other women were out of sight, Morgan turned to him, speaking hastily in Emparian. "What are you doing here, Enparran? Are you mad? You could be killed!"

"I had to come here. It's important," Bellaydin said.

"What do you mean, important?" She grabbed his helmet. "In the name of all that is holy, put the helmet back on before someone recognises you."

Bellaydin did so and attempted to make his case, telling Morgan all he could about his predicament. He told her about the battle, about the

337

Emparian retreat to Castle Wishapton and William's capture. He told her about the sudden withdrawal of the Goriinchians, and he told her of his desire to find and rescue his cousin.

"You are brave, Enparran," Morgan said after he had finished telling her everything. "Foolish, perhaps," she added, smiling, "but brave nonetheless."

"Will you help me then?" Bellaydin, still breathing heavily, looked at Morgan expectantly.

"This is much that you ask of me, Enparran," Morgan said. "You would put my own life in danger, as well as yours?"

"At least let me speak to him. That's all I ask." Bellaydin pleaded.

Morgan's brow furrowed in thought. Then, a few moments later, her features softened. "Come with me," she said.

***

Pain.

It filled William's world.

He lay stretched out on a torture rack, his head secured in place so it faced the sky. The ropes cut into his flesh, rubbing his skin raw. William could not see the many wounds on his body, or the blood that stained his torn and tattered clothes, but he knew they were there. The Goriinchians had beaten, whipped and scourged him, and when they were satisfied that there was nothing more they could get from him, they dragged him to this hill where they promised that he would watch as the carrion birds feasted on his guts.

Another bolt of agony shot through his limbs. Sweat beaded on his forehead. He tried to shut out the pain, tried to ignore the agony that had been inflicted upon him by his captors. He thought of other things, other places. Had not Kytilas, the Shining Divine Martyr, endured death and humiliation at his enemies' hands to save the soul of one mortal child? Had he not drowned the gates of the Underworld with his own holy blood? William felt, for a brief moment, that he could nearly see the god's face, spattered with blood, wielding the flame of righteousness and snarling defiance at the forces of darkness. He tried to smile and keep the image of the god in his mind, but it dissolved, leaving him feeling empty and alone. The gods, the realms above and below, all seemed so distant now, even as he approached the end.

He thought of his youth – the father he'd never known, the kind, warmhearted mother who died when he was young. Then of those who raised him – his aunt, stern, serious-minded, and his uncle, jovial, open, and full of vitality.

He thought of his wife, he remembered holding her tightly as she passed away, her strength sapped from long illness. He remembered the first day that terrible, heavy feeling of loneliness and despair had appeared in his heart, never to leave. His thoughts moved to his daughter, sweet and innocent, pure beyond all other things. William would never see her grow into a woman. He would never be there on her wedding day. He would never know his grandchildren. The thought ate away at him, devouring from the inside.

Delirious with pain, William thought of those still at Wishapton, and whether the town still held. Geoffrey had taken a blow that felled him. Was he alive or dead? Haakon would be leading the survivors if, indeed, he lived. The old man's heart may have already given way. And then there was Bellaydin. The poor boy. Blood, suffering, death – were they to be his introduction to the lands of his ancestors? Better that he stayed with the elves, better that he remain some half-formed elf thing, better he never become a man, any fate was better than this, surely. The Ap'Lydin bloodline was spent, its energy exhausted. What was left?

William coughed, his vision blurring. Somewhere above him the gates of the Realms of Righteousness would soon open, and he would rejoin those who had passed. His father, his grandfather, all the sons and fathers of the Ap'Lydin line, they would greet him there, before the silver throne. He could almost feel it. But it did not happen. They did not open. He saw nothing in the sky but the approaching dusk. Delirium overtook him as he saw a face loom out of the shadow. "Bellaydin..." he croaked. And then spoke no more.

CHAPTER 19

"William… William." Bellaydin called as he arrived at the place Morgan indicated.

"It is as I said, Enparran," Morgan said, her eyes passing over William's prone form.

His chest lurching, Bellaydin ran towards his cousin. "Oh gods," Bellaydin said, his eyes wet with tears, "William, wake up. William!" William's eyes rolled and he muttered a few unintelligible words. "He's alive," Bellaydin said.

"Yes, Enparran, but he is dying," Morgan said.

"But not yet," Bellaydin said defiantly. He tried to loosen the ropes binding William's hands. "What have you barbarians done to him?" Bellaydin snarled.

Morgan regarded him coolly. "This is the Iobair," said Morgan. "It is the punishment reserved for the ultimate crime."

"And what is that?" Bellaydin asked. He continued to pull at the ropes and did not even glance at Morgan.

"Apostasy. Your kinsman rejected the Horned God, even after he was immersed in the full glory of the Horned God's being."

"You people make me sick," said Bellaydin, his back still to Morgan.

"It is the Horned God's will," Morgan said, but without much conviction.

Bellaydin turned to look at Morgan. The girl's expression revealed little, but there appeared to be tears in her eyes.

"Come," Bellaydin said, his voice soft. "Help me untie these ropes."

Morgan again looked hesitant, glancing over her shoulder, as if to see if there was anyone watching.

"Morgan," Bellaydin said. "I do not believe that any god, anywhere, would want to see a man suffer like this, no matter his crime."

Morgan looked surprised and, after a few moments without reaction, slowly shook her head and approached Bellaydin, helping him with William's bonds. "If we are to do this, Enparran, we must hurry," Morgan said, tugging at the bonds as William stirred underneath.

"Stand back," warned Bellaydin. He took the axe from his belt and started to hack at the ropes where they were tied to the rack. "Take care of the ones on the other side," Bellaydin told Morgan as the ropes began to fray under the blows from his axe. Bellaydin was so focused on what he was doing that he was unaware that there was no response from the girl.

"Morgan?" Bellaydin said, looking up.

He flinched just in time as he nearly sliced his nose on the tip of a sword pointed right at him.

"Don't move a muscle, Enparran."

"Father, no!" Morgan cried. "I can explain."

His throat tightening in fear, Bellaydin looked at the figure in front of him. It was Aonghus Culainn, the Goriinchian Warchief.

"What is this, Morgan?" Aonghus said, moving the point of the blade down to Bellaydin's chest. "Who is this infidel?" Even though he addressed his own daughter, Aonghus continued to speak in Emparian. It was clear to Bellaydin that the Goriinchian wanted him to hear and understand everything that was said. If it was meant to intimidate Bellaydin, it was working. He raised his hands in an act of surrender. Aonghus gestured with his sword, ordering Bellaydin away from the rack.

"His name is Bellaydin," Morgan said softly.

Bellaydin closed his eyes, and sighed with relief. He was thankful that Morgan didn't reveal his last name.

"A strange name for an infidel," Aonghus said, eyeing him up and down. "What are you? Spy? Saboteur? Traitor? What are you doing with our prisoner?"

"Please, father..." Morgan said, grabbing Aonghus' arm.

"Stay out of this, Morgan," Aonghus warned.

"But father, this man. It's his —"

Despite the fear that gripped him, Bellaydin's mind worked quickly. They were searching for this "Heir of Lydin". He needed to conceal his own relation to William. Before Morgan could finish her sentence, Bellaydin cut in, "It's my lord and master, William Ap'Lydin. A dear friend and mentor. I couldn't leave him here to die."

Aonghus looked at him sceptically.

"It is the truth, father," Morgan said quietly.

"I told you to stay out of this, Morgan," Aonghus said.

Bellaydin sweated as Aonghus turned back to face him. The Goriinchian's sword was still pointed at his chest, but this time there was a flicker of emotion on Aonghus' face. "You admired this man, Enparran?"

Aonghus said. His tone was sympathetic.

"Yes, very much so," Bellaydin stuttered. "With all my heart and soul."

"He was a worthy foe," Aonghus said gruffly. "Had he chosen the Horned God over the idols of you infidels, he could have been the Prophet-King's greatest warrior." The Goriinchian turned, looking upon William's prone body as he spoke the last few words. "Pity now, he will never get that chance. Even at the end, he could not see the truth." He turned back to Bellaydin. "What is it you want, Enparran? You cannot rescue him now. You are too late. Your lord and master is gone."

"He still lives," said Bellaydin.

"Barely," Aonghus scoffed. "His life ebbs away, even now, as the Horned God wills. All that is left for you is to claim his remains, to take him back for whatever heathen ritual you Enparrans give your dead."

As Bellaydin watched, the Goriinchian lowered his sword, his expression changed. Aonghus came closer, until Bellaydin could feel the older man's breath on his face. "Is that what you want, Enparran? To bring back your master's corpse?"

"He lives," Bellaydin said again.

"But not for long," Aonghus said.

"Father," Morgan said, taking her father's hand pleadingly. "Please…"

Aonghus laughed. "My daughter seems strangely fond of you, infidel. Perhaps she considers you some sort of exotic pet."

"But this," Aonghus said, jerking his head towards William Ap'Lydin, "this was not my doing. I would have preferred to kill him in battle, to bring glory on myself, my clan, and the Horned God. I don't see how this death brings honour to any of those." He lowered his voice, almost to a whisper. "Morgan's uncle, my brother, he is not an honourable man."

Morgan looked surprised at her father's words.

"Why do you say this to me?" asked Bellaydin.

"It is truth. I would say it to anyone, even an infidel. Also, I want you to know that what I say next, I do not say because I feel sympathy for you, but because my brother has stepped out of his bounds."

"What are you saying?" Bellaydin said.

"Go," Aonghus said.

"What?"

"Go, Enparran, take your master with you. I will not stop you."

"What?" Bellaydin repeated, astonished.

With a single blow of his sword, Aonghus cut the last of William Ap'Lydin's restraints. With little care or concern, he lifted the dying Emparian and moved him to Bellaydin, placing the comatose William's arms on Bellaydin's shoulders.

"Go Enparran, before I change my mind."

"Father, I – "

"Stay with me, Morgan," Aonghus said. "We have things to discuss, father to daughter."

Morgan lowered her eyes. "Yes, father."

"Enparran, leave. I said I would not stop you."

Astonished, grateful and a little apprehensive, Bellaydin secured William and departed the camp as quickly as possible. As he staggered away, pulling his cousin with him, Bellaydin was not sure what god had smoothed the way, but whichever one they were, he offered them a silent prayer of thanks. Now, however, came the difficult part. He had to work out a way to get his cousin back to the castle before he died. William was flitting in and out of consciousness as Bellaydin half-carried, half-dragged him, and Bellaydin was not sure how much longer he would last. There were likely

Goriinchian soldiers all around him and no doubt most of them had no idea that their own leader had let Bellaydin go. In fact, they would probably laugh at the idea, were Bellaydin actually fluent enough in Goriinchian to tell it to them. Bellaydin heard groans. His cousin was stirring.

"Bela…" William said.

"William," Bellaydin stopped in his tracks, helping his cousin to lay down on the grass.

"It's too late," William said, weakly. He coughed again, blood dribbling from his mouth.

"William…" said Bellaydin. He knelt down, grasping his cousin's hand. Limp and covered in blood, the warmth was rapidly fading from it.

"Ah, Bellaydin." William said, his voice trembling. "I think I missed the end… Did we win? Or have we lost?"

Bellaydin blinked, and grimaced. "It's not over yet, William. Wishapton has not fallen. Haakon fights on."

William smiled weakly. "A brave man."

"Not as brave as you William," Bellaydin said, smiling. His eyes shone with tears.

"We're all brave men, in one way or another. Whatever happens, I am glad to have met you, cousin," William said. His words were mangled, difficult to understand.

William reached out to Bellaydin with his other hand. He strained, trying to touch Bellaydin's face, but his strength left him, and the arm collapsed back by his side. "The two of us," William said, his chuckle turning into a cough. "I think, I think our grandfather would… be proud, would he not Bellaydin? We've held off the Goriinchians. You'll be as much a hero… as he was."

"You mean, *we* will be," Bellaydin said gently, squeezing his cousin's hand.

"I'm afraid not, Bellaydin," said William, coughing. "I'm not going to leave this place alive."

"But…"

"Oh, don't… don't be like that Bellaydin," William whispered. "I'm no fool. And neither are you. We must accept what has transpired. None of us get to choose the manner in which we pass from this world… into the Realms of Righteousness, Bellaydin. But, if I had chosen mine, I cannot think of a more glorious way to go than defending my people and… my homeland. I… I was never meant to pass away in my bed as a decrepit, diseased invalid… that much is for certain."

"But we need you William. I need you."

William laughed grimly, "Cousin, I never thought you'd say something like that."

Bellaydin smiled, despite himself.

"But regardless, you don't need me. You're more than ready to make your own way in the world. You of all people. You don't need anyone, but there are those who need you. I must ask something of you. You are my cousin, a blood relative, and the last heir of the House of Ap'Lydin. My daughter, Bellaydin, I want you to be her guardian. Protect her until she comes of age and is ready to receive her inheritance. Can you do this for me?"

"I can."

"Swear to me," said William, eyes wide. He was constantly short of breath now, and his voice was punctuated with gasps.

"I swear," Bellaydin said.

"I… I knew you would not let me down, Bellaydin," William said, his voice becoming hoarser and hoarser. "Defend Wishapton, Bela," he then gasped. "Don't let them take it…"

"Yes, William."

"I have one… one more thing to ask of you. When you bury me…"

"William…"

"When you bury me here, on this field, with the rest of my men… do not bury me with Kaltban. I want you to take it with you."

Bellaydin was perplexed. The Goriinchians had taken Kaltban, but his cousin did not seem to be aware of it. He was about to tell William that the sword was lost, but he noticed the look on William's face, and the words died on his lips. William's eyes, feverish, pleaded with Bellaydin.

"William, I can't take –"

"Please, Bellaydin. I want you to have it. It should have been yours anyway. Bear it well."

"I will, William." The lie tasted bitter, but Bellaydin told himself that he was merely easing his cousin's mind.

"Ah," William said. "Now it's just a matter of time. Don't weep for me, Bellaydin. Soon, Kytilas himself will open the gates of the Realms of Righteousness for me. He will take me by the hand, lead me through the shining city of heaven…" He smiled grimly. "I… I just hope that I'm judged worthy." William's breathing slowed, the gasps died away and his eyes closed. William Caradoc Ap'Lydin died, with Bellaydin the only one to know and mourn of his passing.

***

Aonghus Culainn was pleased with himself. For the first time, he had managed to get the better of his brother, and it was easier than he thought. If there was one thing he regretted, it was the feeling that he had used his daughter for his own ends. Morgan was a good girl, loyal, innocent. He regretted that she had to become involved in this. Aonghus reconciled these doubts to himself with the silent promise that he would make it up to her eventually, in some way. Maybe, once he had what he wanted, he could get the soldiers to recapture that Enparran pet of hers. He laid a hand on Morgan's shoulder, protectively, and smiled at her. She smiled back, albeit a little hesitantly.

It was Cathan's doing. Aonghus knew this. *That damned priest's obsession with this Heir of Lydin. It is all they are after. One man! It is ridiculous. The king has brought his most skilled Warchiefs into the fray — an army big enough to flatten this town and continue deep into heathen territory — and yet we still hold back. The absurdity! Once we found this man, this Lord William, the Prophet-King seemed to lose all interest in the war. No doubt that was the doing of Cathan and the other priests.*

They can be convincing, Aonghus admitted. He knew that the reason they were forbidding any of the warchiefs from seeing the Prophet-King was to concentrate their own malign influence on His Holy Majesty.

But now, Aonghus thought happily, *things are different. The boot is on the other foot.* Aonghus had removed the priests' prize from the camp and in a moment he would return to them, telling all present that William had arranged a daring rescue, and escaped back to the fortress. The priests would have no option but to order the Warchief to reorganise the attack. It did not even matter if, as Aonghus suspected, the man died on his way back. All that was required was for the High Priests and the Prophet-King to think that he had escaped and was alive and well. Yes, it had all worked out fairly well for Aonghus.

"What is this? What is going on here?"

Aonghus turned.

A furious Cathan, his face contorted in rage, stormed towards Aonghus. A few of the High Priest's own soldiers gathered behind him, shock registering on their features.

"As you can see, brother," said Aonghus, "your little prize has escaped."

"What? How in the Horned God's name did that happen?" Cathan said.

The soldiers began to chatter amongst themselves.

"It appears you did not watch him close enough, Cathan," Aonghus said. "No doubt the infidel Lord had already planned his rescue before he was captured. They were able to slip in undetected, it seems. No one saw them come or go. But it is clear as the view from the mountains of the south – the Enparran is gone. And so is your token of victory."

"High Priest, the attack must be renewed," one of the soldiers said.

"Without delay," Aonghus said.

Cathan's lips twisted into a sneer. "How convenient for you, brother."

"You know that it must be done, Cathan," said Aonghus. "The infidel is back in his fortress. The king will want it razed to the ground."

Cathan did not respond.

"Tell me I am wrong, your Holiness," Aonghus said archly.

Cathan pursed his lips, his eyes cold and dead of feeling. Finally, after a few moments of silence, he motioned to the soldiers. "You, spread the word, go tell the king that the situation demands that the attack goes ahead again. Tell him the Heir has escaped." He paused, and looked directly at Aonghus. "Or has been let free. Either way, he is gone."

"Yes, High Priest," said a soldier, bowing. One after the other, the remaining soldiers did the same, and then headed back down the path.

"You look at me with suspicion, brother," Aonghus said.

"This unfortunate turn of events seems to be most fortuitous for you, Warchief," Cathan said.

"What are you implying?" Aonghus said, defensively.

"Merely an idle thought, brother," Cathan said. "But I have been hearing rumours around the place of your daughter being seen leading some unknown man up this path. I suggest you keep a tighter rein on those under your protection."

"You leave Morgan out of this," Aonghus said.

"I am sorry, but the truth is plain to see. You are lax in your discipline of your own flesh. But that is between you and the Horned God, brother."

Aonghus grumbled. "Morgan, you are dismissed."

Morgan departed, eyes downcast, leaving her father and uncle alone together. Aonghus turned to Cathan. "If that is all, then I will take my leave. I have a siege to once again plan."

Cathan smiled at his brother. "Of course, Aonghus, but please, I hope that my words were not taken too deeply. You are my brother, after all, and I love you, just as the Horned God says."

Aonghus nodded. "Of course Cathan, and I love you as I would any brother of my flesh."

"Then come, brother, for old times, let us embrace," Cathan said.

Surprised, Aonghus complied, as Cathan enveloped his brother in a tight hug.

"No hard feelings, Aonghus?" Cathan said.

"No," Aonghus replied.

"Good. Now on to your reward, brother," Cathan whispered into Aonghus' ear.

Aonghus suddenly felt a sharp, biting pain in his stomach as something tore through his flesh. "The Horned God damn you!" Aonghus yelled.

"Shh…" Cathan twisted the blade deeper. "This will only take a moment."

Aonghus felt his strength disappear, his legs weakening. He collapsed to the ground. "Why..?" he whispered as his blood drained out.

"As the Horned God wills, brother," Cathan replied.

The last thing Aonghus saw was his brother's booted foot stamping his face.

"As the Horned God wills."

***

Bellaydin cried. His tears were heartfelt, as true as any he had ever shed. It did not matter that he had only known his cousin for a few short months. Indeed, to Bellaydin, a few months was almost a lifetime ago. William had been many things to Bellaydin – the only remaining link to his birth family, now gone forever; a representation of all that was good and all that Bellaydin admired about Emparia, the homeland he had never got the chance to know as a child. All of that was gone now, destroyed. He looked down upon William's body. Despite the wounds, his cousin looked peaceful, almost serene. The pale skin was cold to the touch, yet there was no sign of pain or distress on William's features. It was almost as if his cousin had simply fallen into a deep sleep.

Bellaydin was not sure how long he had been sitting in the grass, guarding his cousin's body, but it was now well and truly dark, the only illumination being the light from the stars above and the small sliver of one of the four moons.

It struck him that it was very likely that, despite Aonghus' promise, Goriinchian warriors would eventually find him, and deal with him in the manner they would any enemy. He wondered briefly what he should do. He needed to get back to the safety of Wishapton, back to the fortress. Complicating the matter was his cousin. Should he build a cairn and cremate him? That would take time, and would attract attention. The same would apply to any attempt to bury him. No, he would have to think of something else. Suddenly he became aware of a sound – a stamping noise from nearby, of feet trudging through mud and dirt. All other thoughts vanished from Bellaydin's mind as he searched for somewhere to hide. He grabbed William's corpse by the arms, dragging the body with him as he searched frantically for a rock, a bush, even a depression in the ground.

Anywhere that would conceal him. However, Bellaydin seemed to be out of luck. No such hiding place seemed to be around. As the footsteps came closer and he began to hear heavy breathing, Bellaydin briefly contemplated lying down next to his cousin and pretending to be similarly dead, but discarded the idea when he did not think he could make a plausible attempt at it. It was too late, however, for the approaching figure stopped near him, a tall, massive shadow looming from the darkness.

"Ap'Lydin," came the voice, scarcely more than a growl.

"Kahlaf?" Bellaydin said, scarcely believing who it was. "Is that you?" The Ahktarran came closer, the moonlight illuminating a vague, inhuman shape against the darkness.

"Indeed it is," he said gruffly. "What is this? Why are you here and not in the safety of the castle?"

Bellaydin said nothing, but frowned as he noticed Kahlaf's eyes coming to rest on William's body.

"Lord William," Kahlaf exclaimed, considerably more animated than Bellaydin could ever remember seeing the Ahktarran.

"He was captured by the Goriinchians. I tried to rescue him, but…" Bellaydin's voice trailed off.

"He is dead then," Kahlaf said.

Bellaydin nodded sadly.

Kahlaf crouched and looked closely at William's body, grunting as he did. "We became separated during the initial battle," Kahlaf said coolly, "and I was cut off from the keep. It was only through luck that I have been able to survive this long. I did not even know William had been captured." He traced a claw over William's face. "He has suffered horribly. I can see that," Kahlaf said.

"The Goriinchians tortured him," Bellaydin added.

"They are honourless curs. The Jinn of the desert have more faith than they," Kahlaf said. "And you, young Ap'Lydin –"

"What about me?" Bellaydin said.

"You, Bellaydin Ap'Lydin. You are a brave and honourable man."

Bellaydin nodded, smiling. He had never expected to ever hear Kahlaf say that about him. "Thank you."

Kahlaf nodded curtly, grunting, then stood, flexing his arms.

"We need to return to the fortress. It is clear that the Goriinchians are preparing another assault."

Bellaydin nodded, but then gestured to William's body at their feet. "What are we going to do? We can't leave William here."

"We shall either have to give him a makeshift funeral here, or take his body with us," Kahlaf said. "Both choices will delay us."

Even now, Goriinchians would be looking for the both of them. They would also renew their attack on Wishapton, if they had not already done so. A great wall of soldiers probably already stood between them and Wishapton. This time, however, there was no chance of infiltrating them. Even if he was confident of his own ability to do so, with the Ahktarran accompanying him there would be complications. There was no likelihood that even the most foolish Goriinchian would mistake the seven and a half foot Kahlaf for one of their own. They were trapped here. Bellaydin dwelled on this unpleasant thought.

Kahlaf was standing some distance away, on the crest of a small hill. His keen eyes, well-suited to seeing in the gloom, were scanning the horizon for any trouble. "The Goriinchians are regrouping," said Kahlaf, "and moving back towards Wishapton." He pointed towards the town, which was oddly quiet and peaceful. The lull that Wishapton's defenders were enjoying would soon be over. "We need to leave," Kahlaf said, turning back to Bellaydin. "Now."

"But what about −"

Kahlaf stepped towards Bellaydin and, muttering a few words, bent down and took William's corpse in his arms. Bellaydin looked at Kahlaf with interest, and the Ahktarran noted the young man's surprise. "It would not befit a Lord to rot in a field so far from his home," said Kahlaf. "And, on my honour, I will see him returned home."

Grateful and surprised all at once, Bellaydin breathed a sigh of relief and followed Kahlaf as they began their trek back to Wishapton.

***

Haakon's heart ached. He stood on the ramparts on Castle Wishapton, directing the last of his troops. They were so few now − under fifty defenders − most of whom had joined the duke on the walls, armed with whatever ranged weapon they had at hand. Haakon had allowed himself a small measure of hope earlier in the day, for the Goriinchian army had seemingly withdrawn, apparently lifting the siege. Now, however, as night enveloped them, the Goriinchians marched back towards Wishapton, this time with their full strength. They would not withdraw this time and they would crush Wishapton's defenders as one might crush an egg.

The elf Neriaos stood next to him, the most experienced soldier still standing. Most of the other surviving troops were militia, firing arrows until their fingers were red and raw. Most arrows were finding their targets but, even so, Haakon knew it would not be enough.

"Keep at it. Don't let them breach the gates! Think of your wives and children!" Haakon yelled, urging the tired and weary defenders on.

Far below the front lines of the Goriinchian forces broke through the outer walls, hurling themselves at the castle gate.

"Oil! Oil!" Haakon yelled.

A soldier pushed one of the heavy cauldrons of oil to the edge and, with the aid of another soldier, tipped it over. Below the Goriinchian line broke,

355

the scalded soldiers jumping into the moat in a vain attempt to put out the fire. It was a small victory. More Goriinchians quickly rushed up to fill any gaps and, as some began to ford the moat, Saldarri rangers began to fire back.

"Enemy archers!" yelled Haakon, taking cover.

Several militia tumbled over the wall, arrows through their bodies. Others moved forward to fill the breach, continuing the barrage of return fire hitting the Goriinchians. Suddenly, Haakon's left shoulder exploded in pain. An arrow had embedded itself above the shoulder, paralysing his entire left hand.

"Your grace," said Neriaos, shouting to be heard above the din. "We must —"

The elf was unable to finish his sentence, also falling victim to a Goriinchian arrow. Neriaos collapsed, blood streaming from the wound.

Pain shooting through his body, Haakon prayed for a miracle and, against all the odds, his prayers were heard. Somewhere nearby a trumpet sounded – a clear, high note, above the noise of battle.

"Soldier," Haakon asked one of the militia. "What do you see?"

The militiaman approached the edge, peering out into the darkness. Haakon strained his neck in the same direction, and glimpsed flickering lights in the distance.

"Well? What is it?"

"Reinforcements, Your Grace," the militiaman said.

Haakon leant back, and breathed out a sigh of relief. "Praise be."

***

When Bellaydin saw the newly arrived forces, he felt a great warm glow come over him, almost as if his entire being was liberated from the fear and anxiety that he had experienced over the last week. Whether it was excitement at the newfound possibility of victory, or just plain relief that he had survived, something had been lifted from him, and Bellaydin felt better than he had in a long time.

At the vanguard of the newly arrived army rode hundreds of knights, fresh and ready for battle. With a stirring battle cry, they rode down the Goriinchians who stood in their way. The darkness aided the Emparian forces. The knights charged out of the shadows, like soldiers from hell and in the gloom, the Goriinchians had trouble seeing the true size of the force arrayed against them. Assuming that they were terribly outnumbered, the Goriinchian front lines broke ranks and turned back towards their own tail, attempting to flee to the safety of their own camp. The panicked mob's attempt to do so only sowed confusion through their own ranks, and soon the entire Goriinchian force in Wishapton had collapsed, with the last remnants of order unravelling as maddened Goriinchians fled in any way they felt possible. What, a few moments ago, had been an undoubted victory for the Goriinchians was now turning into a rout.

Wulfric rode with the other knights, the Highcrown banner fluttering proudly in the moonlight. Wielding a fierce hammer, the old duke showed no mercy to any Goriinchians who stood in his way, dispatching each and every one with the same grim look of determination.

"Kahlaf!" Wulfric shouted, noticing the Ahktarran.

"My lord!" Kahlaf said, dropping to one knee and bowing his head. The duke ordered the other knights onward in their pursuit, and, breaking from the rest of the army, he reined his horse to a stop right next to Bellaydin. "It looks like I arrived just in time," he said as he approached. His eyes lingered on Kahlaf briefly.

"I see you have survived, Kahlaf," he said, "but others…" He looked at the body Kahlaf held in his arms and then, without a trace of emotion on his lined face, Wulfric turned to Bellaydin. "I am sorry for your loss," he said.

Without waiting for a response Wulfric spurred his horse onwards, rejoining his retinue, and driving the last of the Goriinchians from Wishapton. Kahlaf looked at Bellaydin, and Bellaydin was certain it was sympathy that registered on the Ahktarran's face.

"Don't think that the duke is cold to you, Ap'Lydin," Kahlaf said. "That face is but a mask he shows to the world. He fears to bare his soul to others. Too many painful memories. Perhaps one day he will share those memories with you, but for now we must accept who he is."

"I guess," said Bellaydin.

"Come, Ap'Lydin," he said. "We must get ourselves – and the earl's body – into the castle."

Bellaydin looked towards the knights dispatching the fleeing Goriinchians. "Should we not assist them?" he asked.

"There is nothing left to be done. Fatigued and without mounts, we would be of little help."

With the Ahktarran leading the way, Bellaydin and Kahlaf entered Castle Wishapton ignoring, as best they could, the sounds of battle from outside. "Make way," growled Kahlaf as they entered the castle. "Make way for the Earl of Genio!"

"William!" Geoffrey cried out. His voice was strangled with pain.

"Sir Geoffrey, you must rest," The attendant ran after him, but Geoffrey, ignoring his own injuries, pushed forward. "Damn you, let me see him."

Upon seeing William's body, cold and still, Geoffrey let out an agonised scream that reverberated through the castle. The knight stumbled towards William, grabbing the corpse's hand, and holding it tight.

"It is not fair, brother. It should have been me. You had too much to live for. The gods are fickle, they have spared me and taken you."

Geoffrey's voice was quiet and his eyes shone with tears.

"Where is he? Where is he?" came another voice. Haakon had arrived.

"Here," Geoffrey said. The attendant gently pulled him away, and guided him back to his bed.

"Show me," Haakon said, his voice low.

Kahlaf stepped aside, giving the duke a clear line of sight to the body. The duke gave out a strangled cry of despair, and erupted into tears, sobbing openly. "Oh, Willy... no..." Haakon said quietly between sobs. Haakon looked with sadness upon the still form of William Ap'Lydin, his fingers gently brushing over the pale skin of the corpse's face. "How did it happen?" he asked, his voice wavering.

Kahlaf turned to Bellaydin with an expectant look on his face.

"It was the Goriinchians," said Bellaydin. "They tortured him terribly."

"But did not kill him," Kahlaf said. "Curious."

Bellaydin could not be certain, but it almost sounded as if the Ahktarran's tone was slightly mocking of him. "I... I don't know why," Bellaydin said, flustered. "I think they thought he was their Heir of Lydin."

Haakon frowned. "Those Goriinchians are savages," he said, his tone firm. "No man deserves such indignities. Certainly not a man of valour, and righteousness like Willy. And whatever their reasons, they have denied William an honourable death, a warrior's death."

"They are faithless," Kahlaf said. "The man with no soul, he has no honour."

Haakon nodded, but said nothing.

There was a brief, uncomfortable silence, broken only by someone screaming.

"Father, Father!" Maria saw her father's body and broke down, flinging herself on to her father's body. She screamed again, her eyes filling with tears, and her words faded into indistinct sobs.

Bellaydin went to hold Maria, trying to comfort the girl. Maria barely noticed his presence, clinging on to her father's body tightly.

"Let her grieve, Bela," said Haakon.

"William asked me to become Maria's guardian."

Haakon's face relaxed. He smiled gently, and held out his hands. "Oh, Bellaydin…" Haakon put a hand on Bellaydin's shoulder. "I am not surprised, young man," Haakon said. "Willy loved Maria, more than anything else, and I'm sure that she was on his mind in his final moments. And what he asked of you is entirely just and proper. You, Bellaydin, are now the head of the Ap'Lydins."

Head of the Ap'Lydins! The thought struck Bellaydin like a thunderbolt. He did not feel ready for such a heavy duty, especially not now, receiving it in this manner. But Haakon was right. He, Bellaydin, was now the oldest living male Ap'Lydin. And the thought scared him senseless.

CHAPTER 20

Polnygar was not impressed. "We're going to travel like this?" she said, arching an eyebrow.

"What did you expect?" asked Hebu. "A litter?"

Polnygar darkened, scowling at the Nemoi. "I was expecting horses."

Augustin scratched his head. "To be honest, so was I."

"Well, I'm sorry to disappoint you both," said Hebu, "but Lord Aelzandar placed me in charge of acquiring our transportation, and this is what I chose."

Two figures approached the group, swathed in robes, their faces hidden under scarves, though Polnygar could still glimpse pointed ears poking through the gaps in the cloth. They led two large beasts of burden.

"The Selvara, my dear," said Aelzandar. "Distant cousins of the Eldara. They are wanderers and nomads, and excellent guides to take us north across the desert." Aelzandar spoke to the Selvara in low, hushed tones, allowing Polnygar to catch only a few scattered words in elven. The archmage handed over some coins to the Selvara as Polnygar approached one of the braying animals, reaching out to pat its neck.

"What are they called again?" she asked.

"It's a camel," Augustin said.

"They look grotesque," she said.

"Huh," said Hebu. "He probably thinks you look grotesque too."

"There are stranger creatures around," said Augustin. "Just wait till we get to Skurj."

"They won't bite me, will they?" Polnygar said as she tentatively stroked the animal's fur.

"No, it might spit at you, though," Augustin said.

"What?" Polnygar said, pulling her hand back.

"It was just a joke, girl," Augustin said, smiling.

"There's no way I am getting on one of these… *things*," Polnygar said.

"Well, I'm afraid it's either that or walking," Hebu said. "Trust me, you'll all be grateful for the choice once we're spending weeks travelling through the wastelands to the north. Camels are hardy. They'll do better than horses."

"A lot slower though," Augustin mused.

"Hardly," said Hebu, his voice rising in pitch and volume. "Does it perhaps occur to you that even if we were to ride horses across the unforgiving terrain of central Carurlonia that perhaps, just perhaps, we wouldn't be driving the beasts to exhaustion by galloping the entire way?"

Augustin laughed. "Alright, alright, I see your point, gnome."

Hebu turned around. "I am *not* a gnome," he said indignantly.

"Sorry, *Nemoi*," Augustin said, correcting himself.

"Don't you dare say that word again," Hebu said, hands on his hips.

"How do you get on these things?" Polnygar said. "I can't reach."

"Here," Augustin said, coming closer to Polnygar. "Let me give you a hand."

Polnygar didn't want to seem like she needed help. "No, it's alright, I just – "

"Here," said Augustin gruffly, grabbing the girl around her waist and lifting her up until she could reach the top of the camel, and pull herself on to it.

"Thanks," said Polnygar curtly.

Augustin grinned broadly and Polnygar, much to her embarrassment, realised she had felt a small thrill as he had held her. She flushed and Augustin, seemingly noticing her discomfort, smiled even wider. When Hebu joined in, Polnygar went even redder.

"Don't worry," said Hebu, sidling up to the pair. "I know. It's just hot today, correct?"

"Uh, yes," Polnygar said, fiddling with her sleeve. "Quite hot."

Augustin chuckled.

"If I might interrupt – "

Hebu turned around. "Lord Aelzandar," he said, "I didn't know you were here."

"I've only just arrived, Hebu," Aelzandar said, leaning on his staff. "Are these our mounts?"

"Yes, my lord," Hebu said.

Aelzandar looked at the camels sceptically, eyeing them up and down. "Well, my apprentice seems comfortable," he said.

"I wouldn't say that," Polnygar said, trying to stay atop the swaying camel.

"Keep practicing," said Augustin. "You'll get the hang of it."

Without warning, the camel brayed, and moved forward. Polnygar nearly toppled off, and only managed to stay on by gripping onto the animal's neck with both hands.

"Thank you, Hebu," Aelzandar said. "They will suffice."

Hebu bowed. "My lord is wise."

Aelzandar, seeing Polnygar's discomfort, approached the camel and offered Polnygar a hand. She took it and Aelzandar helped her back to the ground.

"Thank you Aelzandar," she breathed.

Aelzandar smiled. "Don't mention it, my dear."

"So, what's the plan?" said Augustin. "When are we going to give Ivellios what he deserves?"

Aelzandar turned to Augustin. "Patience, Baron. Let's not let personal vendettas obscure our vision. Ivellios is a threat, and he has caused much pain and anguish to all of us, but if we are to defeat him, we must make sure we perceive the situation clearly and without prejudice. Ivellios has gone to Skurj, and, if I am correct, he seeks something that would be very bad news were it to fall into his possession."

"And what might that be?" Augustin said.

Aelzandar pursed his lips. "I suppose it is too late now for any further secrets," he said, sighing. "In Skurj another piece of the Tears of the Divine lies hidden."

"What?" said Polnygar. "Another piece? How can you be sure?"

Aelzandar lowered his voice. "I know because I was responsible for making sure it was hidden. And the last time evil forces threatened Skurj, I was responsible for making sure they never found the Tears."

"When did all this happen?" said Augustin.

Aelzandar looked distant, almost wistful. "Oh, a long time ago now. A hundred years, give or take a decade or two."

"Surely the location is long forgotten then," Augustin said, "and the Tears are safe."

"Evil never sleeps, Baron," Aelzandar said. "And where the Tears are hidden is not a place, it is a man."

"A man? Surely he would be dead by now," Augustin said. "Unless he's an elf," he quickly amended.

"No, he's human," said Aelzandar. "And you are correct, he is most likely no longer alive. However it was his family who I entrusted the Tears with, and no matter the generations that have passed, I know they will continue to keep it safe."

"How did Ivellios find all this out?" Polnygar asked.

"That is one piece of the puzzle that still eludes me, my dear," Aelzandar said. "We can only hope that he hasn't learned of its precise location."

"And if he has?" Augustin said.

"Then we may already be too late," Aelzandar said.

"What does Ivellios want with the Tears?" Polnygar asked.

"Simple. Power," Aelzandar said. "Ivellios has always craved it for as long as I have known him. Even incomplete, the Tears hold an amazing pool of arcane energy. If all the pieces were to be found and brought together, then, well…"

"Well, what?" Augustin said.

"The results would be catastrophic," Hebu chimed in.

Aelzandar nodded.

"Then what are we waiting for?" said Augustin. "We should get moving."

"Correct," said Aelzandar. The elf turned to Hebu. "Hebu, send for our supplies and belongings, make sure they get put on our mounts."

"You mean camels," said Hebu.

Aelzandar rolled his eyes. "Yes, the camels. You can correct me another time, Hebu."

Hebu bowed, with a smile on his lips. "You are most gracious, my lord."

"Away with you, rascal," Aelzandar said. As Hebu departed to make the final preparations for their journey, Aelzandar approached Polnygar and spoke to her privately. "My dear, the trip ahead of us will be long and since you have declined my offer to have you returned home…"

Polnygar smiled sheepishly.

"I think we can fill in the duration of this journey productively. There are still many things I have to teach you about the Art," Aelzandar added. "Though I will admit that you have fairly well mastered the small portions I have taught you so far."

"How are we going to write in those spellbooks while we're riding those camels?" Polnygar asked.

Aelzandar chuckled quietly. "Not all of the Art is pouring over thick and dusty tomes, my dear. And not of all it is memorising obscure phrases and mastering archaic tongues."

"Oh no?" Polnygar raised an eyebrow. "Most of it seems to be."

Still smiling, Aelzandar put an arm around her and said, "There is much you still have to learn. Pay attention and you'll do fine."

By early next day, the group was well on its way, and the walls of Ralom were already out of sight. Polnygar had found the first few hours atop the camel uncomfortable and unsettling but now she was beginning to get used to the animal and, surprisingly, was even beginning to find the beast's gait soothing and tranquil. She turned to Aelzandar, and noticed the archmage looking at her with a smile.

"I'm sorry, master, were you saying something?" she said.

"Dreaming, were we? Never mind my dear, we can discuss this another time if you want."

"No," she said. "Please go on."

"Very well. Bring your animal closer to me."

She pulled on the camel's reins and guided it closer to the archmage.

"Now, Polnygar," Aelzandar said as they rode together. "The most crucial thing to remember about magic is that it is, when all is said and done, an art form. That is why we call it the Art. You must sculpt arcane energies as a potter sculpts clay. Scrolls and books can give you direction, but in the end all they really are is instructions. The true master of any art learns eventually to do without his guidebook, and develops his own technique."

Polnygar nodded thoughtfully, but Augustin, listening in on the conversation, scoffed openly.

"Sure. Sounds easy," he said. "But it seems to me that it's far easier to get my hands on clay than it would be to find some magic to shape."

"Well, I wouldn't be too sure of that."

Augustin looked confused, and then shook his head slowly. "I'm afraid you've lost me, wizard. You're telling me magic is as common as mud?"

"Well, those aren't the words I would have chosen," Aelzandar said, "but in a manner of speaking, yes. It is the four moons that power the Art. Their light shines on our world and it is through this light we are able to perceive the fabric of the ether. When a master of the Art draws on his power, what he actually does is shape the energy of the ether into the form he desires. Such energy is around us at all times; the only difficulty is manipulating it. It takes a certain talent to do so."

"One that both of you have, yes?" Augustin said, pointing to both Aelzandar and Polnygar.

"The talent is common in Eldara," Aelzandar said matter-of-factly. "Especially in families of spellweavers. My grandfather was one, as was Polnygar's. Her talent does not surprise me in the slightest."

"What about us humans then?" Augustin asked. "Do any of us get to share in this bountiful gift?"

His tone was slightly sarcastic but if Aelzandar noticed, he did not show it. He answered the question as directly and plainly as he had answered the others.

"Certainly, Augustin," he said. "Though the gift may not appear as commonly in humans as it does my own people, the sheer mass of humanity ensures that human wizards are most prevalent. Some, of course, may have some tiny trace of Eldara heritage that gives them that power. Others... well, let's just say there are many strands that make up the human tapestry."

Augustin chuckled. "Humans . A true mongrel race, gods bless us."

"Yes, well, I hate to interrupt this absolutely fascinating discussion of racial heritage, but I believe we have a problem," Hebu said. "There appear to be some fellows on the road ahead who seem – and I hope no one thinks I'm jumping to conclusions here – to be rather unsavoury."

Polnygar looked ahead, spotting a small group of men some distance ahead of them, blocking their path. The men were dressed in black, their faces obscured and they carried their weapons openly. They had horses with them but were not mounted.

"Maybe we should go around them?" Polnygar suggested.

"Why bother? We can take them," Augustin said.

"Perhaps, Baron," said Aelzandar. "But I would like to exercise caution, just in case. They may simply be lost travellers."

"I wouldn't count on it," said Augustin.

"Let us see, shall we, Baron?" said Aelzandar.

They continued towards the men who eyed them warily as they approached.

"Good day to you. A fine day for travelling, is it not?" Aelzandar said as they came close.

"If only it were, master elf," said one of the men. "Unfortunately, my companions and I have been hampered by a lack of supplies."

"Oh, now that is unfortunate," said Aelzandar. "Perhaps we can help."

The man beamed. "Well, yes, we were hoping you could, actually."

"Let me see what I can do," said Aelzandar, dismounting.

Suddenly, Polnygar felt herself being yanked off the camel, and a sword pointed at her face. She heard a scuffle as Augustin and Hebu were likewise inconvenienced. The bandit held the Nemoi with one arm while he pointed his sword at Augustin's throat with the other.

The Selvara guides drew their weapons, ready to attack, but seeing the bandits had the upper hand, held back for the moment.

"Nobody move," yelled the lead bandit.

"Brigands." growled Augustin.

"In a manner of speaking, yes, outlander," the man grinned.

"You're making a terrible mistake," said Aelzandar.

His voice was calm. Polnygar noticed the archmage showed no sign of fear, even though she was sweating furiously.

"Oh, I'm sure we are," the man said sarcastically. "Where are you going?"

When Aelzandar failed to answer, the man nodded to his companions, who held their blades closer to the prisoners. Polnygar felt metal against her skin.

"I'll ask again. What is your destination?"

"And I'll tell you again, you're making a terrible mistake."

"You have no idea who you are dealing with, elf," the man snarled, barely an inch from Aelzandar's face.

"No," Aelzandar said.

"No?"

"No, it is you who have no idea who you are dealing with." With a single handed gesture, Aelzandar unleashed a bolt of magical energy and sent the man tumbling backwards. Then, with another flick of his wrist, the weapons spun out of the grip of the other men, allowing Hebu, Augustin and Polnygar to escape from their captors. The bandits scrambled to grab their weapons, but Aelzandar was already upon them, and, with a swing of his staff, smashed the leader in the face, knocking him to the ground. Reeling, the bandit pulled a knife from his belt and lunged at Aelzandar, only to have the archmage twist out of his way and strike the bandit again in the stomach. Two more bandits fell to the blades of the Selvara guides.

The remaining bandits, sensing that they were no match for Aelzandar, tried to escape. While Augustin's sword clashed with one of them, the other one pushed Hebu aside, jumping onto one of the horses, quickly urging the steed off in a gallop before Polnygar could reach him. Rather than pursue, she grabbed a weapon and went to assist Augustin. The bandit fought ferociously and, with his avenues of escape gone, he asked for no quarter. Before long, he was dead, having taken a sword thrust below the ribcage.

Augustin and Polnygar rushed to Aelzandar, in time to see the archmage fell his opponent with a final blow. He looked at the prone man, prodding him with his staff. "Oh dear," Aelzandar said. "I may have hit him too hard."

"I must say, archmage," Augustin said, "I'm impressed. I never thought you could fight like that."

Aelzandar chuckled. "Oh, my dear Baron, I've been fighting bandits for longer than either of you have been alive."

"Point well taken," Augustin said.

Polnygar smiled, nodding. She had long since given up being surprised at the feats Aelzandar was capable of.

"Is he dead?" Augustin said, nudging the body with his foot.

Polnygar crouched down, checking the man's pulse. "He's dead."

"Pity," said Aelzandar. "We may have been able to ask a few questions."

Augustin looked around. "By the way the other one fought, I don't think any of these fellows intended to be captured alive."

"For bandits, that seems odd," Polnygar mused.

"To say the least," said Aelzandar. "But I have a feeling these weren't mere bandits." He turned over the body with his staff, flipping the man on to his belly. "There. The mark on his arm."

"What mark?" Augustin said.

"No, I see it." Polnygar crouched down and looked closer at the man's arm. There was a black tattoo inscribed on the skin. As she looked at it, recognition dawned, and she felt a cold chill go down her spine. "It's the same symbol I saw on the cultists who attacked me in Macrodonia," she said.

"Indeed," said Aelzandar. "That is the symbol of the Horned God. These men were not mere bandits."

"The Horned God?" said Augustin. "What in the blazes are his cultists doing here?"

"Isn't it obvious? Looking for us," Hebu said.

"You mean looking for me," Polnygar said quietly.

"Let's not begin to make assumptions," Aelzandar said, but Polnygar knew that was not what he and the others were thinking.

"They know we've left Ralom, that's for certain," said Hebu.

"Yes, but it doesn't look like they know where we're going," Augustin said. "So that gives us at least one advantage."

"One did get away," said Polnygar apologetically.

"Don't worry about that, my dear," said Aelzandar. "That is no one's fault. Besides, the one who escaped didn't learn anything that will put us in danger."

"So, if I understand correctly, we're now being hunted by the cultists of the Horned God and Ivellios?" said Hebu.

"Technically, we're the ones hunting Ivellios," Aelzandar said. "But yes, the principle is much the same. Is that a problem, my dear Hebu?"

"No, of course not, master," Hebu said, bowing. He grumbled quietly for a while in disapproval.

"We should continue on our journey," said Aelzandar. "As soon as we bury these bodies, of course. They may have been our enemies, but that's no reason for us to act like barbarians."

"No sense letting those weapons go to waste either," said Augustin, collecting the swords of the fallen men.

"Good idea," Hebu jumped to assist him.

"And look." Polnygar grabbed the reins of one of the horses. "They left these too."

"Thank the gods," said Augustin. "A real mount."

Hebu looked hurt. "Just what have you got against these camels?"

"Nothing," Augustin said. "I'm more concerned about what they have against me."

Hebu crossed his arms. "Well, maybe it's from having to listen to you go on and on all day. I almost sympathise with them."

"Enough!" said Aelzandar, "We will take the horses with us. Augustin and Polnygar may ride them if they choose. Hebu and I will remain with what we have."

"Yes, master," said Hebu.

The Selvara guides approached them.

"It is time," one said. "We must continue if we are to reach the border."

"What border?" Polnygar asked. She was only vaguely familiar with the geography of Carurlonia. If her brother was here, no doubt he would have known, but Polnygar had not spent nearly as long staring at the map in their mother's house as Bela had.

"These are the Vallistian Marches," Aelzandar explained, "But as we journey they will give way to the great Desert of Despair."

Polnygar wrinkled her nose. "Despair? That hardly sounds inviting."

"It's not," Augustin grumbled. "Damn nearly died there last time I was in Qarld."

Polnygar recognised the name. "Qarld, I think I've heard of that. Is it dangerous then?"

"Qarld is the largest province of the Infinite Caliphate," explained Aelzandar. "Augustin may be exaggerating. We should be quite safe, as long as we behave ourselves."

"A land of sand, slaves and mystics. They're a touchy bunch," Augustin said. "Don't say anything to insult the 'Infinite Faith'." He said the last words with a touch of scorn.

Hebu scoffed. "Gods who take offense at words. Humans cannot conceive of deities who do not share their own fragile vanity."

The conversation continued, but Polnygar was no longer paying attention. She found herself strolling up the hill side, towards a vantage point on the ridge above. She could see the land stretch out in all directions. At the horizon the green plains slowly disappeared as the desert began, as if the sands themselves were devouring the fields around them.

Augustin had come to stand beside her, "Worried about what comes next?"

"Somewhat."

"Qarld can be treacherous, but we'll survive."

"It's not just Qarld."

Augustin raised an eyebrow. "Ivellios?"

"He's out there somewhere," said Polnygar.

"He'll pay for what he's done, don't worry about it," Augustin said.

"Are you with me?" Polnygar asked.

She felt his hand brush against hers ever so slightly. He kept it there a moment and smiled at her.

"To the end."

***

Bellaydin stood silently as the rain fell.

It was the day after the battle. There was neither glorious victory nor terrible, crushing defeat. Only the pain of loss. The dead were numerous but one name stood out above all others. William Ap'Lydin, Earl of Genio.

His men had achieved a great victory in his name. The invasion had collapsed, and Emparia was safe for now, but at what cost? The Goriinchians had fled, that much was certain, and had lost much of their infantry. Of the defenders of Wishapton, on the other hand, all that remained was a pathetic, bedraggled remnant of cripples and invalids. Many would not survive the next week. Most would never bear arms again.

The Goriinchians had lost the battle, but not the war – not by a long shot – and despite Wulfric's brilliantly timed arrival the Emparians were as unprepared as ever. Without a doubt there would be more attacks, even with the Goriinchian losses, and the death of Aonghus Culainn. The Goriinchians had other Warchiefs, and Ygarak had not given up on his dream of conquering Emparia, nor would his priests and warriors let him forget that dream.

Bellaydin looked around. A crowd was beginning to gather, hoping to pay their last respects to William Ap'Lydin. A pyre had been constructed for William's body in preparation for the ritual cremation that would soon occur. Bellaydin wondered how long it would take for them to light the pyre under the rain. He saw Geoffrey Keslin, leaning on a crutch, alongside Kahlaf and surviving knights from Wulfric's force. Maria Ap'Lydin, William's daughter stood with her attendants, a veil of mourning covering her face. She looked towards Bellaydin, tears in her eyes, and he moved towards her, placing his hand on her shoulder. Maria said nothing, but buried her face against her older cousin's chest.

A group of men walked slowly towards the unlit bonfire carrying a bier, atop which lay William's body. His body washed and cleaned since Kahlaf and Bellaydin had brought it back with them, the Earl of Genio looked almost as if he were simply asleep. Haakon de Morcor and Wulfric Highcrown served as pallbearers. Tears streamed down Haakon's face, while Wulfric's was emotionless as ever, stoic even as he carried the body of someone he had known for thirty odd years.

The chaplain stood before the crowd, wearing the red and white robes of Kytilas. "We are gathered here today to celebrate the life of William Caradoc Ap'Lydin, Earl of Genio, and to mourn the passing of that life. We honour the memory of a man who willingly gave his life to defend the innocent, just as Kytilas himself did when he martyred himself to break the grip of the Shadow."

The priest's eulogy continued as Haakon and Wulfric laid William down on the pyre, carefully arranging the body so that William lay in a dignified position, his arms folded on his lap. He was not dressed in the armour he died in. The body, after it was washed, had been clothed in some of William's finest garments, upon which the Ap'Lydin crest could clearly be seen.

"We ask, oh valiant lord, oh divine martyr, that you spread your hand down now, and guide William's spirit to your kingdom, to the Realms of Righteousness, and that you open the celestial gates for him, so that his path into paradise might be speeded. Protect him from the powers of darkness, oh great guardian, and do not let the Lord of the End steal him to the Underworld." With a gesture, the chaplain blessed William's body. "Now we free our friend and brother's spirit from the shackles of its mortal form, and send him on his way to his well-earned reward."

With the other attendants leaving, Haakon and Wulfric grabbed a torch each and, dipping them in a bucket of flaming pitch, held them to the pyre. Despite the drizzle the wood soon caught on fire and within moments, the pyre was ablaze.

"Great lord," the chaplain said, "into your hands we commend his spirit."

The flames burned high and hot, and the rain eased. Within the hour, William's body had disappeared in the flames. His hand stroking Maria's hair, Bellaydin watched as the last few tendrils of smoke disappeared into the air.

"Goodbye cousin."

EPILOGUE

Cathan waited in the darkness.

The glade was isolated, out of the way, and at least a few hours' ride from Wishapton. He was confident that he would not be noticed by the city's defenders. Still, he was taking an awful risk. Unfortunately it was the only place the duke would meet him.

"The duke". That was the only name he knew his contact by. When the duke deigned to meet Cathan, he did so robed and cowled, and in darkness, never allowing Cathan a good look at his face.

Cathan heard a rustling. Cautiously he drew his sword. "Who's there? Did you come alone?" he called out.

"I am here, Cathan," came the voice. "Just as you asked. What is it?"

The duke's voice was brusque, impatient. There was a tone of barely concealed contempt for the Goriinchian he spoke with.

"I want answers," Cathan said. "You are one of us, yet today you fought for them."

"You and your brother forced my hand," the duke responded.

377

"Wishapton should have never been attacked."

"Are you questioning the will of the Horned God, brother?" Cathan demanded.

"Was what happened the will of the Horned God, Cathan, or the will of Culainn?"

"I am the Horned God's voice!" Cathan protested.

The duke was not deterred by Cathan's barb. "You are sadly mistaken if you believe that you can intimidate me, priest. I have served the Horned God since before you were in swaddling clothes. And though we both serve the same master, do not delude yourself into thinking that we are equals. We are not."

"And what then of the Heir of Lydin escaping?"

"That is your brother's crime. But William Ap'Lydin's death was yours. You were told of his importance, that he was not to be harmed."

"But he refused the call of the Horned God. I did as the Horned God's law demands…"

The duke waved a hand dismissively.

"Your excuses are not necessary. You have only avoided punishment because it has become clear to the Horned God that there is another Heir."

"Another? Who?"

"You will not need his name, because he is beyond your reach. He has been delivered to me by the Horned God's grace, and I will guide him to his destiny."

"I am the Horned God's chief priest," Cathan said. "I should be involved."

"You will not touch him!" shouted the duke. "That is the Horned God's will."

Cathan was quiet for a moment. "If that is the Horned God's will, then I will obey."

"See that you do, Cathan. The Horned God has destroyed one Culainn. You do not wish him to destroy another."

The duke turned to leave, but Cathan shot back a remark. "How long will it be then until you can join us openly? How much longer do you plan to hide beneath that mask?"

"Not much longer, I expect. And on that day I will enter Goriinchia with the Heir of Lydin, and Ygarak will embrace me as an equal. I will sit with him at the right hand of the Horned God. And on that day, Cathan, your failure will be complete.

APPENDIX

CHARACTERS

In order of appearance

Bellaydin Ap'Lydin: Orphaned human, born in Emparia, but currently living in Aderilund with his half sister and foster mother.

Ivellios: Lord Spellweaver of Aderilund

Saegralanna li'Saegras: Head of House Aelsar, mother to Polnygar Ap'Lydin and foster mother to Bellaydin Ap'Lydin

Quarion li'Ailnyu: Lord Speaker of the Council of Ancients

Augustin Bauer: Emparian Ambassador

Polnygar Ap'Lydin: half-sister of Bellaydin Ap'Lydin, daughter of Saegralanna

Talan li'Karn-Raka: High King of the Eldara. Husband to High Queen Talina.

Talina li'Aderias: High Queen of the Eldara. Wife to High King Talan.

William Ap'Lydin: Earl of Genio, first cousin to Bellaydin and

Polnygar Ap'Lydin

Oswin Zalltor: Duke of Georgeton. Member of the Privy Council.

Edmund Tallcastle: Duke of Emperor's Palace. Chair of the Privy Council.

Haakon de Morcor: Duke of Alariat. Member of the Privy Council and cousin to the Queen.

Wulfric Highcrown: Duke of Oldharbour. Member of the Privy Council.

Amaryllis de Morcor: Queen of Emparia.

Sir Geoffrey Keslin: Knight Bachelor and sworn sword to the Earl of Genio

Kahlaf el'Lahn: Ahktarran sworn sword to the Duke of Oldharbour

Keras: Mysterious messenger.

Vaerath: Eldara spellweaver

Aelzandar li'Geihnos: Lord Archmage and Royal Mage of Macrodonia.

Hebu: Royal Scribe of Macrodonia

Jagontay V: Pharaoh of Macrodonia

Arhotep: Royal Vizier

Morgan Culainn: Goriinchian girl

Aonghus Culainn: Goriinchian Warchief, father of Morgan

Cathan Culainn: Goriinchian priest, brother of Aonghus

Ygarak: Prophet-King of Goriinchia

The Seeress: Mystic prophetess of Goriinchia

Maria Margaret Ap'Lydin: Daughter and sole child of William Ap'Lydin

NATION STATES AND REGIONS

Aderilund: Southern Land. Part of the Aspen Kingdom – the realm of the Eldara.

Caruillin: Vast empire dominating the north of Carurlonia. Major provinces include Skurj, Lerid, the Heartlands and the Vallistian Marches.

Emparia: Northern Kingdom populated by Emparians. It borders Goriinchia, with whom it has a long history of conflict.

Goriinchia: Southern neighbour of Emparia, inhabited by the Goriinchians and the Saldarri. Ruled by the religion of the Horned God.

Infinite Caliphate: A religious empire ruled by the followers of the Infinite Faith. Qarld is the most powerful province, and the Sultan of Qarld serves as Caliph of the empire.

Lerid: Large province to the south of Skurj. Ruled by the Grand Duke of Lerid.

Macrodonia: Hot, desert kingdom to the north of Aderilund. Ruled by a King known as "Pharaoh", and home to Macrodonians and Nemoi.

Mokeria: City-state to the south of Aderilund.

Qarld: Exotic sultanate to the north-west of Macrodonia and largest province of the Infinite Caliphate. Known for its desert mystics and proud Bedouin tribes. Home to Qardleeans, Nemoi and Ahktarra.

Shadrish Archipelago: Island chain off the western coast of Carurlonia and a province of the Infinite Caliphate.

Skurj: Frigid land in the extreme north. Borders Alfheim. Home to the Knights of the Crux Caruillin.

Tarken: The so-called "Hermit Kingdom", reclusive and secretive realm ruled by "Dragonborn" Emperors.

Vallistian Marches: Southern lands of the Empire of Caruillin that share a border with the Infinite Caliphate.

SETTLEMENTS

Aderial: Capital of Aderilund.

Alariat: City in Emparia. Seat of the Duke of Alariat and the Archbishop of Alariat

Drakeford: Small town near the border of Emparia and Goriinchia, seat of Sir Edric Keslin, Baron Drakeford.

Emperor's Palace: Capital of Emparia. Seat of the monarch and of the Duke of Emperor's Palace.

Genio: City of Emparia. Seat of the Earl of Genio.

Georgeton: City in Emparia. Seat of the Duke of Georgeton.

Gorin: Capital of Goriinchia.

Oldharbour: Large port city in Emparia. Seat of the Duke of Oldharbour.

Harralin: Major settlement in Skurj.

Korfar: Goriinchian settlement near the Emparian border.

Liderial: Ancient city of the Eldara. Situated just north of Skurj. Seat of the elven monarchs and capital of the Aspen Kingdom.

Oldharbour: City of Emparia, seat of the Duke of Oldharbour.

Qar Arrid: City of Qarld, home to the Great Library

Qar Dal: Former capital of the Caliphate, site of the defeat of the archmage Ralur almost two and a half centuries ago.

Qar Udel: Prominent city of Qarld, and seat of the Sultan.

Ralom: The Holy City. Centre of the Triune faith of the Church of Ralom.

Tower of the Magi: Ancient ruin in Goriinchia. Sacred temple to the Horned God.

Tyronsville: Emparian city. Seat of the Earl of Tyronsville

Wishapton: Emparian town. Close to the Goriinchian border and southern-most city of the Earldom of Genio.

Warding: Emparian city. Seat of the Earl of Warding

NATIONALITIES AND ETHNICITIES

Ahktarra: Lizardmen from the land of Qarld.

Caruillani: Humans from Caruillin

Emparians: Humans from Emparia.

Goriinchians: Humans from Goriinchia.

Eldara: People of the Aspen Kingdom. Known to outsiders as "Elves" or "Fey".

Leridians: Humans from Lerid.

Macrodonians: Humans from Macrodonia

Nemoi: A diminutive people from the land of Macrodonia.

Qardleeans: Humans from the land of Qarld.

Saldarri: A Goriinchian tribe of mixed human and Eldara blood. Expert trackers and archers.

Sarrisite: Follower of the Infinite Faith. Named for the Prophet Sarrius, founder of the Infinite Faith.

Soldara: Ancient ancestors of the Spellweaver caste. Believed extinct.

Selvara: Nomadic cousins of the Eldara. Named for Selvaros, who rejected the founding of Liderial by Lideros.

Skurjans: Humans of Skurj.

Shadrish: A dark skinned sea-faring folk from the Shadrish Archipelago, western province of the Infinite Caliphate.

Tarkenese: Humans from Tarken.

RELIGION, CULTURE AND HISTORY

Alarion I: First king of the unified Emparian nation.

Art, The: The term for magic, most commonly used by humans and the Eldara.

Automaton: Animated metal construct in the shape of a human. Created by the Soldara through unknown techniques.

Bahamut: Messenger of the Infinite Faith, considered to have passed the words of the Infinite to the Prophet Sarrius.

Cassian: Archmage and vanquisher of the Night Dragons. Aelzandar's master.

Celestial Architects, The: Religion of the Nemoi, centred on the book *Nemoinomicon,* and without priests or places of worship.

Draconic: The script used for recording knowledge of the Art. Purported to be the language of dragons.

Divine Martyr, The: Also known as Kytilas. God of chivalry, self-sacrifice and valour. Worshipped by the Church of Ralom, centred in Ralom.

Eldaric: Name given to the script and spoken language of the Eldara.

Far-speaking: The ability used by practitioners of the Art to speak to others over long distances.

Fostering: A tradition whereby young members of noble houses are raised in the households of other families to forge bonds of friendship and amity.

Great Fostering, The: A form of fostering specific to the royal court.

Heir of Lydin, The: Prophesised messiah figure in Goriinchian mythology.

Horned God, The: The deity of the staunchly monotheistic Goriinchians. Followed outside of Goriinchia in secretive, subversive cults.

Hydria: Mother Goddess of the Eldara.

Kaltban: Magical sword recovered by Sir William Ap'Lydin during the siege of Ralom. Lost by his grandson, Earl William, after being captured by the Goriinchians at Wishapton

Knights of the Crux Caruillin, The: Chivalric Order headquartered in Skurj and dedicated to the Divine Martyr. Led by Grand Master Agmar Keller.

Lich: A practitioner of the Art who has succumbed to magic addiction and become a creature sustained only by the power of the Art.

Mal-halyth: Eldara pejorative to describe a human or one of human heritage.

Moon-seer: An individual who can use the Art to perceive the future or grant visions.

Realms of Righteousness, The: The heavenly realm believed to exist by followers of the Church of Ralom.

Sarrius: Founding prophet of the Infinite Faith.

Silver Lady, The: Also known as the Queen of Light and Life. The wife of the Sun King and mother to the Divine Martyr. Goddess of childbirth, women and the home. Worshipped by both the Church of Ralom.

Spellweaver: An Eldara Mage.

Sun King, The: God of the Sun, Light and Nobility. Worshipped by the Church of Ralom, centred in Ralom.

Tears of the Divine, The: An ancient magical artefact. Broken into four pieces and scattered around the known world.

Tragedy of Belial'ad-Dīn, The: A folk tale from Qarld that describes the tragic and sad life of a man born the son of a demon and a human woman.

Transcendent Faith, The: Religion of the Eldara, centred of the worship of Hydria, "The Great Mother", and her children – the so-called "Firstborn of Hydria".

Tyron: The "Last Davorean", founder of one of the proto-Emparian kingdoms. Ancestor to Alarion I.

Underworld, The: The hellish netherworld believed to exist by followers of the Church of Ralom and the Infinite Faith.

ABOUT THE AUTHOR

Aidan Hennessy lives in Canberra, Australia, with his wife, two children and two ginger cats. He spends his days fighting that most tenacious of foes, procrastination. This is his first novel.

theaplydinchronicles.wordpress.com